Praise for Kathleen Kent's
The Outcasts

Winner of the ALA/RUSA 2014 Reading List Award for Historical Fiction and a finalist for the 2014 Will Rogers Medallion Award for Western Fiction

"Kent shines not only as a storyteller but as a landscape artist, never better than when describing the sense of a place....Like any Western writer worth her salt, Kent proves that there are endless ways to kill and be killed, but more interesting is when she leaves us in the dangerous, complicated land of the living, where characters yearn for order even as they cause (or combat) chaos."
—Kirk Reed Forrester, *Kirkus Reviews*

"Kent has given readers another strong female protagonist in Lucinda Carter....*The Outcasts* is well written, tightly plotted and full of ingenious twists....Like the rotgut poured at some dusty Old West saloon, this tale has a wicked kick to it."
—Shawna Seed, *Dallas Morning News*

"A rollicking tale." —Steve Bennett, *San Antonio Express-News*

"A talented storyteller....Kent manages to upend expectations through rich characterizations, historic verisimilitude, and a close study of East Texas geography....There are echoes of Cormac McCarthy in Kent's bloody novel....But time and again, largely because of the humanizing attention to women and minority characters traditionally given short shrift in historical fiction, Kent manages a fresh take on a tale that could have been just another redundant entry in the Lonesome Dove sweepstakes."
—Dan Oko, *Texas Observer*

"*The Outcasts* is an engrossing novel set in the American West where no one is perfect and everyone is in search of something. Excellently written…capturing the crudeness and wisdom of old age cowboys and rangers. Incredibly fabulous.…This is the Old West at its best and worst—ruthless, dangerous, wild.…The author has the ability to make the characters bigger than life, real, sympathetic, credible." —Historical Novel Review.com

"Kent's novels never fail to illuminate both the facts of life in the past and the realities of human nature both then and now, and *The Outcasts* is no exception." —Jen Karsbaek, SheKnows.com

"Through the combined perspectives of these varied and multi-layered characters, Kent brings to life a world lived on the edge of everything: civilization, lawfulness, and morality." —Kerry McHugh, *Shelf Awareness*

"This historical fiction is full of the usual tropes of the American western: outlaws, horses, saloons, guns, whorehouses—even some buried pirate treasure. Set in nineteenth-century post–Civil War Texas, *The Outcasts* has two different narratives that run parallel and only collide toward the end. There's Lucinda Carter, a reluctant prostitute who has escaped to be with her lover. He has nefarious plans of his own. Then there's Nate Cannon, a policeman on the hunt for a serial killer. Kathleen Kent is good at evoking the Wild West landscape, and Lucinda is as ruthless as the men in the book. Her hooker heart of gold has certainly been tarnished." —Thuy On, *Sydney Morning Herald*

The Outcasts

Also by Kathleen Kent

The Heretic's Daughter

The Traitor's Wife (originally published as *The Wolves of Andover*)

The Outcasts

A Novel

Kathleen Kent

BACK BAY BOOKS
Little, Brown and Company
New York Boston London

Copyright © 2013 by Kathleen Kent
Reading group guide copyright © 2014 by Kathleen Kent and Little, Brown and Company

Back Bay Books / Little, Brown and Company
Hachette Book Group
1290 Avenue of the Americas, New York, NY 10104
littlebrown.com

Originally published in hardcover by Little, Brown and Company, September 2013
First Back Bay paperback edition, October 2014

Back Bay Books is an imprint of Little, Brown and Company. The Back Bay Books name and logo are trademarks of Hachette Book Group, Inc.

The publisher is not responsible for websites (or their content) that are not owned by the publisher.

The Hachette Speakers Bureau provides a wide range of authors for speaking events. To find out more, go to hachettespeakersbureau.com or call (866) 376-6591.

Library of Congress Cataloging-in-Publication Data

Kent, Kathleen,
  The outcasts : a novel / Kathleen Kent. —1st ed.
    pages cm
  ISBN 978-0-316-20612-9 (hc) / 978-0-316-23988-2 (large print) / 978-0-316-20611-2 (pb)
  1. Brothels—Fiction. 2. Gulf Coast (La.)—History—19th century—Fiction. 3. Travelers—West (U.S.)—History—19th century—Fiction. I. Title.
  PS3611.E674O98 2013
  813'.6—dc23   2013017705

10 9 8 7 6 5 4 3 2 1

RRD-C

Book design by Marie Mundaca

Printed in the United States of America

For Katie, Kelly, and Alyssa

These tales are not creations of mine. They
belong to the soil and to the people of the soil.

—J. Frank Dobie, *Coronado's Children*

The Outcasts

Prologue

For a thousand years, the northern, windward side of the island lay fallow. The sand tracked its way inland along with the bellowing gusts from the ocean and the serpents too that crawled towards shelter in intricate breaststrokes. Bald cypress and pine grew on ancient creek beds, and Spanish moss hung from live oaks, trailing heavily in sweet-water streams. Leeward, along treacherous shallow reefs, a ship followed a northwesterly course, its sails at full rigging, the bow pointed towards the mainland. Twelve miles to the south, on the island's port city, a red house burned.

The *Pride* would make no return to the island; its captain, Jean Lafitte, had been proclaimed a brigand. The great red house had been his — the entire Galveston settlement had been his — and he had torched it rather than give it over to the hard-following agents and hounding merchant marines of the new Americas.

The ship he sailed was over one hundred feet long and fast beyond belief. Shallow-drafted for mobility and stealth, it had been stripped of every bulkhead to make room for additional men and powder, and outfitted with sixteen cannons for killing. It maintained its northerly course through Galveston Bay, slackening its sails only when April Fool Point had been passed.

At the mouth of Clear Creek, the anchor was dropped, and over the side of the ship a longboat was lowered into the water. Onto the longboat climbed Lafitte, followed by two men holding two chests filled with gold coins. They would row beyond Clear Creek into the heart of Middle Bayou.

At sunset, Lafitte returned to the ship without the men, and without the chests. By midnight, the *Pride* was well on its way to the Tropic of Cancer and the Yucatán that lay beyond it like a pale virgin sleeping, reflecting the light of countless stars.

Chapter 1

$\mathcal{A}$ hard fall had come upon Lucinda, throwing her to the floor of her bedroom, chafing an elbow and bruising the skin on one cheek. It had happened on a Monday, so that when the dizzying waves came over her again on the following Wednesday, she stood with her back pressed flat against a door for balance and her hands balled at her sides. A crescent of sweat beaded her lip, and she could taste the salt as it ran into the corners of her mouth. She closed her eyes and waited for the rigors to pass.

There had been a forewarning of this within the first hour of waking. The scent, strange and not altogether pleasant, had seemingly rolled out along with the folds of the gray bombazine travel dress that she unpacked from a box hidden under her bed. She thought for an instant that the dress had perhaps been secretly taken out and worn by one of the other girls, the fabric still carrying the remnants of a too-old perfume. She frowned in irritation and pulled the dark jacket closer to her nose. Then she remembered that the odor was a part of the malady, a sign that was of her and not apart from her. She had seen the beginnings of fracturing lamplight, the hazy yellow globes floating and pulsing at odd intervals, and she had known the aura for what it was. She had gone weeks without such a fit, until the Monday past. It was the stress of the impending travel, she thought, that had brought back her intractable weakness.

She had managed to finish dressing that morning by herself, willing her arms and legs through the complicated layers of laces and hooks of undergarments and overdress, and she was fine until the moment she stepped out of her room. She latched the door soundlessly behind her before her limbs began their jerking, trembling rigidity, her mind sliding towards blankness.

She was damp through her clothes, her forehead slick and prickling, but to move away from the door, even to dab at her neck, could pitch her facedown onto the thin carpet, waking the occupants in the nearest bedroom. She dared to let her chin fall, her eyes downcast and half closed, her lips twitching as though in conversation with her shoes.

The shoes. She saw right away how ridiculous was the turn of mind that had prompted her to put on the high-laced boots of yellow kidskin. They were thin soled with raised heels, and the color flashed from the hem of her skirt like a lighthouse beacon through a storm. They were insubstantial and ill-advised for traveling, but in a moment of stubborn vanity, she had put them on, rather than the sturdy black walking boots that she had packed into her traveling bag.

Next to her feet, where she had dropped it, lay the tapestry bag containing a light cotton dress, a heavier woolen dress, a paisley shawl, her teaching primers, a lady's gun, and a bottle of laudanum. The laudanum had proven useless against the fits, as had bromine, tincture of mercury, and every other apothecary offering. She had once even tried an evil-smelling concoction of herbs and what looked like turtle shells bought off a Chinaman. Boiling the dark fragments into a tea had filled the house with foul odors, driving Mrs. Landry, the house's owner, into one of her own fits. Lucinda never tested its merit, as her landlady had thrown it all into the yard to be pecked over by the hens.

But the laudanum would bring comfort on the nights she couldn't sleep. The Remington offered reassurance of a different kind.

There was an easing of the spasms in her legs and neck, and she felt the edges of her vision expand again to the ends of the hallway on either side of her. The wave of sickness she had felt moments before resolved itself into simple morning hunger. Although the paralysis had been brief, precious time had been lost. It could be only a half hour more, if that, until the woman arrived to clean the downstairs parlor.

The only sounds came from the room next to hers: a gentle snoring and a squeaking of a bed frame as the sleeper shifted.

Still she rested against the door, breathing slowly the stale air coming off the worn carpet. She wondered how many feet had trudged up and down the hallways, day upon day, hour upon hour. Mrs. Landry was not a young woman; she was already well in her forties, although her fondness for wearing false bangs and low-cut, tight-fitting gowns had not diminished over the decade she had run her busy and very profitable house.

How many women and girls had trodden these stairs, each thinking to stay for a short while, to make some quick riches selling the only asset left to her, the garden between her legs, only to find that *quick* and *plentiful* were two different things entirely. It was astonishing really how many of them believed they could be frugal enough, or smart enough, or sly enough in their dealings with Mrs. Landry to save the money required to set up their own shops somewhere else.

She'd seen girls as young as twelve taken in, girls who had already spent months with the camps, following men on cattle drives. Hollow-eyed and detached, even after a stiff scrubbing, they looked in their wet nakedness like wiry boys, their backsides flat as china plates.

And also older women, well beyond their years of first budding, who, because of widowhood, or misuse, or just plain boredom, came and stayed for a bit to change their luck, then disappeared again. What was the same for everyone in Madame Landry's house was the importance of accepting a simple mathematical truth: the law of diminishing returns. The longer you stayed, the deeper in debt you became, through the acquiring of either gowns, doctor's bills, liquor, or laudanum.

There was never any forcing of boarders to stay if they wanted to leave. But every woman was searched foot to mouth before she exited through the always-locked front door, taking with her only what she'd brought into the house. Rarely did a woman depart with any money after her accounts had been settled, and even a trip to the dry-goods merchant or postal office earned a close inspection.

The enforcer in this was Mrs. Landry's German. The German spoke halting English and was never tempted by bribes of any kind, either flesh or money. High-voiced and sloe-eyed as the German was, house gossip had it that he had somehow been gelded as a boy and thus had no weakness for women, even though he shared a bed nightly with Mrs. Landry. He also had fists the size of Easter hams.

Mrs. Landry's bedroom was off the parlor closest to the door, and the trick for Lucinda would be slipping through the door without waking the pair of them. The woman was a notoriously wakeful sleeper and, it was said, could tell the number of times each of her girls used the chamber pots from the squeaking of the floorboards overhead.

For days Lucinda had been greasing the lock and hinges of the door with a feather covered in lard, and she carried in her stays a key made from a mold of the German's own key, a mold she'd obtained by pressing the key into a thin brick of soap hidden in a small tin box.

The German always kept his key on a chain fastened to his belt. But it had not been difficult to distract him with a turn at cards. Lucinda had sat near him, her head bent towards his, the better to patiently teach him the rules of faro. She spoke encouragingly to him, laughing and gesturing extravagantly as she deftly slipped the key from his pocket, pressing it into the soap, and then passed it back into his pocket again before the hand had played out.

She didn't know whether the copied key would even turn the lock, but she would get only a few tries at the door before Mrs. Landry would wake thinking the oily rattling was the cleaning woman come early.

Bending her knees, she dipped down to grasp the top of her bag, and then slowly raised herself again to standing. She pushed away from the bedroom door and used the forward momentum to grasp at the wooden finial at the top of the stair rail. She placed both hands on the railing to steady herself, the bag's handles looped over one arm, and stepped carefully down the stairs, riser to riser, the carpet absorbing the sounds of her progress. At the bottom of the stairs, she rested a moment, breathing through her mouth, waiting for the play of stippled lights inside her eyes to subside. A renewed wave of nausea came and went. The scrabbling of a mouse, or a rat, settling in the walls sounded faintly and then stopped.

At the door, she pressed her forehead against the wood, and the key slid easily into the lock, but she paused one last time to listen for any movement within or without the house. There were no sounds coming off the streets, and she turned the key soundlessly, and felt the heavy bolt slip open.

Through a narrow space, she eased out, and then shut the door gently behind her. She inserted the key in the outside lock and slipped the bolt back into place. Dropping the key into the pocket of her day coat, she turned and walked, carefully at first, and then more briskly, southwards, away from the direction the cleaning woman would come.

Past Jody Strange's sporting house and gaming parlor, she turned left onto Fourth Street, unmindful of keeping her head down or veil drawn. The streets were yet empty and hollow-feeling, as she'd known they would be; the girls of Hell's Half Acre of Fort Worth and their stay-over clients were still unconscious. After the cleaning woman arrived, Mrs. Landry would likely go back to her bed until noon, and it might be another hour after that before Lucinda was discovered missing from the house. But by then she would be several hours gone.

She followed Fourth Street to Rusk, then turned southward again, towards the better hotels and saloons closer to the coach depot and wagon yards. September had been dry, and, instead of the usual sucking mud oozing through the pine planking, the only thing caking her yellow boots was a fine scrim of dust.

She entered the Commerce Hotel, sat in the lobby, and ordered tea and a piece of bread. The clock behind the clerk's head struck the half hour past seven. At eight o'clock the coach would come.

She smiled wanly at the clerk, making sure he took note of her face, and asked if the coach to Dallas would be on time. A few pleasantries were exchanged, the clerk being made to believe that Lucinda would be visiting family there, so that when the German came looking for her, and he would certainly come, he'd be told she was in Dallas, and Lucinda would gain some much-needed time.

She was in fact taking the coach beyond Dallas, through Waxahachie, Hillsboro, Waco, and finally to Hearne; over one hundred and fifty miles. At Hearne she would board the rail line to Houston, a hundred and twenty miles farther on.

She had begun to feel better, only a tightening at her temples and a kind of burning sensation at the back of her skull to prove she'd had the fit. She finished her tea and bread and paid for them with a few coins drawn from a delicate embroidered pouch. When she replaced the small pouch in the carpetbag, her hand instinctively felt for the reassuring weight of a much larger pouch filled with a comfortable sum of money taken from Mrs. Landry's cache under the floorboards of her room.

Lucinda had discovered the hidden place only recently, and by accident, while caring for Mrs. Landry during a brief illness. The madam's fever-pooled eyes had constantly, and anxiously, sought out a place on the floor near her bed, as though by habit, and when Lucinda gently tapped the boards with the toe of her shoe, she heard a hollow sound. After an extra draft of laudanum for Mrs. Landry in the early afternoon, Lucinda made a quick examination of the floorboards that proved her suspicions right: something of value had been tucked away underneath. In a hollow space she discovered a canvas sack filled with hard currency; merchant tokens; and shinplasters, the paper money given out during the war. The heavier gold and silver coins had settled to the bottom and she removed as many as she dared, reducing the size of the bag imperceptibly.

Later today, after Mrs. Landry realized Lucinda was gone, she would immediately check the space beneath the floorboards. A quick count, and the German would be out the door like a baying hound.

Robbery had not been part of Lucinda's original plan. She had merely wanted to leave unmolested, carrying the little bit of money she had managed to hide from the prying eyes of her employer. The old bawd was as tight as a Gulf oyster with her pay, and it was simply happy circumstance that Lucinda had found the hidden cache and the opportunity to take it. Once she had secreted the coins in her own room, she gave herself only a few days to plan and execute her escape. To be caught thieving from Mrs. Landry would most likely bring an unending bath in the Trinity River.

The clerk, who had been staring at her yellow boots, looked quickly back at her face and smiled broadly with the kind of come-on she had grown used to. The town men, even the dullards, seemed to size her up with telegraphic precision. Assessing his frayed coat and collar, she guessed the clerk would have been good for only about three dollars and, at most, thirty seconds of energetic pushing. She turned her head, nullifying him, and stared out the window.

Within five minutes the coach arrived, and, after a hand up from the driver, she paid her fare and seated herself across from a gentleman who, she was pleased to discover, was a doctor traveling to Hillsboro. She immediately closed her eyes, hoping to sleep while discouraging conversation. At least, she thought, she could get proper care if felled by another bout of palsy while in his company.

Four hours later, the coach halted in Dallas and the driver handed his two passengers down, telling them they could rest for an hour, avail themselves of food and drink, while the horses and driver were changed. They were also told that for the next leg of the journey, the driver would be accompanied by a shotgun companion; there were as many gunmen on the road to Hillsboro, the driver said, as there were "teats on a wild boar."

The doctor, who had not spoken a word to Lucinda for the whole of the time beyond the initial introductions, walked immediately to the public house nearest the coach. She watched him as he moved discourteously away and decided that he must be a Methodist, as a Baptist would have spent the greatest part of the trip staring at her bosom.

Taking in the sight of pine buildings, rawboned in their newness and smelling of turpentine, Lucinda crossed the rutted street opposite the coach, carrying with her the carpetbag. In the nearby dry-goods store she purchased a cheap muslin nightgown and a comb. She then walked to the McClintock, a modest hotel at the far end of the street, and paid for two nights. She paused for a moment, and then her lips curled and she signed the registry *Mrs. Landry.*

She ordered a cutlet and coffee to be sent to her room. When the meal came, she hungrily ate all of the beef, pushing aside what looked to be apples fried in lard. She finished her coffee, sipped at some water, and used the chamber pot. She laid the nightgown and comb on the coverlet and sat on the edge of the bed for a while, feeling almost well.

She pulled two letters from her bag, both sent to her through the post office in Fort Worth. The first note read *Come to the Lamplighter when you are able. I will leave word. Ever Yours, by the hour . . .* She smiled and covered the note with her fingers before returning it to her bag. The second letter she did not open, knowing the words by heart, but she let it rest in her lap for a while. It was the letter offering her the position of schoolteacher in a settlement called Middle Bayou. The job would pay twenty-five dollars a month, provide her with a room, and would no doubt be close to the edge of the world: crude, forlorn, and mosquito-infested. She would be astonished if she hadn't contracted malaria within a few weeks.

Having replaced the second letter, she changed her gray suit for the lighter cotton dress she had packed and pulled on the stout walking boots and the shawl. She then picked up the bag and walked downstairs, where she informed the hotel clerk that she would be back after dark, as she was going to have supper with her brother. She strolled the few blocks to the coach and found two additional passengers, as well as the doctor, waiting for the new driver to take up the baggage.

Before she stepped onto the foot rail, she looked to the top of the coach, catching sight of the safety man seated on the driving board. He was cradling a double-barreled shotgun and leisurely smoking. He glanced at her, stubbed out the live ashes of the cheroot against the side of the coach, and gave her a mournful nod.

Once the coach got under way, the dust from the road followed them for miles. Lucinda pictured the German arriving in town after dark, his horse lathered almost to glue. He would look for her, eventually finding his way to the hotel. There he would bribe, or bully, his way into the room she had rented. Seeing the nightgown and comb, he would sit on the bed, hopefully for most of the night, waiting for her to return, his fists clenching and unclenching. She had cast off the heavy travel clothes as well, leaving them scattered about the room; the yellow boots she had reluctantly pushed beneath the bed.

Chapter 2

The horse Nate rode out of Franklin on that morning had had a man's weight across his back only a few dozen times. It was a three-year-old gelding, narrow in the body and neck, with an ill-defined head that would have signaled to the unknowing, or the inexperienced, that the animal himself was as bland as his conformation. In fact, he had been given up for the sausage cart, viewed as unreliable and intractable by the rangers of the westernmost outpost.

Nate knew from the beginning that he had been assigned the horse as a joke: a test for the newly sworn-in Texas state policeman from Oklahoma. The gelding had been yanked at, whipped, blindfolded, and hobbled in an attempt to break him to the saddle, to the extent that even a tightening belly cinch sent the animal into frenzied bucking.

When Nate saw the horse—head down, ears plowed backward, feet splayed—the first thing he did was remove the saddle, blanket, and bit, leaving only a lead rope around his neck. Nate stood by the gelding the remainder of the afternoon, occasionally feeding him a bit of grain and molasses, never looking directly at him, only following close as the animal grazed. The rangers, hoping for a show, had quickly gotten bored after the first hour and wandered away to see to their own affairs.

The second morning, Nate hand-fed the horse at regular intervals, touching him rhythmically in sweeping motions across his back and haunches, even removing his shirt to flag it gently across the horse's line of vision. By midday there was not even a ripple of muscle across the gelding's chest when another ranger passed by.

On the third day, Nate spent hours slipping the rope off and on the gelding's head and neck, snaking it across his withers, even draping it around his belly, tightening it only enough for the horse to feel the pressure. He fed the horse more grain and molasses, and the animal began to follow him around like a dog.

On the morning of the fourth day, everyone in the entire ranger company who was not out on raid duty collected to watch Nate putting the blanket and saddle on the crazy gelding, who yielded quietly, even when the cinch was tightened. The onlookers braced expectantly for action when Nate put his foot in the stirrup, but he only leaned his weight across the saddle and then stepped down again. He repeated the action for half an hour before he fully seated himself. He touched his heels to the gelding, and the horse bucked forward but soon stopped and stood still, only his ears twitching. Nate got off and on the saddle a few more times, led him around by the bridle, got back on, and tapped the horse into an easy canter away from the post. He was gone for twenty minutes, and when he returned, the gelding was lathered but calm. The rangers who had stood around making bets that the horse would come back riderless gave him backhanded compliments and pressed him for information on how to subdue their own uncooperative and clod-footed mounts.

When the captain, a veteran ranger by the name of Drake, asked him how he was able to break the horse, Nate shrugged and told him that working with a horse was like raising up a child. "You build on trust and little tries," he said.

At dawn on the fifth day, he was given the gelding, which would replace his own worn mount, and a commission to ride westward an hour distant to find two rangers in the field, Captain George Deerling and Tom Goddard, and bring them back to Franklin. A killer named William McGill had reappeared in Houston after some absence from Texas, to murderous effect. A man that Captain Deerling, for personal reasons—reasons Captain Drake did not elaborate on—had been chasing for years.

Nate rode west for more than two hours until he saw the irregular bands of gray smoke from a campfire and came upon three men seated together in a companionable arrangement, drinking coffee. If he hadn't seen the leg irons on the man sitting in the middle, he wouldn't have known which one was a prisoner and which ones were rangers.

The only one smiling was the ankle-bound man, his hair poking up in unruly spikes, as though he'd slept with a blanket pulled tight over his head. The rangers must have heard Nate coming from a long way off, otherwise they would have had their Colts drawn and cocked.

He legged himself down from his horse and walked to the fire.

"You George Deerling?" he asked. He addressed himself to the closer ranger, but the man shook his head and pointed to his older companion.

From a middling distance, the two rangers looked remarkably alike, even beyond the sameness of their dress. Hatless, they both wore top boots over home-sewn denim and shirts dyed an approximate indigo. The younger ranger was black-haired with a black mustache, the edges of which drooped into his coffee cup, requiring him to make a backhanded sweep after every sip. The one he had pointed to was an older man, silver-haired with a gray mustache, also of impressive width.

Their hair was cropped serviceably short, and every bit of exposed skin on the two rangers—wrists, necks, faces—and even the color of the eyes seemed sun-blasted to a dunnish brown. The man sitting between them was fully dressed in the same hard-ridden way but was bootless, owing to the bulk of the leg irons.

Nate shifted his good leg so he could stand more comfortably. His hip hurt something awful, but of a certainty he didn't want to appear weak-limbed on his first field day.

He said, "I'm Nathaniel Cannon. Nate." There was no nod of assent or motion of recognition. He added, "Sent by Captain Drake." The last word lilted upwards and came out sounding, to his ears, like a question.

The older ranger said, "I'm George Deerling. My partner"—he motioned sideways with his head—"Tom Goddard. Dr. Tom."

The man in the middle said, "And I'm the goddamn queen of the desert." He yukked and grinned, showing all his teeth, top and bottom.

Deerling, in a sweeping motion, brought his gun out of its holster and applied the butt of it sharply to the prisoner's head. Through the yowling and protestations of foul play, Deerling said, "This mannerless yahoo is Maynard Collie."

Dr. Tom set his cup down and motioned for Nate to sit. "You here to help us bring old Maynard in?"

Even the voices of the two rangers were the same, Nate thought. The top notes slightly breathy and clipped, like air exhaled through short, fibrous reeds.

Dr. Tom smiled. "You already missed the fun. Maynard shot his own horse out from under himself trying to ride and fire at us at the same time."

Nate sat and fingered the dirt as if testing it. "You know, you're awfully close to Las Cruces. We don't have power of arrest in New Mexico." He kept his voice neutral but looked pointedly at Collie.

Dr. Tom looked across the top of the prisoner, who was still rubbing his head with both hands, with an amused turn of his lips. "George, did you know we was in New Mexico?"

Deerling drained the dregs of his cup. "Still looks like Texas to me." He held the cup out to Nate. "You want coffee?"

Nate nodded, grateful for the offer, and the cup was half filled with the last of the coffee remaining in the small tin pot. He sat and watched the rangers begin to break camp and wondered how long he should sit drinking coffee before he broke the news to Deerling.

Collie looked at Nate and asked, "They ready to hang me?" He grinned again but sounded plaintive.

"Shut up, Maynard." Dr. Tom cheerfully nudged him with a boot. "Make yourself useful and cover over the fire."

Nate finished the coffee in the cup and, wiping it against his pants leg, stood. "Captain Deerling?"

Deerling, kneeling and packing his supply satchel, looked up.

"We've gotten word about McGill." A pause. "He was in Houston a week ago."

"And...?" Deerling stood, leaving his pack on the ground.

"And he's gone. Left the town with Crenshaw and Purdy fol-lowin' after."

"What's the butcher's bill?" Dr. Tom asked.

"They took a mail stage and a dock warehouse. Didn't get a whole lot but killed two people in the process. Both gut-shot."

Maynard shook his head sadly.

"While all this was goin' on, seems they were hiding in some settler's house, just north of Houston."

Dr. Tom asked, "Were any left alive?"

"One. The woman lived. But he killed the husband and two children."

"Goddamn kid killers," Maynard said. He scratched at the skin under the leg irons.

"She crawled more than a mile to a neighbor, bleedin' the whole way. Said they were told all along they'd be left alive. And when it came time to leave, McGill just started shooting."

Deerling asked, "Where'd they head?"

Nate shrugged. "The woman said they'd talked about riding to Harrisburg."

"Harrisburg? What's in Harrisburg?" Dr. Tom looked to Deer-ling.

"There's the railroad to Richmond on the Brazos, for one. San Jacinto? Galveston, maybe?"

"And then on to New Orleans." Dr. Tom whistled. "They get to New Orleans and we'll never see 'em again."

"If it were me, I'd go to Mexico." Maynard settled on a hopeful look.

"If it was you, you'd know when to shut it." Dr. Tom hunkered down and removed a key from his vest to unlock the leg irons.

"Tom." Deerling held up a restraining hand. He turned again to Nate. "Did the woman say anything more?"

"She said they were after a stash of Confederate gold some dirt farmer uncovered in the Texas bayous. Or some such nonsense. She was mostly out of her head, I think."

Deerling frowned. "What's the disposition on Collie here, once we get him to Franklin?"

"We're just waitin' for the judge to show up," Nate said. "We got the jury. It could be a week more. Ten days, maybe. Drake knew you'd want to follow after McGill. After you give testimony at the trial, he said. I've got my commission. I can ride with you as long as you need me."

Deerling looked at Dr. Tom for a good while. He said, "We wait that long, we'll lose 'em for sure."

Dr. Tom considered for a moment. "We may have lost them already, George. What do we do with Maynard here?"

"You could let me go," Maynard offered.

"He's gonna be hanged regardless." Deerling talked over Maynard's head, as though he'd wandered off.

Dr. Tom pursed his lips. "You could bring a whole hornet's nest of trouble on us if he comes in lookin' like he was not a willing participant."

"What in the hell...what're you *talkin'* about?" Maynard asked. "I'm sittin' right here, goddamn it."

Deerling looked at Maynard contemplatively. "We bring him in alive, and we're committed to a turn of events outside our control."

Dr. Tom nodded.

"I got a big bite, fifty-caliber, in my saddlebag," Deerling said, looking towards his horse, a large bay cropping grass nearby.

"No, no, no, no . . . I'm *not* willin'," Maynard shouted. "And if you bring me in with a rope-collar burn, or, or a hole in the back of my skull"—he pointed to Nate—"*he's* gonna know it and have to tell God and everyone what you done."

Nate looked from Deerling to Dr. Tom, feeling as though he had dropped off into a deep sleep and had just awakened to find himself in the middle of the conversation.

"I get a trial, right?" Maynard looked around, then settled his eyes back on Nate. "Right?"

Dr. Tom said, "Maynard, you just had one." He tapped Nate on the arm and, grabbing his hat, said, "Come on."

Nate took a defensive posture. Pointing to Deerling, who was digging through his saddlebag, he said, "He's not going to shoot the prisoner, is he?"

"No," said Dr. Tom. "He's not going to shoot him." He looped his arm around Nate's shoulder in a persistent but fatherly manner, prompting him to move away. "He's just goin' to talk to him a bit."

After a few paces, Nate shrugged off the arm.

Dr. Tom rocked back a bit on his heels and squinted up at the younger man in a calculating way. Nate looked over the ranger's shoulder, trying to keep the prisoner in his sights. Maynard was throwing fistfuls of dirt, pebbles, anything at hand, towards Deerling, who had hunkered down at a safe distance and was holding up what looked to be a large shotgun shell.

"You have family?" Dr. Tom asked.

"Yes. A wife and daughter." Nate could hear Deerling speaking in a mostly one-sided discourse with Maynard, the exact words indistinct, but the tone reasonable, comforting even.

"What are their names?"

"Their names?" Nate looked uncomprehending at this line of questioning. "Beth and Mattie, not that it applies to any goddamn thing goin' on here."

Maynard had stopped throwing things and had taken up pleading.

"You love your family, your wife and daughter?"

"Hell, yes, I love my family." Nate backed away a few steps. His confusion was beginning to make him angry. "What the hell's goin' on?"

Dr. Tom gestured with a thumb over his shoulder. "Maynard here kills women. All of 'em whores. But, still, each of 'em started out as someone's sister. Or daughter." He gave Nate a few moments to absorb this fact, and then tapped him on the arm again. "Come on. Let's walk a bit."

Nate turned one last time towards Maynard, who was now holding his head in his hands, listening—or not—to Deerling, who talked on and on. He remembered Maynard's hands holding his coffee cup, the nails bitten down to the quick and stained with something dark. Maybe dirt, maybe not.

He followed Dr. Tom away from the camp and to a slight drop-off by a dried-up streambed, where they stood at the edge, their backs to the sun. Dr. Tom took out a pocket rag and swiped it around his neck. He gestured towards Nate's legs. "You break one a while back?"

"No." Nate crossed his arms, easing his weight from one foot to another. "Horse fell on me. Broke my hip."

"Hurts, don't it?" Dr. Tom smiled. He tugged on his mustache thoughtfully and said, "Old Maynard's got a choice to make, something the poor bastard's probably never had before in his life."

"You think he didn't have a choice, killin' those women?"

"Well, no. Your average killer, yes. He's got a choice. But Maynard"—Dr. Tom tapped his head—"Maynard is beset by the demon of by-God-have-to-do-it-and-don't-know-why. You find 'em every once in a while. I don't think he ever liked the killing part one bit." He dragged the rag around his neck again and hunkered down. To Nate, it looked like he was simply enjoying the view.

Nate stood studying his hands for a bit, considering, and then dismissing, the idea that this was all some elaborately staged rite of passage, like pulling the short hairs on the last boy out of his bedroll. He decided it was not. "Goddamn it," he muttered.

Dr. Tom said, sympathizing, "A hell of a first day."

"What's his choice?" Nate finally asked, lifting his chin back toward the camp.

"The big bite. Or something else, something less pleasant."

Nate thought about the shell Deerling had shown Maynard and about the impact of the blast that a 70-grain cartridge used in a .50-caliber shotgun would make. What the "something less pleasant" would be, he couldn't imagine. "You said the prisoner wasn't going to be shot."

"He's not." Dr. Tom spat between his teeth and watched some buzzards circling high up.

Regardless, Nate strained his ears for some sounds of a struggle back at the camp, bracing himself for the concussion of a shotgun fired off. He wondered what the hell he would say to Drake when it came time to bring what was left of Maynard back into town.

He had only just been sworn in a week ago and didn't think his word on the matter would be taken for much.

"I guess you never heard of a big bite before?" Dr. Tom asked. "Buffalo hunters on the south plains started carrying 'em a few years back. The hunter empties out a cartridge and fills it with cyanide. If he gets close to being taken by Indians, he nestles it between his teeth and bites down. It's pretty fast." Dr. Tom batted at the gnats beginning to swarm around his face. "At least, it's faster than watching your own tender bits cut off by Kiowa."

"Is that what'll happen to him if he refuses to take the cyanide?"

"Oh, I think not," Dr. Tom said. He stood up stiffly, brushed off the seat of his pants, and straightened his hat, as though a train, long awaited, had just pulled into the station. "The big bite's a hell of a lot faster than doin' the hurdy-gurdy at the end of a rope. And anyway, if Maynard cooperates, George will make sure Maynard's kin get the reward that would otherwise go to some latecomer. I think he'll see reason."

"What's it goin' to look like when we bring him back to town?"

"I imagine it'll look like what it is."

"Which is…?"

"Self-inflicted mortality."

"What about the trial? You think no one's gonna ask questions?"

Dr. Tom sighed as though Nate had posed a delicate philosophical question. "The honest truth is, no one is gonna give a damn, except maybe the judge if he makes the trip for nothing." He stood for a while watching Nate shaking his head. "If it makes you feel any better, we could say that you come upon us after Maynard passed on."

"You want to add more lies to a killing?"

"Don't take this personal, son."

"Hell, it's *all* personal."

"I see you feel that." Dr. Tom squinted against the light and crossed his arms, regarding the toes of his boots. He shifted once, and then raised his eyes to Nate's. He wasn't smiling anymore, but there was nothing menacing in his face. "Maynard Collie is a done deal. He slaughtered a few pitiful whores, and most people wouldn't even bother to dig a hole to bury him in. But McGill, see. McGill is still alive and full of malice. You think you know what McGill has done, shooting near a dozen men in the past few years, but you don't know the half of it. We've been following him and his men for over twelve months. We lost him for a short while, but we got the scent again. And you can take it to the bank that this *is* personal to us. Now, you can ride away back to Franklin right now and tell Drake whatever the hell you want to, but me and George need to finish this up, get him back, and head for Houston."

Dr. Tom adjusted his hat and began walking to the camp. "I think it's been time enough."

Nate followed him back, almost expecting to see the prisoner still pleading with Deerling, his hands filled with rocks and dirt. But when he got close he saw Maynard lying on the ground, the leg irons removed, his stocking feet splayed and unmoving. His eyes were open, and a frothy ribbon of spittle rolled down one cheek.

"Well…" Dr. Tom said, looking at the motionless form.

Deerling, tightening the cinch on his horse, looked over his shoulder at Nate. Then he turned to Dr. Tom and asked, "Is he comin' to Houston?"

"I don't know," Dr. Tom answered. He picked up a blanket to cover the body. "Why don't you ask him?"

Nate, peering at Maynard, was surprised to feel nothing even close to outrage, more of a wilting pity than anything else.

"Just tell me one thing. He done this with his own hand?" Nate asked.

Deerling kneed his horse briskly in the belly and pulled the cinch tighter. "I talked. He listened. He saw the sense in not dragging out the inevitable." He tugged a few times at the stirrup and then walked to stand at the remains of the fire.

Looking at Maynard's diminished form now under the blanket, Nate wondered if the prisoner had put out the last of the coals like Dr. Tom had told him to do before swallowing the poison. He believed, almost knew as a certainty, that this was the closest thing to a recounting of the events that he was going to get for a good while, maybe ever.

After a bit, Dr. Tom called, "Nate. Come help me lift old Maynard here up onto the mule."

Nate wiped the sweat off his face with one sleeve, stooped down, heaved Maynard up by himself, and carried him to the mule. He draped the body over the withers, facedown, and secured it with the long ends of the rope.

He mounted his own horse and began leading the mule southwards, back to town. He did not wait for the other two men to trail directly after. He did wonder, though, and often, in the days following, whether he should have pressed Deerling more about what Maynard's other choice had been.

Chapter 3

The coach arrived in Hearne at eleven that morning, having been on the road for over two days, changing horses and drivers every forty or fifty miles and discharging passengers in the late afternoons to whatever overnight lodging they could find and pay for.

Grateful for the few hours before the train was scheduled to depart for Houston, Lucinda walked up and down the main street, carrying her carpetbag close to her body, wandering in and out of the open shops, their shelves filled with goods carted in from San Francisco and Boston. She lingered over some dressmaking cloth and finally bought a jar of gooseberry jam, thinking to eat it all in one sitting. She felt well and strong; hopeful, now that the journey was almost done.

During the first night, there had been a moment when a sudden headache had spawned worries of a coming fit, but a few drops of laudanum judiciously taken in water had given her sleep, and the head pains were gone in the morning.

There seemed to be as much street traffic here as in Fort Worth, with an abundance of men who looked more like merchants than farmers or stock handlers and who had uncallused hands and fresh-creased pants. The men tipped their hats and smiled through their beards at her. She nodded in return, her mind reflexively reducing the distasteful but necessary acts of her profession to the more comfortable rules of mathematics, geometry in particular. Where two bodies in motion, with their collective points, curves, segments, and surfaces, intersecting in the horizontal and the vertical, from above and from below, could be reduced to the abstract. It was a trick she had cultivated as a child when committed to an asylum. Her mind quickly grasped the theorems and concepts and could then distance itself from the terrifying experiences of ice-water baths, forced feedings, and painful restraints by reducing the nurses, doctors, and other inmates to mere points in space.

She had come to stand in front of the plate-glass window of a grain store and paused to study her reflection: a woman in a plain cotton dress and a paisley shawl drawn modestly over her shoulders. A man soon came to stand next to her. She sensed him watching her reflection, waiting for her to smile, to turn her head and speak. Instead she stepped away and walked to a hotel set back from the train station.

She took a room, paying for hot water to be brought for a bath. Soon a large tin washtub was brought in by a gaunt, harried woman, along with just enough scalding water to fill it a quarter of the way. The woman then brought a bucket of well water, a chip of soap, and a cloth for drying. She admonished Lucinda not to overturn the bucket and left in a huff when Lucinda asked for more hot water.

Lucinda removed her clothes and sat waist-deep in the water, her legs drawn up almost to her chin. It was not in any true form a bathtub, and yet the heat on her skin was the most pleasure she had had in weeks. Wrapping her arms around her shinbones, she rested her head on her knees and breathed deeply as though sleeping.

She thought of the letter, and of the letter writer, telling her to come to the Lamplighter Hotel in Houston. She thought of his hands as he wrote the letter, the fingers slender and tapered with beautiful nails like a woman's, and of the long lean bones of his thighs, the hollow of his throat, the jutting ridge of the collarbone.

He had first come to her during her time at Mrs. Landry's, setting his coins in two neat stacks on the dresser. They had lain together twice with hardly a word spoken apart from the erupting sounds of release and polite good-byes. He was clean, restrained, mannerly.

But on his third visit, a violent fit had overtaken her as she began to undress, and, panting and jerking, she begged him to leave. The few men who had previously witnessed the onset of symptoms had scrabbled for the door as though she had called out, *Typhoid.* But he carried her to the bed and laid her down, stripped her until she was fully naked. He lay on top of her, still wearing his trousers and jacket, holding her thrashing head cupped tightly between his palms. He brought his face close to hers and tracked her eyes with his own.

He asked, "Are you dying?" His breath was over her grimacing mouth, and she believed that she was. His palms pressed more tightly into her temples to stop the spasms, and he asked her again if she was dying. She was in the full measure of her sickness, with no control of any part of her body other than the erratic pumping of air in and out of her lungs. His weight had become unbearable, even with the bucking movement of her body, but when she closed her eyes, he pried the lids open with his thumbs, saying, "Look at me."

He smiled, his lips parted with a kind of wondrous expectation, as though he had come to peer into a small pit but instead found a fissure of unknowable depth. He spoke to her, saying, "Here, here," not the calling of a parent to a wandering child but a demand for her to keep her eyes open and focused on his.

That she would die from her malady, Lucinda had no doubt. Uncontrollably pitched from a landing, or stairs, or even from her own bed, she would one day strike and crack her skull. Perhaps she would lie in the bottom of a bathtub, flailing and twitching, like some boneless sea creature, slowly drowning in terrified helplessness.

But as he pressed himself over her, the dark irises of his eyes inches from hers, she began to feel a retreat from fear, a blankness of soul. She never fully lost consciousness and was keenly aware of the skin of her belly incised with the sharp edges of his belt, the buttons of his coat imprinted on her ribs and breast.

The entirety of her life up to that moment had been a torment, a restlessness of mind, as though her brain were a frightened, overly large fish inside a brittle bowl. His near-ecstatic study of her eyes dancing on the edge of nothingness had in the instant changed that balance, rendering her mind becalmed and her body agitating for even a careless, wounding touch.

When she had quieted, he undressed and lay back on the bed, then ran his nose along her skin as though sniffing out the source of the illness. Then he touched her for a length of time and brought her to another kind of shuddering.

A sudden, hard knock at the door signaled the hotel woman's return with the hot water, and Lucinda called her in. The woman closed the door behind her and walked farther into the room before she realized that Lucinda was naked in the bath. She drew herself up short, quickly turning her head away in embarrassment, her face pinched and disapproving. Lucinda asked her to bring the bucket closer, and, as the woman drew near, Lucinda, smiling sweetly, let her knees draw apart to the sides of the basin, showing through the shallow water the private hair between her legs. Dropping the bucket onto the floor, the woman fled the room.

Lucinda finished her bath and dressed in the clean, heavier woolen dress from her bag. She would buy more dresses in Houston and so left the soiled cotton dress behind in the room. Before leaving, she spoke with the hotel clerk, an aging man with inflamed red eyes, and asked him about the dangers of riding the ferry to Galveston. If the German happened to find his way this far south, there was no harm in pointing the trail away from her true destination.

Lucinda boarded the train's passenger car behind a stout, respectable-looking woman with two small children. She sat facing the little family and smiled pleasantly at them. The ride would be six hours, and she settled back on the bench to look out of the window. The train lurched twice and then slowly began to gain momentum once it had passed the abandoned cotton gin on the outskirts of town.

A few miles south, they slowed for a bridge crossing, and a man in a long frock coat and feathering silver beard walked from the underpass and came to stand near the tracks. He held up a large board as the train's passenger cars came abreast of him. Printed with hand-blocked letters, the board read *God Is Coming. But He Is Not Here Yet.*

The woman clucked in agreement and, speaking with the heavy accent of some distant place, told Lucinda she was going to Houston to be married, her first husband having died the year before. She had been a lady's maid once, but after the chaos and ruin of the war, she had been hired by an undertaker to do the hair and face-painting of the dead. Business had been very good for a few years, but of late the undertaker's establishment had gone into a decline. She still had nightmares of the dead coming to life and grabbing her around the wrist as she worked on them, but she told Lucinda, "One does what one must to live."

Lucinda agreed with her. The woman soon fell asleep with the rocking of the train, and Lucinda looked out the window again at the slanting light blazing the grasslands and prairies and thought, *Yes, one does what one must.*

Chapter 4

Nate looked east across rolling terrain carved deep with escarpments and punctured by thorn grasses, mesquite, and cholla, the thorns of which seemed to leap off the cactus onto passing horse or man. He remembered thinking on his initial ride to Franklin that he had never seen such country. He had been through the Big Thicket and longleaf piney woods of East Texas, gone farther east into the wilds of Arkansas, with its mountains of boulders and sheer drop-away cliffs. And he'd been over the vast expanses of Oklahoma, where he was born, the surface planes of which seemed often molded to a concavity, such was the weight of its flatness.

In Oklahoma, the ground had always appeared to him to be resting. It was solid, packed firm under the hooves of countless horses, bison, and cattle, its ancient upheaval already done. Here in Texas, the ground first buckled and then plunged away, lowering to canyons or surging up into mesas, as though still in the act of formation.

The Sierra Vieja stood at his back as he watched Deerling and Dr. Tom riding a short way ahead. From the time they had left

Franklin, following south the floodplains of the Rio Grande to their first supply stop at Eagle Springs, Nate had instinctively lagged behind. It seemed somehow an imposition on seniority to ride next to them, although it wasn't only his junior status that gave him pause. It was more the sense of violating an unspoken social pact that made him loath to come within earshot.

Watching the rangers together, he was struck again by their similarity or, more to the point, their relatedness, although he knew for a fact they were not blood kin. Upon Nate's being sworn in to the Texas State Police, Captain Drake had spoken of Deerling's and Goddard's long career of rangering—twenty years together, almost as long as Nate had been alive, border wars and Indian chasing for half their own lives. Drake had told Nate personally that if he chose to make a career of the law, he could do no better than attach himself to Tom Goddard and George Deerling.

On occasion, Dr. Tom would drop back and point out animal markings in the sandy loam or a weathered imprint carved into the rock. Often it was to warn Nate to look sharp, to scan the slight rises or abutments of rock for signs of movement from Mescalero Apache or even Comanche raiding south from the Llano Estacado. Earlier, Dr. Tom had taken him to task for his old Dance revolver and his Henry repeating rifle, asking when Nate would grab some sense and be reborn into the religion of Colt and Winchester. He warned Nate, "Someday when you don't need it to happen, some piece of metal's going to get fouled under the hammer of that cap-and-ball pistol. You wait and see."

Nate had to admire the wicked beauty of the brass, self-contained cartridges of the rangers' converted navy Colts. But he'd never give up his Dance cap-and-ball pistol. It had been given to him at the outbreak of the war by a man closer to him than his own father. He did, however, admit that he would gladly give over the old Henry hanging in a scabbard at his side for a .44 Winchester as soon as he had the means to do so.

The sun set in slow measure, warming their backs until the light was snuffed out and the elevated plain turned cold. They passed through Fort Davis, a dirty, mean, nearly abandoned fort manned by black soldiers left over from the war. They had been assigned to guard the coach and wagon trail routes frequently raided by Indians because of their training in conflict but also because these soldiers had nowhere else to go. No funds were available to keep the fort in good working order, so its window frames stood empty of glass, its barracks empty of doors.

Deerling did not stop at the fort but rode purposefully through the town, saying they would bedroll at Limpia Creek a half mile away. The soldiers stood quietly in groups in the alleyways, hovering around fire pits, their impassive faces turned towards their shoes.

They ate jerky and pan bread next to a fire built up from mesquite wood under an overhang. Dr. Tom pulled from his pack a much-abused news sheet and squinted at the variegated print in the half-light. Nate tossed out the last of the grounds in his cup and started to pull off his boots.

Deerling said, "Don't do that."

Dr. Tom pointed to the overhang. "We get a visitation, you don't want to have to make a run for it in your stocking feet."

Deerling lay supine on his bedroll, his shotgun cradled like a child in his arms. Closing his eyes, he said, "Tom, take first watch. Then Nate. Then wake me."

Dr. Tom squinted hard at the newsprint, but the fire had grown too weak, and the wilted sheet was refolded and put back into the pack.

True to their word, the rangers had seen to Collie's burial. They arranged for the local undertaker to claim the reward and sent the balance, after expenses for box and shovel were met, to Collie's wife in Van Horn's Wells. There had been no inquiries made in Franklin by Captain Drake or anyone else; no questions, no delays in leaving. Collie was dead by his own hand and that was that. The judge would be intercepted by a rider on the San Antonio mail road. The rangers were asked only to make their reports by telegram to Drake. Nate would do the same to the state police office in Austin.

Dr. Tom rubbed his hands together. "There'll be snow on the ground soon. We need to be in Fort Stockton before that happens."

Nate nodded. "My hip's tellin' me that's so."

"We'll need to get an early start. If we don't get held up by you repacking powder in that old Dance."

"It shoots just fine."

Nate pointed to Dr. Tom's pack. "Any news of the world in there?"

"Oh, that's old. From a Boston paper last year." Dr. Tom leaned back and recited, "'No landlord is my friend and brother, no chambermaid loves me, no waiter worships me, no boots admires and envies me.' It's Dickens."

Nate shook his head, having no idea who Dickens was.

"An Englishman. A writer of books, some of them printed in newspapers. I was going to travel all the way to St. Louis a few years back just to hear him stand on a stage and read." Dr. Tom laughed. "But the train from New York was too much of a hardship for him."

Deerling said, keeping his eyes shut, "Your talking is a hardship for me at this very moment."

Dr. Tom nodded to Nate to take to his bedroll and sleep. When Nate was awakened a few hours later, he emerged from his stiffened blanket, feeling with the naked palms of his hands and the soles of his boots the crusted mantle of frost covering the ground. He heard the horses stamping and chuffing in the dark air against the thin dusting of ice crackling away from mounds of basket grass under their hooves. After arranging the blanket around his head and shoulders, he pulled two of the horses together and stood between them for warmth, his carbine downturned against one thigh, the revolver tucked into his belt. Having no pocket watch or any light to see it by even if he'd had one, he counted the passage of hours in the movement of the moon toward the ranges to the west. He heard once the discontented flight of a bird breaking free of brush atop the overhang but no other sound that would have signaled a threat.

He revisited the accounts Deerling had given him earlier that day, of McGill's murderous path through Missouri, Kansas, and Texas. He had killed both men and women, a sixteen-year-old boy, and even two lawmen who had been on his trail. Most of them had been shot during the course of a robbery or at a card game gone bad. But a few of the killings had seemed random and pointless: a careless word, an incautious step, a shadow thrown over the killer at just the wrong time. And now, after the murder of the settlers in Houston, McGill could add two children to his tally.

To dispel those images, Nate thought of his wife in the garden, her fingers smelling of fall okra, green and tender-hulled, and he decided to post a letter to her from Fort Stockton. He thought of the stories of raiding Comanche and Kiowa and ruminated on the wisdom of carrying cyanide.

Just before dawn, he walked to Deerling's bedroll to wake him. But the man's eyes were already open and cleared of all sleep, as though the ranger had been wakeful in the dark for some time.

The three riders entered Fort Stockton, sixty miles on from Fort Davis, to acquire food and ammunition. As with Fort Davis, buffalo soldiers supplied the bulk of the outpost troops. But where the former station was poorly situated, Fort Stockton was armed and well provisioned, behind stone walls and stockade fences with lookouts.

Dr. Tom nodded with approval. "They don't call this Comanche Springs for nothing."

The officer, a young, tubercular-looking white man in a too-large Union coat, warned them that raiding parties had been seen in increasing numbers through the Edwards Plateau, following the Pecos River Valley.

"Fort Lancaster is completely unmanned now," he said. "If you are engaged, there can be no help for you."

Deerling thanked him and they rode on to the nearby town of St. Gall for a bath and a decent bed for the night.

They tossed a coin for first to the bath, Dr. Tom winning both throw-downs. He clapped his palms together, smiling. "Dress and delight, boys," he called out to them as he pulled a clean shirt from his pack and headed for the door. "Dress and delight."

Nate called after him to ask when they'd be riding out in the morning, and Deerling, sitting in a chair pulling at his boots, gave Nate a hard eye.

"Tomorrow's Sunday," Dr. Tom answered, nodding towards the chair where Deerling sat. "George is rather touchy on the subject of keeping the Lord's day." He closed the door and walked down the hallway, hitched and flat-footed.

"Don't you go to church?" Deerling asked Nate.

"It's been some time since."

"Didn't your mother raise you up to it?"

"She was raised with a mission church. She wasn't too fond of it."

"You a Catholic?" The hard eye returned.

"No," Nate said, standing up from his place at the floor, where he had been sorting through his pack. "Baptist."

"A Baptist?"

"Yes, an Oklahoma Baptist, if that's all right."

"Well…all right."

"Glad you can accommodate that." Nate turned his back to Deerling and kneeled down to resume looking for a less soiled shirt. After a while he added, "It seems to me that a man's beliefs are his own affair."

Behind him from Deerling he heard a grunt, although whether it was a noise of assent or merely of physical exertion he couldn't be certain, as it was followed by the sound of a boot clattering to the floorboards.

Nate sat on the bed with a piece of paper and a stub of pencil and commenced writing to his wife.

Dear Beth,

We have arrived in St. Gall, having safely passed through Forts

Davis and Stockton. The countryside is mostly scrub and desert and a hardship to our horses as, at times, they were fed only cactus pears with the thorns knocked off. We have seen no Comanche, but buffalo soldiers aplenty posted on the Government Road for the protection of all and for the gain of everyone but themselves. There is early frost on the ground out west, and snow in the sierras, which turn blue at night and orange with the sunrise.

The two rangers I am commissioned with, Tom Goddard and George Deerling, are experienced men of resolute purpose, but I fear their years on the borderlands have made them at times...

Here he paused, searching for the correct word. He didn't want to seem disloyal, but the memory of Maynard Collie's death still pulled at him. He thought about writing *unheeding of due process* but decided it would alarm his wife and wrote, instead, *hasty.*

Tom Goddard is a medical man from back East but knows more than any man I've ever met about the ground we walk on, its history and its beginnings. He is a reader of books and can imitate any bird or animal by breathing through his clasped fingers. His cougar call is a wonder and would make you blanch to hear it.

George Deerling has personal reasons for wanting to capture or kill the murderer William McGill, but what those reasons are, I cannot guess.

We are following McGill to Houston, which will take the better part of a month. But be assured that I will write you as often as circumstances will allow.

Send my love to Mattie. My hope is to see you both in early spring.

My love always, Nathaniel

After consideration he added a postscript telling her to write him in care of the postmaster in Austin and saying that he would be attending church in the morning, knowing it would bring a slow creeping smile to his wife's face.

When it was his turn, Nate paid for a half bath, the price of the full bath being too steep. The bathhouse was a large tent behind the main house with a tub, a washstand, and a small mirror nailed to a support post. He washed standing up and then combed his hair and shaved at the mirror. He observed that his hair was too long for ranger service and would soon need cutting. Since the war, he had worn it full, in pride of the Confederacy, but also because cropping it, he felt, would make him appear too young and inexperienced.

He scraped the razor over his cheek, breathing in the mustiness of the canvas sides, and realized that the tent had most likely been used in the field. He turned to observe the spray of darkened stains on the lower half of the far wall; it told him the tent had been in hospital service. When he turned back to the mirror, he saw reflected on the mottled glass what his naked eye had missed: one rust-colored blot on the canvas, vaguely the shape of a man's palm. He stared at the reflection for a good while, the razor poised in his hand, and thought of the field hospital in Arkansas in which he had spent some time, and of the men lying in it, suffering typhoid and dysentery and pneumonia, men and boys who had yet to see battle or even fire a gun but who were dying just the same.

Finished shaving, he quickly dressed, giving his work shirt to the boardinghouse lady to be washed. When he returned to the room, the two rangers looked awkward, as though their conversation had been cut off abruptly upon his entering.

Dr. Tom stood up from the bed. "Well, Nate. We thought you'd run off with the woman of the house."

The three of them walked the short distance to the public house to eat dinner, a meal composed of pot squash and steaks of indeterminate origin. They ordered three whiskeys and all stared for a long moment in appreciation of the warm oaky color and burned-barrel scent before draining their glasses.

They looked around at the empty hall and watched the barkeep cleaning used whiskey glasses with his tongue. The barkeep pointed to a sign over his head, which read *Dances, Two Bits*, and told them that the dancing would commence at eight o'clock, along with music the likes of which, he was certain, they had seldom heard. The girls, he assured them, were genuine hurdy-gurdy girls from Europe, and no common whores.

He added, "These foreign-born like dancing more than you've ever seen. You'll see. It gets rigorous."

As the barkeep had promised, within the hour, a small group of men and women quietly entered the public house and seated themselves on benches set against the far wall. One man unpacked a fiddle and another a squeezebox, and they began to play a song. Three young women, the hurdies, dressed in full skirts hemmed just above the ankle, nodded to the music, their old-fashioned sausage curls coiling and uncoiling in time with their bobbing heads.

Soon more men and women began to enter the public house, Irish, Mexicans, and Rhinelanders among them, each in his own dress, all speaking incomprehensible languages. Most of the men, and a fair share of their women, bought small glasses of beer and crowded the open area to hear the music that was played in ever-increasing tempos. Eventually, a couple of men bought their dance tickets from the barkeep and shyly approached the hurdy girls. Like the men were draft horses, Nate thought, too long at pasture.

The seated girls chosen to dance smiled and led their callers onto the floor, where they guided the men through a near approximation of reels, polkas, and galops, their partners changing after every song. Swiping his mustache, Dr. Tom walked to the bar and bought two tickets. He chose his partner and commenced an admirable waltz.

Nate turned to Deerling. "You gonna dance?"

Deerling took his hat, which had been balanced on one crossed knee, and set it on the table. "Never much cared for it. You?"

"No."

"Your wife don't miss it?"

"She didn't marry me for my dancin'."

"What did she marry you for?"

Nate saw it was a friendly-enough question. "She told me I was constant."

Deerling considered that for a moment. "Constancy in men is like fidelity in women. Much to be desired, but seldom found." He stared at Nate for a brief moment before shifting restlessly in his seat.

"That's a hard line to take," Nate said.

"No. It's not." Deerling stood up and faced him. "Oklahoma, I'm sure your wife is as faithful as the North Star. From what I've been told, you're not much for farming, but you know horses better than most, and we fight for the same side. But I didn't spend the past twenty years of my life learning to appreciate the merits of mankind. You're young. You'll learn." He fit his hat carefully back on his head and said, "Church is at nine."

With a nod to the barkeep, Deerling walked out of the hall just as Dr. Tom finished his first dance and returned to the table. Clapping Nate on the shoulder, he moved his chair around to better see the floor, now crowded with a dozen or more couples wheeling about the room.

Dr. Tom leaned close to Nate and said, "I didn't understand a word that girl said, but she could sure wing a lively one." He smiled and looked around. "Where's George?"

"He left. I think I put him awry."

Dr. Tom crossed his arms. "Oh?"

"He holds a darkened view of humanity."

"One thing you'll discover about George is that he takes his time with people. When I first rode with him, it was near a year before we had more than a passing of words. Just keep a steady path and he'll soften up."

Dr. Tom took a sip of whiskey, then thoughtfully sucked the remainder from the bottom of his mustache. "Listen," he said. "More than any other man I know, George would give his life for a friend. We were forty miles into Mexico—oh, this was in 'fifty-five—chasing some Lipan that had been raiding in Uvalde County. There were about a hundred of us, but we got pinned down at a stream called Rio Escondido by about five hundred Mexicans. George waded into that stream four times to pull out wounded men. Got shot in both arms. We thought he was going to have to pull the last fellow out with his teeth."

Nate smiled. Ranger lore, more than any other kind, valued the power of understatement.

Dr. Tom danced one more time with a different girl, and then he and Nate walked in amiable silence towards the boardinghouse.

The sky was dark and filled with stars, and Dr. Tom stopped once and rocked back on his heels to look up. He said to Nate, "Makes you feel small, doesn't it."

"Yes, it does." Nate watched Dr. Tom watching the stars. The ranger's mouth was open in awe, like a kid's, which made Nate smile.

Dr. Tom traced the arc of a shooting star with his finger. "Celestial wanderers," he said. "Sort of like me and George." He looked at Nate. "It's hard to imagine, seeing how crowded the sky looks tonight, how far away one star is from another. Like people, really. We can appear to be standing right next to each other, and yet in our minds, we can be thousands of miles away, lost to the outer reaches. But we're all together in the same black soup, which makes us all related somehow." Dr. Tom shook his head. "George rags on me about my pondering such things. It's good to have a sympathetic ear, though."

They walked up onto the porch and Dr. Tom placed a hand on Nate's arm. "Tomorrow, after George gets his church, we pick up the pace. We didn't want to run breakneck through the desert, but now there's more water and graze for the horses, we'll be riding fast."

They entered their room quietly as Deerling seemed to be sleeping, though the lamp was still burning.

Nate removed his clothes down to his long underwear and crawled into the bedroll. His ear pressed close to the floorboards, he could hear the woman downstairs stepping around the parlor, locking up and humming to herself. His wife would often hum.

Sometimes it seemed to Nate that the same strangely lamentable song had stretched out over the entire five years of their marriage. Strange because his wife was always smiling and seemed, more than anyone he knew, to be satisfied in full with her life, although she'd had troubles enough to be dour. Losing three babies from her belly in as many years could have made her bitter and resentful. But she rose cheerfully in the morning and smiled secretly against his fingers in the dark of their bed at night.

He turned over once to still those thoughts, and slept.

Chapter 5

The river barge, the *Emmelda Tucker,* slipped easily through a fog bank, eastbound with the tide on Buffalo Bayou. Lucinda had boarded at Allen's Landing in Houston early that morning with a dozen other men and women traveling to Harrisburg or Lynchburg or even farther on across the bay to Galveston Island, more than sixty miles to the south. An early-fall rain had soaked the cattails growing on the banks, and when the sun broke through, the matted rushes spilled mist over the river like smoke from a shanty fire.

Lucinda put a hand to one cheek, felt the tacky, saltwater air from the Gulf covering her face like a second skin. She stood on the bottom deck and, closing her eyes against the glare off the water, leaned against one wall of the barge's passenger cabin. Above her, on the hurricane deck, the men walked about, smoking and laughing good-naturedly about the fine weather, expressing hopes or giving assurances that the passage would prove calm.

From within the passenger cabin, she could hear some women talking, enjoying an effortless voyage where they could sit at their ease. It would be cooler inside, away from the press of the sun, but

Lucinda had no desire to talk mindlessly for hours about children, husbands, relatives soon to be found or lost, tatting, quilting; the disasters of small days, the tragedies of long nights.

She had waited for three days at the Lamplighter before her suitor had come. By the evening of the second day, she had been close to panic, pacing her room, parting the curtains to watch the streets for him. He was a cautious man, but he had always been punctual in his habits with her, and a vision of his possible injury or death sent her searching for the laudanum bottle to ease her into sleep.

On the third day, she sat for hours in a chair, certain he had abandoned her, and now her troubled visions were of herself alone, sick and discarded. She stared at the laudanum bottle, still half full, and considered drinking it all. She returned to her bed and lay, unmoving and cold, trying to recall his touch, or any touch in her brief life that had not been prompted by anger or empty, ungratifying lust.

He slipped into her room on the evening of the third day, well past dark, making his way soundlessly to the bed after she had already fallen into a drugged sleep. She woke as he was easing himself naked under the quilts next to her. He clamped his hand over her mouth, his quiet laugh in her ear, and he whispered, "You didn't wait up for me."

He raked up her nightdress with his other hand and then covered her eyes as well as her mouth but made no moves to have her until she had molded her body willfully against his. This initial withholding on his part—the momentary passivity so contrary to his restless animal strength—always excited her. It gave her a fleeting sense of control, a temporary feeling of safety, which was replaced by the even greater excitement of his forceful lovemaking.

Afterwards, they lay for a while, not speaking. She turned her back to him so that he wouldn't see her tears of relief and biting anger. "You left me alone here for days," she said. "With no word of where you were, or when you were coming."

He traced a fingernail against one shoulder blade. "The vagaries of surveying, my dear. You must be patient." He yawned as though he were falling asleep, but then he asked, "You've secured your position at Middle Bayou?"

"Yes," she answered. "I've written that I'll be arriving in two weeks' time."

"Good."

She turned to face him. He was motionless, but she could see the partially opened lids, the eyes watchful. "You'll come soon for me?"

He smiled and said, "You look flushed. Is it another fit coming on?"

She frowned and flopped away from him again, lying on her side. He pressed himself against her back, palming one breast. "Lucy," he said, the nickname that was his alone to use. "You know I'll never leave you. I'll never abandon you, but you shouldn't question me. Do your job. Write to me of your progress, and, when the time is right, I'll come for you." He expelled air into her ear mirthfully. "Then, when I introduce you to my mother, I can truthfully say that my wife has been a teacher, not a whore."

"I thought you liked the whore."

She could feel his lips curling against her shoulder. "Oh, make no mistake. I like the whore just fine. One might even say I like the whore better than anything." He rose up on one elbow, looking down at her. "The whore neither spins nor sews, but neither is she idle. She is not deceitful in her chosen enterprise; she is not puffed up. She is what she seems to be. Purely the embodiment of both commerce and discourse, pressed and distilled to a place no bigger than a sparrow's nest." He stroked her hair and slipped his fingers between her thighs. "Why, the only difference between you and our family deacon is the fob watch..."

Now, a movement next to her as she stood on the barge pulled her thoughts back to the river, and she saw a man standing close by in a startling orange-and-brown-plaid suit, the tight-fitting coat long to his knees. He removed his hat, nodding to her awkwardly, his hair nearly as orange as his jacket. She suppressed a smile, imagining his tailor convincing the man that the mirroring colors of the cloth were complimentary to his person as well as fashionable.

He pointed to the riverbank and said, "It's beautiful, isn't it?"

She followed his gaze and saw a large persimmon tree, the ripened fruit like scarlet globes of Italian wedding glass, perfect and seemingly untouched by birds.

"Yes," she said. "It's beautiful." She looked at his white, spotted profile and pale hands and realized he was closer to a boy than a man. "I've only ever tasted one, and it was near heaven."

He looked at her for a moment and then began to unbutton and remove his coat. "Shall I swim over and get you one?"

She laughed, shaking her head no, but to her amazement, he smiled more broadly and began to remove his stiff collar and shirt as well. He drew laughs and shouts from the men above, which brought the women out of the cabin, looking to see what the excitement was about. Lucinda held her hands over her mouth in disbelief that he could be so foolish—perhaps he truly was a lunatic.

He began pulling off his boots with some difficulty, and she then realized that he had been drinking, most likely fed whiskey by one of the other men. The women squealed in protest, and, while the men shouted encouragement, Lucinda fell helpless with laughter watching the boy stripping down to his undergarments and preparing to crawl over the railing.

The captain shouted a warning at them from the steering house and climbed down the ladder holding a rifle. He grabbed a handful of the boy's undershirt and quickly hauled him back off the rail and onto the deck. The captain whistled shrilly, and his dog, a black spaniel, leaped into the water and began swimming towards the shore.

The captain turned to the boy and said, "Watch and learn."

The dog had not swum ten yards before the water under the reeds started to boil, and the logs that had rested against the bank, bobbing gently with the current, began to move purposefully toward the center of the river. The captain whistled again and the dog turned and began paddling back to the barge.

The once-featureless logs resolved themselves into leviathans with churning legs and tails, three of them swimming rapidly to where the dog, his narrow-snouted head showing above the glassy surface of the river, was treading water in a way that seemed to Lucinda too languid for safety.

The passengers, men and women, came to stand at the railing to watch the dog's progress, the near-naked boy forgotten. The alligators had closed the gap between themselves and the dog by a good twenty feet when the captain took aim with his rifle and fired. The bullet struck the first gator in the broad space between the eyes. The impact of the bullet on the skull made a sound like a mallet against a watermelon, and the creature sank without a struggle.

The ship's fireman, his face and arms blackened from stoking the engine's furnace, joined the group, and he swung open the boarding gate and hunkered down, readying himself to pull up the dog once he breasted the hull.

The remaining two gators had closed the distance farther and Lucinda quickly calculated the amount of time left before the precise meeting of the surging bodies. The dog had, at most, only a few minutes. All eyes were on the captain, who stood poised with the stock of the rifle against his shoulder.

The dog was within a few feet of the boat, the gators perhaps the same distance behind, when the captain finally discharged the rifle, striking the closest creature midback. The wound, at first as white and dense as a man's thigh, soon bubbled blood like a fountain, and the gator's companion, without hesitation, turned and began to tear at the exposed flesh.

The dog swam abreast of the deck, and the fireman reached down, grabbed the long, wet fur with both hands, plucked the animal out of the water, and put him on the deck. The dog shook himself mightily and went to lie down, unperturbed by the events, in the shadow of the passenger cabin.

The men, and a few women, continued to watch as the remaining alligator ferried the carcass across to the far side of the river.

The boy had collapsed onto the deck, and the captain leaned

over him and said, "Here ends the lesson." The captain climbed back up to the steering cabin, and the boy gathered up his clothes and was helped inside by two of the older women.

Lucinda watched the dead gator float for a moment in the shallows and then saw it pulled under, with barely a resulting ripple, the persimmon tree on higher ground yet glorious and unmolested.

By midafternoon, the last of the passengers had stepped off onto the landing at Lynchburg, and she was alone, apart from the captain and fireman, for the last leg of the journey to Morgan's Point at the true beginning of Galveston Bay. From there, she would be met by a cart sent to fetch her overland to Middle Bayou.

After the boat docked at the old Confederate pier, the captain handed her off the barge, along with her bag, and she stood in the shade of some abandoned barracks for a while, watching the road for an approaching rig. There was not another being in sight across the grasslands to the west and the marshlands extending far to the south.

Bored with waiting, she walked onto the pier and looked out across the greater bay. A cooling breeze whipped at her skirts, and she watched the sky haze over with mackerel clouds tinged pink with a late sun. A coral snake, disturbed by her footsteps on the wooden planks, swam into the deeper channel, and she wondered what form of gnawing, rending, stinging death would claim her if she were to jump into the water.

The clapper in the old kitchen bell stirred with the breeze, a resonant sound that put Lucinda in mind of a ship's bell. She allowed herself to imagine a water voyage across the Gulf to

Galveston, and then on to New Orleans, away from the grinding dirt and dust of beggared towns. Soon, he had promised her, they could go wherever they liked.

She heard the sound of a horse approaching and turned to watch a buckboard carriage with two occupants, both female, pull up the long, flat road to the barracks. She had expected her employer, a planter named Euphrastus Waller, to meet her. But when the carriage drew to a stop next to her, the driver was an unremarkable young woman with light hair and eyes, no older than seventeen. The younger girl sitting behind her, with arms draped around the driver's neck, smiled, and Lucinda caught her breath. Through Kansas City and Abilene, she had seen women of wealth and status stand heel to heel with high-dollar whores, but she had never seen a more beautiful girl. If a virgin—and undoubtedly she was—this girl could earn more than a thousand dollars in a night over one bloodstained sheet.

"Are you Miss Carter?" the older girl asked.

Lucinda nodded. "I was expecting Mr. Waller to come for me."

"This is his carriage. I'm Jane Grant. And this python about my neck is my sister, May."

The girl unclasped her arms and sat back against the rear bench. "Mr. Waller is certainly not with us." She laughed and patted the place beside her, saying, "Come sit here."

"No, May. Miss Carter is sitting next to me." Jane motioned for Lucinda to put her bag in the cart and climb onto the front bench.

No sooner had Lucinda settled herself when she felt May's arms wrap tightly around her own neck. Jane waved her sister away and gave the reins a shake. "It's nothing, Miss Carter. Her mind is often elsewhere."

They rode in silence, shielding their eyes against the sun flattening itself on the western grasslands. The shadow of the cart followed behind them like a run of tar flowing into the general darkness of twilight. They stopped only once, when a feral pig, massive and tusked like an elephant, rushed onto the road. Its glistening snout, open-holed and almost obscene in its suppleness, tested the wind, but it was too weak-eyed to make a charge, and soon it waded into the tall brush on the other side.

For miles, Lucinda looked about for cabin light or campfires, but there was nothing man-made beyond the pale road she saw stretching ahead between the horse's ears.

Chapter 6

Deerling sat with a map spread out in front of him, positioned so that Nate and Dr. Tom could see the planned route. They ate supper while they studied it, finishing the last of the food packed by the boardinghouse woman in St. Gall. They had set up camp in the abandoned stone buildings of Fort Lancaster, and they were spent, having made fifty miles in three hard days, riding through country of steep mesas and hardscrabble depressions, crossing the mostly dry riverbed of the Pecos without incident. Barring accident or injury, they would be in Austin in a few weeks. From there to Houston was another one hundred and sixty miles.

Deerling pointed over the map. "We'll pass through Forts McKavett and Mason, right through the heart of Edwards Plateau."

"With full Comanche presence up this corridor until we get due east of Mason," Dr. Tom said, sweeping his finger south to north. He turned to Nate. "You ready for this?"

Nate grinned; Dr. Tom had seen such a look of eagerness in boys looking to put a hammer to a percussion cap. "I imagine so."

They sat for a while in the quiet, enjoying the last of the cornbread, which they dipped into their coffee. It seemed to Nate that

Deerling was more at his ease, or perhaps only less guarded, after the Sunday in St. Gall. They had spent the entire morning at the immigrant church, housed in a large tent set with an odd assortment of chairs provided by the parishioners. An older settler standing at the front suggested to Deerling in broken English that he leave his guns outside. Deerling ignored the old man and found a place in the front row, where he sat with his arms crossed, as if preparing for an argument.

Soon after the preacher began his sermon, a group of large, kite-eared boys began to laugh and talk loudly.

Dr. Tom leaned towards Nate and whispered, "Hellfire's comin'."

Deerling stood up, passed in front of the preacher, who faltered in his sermon, and calmly walked to the row of chairs where the youths sat. He pulled one of the Colts from his belt and tapped the boy nearest to him none too gently over the head with the butt end. In the shocked silence of the tent, Deerling walked back to the pulpit, coming to stand behind the sermon giver. The ranger directed the shaken preacher, "Go on ahead with your lesson. Just think of me as the angel Gabriel."

From that Sunday forward, Deerling had appeared as close to cheerful as Nate had yet seen him.

The food was soon swept away, and the weapons were brought out for inspection.

Deerling gestured to the Dance revolver and Henry rifle that Nate was cleaning and said, "You're going to need to get more firepower than that."

"I will when I can pay for it." After a pause he asked, "You think we'll see any play?"

Dr. Tom shrugged. "We don't want to linger here any more

than we need to. What's the farthest distance you've ever gotten out of that Henry?"

"A few hundred feet, maybe more."

"Or maybe less." Dr. Tom laughed.

Deerling looked at Nate for a moment as though deciding something; then he got up, walked to his bedroll, and reached for a long leather case. Nate had seen the case strapped to the mule and guessed it was a rifle but had not yet seen what kind.

Out of the case, Deerling pulled a Whitworth and handed it to Nate.

Dr. Tom said, "Well, this is a kiss-and-make-up. He don't even let me hold that rifle."

Nate had never seen a Whitworth rifle, much less held one. A few Confederate sharpshooters had used them to great effect, but they were rare, and a one-shot deal in a hard engagement. Of all the weapons spread out before him—including two navy Colts, a Smith and Wesson top-break pistol, two Walker Dragoons, and two Winchester rifles—the Whitworth was worth the most, more than all of them put together.

"It's light," Nate said, surprised.

Deerling nodded. "I've got only six bullets left for it."

Nate sighted down the barrel, swept it in a slow arc from window to door. He then passed it back to Deerling. "Where'd you come by it?"

"I negotiated heavily for it."

Dr. Tom slapped the table. "He liberated it from some old reprobate perched on a gully firing at the Henderson town sheriff a quarter mile away. That rifle shoots twice that distance without breakin' wind."

Deerling carefully returned the rifle to its case, and Nate thought he looked pleased by the memory. Deerling added, "Maybe I'll let you fire it sometime. We get to Austin, we'll draw pay and see about you getting another rifle."

Nate nodded his genuine thanks and he sat comfortably for another hour in the shadows cast by the oil lamps listening to commentary, mostly by Dr. Tom, about the distances yet to be traveled, the streams and rivers and wide-gaping arroyos to be crossed. About how the land would change, from sand and rock to hills of black soil and prairie, the bands of colors changing with the ground from the damnation red and purple of the desert to endless shades of yellow and green of grasslands.

Having little hardware or tack to clean, Nate crawled into his bedroll and left the two rangers to finish their business. When he woke, it was to the milky, diffused light of dawn. Through sleep-gummed eyes, he became aware of a figure standing next to his bedroll.

Deerling said, "We've got to leave now. Tom's out readying the horses."

Nate drew his head back like a tortoise, rubbing his face and squinting to better see. Deerling hunkered down next to him and held out, between the fingers of one hand, a large-bore rifle shell. He had Nate's full attention as he balanced the shell upright on the ground next to Nate's head, the faint smell of almonds wafting over the tang of the lead casing.

He told Nate, "Let's hope you never have to use it."

The tone of Deerling's voice was as flat as a capstone to a building, but the image of Maynard's stiffening body filled Nate's mind. Within minutes, he was dressed, and after grabbing up his bedroll, he followed Deerling out the door, the big bite dropped into his pack.

They filled their canteens at the runoff of Live Oak Creek and rode east, towards the ascent of Government Road, which wound its way up a steep hill to the plains beyond. Deerling led the mule, but after a few hundred feet, the creature balked at the incline, and Dr. Tom had to take a prod to his bunching hindquarters to edge him up to the summit.

At the halfway mark, Dr. Tom directed Nate to stop and rest his horse on a flattened stony shelf that jutted out a few feet from the mesa wall. He pointed to the striations of rock, reddish bands on ashen gray, revealing to Nate that the whole of the valley had at one time been a vast inland sea with creatures of shell, more than any man could count, that swam through it. He gestured to a swath of black cutting through the rock face and said, "The grave-yard of this whole world pressed to the size of a lady's ribbon. If you know the history of rocks, you know the history of the world." He spurred his horse back to the ascending road; loose pebbles were kicked out behind him like stinging missiles.

Nate held back a bit before giving rein, wondering what Deer-ling thought of Dr. Tom's theorizing on ancient seas, theories that might fall outside of the biblical word. "Are you really a doctor?" he called up the path.

"Oh, that's been George's doing, in the main. I went to medical school in Baltimore for a term. It wasn't for me, though. I left and came down here, and he got to calling me Dr. Tom. A year spent with medical men, and their potions and devices, and I've done my best since to stay away from the whole lot of 'em. I get shot, I'd just as soon visit the local baker than the surgeon." He looked briefly over his shoulder at Nate. "I did, however, keep my medical kit. Never know when someone will need a good wrist saw."

Once they reached the apex of the road, they sat for a few minutes looking down at the valley spread out before them. Dr. Tom took field glasses from his saddlebag and scanned the entire broad expanse in a sweeping motion of his head. He offered them to Nate, who took them and looked down at the stone buildings of the fort.

Dr. Tom said, "It didn't look so small coming from the western approach, did it?"

Nate agreed, took one last pass with the glasses across the southern basin, and saw a puff of dust wafting upwards. Traveling animal, he thought, coyote or wolf. The early sun had not yet thrown light fully onto the valley floor, and he couldn't see a defined silhouette at such a distance. He waited a moment more, aware of Dr. Tom's hand outstretched to take back the glasses.

Deerling's horse shifted. "Come on, Nate."

Several more dust funnels appeared, like small tornadoes forming in reverse, and he thought he saw dark shapes moving through a distant stand of oak. He brought both hands up to the glasses to steady the view.

"What is it?" Dr. Tom asked.

"I don't know." Nate pointed to the southwest where he had seen movement and gave the glasses to Dr. Tom.

Deerling pulled his horse back to the lip of the ridge. "Tom?"

"Hold on. Not sure yet."

Nate could see the tiny spray of dust expanding, and a moving band of animals cleared the trees, following a dry creek bed.

"Wild horses?" Nate asked.

After a moment, Dr. Tom said, "Comanche raiders." He lowered the glasses and handed them to Deerling, who looked for a brief while, and then dismounted.

Nate recalled that only a few years back, Deerling and Goddard had been a part of the skirmish at Dove Creek. Two ranger companies, along with a few hundred Confederate troops, were outgunned and outmaneuvered by seven hundred Kickapoo Indians. That the Kickapoo had been mistaken for fighting Comanche or Kiowa and had been seeking only to escape the ravages of a civil war did not lessen the surviving rangers' desire to kill any Indian, regardless of his origin. The remnants of the tribe were chased into Mexico; often they were shot in the back, or, as some of the rangers referred to it, the "northward side." Dr. Tom had told Nate he never cared for that tactic or the expression—"unbefitting," he called it, a shameful comedown for those in service.

Deerling said to Nate, "Follow me down to the ledge, and bring my Winchester along with your Henry. Tom, keep watch here." Deerling yanked the Whitworth from its case on the mule and they began quickly sidestepping down the hill off the main road.

Once he'd gained the ledge, Nate flattened himself next to Deerling, who used the glasses to watch the approaching horses. They were still more than a half a mile distant, traveling north, but Nate could make out four men on horseback driving the herd of about twenty horses at a fast walk. The outcropping where the two men lay was in shadow, but the valley was now torched with clear light.

Deerling said, "They'll switch course to the runoff." He passed the glasses to Nate, who watched the herd soon being driven to the creek.

As the horses waded into the water, their heads bent to drink, Deerling asked, "What do you make it?"

"Between a hundred, hundred fifty yards from the base road."

"And we're two hundred yards up?"

"Maybe less."

Deerling removed his hat and carefully raised himself to a one-kneed position, then sighted down the side scope of the Whitworth. He adjusted it and gave Nate the rifle to shoulder. "In a minute, one of those bucks is likely to cross the stream to our side. Take a look."

One of the riders broke off from the group and splashed through the stream, scanning the rise. Through the scope, Nate could clearly see the pearl-white buttons on the man's shirt. After a moment, the rider turned his horse around and sat loose in the saddle, his back to the cliff.

"I don't have a fork for the barrel," Deerling said. "So you'll have to hold firm for the kick."

Nate pulled his eye away from the scope and peered sharply at Deerling.

"You only get one shot, so make it count."

"They don't see us, there's no cause to shoot."

Deerling sat back on his haunches and stabbed a finger toward the herd. "All of those horses are branded. When you joined the force, it should have been explained to you that a horse thief is a man just waiting to be dead. Now take the shot."

"Christ Almighty. They're not a danger to us—"

Deerling put his face close to Nate's. "I'm not telling you again. When that gun goes off, and he goes down, the rest will scatter with the horses. You miss, and they're likely to regroup and kill us on our descent. Fire the weapon."

Nate sighted down the scope and watched as the rider kicked

his horse forward and the three men on the far side of the stream began waving the herd into motion again. His finger slipped inside the trigger guard and curled around the trigger, but an instinct as strong as breathing made him pause.

The rider had crossed the stream, and Nate lowered the gun. "I'm not shooting a man in the back, horse thief or no."

Deerling pulled the Whitworth from Nate's hands. "You just failed your first test." He stood up, and with the rifle shouldered and carefully aimed, he whistled through his teeth, as if he were calling in a field hand. The rider yanked the reins, wheeling the horse about, and Deerling fired. Following the shattering boom of the Whitworth, the man was thrown backwards into the water, a red mist scattering where his head had been moments before. Several rifle shots from Dr. Tom were discharged from the summit above them, the bullets tearing clods out of the streambed.

The three remaining riders flagged the horses into a panicked run, and they raced north again up the valley, leaving the body in the shallow current. Deerling turned and began climbing towards the top of the road.

Nate sat on the ledge watching the distant body floating in the stream. The riderless horse had stampeded away with the herd, and a turkey vulture circled in ever-tightening spirals in the warming updrafts. By the time he had gathered up the two rifles and started back up the mesa, the sun had come to shine on its western face and he didn't know if the two rangers had waited for him or if he would breast the hill and find himself alone.

Chapter 7

The Waller family sat facing Lucinda as though they had
been elaborately posed for a theatrical performance or da-
guerreotype. Euphrastus Waller was a large, somber man dressed
in a dark woolen suit with a black silken tie drooping beneath
his chin. His ample haunches looked to be uncomfortably
planted in an ornate, tufted chair, and Lucinda suspected, from
the way his coat stretched across his chest, that he was wearing
a corset.

His wife, Sephronia, sat to his left on a low bench. Her hair was
in a tight knot at the nape of the neck, her scalp an unblemished
white through the exactly centered part. Her dress was also of silk,
although the hem was frayed, and she had voluminous petticoats
under the skirts, the likes of which had not been seen since the
fall of Atlanta. The daughter, Lavada, sat in an even lower chair
to his right.

Good God, Lucinda thought. *The girl's wearing gloves.*

Next to Lavada, close to a window, was the Wallers' son, Elam.
He sat motionless in a wheeled, cane-backed chair, his face towards the light, his half-open eyes focused on nothing. Lucinda

must have looked overly long in his direction, as Lavada offered, "Brother has had a hard life."

"My son…" Euphrastus began. His voice trailed away and he cleared his throat.

"Our son was wounded at the Battle of Vicksburg," Sephronia said pointedly. "He has been in a decline."

"It was a siege," Euphrastus corrected. He glanced briefly at his wife, and she blushed under his scrutiny and looked down at her hands.

"Ah," Lucinda said, focusing on the wall above their heads. It was a small parlor, but it had high ceilings, and the maroon-and-green-striped wallpaper gave the room extra height so that she felt a momentary sense of dizziness, as though the floor were falling away from her chair. To counter the effect, she moved her gaze to the mantel behind Euphrastus and saw perched there a stuffed and mounted owl with amber glass eyes.

Euphrastus said, "I suppose that, as it was dark when you arrived last night, you will be eager to see the school."

Sephronia nodded, as if it were a startling, momentous observation. Lucinda was uncertain whether or not this was her cue to leave, so she nodded as well, and waited.

He continued, "And to the subjects being taught?"

"As I wrote in my letter," Lucinda said, "reading and penmanship, mathematics, geography—"

"From what map?" Euphrastus muttered.

"And, of course, the natural sciences."

Sephronia's head came up. "Miss Carter, are not all sciences natural?" She smiled at her own cleverness, and Lavada stifled a laugh behind one gloved hand.

"And elocution, Miss Carter?" Lavada asked.

She handed Lucinda a slender volume engraved with the title *The American Speaker.* Lucinda opened the cover to the table of contents and read the first two entries: "Religion Never to Be Treated with Levity" and "The Folly of Misspending Time."

Euphrastus stood abruptly. "I think we should show Miss Carter where she will be teaching."

He led Lucinda down the front-porch steps and onto the path away from the house, and she could see what had been hidden in the dark: a whitewashed two-story house, hastily built, with the wash already peeling.

Behind them, the two women pushed the wheeled chair down a ramp, Elam seemingly insensitive to the world around him.

Euphrastus gestured to the north and the south of the path as they walked, naming the homesteads and farms. Behind them, to the west, ran Middle Bayou, with live oak and magnolia growing in abundance, and crape myrtles newly planted for color.

He told her that he was growing cotton and planned to plant cane for a sugar mill.

She allowed him to take her elbow as she stepped over a deep rut in the path, observing that he was mindless of the women struggling with the wheeled chair. She let his eyes linger over her naked fingers.

Turning her face slightly to him, she curled her lips upwards and asked, "Is that what you did before coming to Middle Bayou?"

"Yes. I had twelve hundred acres of cotton and tobacco in Mississippi. Before the war."

He stared off down the road, his eyes fixed and tormented-looking, his momentary silence testament to all he had lost. He released his grip on her elbow and pointed out the Grant farm in the distance. The main house was a small, misshapen affair but situated in a field of flat-leaved grasses that reflected sunlight off their wavering tips like an ocean of copper mirrors.

Approaching Red Bluff Road, Lucinda saw the schoolhouse and was surprised. She had been prepared for a refitted barn or disused carpentry shed, but at the juncture of the Middle Bayou Road and Red Bluff was a new pine building, the boards still oozing sap. The women positioned Elam in the shade of a tree and followed Lucinda inside.

There were only a few windows, and they all stood quiet for a moment, letting their eyes adjust to the darkened room.

"The desk was brought from my own office," Euphrastus said. Lucinda ran the pads of her fingers appreciatively over the carved surfaces, allowing one forefinger to slip lingeringly into a bit of scrollwork.

Euphrastus, watching the movements of her hands, became short-winded and made a show of studying the view from one of the windows before sweeping his wife and daughter to the door. "We will accompany you tomorrow morning, Miss Carter, to introduce you to your pupils."

She watched them walking homeward for a while, standing at the same window Euphrastus had been looking through. This time, Euphrastus pushed the wheeled chair. Lucinda stretched her arms and pulled off her bonnet. She examined the readers and workbooks stacked precisely on the desk and counted thirteen sets of each.

There were three rows of sturdy benches with long, unbroken

planks in front of them, raised and tilted, for writing. She sat in the wooden chair behind Euphrastus's desk and let her mind wander. *Only a few weeks of this,* she reminded herself, *so it hardly matters what I stuff their heads with;* she would teach the farmers' offspring what she liked, and put laudanum in the water bucket for the troublemakers.

She shifted her gaze and saw May in the open doorway. The girl wandered in and came to stand in front of the desk. She was wearing a dress of cornflower blue, the same startling color as her eyes. The dress was ten years out of fashion but capably reworked to fit her small frame.

May picked up a reader and pretended to study it. "Do you want to know a secret?"

Lucinda smiled. "Only one?"

May slipped onto one of the benches and rested her elbows on the writing board. "My name is not really May."

"Oh?"

"It's Jane."

Lucinda cocked her head. "Isn't that your sister's name?"

"It *is* Jane. We're both Janes." May stage-whispered the last and, laughing, sprang from the bench, coming to alight on the desk in front of Lucinda. "My mother, who was the second Mrs. Grant, had her way and named me Jane also. It was the only name she said she'd ever wanted for her girl. Father couldn't abide having two Janes under the same roof, though, and took to calling me May, the month I was born."

"And what does your mother call you?"

"My mother calls me nothing. She is not with the living." May slipped off the desk and Lucinda watched her progress about the room, examining and overturning every item, looking into each corner. Lucinda reminded herself to be cautious with this one.

"The last time I saw my mother," May went on, "I was four years old. She sat next to Father in a buggy headed to Little Rock. Father had told us that she was very ill and he was taking her for the doctor. She was wearing a bonnet, one with colored ribbons. He returned later that night, alone, my mother's bonnet hanging by its ribbons from the struts. There's a big river on the way to Little Rock, you see."

Lucinda did not see, but May suddenly said, "I hear Jane calling." She darted for the door, but before leaving, she stopped and turned, smiling through bowed lips.

Lucinda watched her hurtling down the road and off into the fields, her dress showing in blue, vibrating swaths through the tall grass.

She stayed at the school until the supper hour and then left, latching the door, thinking she had forgotten to ask Euphrastus for the key. But there was no lock on the door—nothing but knowledge to steal—and, arranging her bonnet on her head, she walked down the road back to her room at the Wallers'. There had been biscuits and cornmeal for breakfast. She hoped there would be meat for dinner.

Chapter 8

$\mathcal{T}$he weather had turned: the men rode the last ten miles to Austin in rains that were near horizontal. The storm had come in from the northwest, and the frigid rain ran in sluices down the collars of their oiled coats.

When they got to the banks of the Colorado River, they saw that the bridge had been washed away and the ferry was gone, probably swept downriver. They watched the surging waters and the things chased along with the current—bits of wood and sacking, the upright hooves of some cloven animal—and then they turned around and made for an abandoned house they had seen a quarter of a mile back.

They found it after a few pass-bys and saw that it had a lean-to shed on one side. But the shed was too small for the three horses and the mule, so they stripped the horses of tack, stored the supplies in the shed, and left the animals standing together, huddled and spring-footed, beneath the overhang of the porch.

The house had not long been abandoned, and the roof was mostly intact, the floor with dry areas large enough to sleep on. The stove was old, but the wood from the bin was sufficiently dry to catch a small flame, and the men stripped down and shivered close to the frail warmth as they searched for dry shirts and long underwear. The steam rolled off their bare backs in wisps. "Like smoke off bacon," Dr. Tom observed.

Nate lit a lantern, and his boot caught the edge of a bottle, sending it rolling against one wall. He picked it up and saw it was a nearly empty bottle of Argyle Bitters. The label claimed the contents would *carry away the bile, rendering the patient less distempered,* and he wondered if it, or anything, could lessen the punishing silence from Deerling the past two weeks. The only human voice he had heard speaking directly to him was Dr. Tom's.

A few times, he had tried to write his wife about what had come to pass, but he couldn't find the words to tell her. He had revealed to her long ago the sum total of his service during the war: the one summer spent in Arkansas, where he had arrived at sixteen as part of a mounted cavalry force from Texas. Where, within the space of a month, he had been officially dismounted, forced into infantry status along with thousands of other Texans, brought low with dysentery, and finally sent home with all the other men under sixteen or over forty.

But there appeared to be no foothold by which to regain Deerling's confidence. The man seemed to discount and undermine him at every turn. It was more than just the silence, Deerling refusing to speak to him, as though Nate were a ghost haunting the campsite. There were the deliberate actions designed to unseat Nate's nerve.

Two days after the shooting at the creek, the men had been hunting for rabbit and quail, anything to supplement the constant rations of jerky. Each man had picked his own path away from the road, and Nate followed a trail into a rocky gully, where he spied a mottled gray rabbit settled on a large boulder. He took aim, but a rifle blast behind him made him flinch wildly and misfire. He jerked his head around in time to see Deerling at a distance behind him lowering his Winchester. The ranger moved past him, grabbed the dead rabbit by the hind legs, and returned to camp, all without a word.

Nate was by turns angry and frustrated, and, worse, he was rendered indecisive. At another time, a man firing over his head like that would have earned that man a beating. Even Dr. Tom had grown more quiet and reflective as the days progressed, offering no comments or observations about the actions of his partner.

Nate fed small pieces of wood into the badly smoking stove and they set about eating a cold supper of day-old cornbread and some canned peaches. With their clothes hanging on pegs to dry, they waited for the coffee to warm while listening to the rain turn to hail on the roof. There was an occasional buzzing from the wall behind the wood bin as well, as though the wind were shaking something loose in short, rapid bursts.

Dr. Tom worked at the damper in the stove, and Nate saw a red, puckered crater in the skin on the underside of his arm.

"That," Dr. Tom said, following his gaze, "was gotten as a child. Pitched from the hay wagon. The baling hook trailing behind sliced into my arm and dragged me for what seemed miles. I almost drowned in the mud before my brother realized I had fallen off." He smiled, then tilted the can of peaches to his mouth; peach juice dribbled down his chin. "Who says farming ain't dangerous?" As he lowered the can and wiped his mouth, the buzzing sound came again, and the three of them listened for the source.

After a time, Dr. Tom stood up and reached for more wood in the bin. *"Shitfire,"* he yelled, throwing himself to the side. "Snake."

Coiled, with head raised, the diamondback at its thickest was as big around as Nate's wrist. The strike came, missing Dr. Tom by a handbreadth, and the head recoiled again, but higher up, raised a good six inches against the wall; the rain-dampened rattler buzzed fitfully.

The three of them backed out through the door and stood shirtless under the dripping eaves with the horses.

Dr. Tom said, "It's not like it hadn't been warning us for the best part of an hour."

Shivering, the three reflected for a moment, considering their options. Deerling finally said, "I'll go back in and get the pistol."

Dr. Tom shook his head. "Tell it I said hey."

Nate said, "No. I'll do it."

He walked back into the house, grabbing a sodden shirt off a peg. The lantern light was weak; he couldn't see the snake on top of the bin anymore. He hoped it had slipped back between the kindling and not onto the floor nearby. He stood quiet for a moment and listened. There was an empty rain bucket close to the door, and Nate picked it up and gently toe-heeled towards the stove. A renewed buzzing low down told him the snake had crawled back into the wood bin and would have to be coaxed, or driven, out. It was cold in the room, so they couldn't sleep in the house without expecting the snake to make for the warmth of their bedrolls.

The stove had little wood in it and had already smoked itself out. Nate opened the wood latch and, using the wet shirt, scooped up a few pieces of wood, still glowing and hot. He dropped the steaming, wadded shirt with the embers into the bucket and closed the wood latch and the damper. He then set the bucket on its side, some distance from the stove, with the open end toward the bin.

Dr. Tom called, "Nate? It's cold out here..."

Nate looked out the open doorway onto the porch and saw the two rangers wrapped in horse blankets and shivering. He picked up his Henry rifle and, with the butt end, began striking the woodpile, opposite the side where the bucket lay. He heard the distinctive, angry buzzing, and soon the snake emerged at the far end; it crawled towards the warmth of the embers and into the mouth of the bucket.

In four strides Nate had his boot on the bottom ridge of the bucket, upending it, trapping the snake inside. He secured the bucket with several heavy logs and stepped to the door, motioning the rangers back into the house.

Dr. Tom stood over the bucket. "Now, that's one I haven't seen."

"Don't thank me yet. It's your shirt in there with the snake." Nate sat down on the floor, rubber-legged.

"What do we do with it?" Deerling tapped the bucket with his foot, setting off the dull thud of a strike from inside.

"We go to sleep. He's not goin' anywhere."

"You gonna kill it?"

"No, sir." Nate reached over and grabbed his bedroll, then pulled it around his shoulders. "I believe I'll leave the killing to you. You seem so eager for it."

He crawled to a dry spot, lay down, and shut his eyes. Behind closed lids, he thought of his wife. He remembered a day in the first few months of their marriage, remembered her crouching with him outside their small field of corn. Her face was close to his, her breath fogging the morning air. She whispered, "This is the way the grandmothers do it. You don't kill the snake. He eats the mice that eat the corn." One of her arms encircled the capture barrel, the thin silver bracelet he had given her bright against her skin. "You make him rest beneath the barrel for an hour while you pick what you need." She pointed to the warm embers inside the bucket. "The snake is drawn to the warmth.

"Like all living things," she had said, her fingers tracing heat across his forehead, proving the point.

Chapter 9

The students of Middle Bayou were twelve in number, eleven on the frequent days that May did not attend. The oldest was Lavada Waller, a girl who, in Lucinda's estimation, was almost stunningly thickheaded; the youngest, a sweet, placid boy named Pete who stuttered badly.

On Lucinda's first day, Euphrastus presented her to the community with an introduction so lengthy that half the students, along with a good number of the parents crowded into the over-heated schoolroom, nodded off. He intoned a speech on the virtues of Southern education, which had been cut short during the "War of Northern Aggression," and revisited in agonizing detail the resultant evils of Federalism, reinforced by Reconstruction.

Lucinda looked over the sad, wilted gathering of settlers, the women in faded dresses, the men in their work denim, and recognized in all of their faces the tenuous look of hope, pale and limpid, painful in its degree of uncertainty, inadequate as a counterweight to the years of starvation, of violence, of sudden death.

During the war, she had worked for a short time nursing the

amputees who filled Confederate hospitals. Their missing limbs horrified many of the other volunteers, the women preferring to dote on the soldiers whose wounds were less disfiguring, finding comfort and purpose in feeding their hopes of a return to life as whole men.

To Lucinda, the amputees' rage—at their dependencies and helplessness, at the dawning knowledge that they would never reclaim their lives as they had been or be without their graceless infirmities—was as familiar and unthreatening to her as her own face. She had recognized the fearful, condemning looks given to them by the hospital visitors and felt her own rage welling up in sympathy. She remembered all too clearly the faces of onlookers and curiosity seekers at the asylum where she had spent her youth. Gawkers who were repulsed and yet fascinated by her wild contortions during a fit and who were irrationally fearful of contracting her violent tremors and deathlike stupors as they might a camp fever. She had learned as a child that nothing could unseat the God-fearing volunteers from their ministrations as quickly as the discovery that they were in close proximity to an unexplained illness.

She had played cards with the soldiers; had held their hands or their arms, or their shoulders if their hands and arms were gone; had changed the seeping bandages on their lower extremities without blanching or turning away. She had fought on their behalf for a fair share of blankets, of food, of medicine. And in fighting for them, she had claimed what had been denied to her as a child.

But she had to look away from the terrible rawness of the settlers of Middle Bayou as they gazed in pride at their offspring, their thin, ragged hopes for the future, and focus her attention back on Euphrastus's droning speech. When it ended at last, the farmers clapped politely and, after shyly wishing Lucinda well, walked back into the light, away to their fields and homes.

When she turned to face the children, Lucinda was surprised to see that the Wallers' son, Elam, was still at the back of the room. Sephronia reappeared at the door uttering apologies, saying she had walked halfway down the path home before she remembered her stranded invalid. She cheerfully waved and then wheeled the chair from the schoolhouse as though she had merely forgotten a tea cart after a party.

In the silence that followed, Lucinda wrote on the slate board balanced on an artists' easel *Miss Carter.* She then turned to her students. "Over the course of weeks, you will be practicing reading and mathematics, geometry, in particular. Nothing of nature or in man's designs for roads or bridges or even surveying can be appreciated without an understanding of the spatial relationships between one thing and another."

She smiled at their blank, uncomprehending faces and then turned once more to the board. Below her name she wrote, in elaborate looping letters, *In one page, describe your greatest hopes and fears.*

Having handed out the copybooks, she seated herself in the chair behind the large desk. For the better part of an hour, she watched her charges struggling to put their thoughts into words, brows furrowed, lipping pencil nubs like anxious horses. She occasionally nodded encouragement and answering a few simple questions from the younger children. When the last child had completed the assignment, she collected the books and, to the students' delight, turned the class loose for the day.

She stood in the door waving good-bye. Experiences with her

own teachers had shown her that there were no greater tools with which to control young minds than their weaknesses and their fears.

As the days passed, she learned their names, their habits, and their histories. Several of the students were bright; most gave no trouble. The two oldest boys, fourteen and sixteen, were brothers, and aggressive in their early defiance of her. But after Lucinda complained to Euphrastus, the older, Jack, was severely caned. For a week following the caning, she went out of her way to show excessive kindness to the younger brother, Sam—praising him for his work, ruffling his hair, smiling at him fondly—ensuring that the brothers' grudges and resentments would be turned towards each other.

At the end of the week, the resulting fistfight in the yard saw both of them expelled entirely from the schoolhouse.

Her cleverest student was Pete. He was no more than nine or ten but had the eyes of an old man. He had a bad stutter, but she found that if she stood behind him with her hand placed firmly on his shoulder, he could speak reasonably well. Those who teased him for it were given the onerous task of cording wood for the schoolhouse stove or liming the outhouse.

She let the majority of the students pursue their own interests and spent the most time with those few inclined to mathematics. In this regard, May was bright, but easily bored, often wandering away without permission or explanation.

At the end of the second week, on a rainy afternoon, May lingered after the other students had left. She was bent over her workbook, her face close to the page, completing the last of the day's assignments: an essay on the legends of Middle Bayou. Lucinda in that instant realized that May was quite shortsighted. It made the girl seem vulnerable, and Lucinda was surprised to feel suddenly protective, knowing that the otherwise perfect girl had such a flaw. She asked, "Are you near finished?"

May looked up, stretching her neck. "I could go on and on."

Lucinda reached out her hand for the return of the book and smiled warmly. "I'm certain you could."

May shut her copybook and returned it to Lucinda. She sat on one corner of the desk, swinging her feet, the hem of her dove-gray dress hiked above her knees.

Lucinda asked, "Another new dress, May?"

May pursed her lips. "It was La-va-da's."

Lucinda laughed at the near-perfect imitation of Lavada's drawl. "That was kind of her."

"Kind had nothing to do with it. Her mother was going to pitch it in the rag barrel." May leaned back on her elbows. "It kills her that it looks so fine on me."

Lucinda reached out and slowly pulled the hem of the dress down over May's knees. May arched her brows and laughed. "Do you have a gentleman friend, Miss Carter?"

Lucinda shook her head.

"I only ask because I saw that you'd gotten a letter." May pointed to a pocket in Lucinda's dress.

A cautioning reflex held Lucinda's expression in check. A letter had been delivered to her the day before, and she had kept it hidden in her clothing, reading it only when she thought she was alone. "Why would you think it from a gentleman?"

May shrugged. "Receiving mail in Middle Bayou is as eventful as the slaughtering of the autumn hog." She smiled, a sly curving of the mouth. "I saw the writing on the envelope."

"As it happens, it's from my brother."

May looked disappointed at the news but asked, "Is he handsome?"

"Yes, I think so."

She shifted onto her side, lying full out on the desk as though it were a couch, her head propped up on one hand. "Mr. McKenzie, our neighbor, is handsome, or would be if he wasn't frowning all the time. He has only one arm, you know, from the war, and his place has been reduced to a few pitiful acres, though he had thousands in Georgia. I think I should let him kiss me if he had two arms. What must it be like, do you think, to be kissed by a one-armed man…"

"May." Jane stood in the open doorway. She saw her sister reclining on the desk and frowned. "I've been calling and calling." She held out a hand.

Diffuse sunlight from a breach in the clouds haloed around Jane's face and hair as she stood in the doorway, and Lucinda thought that she was actually pretty. Then May came to stand next to her, and the impression was diminished.

Jane asked, "Miss Carter, would you please have supper with us tomorrow at six? My father has yet to meet you."

May circled one arm tightly around her sister's waist and added, "And we have a piano, so afterwards I can sing for you."

Lucinda tried to imagine a piano within the forlorn walls of the Grant home; her most recent sampling of such entertainment had been inside a bordello, the songs explicit and, for the less knowing, instructive. Any opportunity to avoid the lackluster talk at her employer's dinner table, though, would be welcome. She inclined her head in acceptance and, gathering up the copybooks to read in her room, said good night to the sisters.

After closing the schoolhouse door, she walked down the path to the Waller settlement. A short distance away, she stopped and slipped inside an old greenhouse. It had been used only for storage by the family but, as some of the glass was broken, nothing of value had been placed inside, and the door was never locked. Lucinda had taken to hiding in it occasionally, to write and read her letters unobserved. Her room in the Waller house was sometimes unexpectedly invaded by Lavada or Lavada's mother wanting to engage her in conversation, and the little shed was the only place that gave her the quiet that she craved; a counterweight to the years spent with no privacy, no solitude, no peace.

She sat on an old piece of burlap and took the missive out of her pocket. The distinctive writing on the envelope, its letters controlled and angular, was decidedly mannish, but May's observations had disconcerted her. The letter inquired about her progress in the settlement; it was cordial enough, and yet a note of impatience was already in evidence.

She then opened the first few copybooks and scanned the sometimes precise, sometimes uneven essays completed in class, mostly to do with the legends of the local islands. "The Legend of Wild Man Island," "The Tale of Red Horse Island," "The Story of Broken Neck Island"—as though the flowing stream of notable history had been trapped and congealed on those small bodies of land surrounded entirely by the brackish waters of outlying bayous.

She picked through the books until she found May's essay and she began reading. Halfway through the second page, Lucinda smiled and whispered, "Good girl."

The rain was dissipating, blowing southward, and Lucinda looked through the murky glass that made up the ceiling. *Enough blue to patch a Dutchman's pants,* she remembered her father saying, his description of a clearing sky.

As she looked, she became aware that she could see the outline of a man in one of the small panes of glass. Or rather, the pane contained the reverse image of a human silhouette, hazily white against a darkened background.

She let her eyes focus on an adjacent section of glass and realized it, too, had the faint but unmistakable figure of a man. She stood up, the hairs on her arms rising, and strained to see the images more closely, finally coming to understand that every pane was a photographic negative of a soldier in uniform. When she visited the shed earlier, the cloud cover had kept her from perceiving the original purpose of the glass; she had thought the darkened areas of the ceiling to be the grime of years.

She stepped onto a crate to examine the negatives more closely. The boxed-in panes of glass showed men of all ages, and more than a few boys, each posing in front of the same static background, some sporting pistols, others holding rifles, all hinting at the prideful, boastful sentiments in those moments before they had ventured into armed conflict. If the resulting photographs had been printed and framed, elaborately or simply, draped with medals of sacrifice or bands of black crepe, they would have held a kind of paradox: the appearance of life but inexorably a proof of what had departed, never to return.

The sun had begun to bleed out the images of the soldiers. It had been five years since the end of the war, and some of the portraits would have been made at the start of the conflict, in '61. Soon the plates would be scoured clean, and it would be a kind of second death. She would never again believe the glass was merely dirty. She would always see the men floating above her head.

Lucinda stepped off the crate, imagining ghosts and the legends of ghosts. She would have the chance the following evening to question May about the topic of her essay: the story of pirate's gold—chests full of it—buried within a few miles of the settlement.

She picked up the scattered books and stepped out of the greenhouse. She smelled the tang of tobacco filling the air and, curious, followed the scent. On the ground, still smoking, was the discarded butt end of a crudely rolled cigarette. A motion caught her eye, and she saw a black man walking quickly across the fields. She watched him for a while before he turned briefly to look back, but he soon disappeared into a stand of trees close to the water. She stamped out the glowing end of the cigarette with the ball of her foot and continued on her way to the house.

Chapter 10

The men spent three days in Austin. One day for church, and two to allow Dr. Tom time to recover from a damp lung the cold rain had inflicted. They slept in barracks shared by a few federal soldiers and local policemen. Nate was left on his own for a good deal of the time—Deerling restlessly joining the local police on surveillance rides to the south—and, after making his official report, Nate walked up and down the streets, in and around the main thoroughfares, looking at the saloons, dry-goods stores, and hotels filled with men and women finely dressed. They had a boldness about them that the small-town settlers lacked. Congress Street, the main road that was plotted from the river all the way to the capital building, had, Dr. Tom said, grown so rapidly in the past few years that he hardly recognized it.

The morning of the third day, Nate waited at the door of the post office for a half an hour before it opened at eight o'clock. He was disappointed not to find any mail from his wife, but he convinced himself that he had outpaced the mail wagon from Oklahoma. He posted one long letter to her describing all he had seen in Austin, Dr. Tom's illness, and the incident with the snake, knowing she would be pleased with what he had learned from her. He also added instructions for her to send all future letters to Houston.

In closing, he wrote,

The city is filled with building works and wonders of comfort for man and beast. Yesterday, in a dry-goods store, I saw a device with serrated teeth, which, when cranked, will cut off the top of a tin can in a moment flat. But the city is not at peace with itself. The governor is roundly hated. Everyone is bristling with firearms, ready at a moment's notice to begin shooting at any imagined threat or cross word, and though Governor Davis has given me a policeman's job, I will be happy to be on my way to Houston. My love always to you and Mattie.

Inside the letter he placed a braided horsehair necklace strung with a few colored beads for his daughter. He had bought it from a dignified black woman, her cart of beaded wares set up at the first light of morning. The sign on the cart read *For the Wheatville Girls School*. She accepted his quarter with long, graceful fingers, smiling broadly when he tipped his hat to her.

He walked to Scholz Garden on San Jacinto Street and paid for a beer, the first beer he had ever drunk alone. He eyed the hard-boiled eggs floating in clouded water in a large glass jar and declined the bartender's offer of them, even though they were free to drinkers. He picked up an old discarded newspaper left on the bar and read about events that had happened a full year ago: "John Wesley Hardin Kills Three Soldiers," "Treaty of Medicine Lodge Violated by Comanche," and one article about a knife fight in an Abilene saloon headlined "You Are a D—d Liar, Sah!"

The saloon was dark and quiet, and he reflected on his uncertain position with Deerling. After the incident with the snake, the ranger had continued to ignore him, but true to his word, after they had drawn their month's pay, he left the barracks abruptly and returned an hour later with an early-model Winchester rifle. He handed it to Nate, saying only "Pay me when you can."

Nate heard a whooping noise from outside the beer hall, followed by the clattering sounds of a group of riders approaching. He walked with the bartender and the few other patrons to the shaded porch and watched the thirty or so men approaching on horseback.

The riders wore long robes, bed linens or lengths of sewn muslin, all of it white; their faces were covered with hoods, holes cut out for their eyes. A few had conical caps shaped like inverted funnels on their heads, and Nate turned, openmouthed, to look questioningly at the bartender by his side.

The bartender spat a long stream of tobacco juice into the dirt. "The Klan has made it all the way from Tennessee. There won't be a nigger safe from here to Uvalde County." He turned and walked back inside, and Nate watched the riders being cheered down the length of San Jacinto.

Returning to the barracks, he did not see the black woman with the cart.

He entered the bunk room quietly but saw that Dr. Tom was sitting up reading with a flannel wrapped around his throat. Nate told him what he had seen on San Jacinto.

Dr. Tom shook his head. "Grown men wearing bedsheets." He put his book aside and looked closely at Nate, who was sitting on a chair, frowning, chewing at his bottom lip.

"You're still worrying on George's good opinion of you, aren't you? Well, the thaw is coming. You'll see. Although a little bravado on your part might grease the wheels."

"Bravado," Nate said.

"Some action that shows some nerve. The snake in the bucket was a good beginning."

"Actually," Nate began and then paused. "I want to know how it sits with you, Captain Deerling shooting that Indian back on the Government Road."

Dr. Tom tightened the flannel around his neck and regarded his hands, clasped in his lap. "You know I don't make commentary on my captain's decisions." He looked at Nate. "It's disloyal." He let that sink in and then added, "But son, you want to believe me when I say you would not have wanted to meet those horse thieves on the other side."

Nate nodded and stood, but Dr. Tom gestured for him to stay. "You know," he said, "it occurs to me that I know nothing about you, and here I've been chewing your ear off for weeks. George said you're a wonder with horses."

Nate sat back down, acknowledging the change of tone.

"Hold nothing back," Dr. Tom said. "I've got nothing to do and all day to do it."

So Nate began to tell him of his past, of how he'd been born in Oklahoma to a mission-raised mother and a father who worked with horses and knew no other way than to break them hard, as his own father had done. And when a man gets accustomed to roping and tying a horse with a mean-set mouth and an unforgiving hand, he often gets used to treating his family in the same fashion. When Nate was fourteen, he left home and came down through Texas to Lancaster and began working with the renowned Steel Dust horses, learning from the trainer who could ride a green colt with only a rope bridle and lead after fifteen minutes of just talking to it.

Nate broke off telling his story and looked to Dr. Tom, half expecting him to be bored or restless, but the ranger smiled and nodded for Nate to continue.

The man's name in Lancaster was McNally, Nate said, and in 1862 he joined with McNally for the Confederate cause and rode into Arkansas. Hundreds of Texans on horseback went with them that summer out of East Texas, the July that Nate turned sixteen. He rode a Steel Dust colt on a Mexican saddle he had earned with his pay and carried with him the only weapon he had, a Dance revolver given to him by McNally.

They rode through country so wasted by drought that McNally exclaimed that the horses could have found better forage from the ashes in a cookstove, and if not for the numerous rivers that were too wide and deep to disappear, the stock would have dried down to hide, teeth, and manes. The heat was murderous, pitching dozens of men from their saddles, men who then lay on the ground senseless, as though felled by a cudgel to the head.

There were uneasy rumors that Helena, the center for Confederate operations in Arkansas, was now in the hands of the Unionists, and that dysentery, typhoid, and malaria raged through the soldiers' ranks, regardless of anyone's loyalties. It was also put about that if the Confederate officers in charge had been more attentive to the well-being of their men instead of to cotton speculation, Helena would not have fallen.

In Hot Springs, McNally and Nate were attached to the Nineteenth Texas Cavalry, but many of the other Texans were quickly dismounted to serve in the infantry with other divisions. Some of the horseless riders, men deemed too young or too old to fight, were sent back to Texas.

Nate was released from service, but dysentery laid him low for weeks before he could depart. McNally nursed him as best he could between his own training and foraging for food. He told Nate that he considered himself most fortunate to remain mounted, as the Texans afoot were to be sent farther east, to the meat grinder of the Southern battlefields.

One night, McNally sat next to Nate as he lay on his hospital cot and told him that the Union had surrendered Little Rock; the Confederate army, along with the governor, would be reclaiming the capital. An order had gone out that three hundred army horses, the best of the herd being Steel Dust horses, had been requisitioned and would be driven up to Fort Smith and placed with the Confederate cavalry, who were determined to contain the boys in blue in Missouri.

"Nate," he said. "I've got some pull with the quartermaster and have put you forward for the job. You're not officially enlisted anymore, so what I'm about to ask you to do isn't actually treason. Our whole future is in the bloodline of those stallions. We send them north, and we'll never see them again. I want you to drive all three hundred horses back to Texas."

He placed his hand on Nate's shoulder. "Will you give me your word, as a son to a father?"

Nate made his promise, and when he was well enough to ride, he left Hot Springs with a dozen Texas boys his own age and headed with the herd northward, as though he were following the ordered plan: to go along the Arkansas River Valley, between the Boston and Ouachita Mountains, to Fort Smith. But then he drove the horses instead across the Ouachita River and headed south on mountain trails toward the Caddo Narrows, through thick forests of pine and white oak.

The herd was led by an old hammerheaded stallion with still enough fight in him to matter, and the line was sometimes strung out single file for miles. The drovers were mostly farm boys used to sleeping rough; they were decent enough in the saddle, but a few had only ever seen a horse from behind a plow. Unlike driven cattle, the herd was quiet, and Nate devised a series of whistle calls to signal trouble. For the first few days, there were signals only that all was well. On the third day, though, one stallion ran afoul of another in front and was kicked off a ledge. By the time Nate had worked himself against the line to see, the horse was dead in a ravine. He was glad he hadn't had to try to shoot it through the tree line, but he thought it a poor start to the journey.

They came to the narrows after four days and crossed the Caddo River at a mill. Almost every homestead they passed had been deserted, the fields abandoned, but as the first dozen horses forged the Caddo, a man came out onto his porch and called out, "Any horse that shits while crossing and fouls my stream is mine." Nate rode forward to talk to him, but the man had seen that all the drovers were young, and he challenged Nate, accusing him of stealing the horses. Nate kept the line going even when the man brought out a shotgun.

Nate told him, "All these boys can shoot. You kill me, you better go on and drown yourself in that river before they come after you."

After a time, the man went back into his house, but Nate followed at the rear of the herd, looking over his shoulder, for the rest of the day.

They followed the Caddo River to its tail end and, where the mountains skirted behind them, came upon an open valley. The horses spread out to pick at the meager, yellow-white grasses. A horse struck on the cheek by a rattler the size of a man's arm spooked the rest of the herd and they scattered for miles, galloping until they were tired, their heads lowered, stained with the heat and dust. Before long, the hide and hair around the wounded horse's snakebite began to slough away, but the horse lived and there were no more stampedes.

South of Acorn, close to the Oklahoma border, Nate came upon three men on horseback sitting in a small copse of trees. He didn't see them until he was almost on them, and the way they studied the herd prompted him to whistle a warning to the drovers.

The three riders approached, their mouths tense, their eyes searching, like men used to being guarded and watchful at all times. The leader was a spectral-faced man in a coat too weighty for the heat, and when he smiled, Nate rested his hand over the Dance.

"The name's Hettrick," he said, draping his hands easily over the saddle horn. His voice, pushed through thin lips, was high-pitched and constricted, like he was being slowly strangled by his own collar. "Been with Quantrill in Missouri these past few months. Harassing the Union." He looked at Nate's horse while he spoke, then rubbed his hand over his chin and smiled, showing more gum than teeth. "Our horses are played out. We're in need of fresh ones."

A few of the boys had ridden up behind Nate, and he told the man, "These horses aren't for sale."

Hettrick grinned wider and said, "I'm not offering to buy them."

One of the drovers, a redheaded boy named Connie, moved closer to Nate, spat, and said, "Bushwhackers."

From somewhere in the recesses of the man's coat, the barrel of a revolver appeared and flashed, and Connie lay behind his horse on the ground. If Nate had blinked, he would have missed it.

Hettrick next pointed the barrel at Nate. "Hate a fresh-mouthed kid. Anybody else have anything to impart?" He looked around, sweeping his gun at the collected boys, and settled his eyes back on Nate. "I'll start with taking the horse that you're on. Unless you've got something you want to say to me."

Nate got off his horse; the leader then ordered his men to pick out two horses each, and they rode away before Connie had stopped bleeding.

They buried the boy in a creek bed in soil soft enough to part under a shovel. Nate took two drovers who could shoot, wild-wooded cousins from Tyler who had joined the Confederacy together, and the three of them, riding stumpy-legged horses that could climb and wouldn't tire easily, followed the raiders north through the Ouachita forests. They trailed the men for days before Nate would risk an attempt to retrieve the horses.

On the third morning, Nate on horseback was scrambling up a steep embankment, the two cousins following after, when the three raiders rose from their hiding place on the ridge above and began firing on them. Nate's horse was shot in the neck and it reared and plunged back, pinning Nate in the mud of an old streambed below. More shots were fired and Nate witnessed the younger cousin riding to his left fall and then heard a strangled cry from his horse. Nate couldn't see where the other boy was, but there was no sound apart from the pebbles sliding down the embankment.

The spectral-faced man thudded a stone onto Nate's horse. "Hey, I believe your back may be broken. Hell of a fix. I'll shoot ya if you ask me to. No? All right, then."

The faces of the raiders disappeared from sight, and Nate lay panting and staring at the sky, his legs caught beneath the horse, in a hot agony of pain the center of which seemed to be in his middle, and yet when he put his mind to any one part of his body, the pain seemed to swell like a grinding of glass into the flesh and muscle down to the marrow of his bones.

Another face appeared over him and Nate threw up a defensive hand until he saw it was the older cousin, Owen. The boy had a bullet hole low in the crown of his hat. He was crying, and a thin trickle of blood ran onto his forehead.

"Goddamn," he said. "Goddamn, but they like to've shot me in the head."

It took a rope tied to the dead gelding's legs and then wrapped around a tree for leverage for the boy to pull the animal off Nate. He could move all his limbs but he was certain from the pain that he had broken his hip. The younger cousin had not been so lucky and had taken a bullet in the chest. They covered him over with rocks and branches so they could find him again and pressed on, with Nate riding the dead boy's horse.

After a day's ride, they discovered the raiders at an encampment on the Forche la Fave River; the rushing waters masked the sounds of their approach. Hours after the three men had settled under their sleeping rolls, Owen whispered to Nate, "Blood for blood."

He showed Nate his hunting knife and his determined, vengeful face, and then he crept toward the man sleeping closest to them. Nate watched the boy crab-crawling slowly over the ground and held his revolver ready, uncertain he could hit the other two men in the dark at that distance if they woke, uncertain as well if he could again stand after lying on the ground for so many hours, his broken hip tyrannizing his legs to jerks and spasms. The sky was clear; the three-quarter moon shone with unnatural brilliance off the river, and it revealed Owen's profile in sharp detail.

The boy bent over the closest bedroll and, with little hesitation, made a jab and then a hard sweeping motion with his knife over the man's neck. The man kicked his legs as though in restless sleep and then lay still, and Owen waved his arm for Nate to come on. The boy then pulled his cap-and-ball pistol from his belt, and when the second raider stirred and sat up, Owen shot him.

Hettrick reared from his blanket like he'd been yanked vertical by a rope. He pulled from his heavy coat two pistols and began firing blindly at Owen, who scrambled across the ground towards cover, the bullets carving out pieces of dirt and rocks surrounding him.

Nate pulled himself up to standing, and, supported by a tree, he took aim. Some sound, the creaking of wood or the cocking of the pistol or Nate's own agonized breathing, brought Hettrick's attention away from Owen, and he jerked a shooting arm towards Nate. Nate fired once, and the remaining raider fell as quickly as he had risen.

Nate collapsed to the ground, his hip no longer able to support him, and crawled cautiously to where the leader lay motionless, facedown, his coat spread out around him like shabby wings. Nate turned the body over and saw that his one shot had hit the man squarely in his forehead; he figured he would probably never be able to make a shot like that again, not even at half the distance and in full daylight.

A brief, exultant surge from the most primal part of himself, fueled by fear and pain, made him yelp out a call, a poor rendition of the rebel yell he had heard from men in the battlefield but a tribute all the same to the reflex that had moved his arm to fire at the exact killing spot.

In the morning, the two gathered together the stolen horses, and after giving Owen's cousin a more fitting burial, they rode for days back to the herd and the drovers waiting for them at the Oklahoma border. They traveled south to Texas through Indian territory unhindered, and were even accompanied some distance by the First Choctaw Regiment of the Confederate army.

On the twenty-seventh of August, the hottest day anyone could remember, the drovers, led by Nate, entered Dallas and herded the two hundred and ninety-eight horses down the main street. And every boy who had made the ride and could boast of surviving stampedes and snakebites and horse-thieving raiders rejoined the war when he was able.

Nate's broken hip, further fractured by a week more in the saddle, took a year to heal, and after that he was considered unfit to serve. He stayed in Lancaster training Steel Dust horses but heard from returning Texans of the fates of his friends, and every young drover to a man was killed in some battle or another.

McNally fell at Vicksburg after serving with the Nineteenth Cavalry for two years. Owen was downed at Blair's Landing in Louisiana while firing his old cap-and-ball pistol on a Confederate gunboat run aground on the Red River, the same gun he had used to kill the horse thief.

When Nate finished talking, he was certain Dr. Tom must have nodded off. He had surprised himself speaking for so long, in so much detail, and he'd spent the last half hour staring at his boots, too self-conscious to look the ranger in the face. Dr. Tom had not said a word for over an hour, but when Nate finally looked up, the ranger was gazing at him, his arms crossed, his mouth curled in a smile. Nate realized that prior to this, he had not told the story in its entirety to another soul besides his wife.

Nate stood abruptly, suddenly shy in the too-quiet room, and said, "Well, I guess I'll see what use I can put myself to."

He walked to the door but turned when he heard his name called.

"Nate," Dr. Tom said. "You're going to make one hell of a good lawman."

The following morning early, the three left Austin, stopping first at Hillyer's Photographic Studio at Dr. Tom's insistence. "Hell, I've got on a new shirt, thanks to Nate. Might as well capture the day."

Hillyer posed them in different configurations, finally settling Nate in a chair between the two rangers, his new Winchester across his lap. Dr. Tom placed one hand on Nate's shoulder and held his Colt aloft with the other. Deerling stood to the other side, giving a heated stare to the photographer as he took his time adjusting the boxy camera. In the moment before Hillyer removed the lens cap, and while he was admonishing the men to stay perfectly still for the count of a full minute, Nate felt Deerling's hand come slowly to rest on his other shoulder.

The photographer nodded to them when the image had been captured and they could move again. He said, "I'll have the prints made from the glass negative within the hour, gentlemen."

Deerling shook his head, already walking to the door. "We don't have time to wait. We'll take receipt of the prints when we return."

The trip to Houston would take another fifteen days, and they hoped to bypass the main city, riding for the small settlement of Frost Town on Buffalo Bayou to the north. There, Deerling would speak to the woman who had been shot and whose family had been killed by McGill's men.

The journey began favorably, the weather mostly dry and temperate, so that sleeping outside at night was a pleasure, though the first few evenings Dr. Tom began to run a fever and coughed his way through till dawn. He had quickly pitched into the bushes the respiratory cure given to him by the doctor in Austin, saying that there were enough opiates and alcohol in the syrup to stun a horse. Deerling and Nate slept little themselves, listening to the wet rumbled hacking that sounded ominously like pneumonia settling in.

Deerling asked after his partner's health so often that once, when the captain handed Dr. Tom his morning coffee, he responded by saying, "Thank you, dear."

The Blackland Border, as Dr. Tom called it, was hilly at first, then gave way to gently rolling pastures abundantly watered with streams and aquifers. On the banks of lakes were farmhouses and barns made of chalky white stone and timber collected in tight, defensive formations against Indian attack, like mushrooms sprouting after the rain.

They followed the path of the Colorado River southeast through sycamore and willow, carefully easing around the giant cutbacks, the eroded earth chopped away from the banks during the recent flooding. As the land flattened, the sky opened up with only a few wisps of clouds, stretched to near transparency with strengthening gusts of wind.

Dr. Tom sat in the saddle with his head down, one hand supporting his lower ribs, his face drawn and pale.

Nate rode closer to Deerling and asked, "Is he all right?"

Deerling turned briefly to look at his partner and frowned. "He's fine."

"He doesn't look fine."

Deerling craned his neck around once more, but kept riding. "He'll tell us if we need to stop. We'll find a doctor in Columbus."

But the townspeople there informed them there was no doctor, only a retired quartermaster living a few miles away who had had some field-hospital experience during the war and who, it was rumored, kept a stockpile of grain alcohol in his barn from which he was known to sample frequently.

They camped on the outskirts of town. Deerling rode away to the south and returned an hour later leading a squalling, unhappy man tied to a horse. The man had the bulbous, pocked nose of a lifelong drinker, and when he was untied and pulled from his horse, he commenced complaining to Nate how he had been roused from his bed, hit over the head, and kidnapped.

Deerling put a finger in the quartermaster's chest. "You've been paid for your time." He then pointed to Dr. Tom, shivering under a blanket. "Mr. Odum, there's your patient. If you don't want another rap on the head, I'd suggest you see to him."

Odum bent over Dr. Tom, blowing his sour-mash breath into his face, and poked around the ranger's middle, feeling under tender ribs until Dr. Tom waved him away, saying, "Hell, George, a horse doctor would have done me better."

"The patient has pleurisy," Odum announced. "He'll need a mustard plaster under flannel." He then walked to his horse and pulled a bottle from his saddlebag. He handed it roughly to Nate and, after a few missed tries, got his boot into a stirrup and rode off in the direction of town.

The following morning, at Dr. Tom's insistence, they continued on, following the road due east to Houston. At night, Nate gave Dr. Tom his extra blanket, and he did what he could to provide food the sick man could easily swallow, simmering cornmeal to mush and boiling dried jerky in water for a soup. Five days after leaving Austin, they camped at the crossing of the Brazos. Dr. Tom was barely able to sit in his saddle from the fever shakes.

Nate watched him that night as he huddled under a blanket close to the fire. Dr. Tom's usual banter had ceased the day before, and the ride was silent except for the sound of labored breathing. Deerling pulled Odum's bottle from his pack, uncorked it, and made his partner drink.

Dr. Tom swallowed and gaped. "That's pure grain alcohol. I may go blind."

"Tom, if you don't get some sleep tonight, I won't either, and I may just be mean enough tomorrow to put you out of your misery myself."

When Deerling went off to find more wood, Dr. Tom gestured for Nate to come closer. He took Nate by the arm and said, "We get to Houston, I'm staying. You go on with George. Don't let him quit on my account. I'll catch up later, if I can."

Nate nodded and Dr. Tom handed him a folded piece of paper. "The damnedest thing about having some medical knowledge is knowing how sick you are when you do catch something. I have pneumonia bad. In both lungs, most likely. I'll either get well fast, or not at all. Take this letter. If I'm dead when you get back to Houston, give it to George. But don't tell him you have it in the meantime. He's got no patience for waiting, and he'll want to read it right away. And then, if I'm still alive, I'll have to live with him bein' awkward and stony-faced all the time."

Nate took the letter and tucked it into his coat. "What's driving all this, Tom? Why are we riding all this way for some man-killers that the county sheriff could just as well chase after?"

"We have our reasons. George most of all."

Nate opened his mouth to speak but Dr. Tom held up a hand. "It has to do with family and that's all I'll say about it. It's up to George to tell you, when he's ready." He curled away into his blanket and promptly fell asleep.

In Houston, Nate and Deerling helped Dr. Tom into a physician's home, where he was placed in a sickroom in a clean bed with a fire built up to bring on the sweats. Nate sat, and Deerling paced awhile, restless and breathing through his nose impatiently, uncertain what to do. He finally pulled the old newspaper from Dr. Tom's pack, which had been thrown into a corner of the room, turned to the page with the Dickens story, and placed it on the bed.

Dr. Tom wiped a hand over his sweating face. "You are about as much help as a pig on fire. Either read it to me or get gone."

Deerling pulled a chair over to the bed and positioned the paper in the lamplight and began reading in a slow and halting way, as though he were having difficulty seeing the words. "'And yet, proceeding now, to introduce myself positively, I am both a town traveler and a country traveler, and am always on the road. Figuratively speaking, I travel for the great house of Human Interest Brothers, and have rather a large connection in the fancy goods way. Literally speaking, I am always wandering here and there.'"

"George," Dr. Tom said, "you need glasses."

Deerling put the paper aside. "My eyes are as good as they've ever been…"

Nate listened to the back-and-forth for a while, the rangers' voices sounding like smoked bees, all buzz and no sting, and then he stood quietly and left the room. He saw to the horses and then bedded down at a boardinghouse, waking only to the sound of Deerling coming in for the night. But Deerling walked to the window, leaned against the sill, and remained there as Nate fell back to sleep. When Nate woke the next morning, Deerling was still in the same place, looking out over the street, his face lined and pale with worry, his chin unshaven for days.

"Tom says to go on without him," Deerling told Nate. "We'll ride to Frost Town to talk to that woman that survived McGill's last shooting. There's not much we can do here today."

They reached Frost Town in a few hours—a German settlement with its own post office and school—and were directed by a livery hand to a large farmhouse fronting the bayou. The farmer who lived there was named Muller, and he led the men into the simple parlor, where his wife served them coffee and warm biscuits.

Muller said, "Mrs. Shenck has been deeply marked by the deaths of her husband and children. She is better in the body, but in the mind..." He pointed to his head and twisted his finger against his temple, like a screw being worked into a board.

Muller's wife led them upstairs to a bedroom, and, after knocking softly, she opened the door and gestured them into the room. Nate followed Deerling and saw a woman reclining in a small bed, propped up against several pillows, staring out the nearest window. She turned her head to look at them with swollen eyes, and Nate removed his hat. He lingered by the door, not sure where to stand, but Deerling took the one chair in the room, moved it next to the bed, and sat.

"Mrs. Shenck, I'm Captain Deerling of the Texas Rangers, and this is Officer Cannon of the Texas State Police. We're here to talk with you about the men who killed your family. Are you well enough to tell us what happened?"

She nodded uncertainly but remained silent. Nate watched the subtle movements of her body turning away from Deerling, and she placed a shielding, protective hand over her chest. Nate would have approached the woman more carefully. As with a battered horse, a wounded person had scant resources left even to keep the body upright, the eyes directed forward, and the mind balanced. He thought a good place to start would have been just to hold her hand for a while.

Finally she said, "There were three men. They came into our house one day. They had guns." Her voice was low, the words softly accented. She took a sip of water from a glass next to the bed with shaking hands. "They said if we caused them no trouble, if we didn't try to run away or tell our neighbors, they wouldn't kill us."

Deerling asked, "How long did they hold you?"

"They stayed for five days. I and the children cooked for the men, and they would come and go, two men leaving and one man staying behind."

She became silent again, her focus softening as her head tilted towards the window. Deerling placed a hand on her arm, startling her.

She licked her lips and reached for the water once more. She said, "One night we heard them talking about a farmer who found gold coins on his land. Some sort of pirate treasure, he said. They bought him whiskey, to make him careless. But the farmer wouldn't say precisely where the gold was."

Deerling asked, "Who was the farmer?"

She shook her head. "They never said his name or where he was from. The leader of the men, this McGill, became angry with them for speaking of such things in our presence. But seeing I was scared, he took my hand and looked into my eyes and promised me that no harm would come to me or to my family."

She clenched and unclenched her fingers entangled in the shawl around her shoulders. She stared wide-eyed at Deerling and said, "I believed him."

Watching her pale and disbelieving face, Nate remembered seeing the same expression come over a Confederate deserter, a man at the end of a line of deserters about to be shot by his former comrades and thrown into a ditch. He thought of his own daughter and tried to imagine what her dying would do to him. And then he tried to imagine her being shot in his presence.

To comfort the woman, Deerling reached out and clasped her two hands in his. "Mrs. Shenck, thank God, you're still alive."

She began to breathe queerly, her gaze panicked, and Deerling stood up, alarmed. "Are you in pain, Mrs. Shenck?"

The woman thrashed on the bed, making sounds like an animal in agony, and Nate thought to fetch Mrs. Muller, but the woman fixed her eyes on him and he became very still, the hairs on the back of his neck prickling. He saw clearly the bruised flesh on her face and wasting tautness of the skin on her arms, and she whispered, "I am not alive."

Mrs. Muller appeared at the door and ushered the men from the room. They went downstairs and were joined on the porch by Mr. Muller. The three stood for a while absently watching the looping banks of Buffalo Bayou, listening to the shrill weeping from the woman upstairs.

Muller said, "The devil shot her last of all. First the husband, and then the two children. The killer made her watch."

Deerling asked, "Do you have any idea where these men went?"

Muller said, "In her ravings she said Harrisburg, but…" He shrugged, turning the palms of his hands up.

Deerling worked his hat in his hands. "Take the train west from Harrisburg and it stops at Alleyton and a few cotton farms. To the south, the railroad goes to Galveston." He turned to Muller. "There's nothing important in Harrisburg except the railroad depot." He stopped for a moment, gnawing the inside of his cheek, and looked at Nate. "What do you think?"

"Well," Nate said, shifting his weight to the stronger leg,

"there must be drinking places in Harrisburg. Places where cotton farmers who have money to spend gather. Maybe our farmer is close by."

Deerling nodded and said, "That's where we'll start, then."

The two men thanked Muller, and within a quarter hour, they had turned south again, heading to Harrisburg.

Chapter 11

*L*ucinda sat, listening to May sing. While the girl's voice was not unpleasing, it had a curious lifelessness to it, as though the words were devoid of meaning. She was singing "Lorena," a tune over which Lucinda had seen hardened men weep, thinking of their lost wartime loves. This in the cathouses where they were being entertained, their hands on the whores they had just had or were about to have.

Jane played the accompaniment on the square piano that had been shipped by barge from Galveston a few months earlier and that, surprisingly, had held most of its tuning.

Lucinda stole a look at Bedford Grant, the girls' father, standing next to Jane and turning the pages of the music folio. He had been stiff and formal at dinner, a meal of chicken and mainly dumplings, and it had taken a great deal of effort on Lucinda's part to help him keep his half of the conversation alive. She suspected that he had not had female company at his dinner table, other than his daughters, in a good while. She also suspected that his looser manner after the meal and his ruddy complexion were thanks to a furtive trip to a whiskey jar kept somewhere in another room.

He looked up at that moment and smiled, the open grin of a father's pride. Lucinda gave him a slow smile in return, and he blushed a deeper crimson, quickly returning his attention to the sheet music.

After acquainting herself briefly with Bedford, she thought him a shy but intelligent man, flattened and embattled by the brutal uncertainties of life. He had, it seemed, failed at everything he had ever set his hand to, as speculator, merchant, and now probably as farmer, although, in recounting his past to Lucinda, he had framed his failures as "mistimed ventures" brought to unsuccessful ends by the inability of the South to secure secession.

For a short while he was even a bookseller, which explained the sagging shelves filled to overflowing with books. It also explained why May, who came so rarely to the schoolhouse, was so informed. Both sisters had the best possible library on subjects as varied as history and the natural sciences, and there were more than a few novels.

Earlier in the evening, Lucinda had pulled one of these novels from a shelf, its spine partially eaten by mice, the pages spotted with black mold grown from the damp air, and read the title: *The Woman in White.*

May, standing next to her, exhaled dismissively and asked, "Miss Carter, have you read this one? Well, don't bother. It's a very tiresome plot about madness and confused identities." She pulled another book from the shelf, *Lady Audley's Secret,* and handed it to Lucinda. May traced the title with a finger and whispered into Lucinda's ear, "She is a very bad woman." Lucinda quickly looked at the girl's face and saw her eyes creased in mischief, and they laughed together.

Lucinda, lost in these thoughts, became aware that May had finished singing. She clapped politely and, rising, said, "Thank you, May. That was quite lovely. But it's late, and I should leave. I thank you for your hospitality, Mr. Grant."

He stood staring at her blankly for a moment while his daughters looked expectantly at him until he realized he was supposed to do the gentlemanly thing and walk her back to the Wallers' home.

She said good night to the girls and, for the first fifty yards, tried to match Bedford's rapid pace. It was a clear night, but the path was still pocked from the recent rains. She slowed and finally stopped, calling out to him to assist her.

He ran his palm over his forehead, saying, "How thoughtless." He held out his arm for her to take and slowed his stride. "You must forgive me, Miss Carter. It's been a while since we've had a guest."

"Not at all, Mr. Grant. I am, I'm afraid, all too used to the pace of the country." She tightened her hold on his arm. "And you have been accustomed to the rattle of cities. What an interesting life you've led."

The corners of his lips turned downward. "If penury can be called interesting, then it has certainly been that."

"But you've provided a wealth of experience and knowledge for your girls." She slowed her walking even further; they were approaching the Waller house too quickly.

"Yes, I have given them that, but my rootlessness has also made them easily distracted and, in May's case, a bit feckless."

"May is my brightest student, Mr. Grant." She paused, leaning slightly into his arm. "When she is in school." She smiled up at him, and for the briefest instant, he stopped walking and stared openly at her face.

Blushing, he abruptly let go of her arm and gestured for her to continue in front of him. She walked ahead, listening to his uneven breathing, taking note of his sudden embarrassment. The Waller house appeared at the end of the road, lantern light streaming brightly from the front windows, as though the house had been readied for a battery of holiday guests. She knew that the family would be waiting up so that Lavada and Sephronia could press her with questions about the evening.

She stopped and turned. "Mr. Grant, May has written a very good essay on one of the local legends. I'd like to submit it to the newspaper at Harrisburg. But..." She paused.

"Yes?" he asked, taking a step back.

"It's about the legend of Lafitte's gold in Middle Bayou. Are you familiar with this legend, Mr. Grant?"

He looked at her, his features indistinct in the dark. "Bedford. Call me Bedford, please."

"Very well...Bedford. Do you know this legend?"

"Yes," he said.

"Well, May has a tendency to embellish. Before I sent the story to the paper, I wanted to make sure it was..."

"True?"

"Yes, true." Lucinda inclined her head, waiting for his answer.

"Yes," he offered absently, staring at the tips of his shoes.

A yipping sound from behind caused them to turn, and they watched a coyote trotting across the road. The animal looked at them, head lowered, with a sly, open dog-smile.

"An opportunist," Bedford said quietly, watching the animal disappear into the tall grasses.

Lucinda looked at him, unsure of his meaning.

"He's hoping we'll weaken. He wouldn't attack us outright, but he's watching, waiting for us to become…compromised." He turned to face her again. "We have a very thin hold on civilization here in the bayou, Miss Carter. There are twenty ways to die from one Sunday to the next." He lifted his chin in the direction of the Waller home. "Despite the efforts of Euphrastus to keep life civilized."

Lucinda looked at the house and discerned the outlines of three of the Wallers peering through the windows watching them, the two women from the second floor and Euphrastus parting the curtains at the parlor. Like dolls propped up in a dollhouse, she thought.

She felt Bedford's eyes studying her, and when she turned to face him, his lips turned up sadly. "We're all opportunists in a way, wouldn't you say, Miss Carter?"

She answered his smile cautiously. He held out his arm for her to take and then walked her to the door.

He placed two fingers lightly on her hand to still her. "I would ask if I've troubled you with my talk, but I believe I have not. I will request of you, though, not to send May's essay to Harrisburg. May is repeating only what she has heard the locals say. She knows nothing beyond that."

She looked at him, a knot of disappointment in her throat. "I see. Then the story of the gold coins is not true."

"On the contrary, Miss Carter, it's quite true."

Her breathing quickened, but she worked to keep her face calm. "Call me Lucinda."

He ducked his head, pleased. "Lucinda."

"And just how do you know it to be true?" She put her hand gently on the sleeve of his jacket.

"Because…" He stopped and cleared his throat. "Because I've seen it."

Her grip tightened on his arm. "What have you seen?" she asked, her eyes wide.

He stepped abruptly away, looking stricken, almost fearful. Touching the brim of his hat to her, he said, "Someday perhaps I will show you. Good night, Miss Carter. Lucinda."

Lucinda watched him for a while from the doorway as he walked rapidly along the path. When she entered the parlor, she saw that Euphrastus had abandoned his post at the window.

The next morning included the usual Sunday prayer service and Bible reading by Euphrastus. The women had been uplifted in their excitement about a possible blossoming romance between the new teacher and the widower. When questioned, Lucinda smiled serenely and told them what a kind and intelligent man Bedford Grant was.

Euphrastus, however, seemed put-upon and dour, casting long reproachful looks in her direction. She had been aware, of course, of his desire. He had sought every opportunity to encounter her alone: at the school, on the paths, and even inside the house. He came upon her once, seemingly by chance, as she was coming down the stairs. Nodding politely, he brushed past her, his arm trailing along her thigh.

Normally, she would have encouraged this behavior. The man was a fool and could have been easily handled. But she didn't need him, only the good opinion of his wife, who would, no doubt, fan the rumors of a budding courtship between Lucinda and Bedford, thus helping to make it so.

She had woken up that Sunday morning with a headache, and she struggled to keep the impatience from her face as Euphrastus read to them Colossians: "'Put to death, therefore, immorality, impurity, lust, evil desires and greed.'" She had a rush of compassion for the Wallers' son, Elam, imprisoned in his chair parked next to his father, forced to listen to interminable lectures and punishing Bible readings, week after week, month after month.

As soon as she could, she walked along the path to her hiding place, welcoming the warmer air of the greenhouse pressing against her skin. The weather had begun to hold the biting tang of coming winter, and the low, heavy clouds were returning.

She seated herself and began writing a letter, but soon she heard a rustling sound, as though an animal was rooting around behind the greenhouse. She picked up a loose board as a club and opened the door, then cautiously walked behind the building.

Seated with his back pressed against the wall was the black man Lucinda had seen crossing the field. He was smoking, and he gave her a heavy look.

They regarded each other for a moment. He said, "This is my place."

"Oh?" Lucinda crossed her arms. The odor of tobacco made her want to smoke as well. "I thought this belonged to Euphrastus Waller."

He snorted through his nose and continued looking at her. "Do they know you're a sportin' woman?"

She thought perhaps she had misheard him, but the throbbing

band of the morning's headache tightened and turned sharp, stabbing her behind her eyes.

"I'm not passin' judgment. I'm just askin'." He flicked ash away with his fingers, watching her closely.

She stood transfixed by the expanding glow of the lit end of the cigarette, her mind frantically searching for the ways in which she could have revealed her true profession in Middle Bayou. The blood pounded in her face and she raised her voice in outrage. "How do you dare to insinuate—"

He shrugged. "Myself, I could give a goddamn. It's not my business." He stared off across the fields, dismissing her as though she'd become invisible.

The smell of the tobacco had turned acrid, making her nauseated, and using the walls for support, she turned and walked back into the greenhouse. She bent down to pick up her things and leave, but she felt light-headed, and empty spaces began seeping into her field of vision. As she reached her arms out for balance, her legs weakened, and she fell hard onto her backside, breathing raggedly. The familiar heaviness at the back of her tongue was followed by spasmodic shakes in her legs and arms, the small muscles at the base of her neck.

Her head jerked back, the rest of her body following the momentum, and she was vaguely aware of her head grazing the sharp corner of a packing crate. She lay faceup, twitching, looking at the glass ceiling, at the images of the dead soldiers floating disconnected above her, the blank spaces where their eyes would have been pale and ill-defined.

Chapter 12

Nate rode next to Deerling, worrying the edges of Dr. Tom's letter in his pocket with his fingers. The talk with the German woman had spooked him badly. He'd begun to imagine disasters in many forms visiting his own family. That he hadn't yet received a letter from his wife served only to strengthen his growing disquiet.

Deerling had decided to travel directly to Harrisburg without stopping in Houston. Nate suspected it was his way of putting off hearing possible bad news about his partner, and Deerling remained quiet for a good while, his mouth downturned in thought.

Riding singly with the older ranger, without Dr. Tom's affable, relaxed commentary on the weather, the terrain, or past events, with his head swiveling from side to side in constant movement, Nate observed how differently Deerling sat a horse when Dr. Tom wasn't there: his face fixed in forward alignment with that of his mount, both hands on the reins, leaning into the rapid gait. Part of his alertness, Nate suspected, had to do with the horse itself, the stallion being young and more content to run than walk. But

Deerling's eyes swept the landscape in ceaseless fashion, as though he expected disaster at any turn.

Spending the few hours in Deerling's company without the buffering presence of Dr. Tom had begun to make Nate's nerves feel thin and spidery. He tried composing a letter to his wife in his head and was caught off guard when Deerling finally spoke to him. They had been riding for hours in silence and Nate twisted in his saddle to face him. "What?"

"I said, I should have let you talk to that woman. I'm too practiced in questioning violent men."

Nate nodded, remembering the woman's self-protective gestures. "She was scared."

"With good reason. I've known McGill to backtrack and shoot a survivor. In Houston, McGill shot a man in a card dispute. The man survived and was taken to the same doctor's clinic where Tom is now. McGill walked through the doctor's front door, went up the stairs, and shot the man in the heart while he lay in bed recovering."

Nate took note of the satisfaction in Deerling's retelling of the story, his grim enthusiasm for the efficiency of the perpetrator, and he said, "I guess it was a good idea, then, your not telling Mrs. Shenck that, or Tom."

Deerling cut his eyes to Nate but he finally pointed to Nate's new Winchester and asked, "You fired it yet?"

"Not yet."

Deerling legged himself off his horse and motioned Nate down as well. "Let's see what distance we get out of it."

Deerling paced off a hundred yards and Nate fired a few rounds into the trunk of a tree. He was pleased with the compactness of design, the ease of the lever action, and the accuracy. Deerling then walked out another fifty yards and Nate toppled a choke-berry tree, splitting the narrow trunk in half.

The ranger returned, held out a hand for the rifle, and fired twice into the nearer tree, splintering bark both times. "You may squeeze out a few more yards," he said, handing the rifle back to Nate, "but you're not likely to be doing any great distance shooting with it anyway." He pointed with two fingers to his eyes. "You'll want to be close up when you engage."

Nate held the rifle upright at his side, resting the half-moon curve of the stock on his thigh. "Thank you for this."

Deerling nodded, shifting self-consciously, and looked away. "Many a time the thing that saved me was not my accuracy but the sheer number of weapons I had to hand, the number of rounds I could fire off. We'll make sure, Tom and me, that you're outfitted properly."

They watched the clouds approaching from the Gulf, moun-tainous, gray, and featureless on the underside, but white and rounded high up, covering over the morning sun and diffusing the light. And yet the grass and a few large cedar trees on the eastern horizon showed in sharp relief.

"Tom looked bad when we left," Deerling said. "I think he's appreciated all your consideration. I know I do."

He put his back to Nate for a moment and then walked to his horse and pulled the Whitworth from its saddle case. He pointed to one of the bare trees in the distance and asked, "Would you say that's a good quarter mile away?"

Nate considered the distance and said, "About."

Deerling then handed him the rifle. "Here, why don't you take a shot. You'll be one of the few men who can say he's fired a Whit-worth."

Nate, awkward with this unexpected gesture, managed to smile, and said, "Thanks, Captain."

Deerling showed Nate how to sight down the brass side scope and explained how to load the powder and wadding and how to ramrod the hexagonal bullet down the barrel.

"You'll be able to take one shot, and one shot only. I have just five bullets left," Deerling said.

He let Nate take his time centering the target within the reticles of the scope. Nate pulled back the hammer, but before he could squeeze off the shot, Deerling placed a hand on his shoulder.

"I just need to know one thing, Nate," Deerling said. "I need to know that whatever order I give you from now on, you're going to follow it, or it will not go well for one of us."

He took his hand away and Nate kept his eye focused on the scope. Deerling's voice had been carefully neutral, but every gesture the man made seemed to be a show of strength, couched in a warning and tethered to some vague threat, like the big bite, given to him under the guise of merciful relief for some unforeseen danger.

Nate exhaled slowly, resighted, and pulled the trigger; his shoulder jerked violently with the explosion, and the ridge around his right eye smarted from the scope's recoil into his face.

They walked to the tree, leading their horses, counting off the distance—over six hundred yards. Nate saw that although he hadn't hit the center of the tree, the shot had torn the bark off its side like an artillery shell.

Deerling scratched at the splintered wood with a fingernail and smiled. "Not one man in fifty could have made that shot, Nate. You'll be useful yet."

They mounted and rode at a faster pace, making Harrisburg before noon. After settling their horses into the stable, they walked up the main street and into the marshal's office.

The marshal, a big man named Prudone, listened to Deerling recount their search across the entire state and then regarded them in frank disbelief. "Where did you say you started from?"

"Franklin," Deerling said, casting a critical eye at the man's desk, which was scattered with papers and the remnants of past meals.

"You must want McGill bad." The marshal shook his head. "That was cowardly business in Houston. But he's long gone."

"I don't think so."

Prudone appraised Deerling with a half smile. Nate had initially thought the marshal looked like a man whose greatest battle in recent years had been finding a way to fasten his belt. But now, looking closer, he wasn't so sure that was the case.

Prudone made a dismissive gesture with his hand. "Believe me, if McGill was still in the county, I'd know about it. I've got reliable scouts and more than a few deputies. There's been no upset within the past month other than the cattle thieves we adjudicated yesterday. The six of them are stacked up like cordwood now outside the undertaker's."

A small vessel under Deerling's eye pulsed. He said, "Then you won't mind if we spend the night in your quiet town."

"No, Captain, you're certainly welcome." The smile had disappeared. "We have two fine saloons, a beer hall, and a bordello that is, so I've heard, clean. Just a couple rules, and one suggestion.

First, don't carry your guns into the cathouse. It annoys the regulars. Second, no card-playing past midnight, because it annoys me. And finally: I'm a federal marshal. I trump both you and your governor-appointed friend here. My suggestion is you remember that."

Deerling looked at the marshal for a moment but then nodded and motioned for Nate to follow him out. Halfway down the street, Deerling and Nate crossed to the other side, and the two of them stood in the shadow of a storefront, watching the door to the marshal's office.

Nate asked, "What're we doing?"

"Wait and see."

The door opened and the marshal walked in the opposite direction from them, then entered a building with a sign reading *Texas and New Orleans Telegraph Company.* A few minutes later, he emerged and returned to his office.

Nate followed Deerling back up the street to the telegraph office, and they stood for a moment outside, peering through the window. The operator, a man with the creased and worried face of a hound, was sitting behind a shallow counter, alone in the room.

Nate said to Deerling, "Just find a way to give me a moment alone in there, without him in the room."

The ranger nodded and they walked in and greeted the operator.

Deerling said, "I'd like to send a message to a fellow ranger at Company E at Fort Inge, but I don't know if the telegraph goes that far."

"Fort Inge?" the operator said. "God help your friend, then, sir. They were just attacked by about five hundred Comanche and Lipan. I can send the telegraph to Austin, but that's as far as it goes. Then it's mule relay."

Deerling engaged the operator for a while, listening to the gruesome particulars of the attack, the number of injured and killed. Finally, he asked the man to point out the best place for a meal and led him onto the porch. It took only a moment for Nate to peer over the counter and read the destination of the previous telegraph sent by the marshal.

The men thanked the operator, and when he called after them asking if they still wanted to send the telegram, Deerling shook his head somberly and said, "No. I don't believe my friend will need it now."

Twenty paces on Deerling asked, "Well?"

Nate said, "Lynchburg."

"What did the message say?"

"Just three words. *Texas law here.*"

Deerling sucked air through his teeth and for the second time that day put a hand on Nate's shoulder. "We're close."

They wandered in and out of the two saloons but it wasn't until the beer hall that they got anything beyond cold stares and nervous tics. There were a few older men seated at a table; the rest of the room was empty.

Once the barkeep had heard their story, he looked grim. He rested his elbows on the bar, keeping his voice low. "I heard what happened to that family. The woman lived, you say? Well, I don't know what kind of blessing that is, seeing her husband and children are dead.

"Listen, I was sheriff in Goliad before I opened this place. It steams me no end to see what's goin' on."

The barkeep was quiet for a moment, letting two of the customers shuffle past and out into the street.

He then leaned over the bar towards Deerling again and said, "McGill was here, him and two others, a few months ago. McGill has more than a nodding acquaintance with our marshal. Prudone gives them protection and they give him a take. I tell you, one of these days someone is going to settle on Prudone with a bullet to the skull."

"McGill have any keen interests the last time he was here?"

The barkeep walked to the far end of the bar, squatted down, reached behind a salt barrel, and pulled out a small sack. He put his hand in the sack and palmed something. Making sure the customers weren't watching, he placed what he was holding on the bar in front of Deerling. It was a gold coin, larger than a quarter, nicked and slightly concave, as though something of great weight had rolled over it.

"A man came in here a few times. He was some kind of farmer, and not a very successful one. Drank a few beers and he started talking. Tellin' everyone within earshot that he'd found gold on his land. I didn't pay him any mind, but the story must have spread, because McGill showed up and started buying him whiskey at the saloon, trying to make him talk more. Something about it rattled the farmer, though, because he left town. But not before stopping off for one last beer. He didn't have any money left except this. Well, he plops it down on the counter and I just about broke my jaw. I don't know much about coins, but I know it's old. He said it was just one of many. A whole treasure's worth. He paid for that last beer with this."

Deerling picked up the coin and turned it in his hands. He

showed Nate the markings on the coin, and Nate said, "That's not any Confederate money."

Deerling asked the barkeep, "You gonna find some trouble over this?"

"Not if you don't tell anyone."

"What was the farmer's name?"

"I don't know, and that's the honest-to-God truth."

"Where'd he come from?"

"Not sure. I'd never seen him before." The barkeep took the coin back from Nate. "But he might have told McGill where he was from. He was sure drunk enough. And in that case, if that farmer is still alive, it's only because McGill hasn't found his gold yet."

They thanked him and walked a ways, looking for a place to eat their dinner. They found a small boardinghouse with a dining room, ate, and lingered for a while drinking coffee. It was growing dark as a man came in and sat at an empty table. From time to time he snuck a look at Deerling.

Nate started to say something, but Deerling said, "Yes, I see him."

Nate angled his face away from the watching man. "How did you know Prudone was lying?"

"Just a sense." Deerling took a drink out of his cup. "On principle, I don't trust any man that would use the word *adjudicated*."

"Are we leaving tonight?"

"I think we should."

"We goin' to Lynchburg?"

"No, we need Tom on this. We'll ride back to Houston and start back as soon as he can sit a horse."

"You think he's going to be all right?"

"Why? You know something I don't?"

"No. He just seemed pretty sick."

"Tom's a tough bird."

They paid for their meal and, after retrieving their horses from the stable, rode for Houston. The night was clear, with the lingering kind of light that turns the sky turquoise before it goes black. A Roman sky, Dr. Tom had once called it, which to Nate's mind sounded fanciful, a description Dr. Tom had probably read in one of his books.

There was no moon, but the brightest stars were beginning to appear, and the road was level and worn fine. A cold wind coaxed the horses to a fast walk, Deerling's big bay straining at the reins to outpace Nate's gelding. They would be in Houston before midnight.

Deerling said, "You did good back there."

Nate felt his face redden, but he was pleased.

"That was quick thinking with the telegraph man. Saved me from having to bang him over the head to get what we needed." He drew a pouch from his pocket and pinched some tobacco into his lower lip. He offered some to Nate, but Nate declined.

Deerling said, "Guile. That's the way of the world now. Pinkertons and federal agents asking questions, stealthy-like. As if you could talk a John Wesley or a Mescalero Apache out of his gun."

Nate watched Deerling's profile, certain his sudden talkativeness had more to do with the excitement of being near to capturing McGill and less to do with his being impressed over Nate's initiative. Dr. Tom had told him that bold action would go a long way towards salving the disappointment Deerling had felt over the horse-thief incident, but Nate figured that his sneaking over a telegraph counter was hardly enough to earn his way back into Deerling's good graces.

As though he'd been reading Nate's thoughts, Deerling asked, "I imagine you were too young to be caught up in the war?"

"Well, I didn't fight, if that's what you mean, but I did get caught up. I was sixteen when I volunteered with the Nineteenth Mounted Cavalry. I'd no sooner got to Arkansas when they sent us back to Texas. Me and a few other boys, and three hundred cavalry horses from the dismounted troops."

"You herded them back to Texas?"

"Yes."

"How many'd you lose?"

"Two."

"Two?" Deerling reined up the bay and looked at Nate. "You lost only two horses out of three hundred? You drive them straight into Texas?"

"No, sir. I drove them into Oklahoma first, south of Fort Smith, and then down to Lancaster."

"How many miles is that?"

"I don't know. A couple hundred."

Deerling stared at him for a moment, then spurred his horse into motion. He spit off to the side and was silent for a while.

Nate added, "The man I'd joined with was fatherly to me. Some of the best stock was his. There were rogue troops in Arkansas, Union and Confederate, and I didn't want the horses taken."

Deerling chewed on that for a while, along with his plug of tobacco. He asked, "You ever shoot a man, son?"

Nate looked at him and said, "Yes."

"Did it have to do with losing those two horses?"

"Yes."

"Then it comes as a surprise to me that you were so upset by my killin' a horse thief. One, I might add, that would've made soup from your guts if he'd had a chance."

"Would you have shot him like that from the ridge if he weren't Indian?"

"Probably not." Deerling spit again, then backhanded his mustache. "That what bothers you?"

"It does." Nate felt his jaw beginning to set.

Deerling grunted and shifted in his saddle impatiently. "And I guess you'd tell me why, if I was to ask?"

"Yes, sir, I would."

"Yes, I bet you would. I see you're just burstin' to tell me why it's wrong to kill an Indian, you bein' from Oklahoma and all."

"What's that supposed to mean?"

"What do you think it means?"

"I think it means you're diggin' awful close to the bone with that stick you call your tongue. Go on, ask me about my mission-raised mother, and while you're at it, why don't you go insulting my wife too!"

"Hold on, Oklahoma—"

"No, you hold on. I went along with the mishandling of a prisoner, and I'll keep my mouth shut about your shooting a horse thief, but you keep riding me about my people and, captain or no, I'll knock you off that big bay. So you go ahead and ask me about my Oklahoma-reservation kin."

A look of dawning understanding passed over Deerling's face.

"Whether or not you were raised on a reservation is no matter to me."

"Well…all right, then." Nate reined his horse abruptly to the far side of the road.

"All right, then."

A good quarter hour passed with no words exchanged, but Nate kept watch on Deerling out of the corner of his eye. He was angry, still itching to confront the ranger, to bring it to balled fists on a flat piece of earth if need be, but he also felt brought down, deflated, and he thought it would probably always be this way with the ranger: three steps forward and two steps back. He struggled to calm his breathing, focusing his mind on the road ahead.

"I had a daughter," Deerling finally said, surprising Nate with the suddenness of a statement that sounded more like a confession than a revelation. The ranger had slowly eased his horse to the middle of the road, and to Nate, Deerling's words felt like the closest to a peace offering he'd get that night. Deerling's face was composed, no longer heated, but Nate caught the whiff of remorseful sadness, the downturned mouth and hunched shoulders.

"It happened a while ago. But you never get past it. I regret now not being softer with her. I'm told I'm sometimes…." Deerling looked at Nate briefly, exhaling a breath through his nose. "Unyielding."

Nate nodded sharply once in agreement, but said nothing. Talking to the widow must have stirred memories for the old man, but it came to Nate that neither Deerling nor Dr. Tom had ever made mention before of having wives or children, other than Dr. Tom's saying that the hunt for McGill was for family reasons.

It had seemed only natural to him that a life spent so long in rangering would mean forgoing such attachments.

He was going to ask Deerling how he came to lose his daughter when a pistol blast caused Nate's horse to rear up, and he saw Deerling knocked back over the bay onto the road. As he struggled to keep his own horse under control, Nate heard a second blast, and then the gelding collapsed to his knees, pitching Nate to the ground. The fall sent a pain like a white phosphorus flare striking across his bad hip and the back of his head, and he lay on the ground stunned and half conscious.

The gelding's hooves were flailing nearby, blood coursing from a wound in his side, and Nate rolled over, pulling himself away from the injured animal, trying to keep the horse's body between himself and where he thought the shooter was. The only cover for an ambush was in a stand of trees nearby, and he pressed close to the ground, hoping their attacker would think them both dead and reveal himself. Nate pulled the pistol from his belt and cocked the trigger.

Two more shots were fired. The first bullet struck the gelding in the haunches; the second shot tore up the dirt close to Nate. He pressed his free hand over a gash at the back of his head to stanch the bleeding, and soon after, he heard the rider pounding past him on the road. Nate stood, taking aim at the assailant, recognizing the bulky rider as Prudone, the marshal from Harrisburg. But it had grown too dark, and his vision too watery and dim, for him to aim and shoot with accuracy, and he was afraid if he missed, the marshal would circle back and renew his attack.

He fell to his hands and knees, dizzy and sick, and then

crawled to where Deerling lay. Hit squarely in the chest, his wound pumping blood, Deerling had torn open his shirt with both hands and was pedaling his legs as though trying to walk away.

Nate could see awareness in Deerling's eyes, and he pressed both palms over the wound. His fingers were soon too slippery for traction, and he tore off his coat and used it as a bandage.

Deerling opened and closed his mouth a few times, blood from his lungs mixing with spittle. "Did you see...?"

"Yes," Nate said, his breath ragged and hot in his throat. "I saw him."

Deerling pressed his hands over Nate's, as though their combined strength could stop the urgent bleeding, but soon Deerling's fingers lost their hold, and his hands slipped from his chest and lay twitching on the ground.

When Nate looked into Deerling's face again, he saw the man's eyes were open and fixed, but he kept his weight on the coat in a momentary belief that some remaining reservoir of blood or wellspring of his own desperate vitality could reanimate the man. After a time, he realized that he had been pumping the dead man's chest, straight-armed and mindlessly rhythmic, as though prodding a sleeping man to wake, and he stopped and sat back on his haunches.

The night had been quiet, no wind or foraging night creatures, and Nate, buffered by shock in the first moments of violence, had been unaware of any sounds around him other than his partner's last utterances. But he heard the screaming of an animal in pain and he realized that his horse was still struggling to stand. Nate staggered up, almost falling, pointed his pistol and fired. He missed the first shot, the blood coating his hands slicking the grip, and he took a second, killing shot.

He pulled Deerling off the road and sat with him for a while, unable to move, gutted by fear, bewildered beyond a ready acceptance that the ranger who had survived hostile attacks for two decades had been killed in his presence by a single assassin who was himself a lawman. But even lifeless, the ranger's face appeared unrelaxed, was still compressed into lines of wary reserve. Nate reached down and closed Deerling's eyes.

Shivering from the cold and his own injuries, he managed after an hour to catch hold of the bay. He calmed the horse and then lifted his partner, facedown, over the saddle. He gathered the reins and began walking towards Houston, Deerling's blood drying on his coat.

Chapter 13

A white vapor filled Lucinda's head. She was conscious enough to know that her eyes were closed, but somehow she was unable to open them. A loud twanging made her stir, and in her disoriented state she thought the sound resembled the strings of a guitar being plucked unnecessarily hard. The noise seemed to come from over her head, and soon another metallic slapping noise jolted her, and her eyelids finally opened.

She was in a bed that she didn't recognize; it certainly wasn't in the Waller home. The room was in want of paint and new plaster, and, when she turned her head slightly towards the window, she saw the wisping threads of a cobweb in one corner. She turned her head away from the window and saw Jane standing at the bedroom door. The girl seemed to glow in the hazy light, and when Lucinda tried to speak to her, she found she couldn't form the words.

Jane came to the bed and sat on the edge. She said, "You're awake. You've been sleeping since yesterday."

After a bit Lucinda managed to ask, "How…?"

"Tobias brought you here. He's the Negro man who found you

at the Wallers' old storage house. He's been here twice to ask after you."

Jane seemed to glow brighter, like some pearl-white lantern with the gas key turned up high. The slapping sound came again and Lucinda's gaze went to the ceiling.

Jane patted her arm. "That's the prickly wire Father has strung across the roof to keep the buzzards off. But they continue to roost. When they fly away, they hold the wires in their talons until the very last moment. May calls them the celestial choir."

It seemed to Lucinda that the words being spoken had started to slow down like an overwound clock, and the brilliance from Jane's skin was scalding her eyes. She felt a tremor beginning in her legs, her back arching involuntarily. Before she lost consciousness, she heard the slapping of the wires playing a tune she thought she recognized.

When Lucinda opened her eyes again, Jane was standing by the bed, holding a bowl and a spoon.

"How long have I been here?" Lucinda's mouth felt dry and cottony, but the light had resumed its normal intensity.

Jane set the bowl on a bedside table and helped Lucinda prop herself up on the pillows. She picked up the bowl and began to spoon soup into Lucinda's mouth. Lucinda thought her stomach would rebel against any food, but the warmth and saltiness sharpened her hunger and she sucked at the broth greedily.

Jane said, "Today is Tuesday. You've been ill since Sunday."

Lucinda looked at her, startled. She had lost two days. She couldn't remember the last time she had been so sick.

She maneuvered herself up onto her elbows and asked, "Why did Tobias bring me here?"

Jane's face reddened and she looked down at the bowl. Lucinda's mouth twitched and she said, "Ah, I see. Well, the Wallers aren't the first to believe that what I have is catching."

Jane fed her another spoonful. "It's ignorance, plain and simple."

"You're not afraid?"

"You have fits, not the plague." She fed Lucinda more of the soup. "The Caesars of Rome had the falling sickness."

"The falling sickness. That's a pretty phrase." Bedford had said that there were twenty ways to die from one Sunday to the next in Middle Bayou—from alligators, poisonous snakes, the perfidy of men. And yet her greatest threat came from within her own body.

Lucinda shifted again, looking around. "Where's May?"

Jane arched a brow. "She's teaching in your stead."

Lucinda said, "Oh, dear."

A movement at the door made Lucinda look up. Bedford was hovering at the entrance, looking worried. She was pleased to see his distractedness and the days'-old stubble on his face. Lucinda had not seen herself in a mirror yet, but she put on what she hoped was a grateful smile. "Bedford."

"Miss Carter. Lucinda. Are you feeling better?"

"A little, thanks to your care."

"I'm…we're happy to have you here for as long as you need to be. Until you are well."

There was a pause, and Lucinda felt Jane's eyes studying the both of them, the spoon poised over the soup bowl. Her attentiveness had changed the moment her father called Lucinda by her first name. If anything good had ever come from her sickness, it was her being placed inside the Grant home as a patient to be cared for and fawned over. Lucinda knew that in her attempt to gain Bedford's trust, his older daughter—who acted in all ways save one as wife to her father—could be her greatest ally or her greatest obstacle. She'd known many women like Jane, women who gave up their own lives to be caretakers and who could find surprisingly inventive ways to fend off those who tried to usurp their hard-earned places.

Lucinda looked up at Jane and, reaching for her free hand, said, "I have the best possible nurse."

For days, both Jane and May brought meals to her room and small parcels of food, preserved fruit or baked things, from the settlers wishing her well. May would leave in the mornings for the schoolhouse but stay with her in the afternoons, telling her of each student's progress or slide towards unruliness. The girl would sit, or lie, at the end of Lucinda's narrow bed, and after she gave her reports, she would press Lucinda for details of towns and cities far away or of the latest modes of ladies' dress and hairstyles.

Several times a day, Bedford would appear at the bedroom door, awkward and concerned, staying only a moment to ask after her health.

On the third day of her recovery, she walked with May out into the shorn fields surrounding the house, their rustling progress flushing mourning doves from their hiding places. When Lucinda felt tired, they lay together side by side, the air cool, the earth radiating the sun's heat like an oven-warmed plate. They could hear Jane calling them back inside, and they shushed each other and laughed like rude children hiding from a playmate. Lucinda turned onto her back and looked up at the clouds, and May rested her head on Lucinda's shoulder, like a sweetheart. They lay so still that soon they could hear the renewed burring of doves nearby.

Lucinda then whispered into May's ear the story of her own father taking her out into their hay field when she was a child and placing into her hands one tiny dove's egg plucked from a nest that only his hunter's eyes had seen.

"The egg burned in my hand with a surprising weight for so tiny an object," Lucinda said. "A pulsing globe with the hidden warmth of the chick about to hatch." She reached over and stroked May's cheek. "He told me that I was like the dove, trapped in the shell of my infirmities, but that someday, if I was good, if I cleaved to God and all His admonitions, I would escape, perfect and whole."

"But you did not escape," May said.

"No, I did not escape." The shell remained, Lucinda thought. Not the brittle casing of a dove's egg, but an elastic, permeable membrane, one that accepted light and air, sounds and awakenings, but that kept her body imprisoned. "He committed me to a madhouse," she said.

"Oh," May cooed, and she wrapped one arm more tightly around Lucinda's neck.

Lucinda's eyes closed with the pleasure of the embrace and the ambient warmth of the ground, and impulsively, she kissed the girl's forehead. She then stood and gave her hand to May to preclude any more conversation, and they walked back to the house together.

Later, Lucinda sat alone for a while on the porch, wrapped in a blanket, savoring the fragile warmth of the November sun. Lucinda could see, in the distance, Lavada and Sephronia pushing

Elam's wheeled chair on their daily walk, the twin bell-like motions of their skirts sweeping up the dust of the path. May stepped out onto the porch holding a hairbrush and watched the women.

She said, "You would think they never had buzzards on *their* roof. But they do, and I've seen them."

May unpinned Lucinda's hair and began to brush it. It had become an afternoon practice, and Lucinda, who most times did not relish being touched, had come to look forward to the ritual. The brush was made of old embossed ivory, the boar bristles gentle on her scalp.

May said, "I've spoken to Father and told him I think you should stay with us. So we can care for you."

Lucinda had tipped her head back and closed her eyes, drowsy and relaxed. "And what did your father say to such a scandalous suggestion?"

"Well, he didn't say no." She continued brushing Lucinda's hair for a moment, and then said, "I found the letter you were writing to your brother."

Lucinda opened her eyes, her drowsiness gone. "Which letter?"

"The letter you had been writing in the little storage house. Before you had your fit."

Lucinda searched her mind for her last few moments before losing consciousness. She remembered being inside the shed, but she had forgotten about the letter until May reminded her of it. And there was no clear memory of what she had written before hearing the noises that led her to find Tobias.

May set the brush down and moved to sit on the railing across from Lucinda.

Keeping her face expressionless, Lucinda asked, "Where is the letter now?"

"In a book by your bed." May tilted her head and smiled in a way that made Lucinda clench her teeth. "I put it there to keep it safe."

Lucinda's tapestry bag had been delivered to the Grant home by Euphrastus during the first few days of her illness. As soon as she was able, Lucinda had searched to make certain that the money she had taken and the gun were still at the bottom of the bag. She had not thought to assure herself that her letters had not been discovered.

May had been swinging her legs, idly kicking the railing struts, but she stopped abruptly. "I think I've tired you out. I'll help you back to your room."

May led Lucinda up the stairs and into bed. After smoothing the bedcovers, she leaned down and kissed Lucinda on the cheek. She stood, brushing the hair from her neck, and asked, "What's your brother's name?"

Lucinda paused for a moment before answering. "Bill," she said.

"Will your brother come and visit, do you think?"

Lucinda reached out and cupped May's face in one hand. "He may need to."

As soon as May had left the room, Lucinda picked up the book and saw it was one from Bedford's library. She found the letter, pulled it out, and read what she had written: *I progress as the Trusted Teacher. You will be pleased to know that I am now friend to the one who is of interest to you...*

Her impulse was to laugh out loud with relief. She couldn't

have written a more innocuous beginning to a letter if she had tried.

Bedford appeared at the bedroom door, and seeing Lucinda reading the letter, he started to leave. But she called him back and he stayed for a while, talking of inconsequential things. The fading light cast doleful shadows under his eyes, and she thought perhaps he'd been losing sleep on her account.

He told her, "Your stay in this house has, for me, been a gift." He looked shyly down at his hands and she waited patiently through the long pause for him to continue.

Finally he asked, "May I continue to call on you once you have returned to the Wallers?"

She lowered her chin modestly and said, "Yes."

The next day, May insisted on a picnic by the bayou, and she packed a basket with the best of the neighbors' gifted food for Lucinda, herself, and Jane. They moved quietly while passing the Waller house, May whispering to Lucinda, "Lavada will want to come too if she sees us, and it will be tedious beyond endurance."

They walked close to a mile along a narrow path to a clearing surrounded and shaded by tall trees, and Lucinda was astonished to see Elam sitting in his wheeled chair unattended. He was situated facing the water, rigid and motionless as usual, a quilt tucked around his lap.

Jane shook her head. "They leave him like that, sometimes for hours. Mr. Waller says there are too many women in the house, and that solitude builds fortitude for Elam. It's cruel."

Turning her back to the chair, May said, "It gives me the willies."

They began to eat the roasted meats and pickled vegetables,

salty and still tasting of summer, but Lucinda watched Elam's unmoving form, believing he was not as insensible as the women in his family believed him to be. Once, when he had been parked outside the schoolhouse, Lucinda noticed that he was in full sun and went to move him into the shade. She waved her hand across his face to chase away a wasp, and his nostrils flared at the smell of the scent on her wrist. She brought her face level with his and thought she saw the slightest gleam of recognition in his eyes. She told him, "I know what it's like to be made a prisoner in your own body."

Watching him sitting alone and helpless at that moment caused a sudden anger to fill her chest.

"My own father couldn't tolerate the sight of me," Lucinda said. Jane averted her eyes at the outburst, but May looked at her, intensely curious. "When I was eleven, he sent me to an asylum for the insane, the simpleminded, and the crippled. In the mornings, we shook scorpions out of our shoes, and at night we chased the rats up and down the hallways. We were beaten when we didn't improve. My father saw my weakness as his personal failure."

She stood up abruptly and walked to Elam's chair. She wheeled him about, pushed him close to where they were eating, and sat down again.

She was about to offer to feed him or at least try to give him some water when Jane, looking over her shoulder, said, "There's a man walking in the trees, watching us."

Lucinda turned and saw that the man was staring at her as though he knew her. He was moving rapidly, almost sprinting, and was only a few yards away when Lucinda realized it was Mrs. Landry's German.

He grabbed her, pulling hard at her clothes, scattering food off the blanket with his heavy boots. May screamed, her hands defensively over her head.

"You bitch. You goddamn bitch."

He yanked Lucinda partway off the ground, held her two-fisted by her collar, and shook her. She felt the back seam of her dress giving way.

"Where is it?" His face was over hers, spittle flecking his mouth, lips cracked and raw. Fresh, knotted scabs threaded their way over his forehead and cheeks, as though he had fallen into a mesquite thicket.

"Where is it?" He shook her again, brutally, causing her teeth to pierce her tongue.

As he opened his palm to slap her, a small red crater appeared below one eye, accompanied by a meager popping sound. He staggered once, dropping Lucinda onto the ground. He touched his face with one hand; his fingers came away bloody, and he moved his mouth as though chewing taffy. Then he pitched over backwards and lay utterly still.

Lucinda pulled her knees up to her chest, struggling for air. The whole attack had lasted less than a minute and yet food and broken cutlery were scattered everywhere; her dress was torn, her throat raw and burning. Both May and Jane were breathing raggedly, hollow-eyed in terror, but they weren't looking at her—they were looking at something behind her, their mouths slack with disbelief. Thinking of another attack, this time by someone with a gun, Lucinda jerked her head around and saw only Elam in his chair, but he had his right arm outstretched. The lap quilt had been thrown to the ground, and in his extended hand was a small pistol.

Whatever emotions had been resurrected in him during the attack still played across his eyes and mouth but were starting to evaporate, like water off a glass. In the few seconds it took Lucinda to get to him, his face returned to an expressionless mask. She gently pulled the gun from his outstretched hand, and the arm fell heavily into his lap. She stooped down, retrieved the quilt from the ground, and settled it around his legs. She put the derringer back under the quilt.

She turned to the sisters, still clinging to each other in fear. Remarkably, she felt no signs of a coming fit, no trembling or heaviness in her limbs, only the exhilarating jab of rage. She had complete mental clarity and could envision the sequence of necessary actions, see them falling into place, like the solutions to familiar mathematical equations.

Lucinda knelt in front of them and took both sisters' hands into her own. "I knew this man from Fort Worth." Her words sounded thick, and she realized that her tongue was beginning to swell. "He was a day laborer assigned to repair the schoolhouse where I taught." She was warming to her fabricated story, the particulars unwinding as easily as thread off a spool. "I didn't know how dangerously unbalanced he was until he mistook my kindness for permission to make advances towards me. He followed me everywhere and became the main reason I had to leave."

"He became obsessed with you," May whispered, her color high.

She's finding the story exciting, Lucinda thought. *Like a passage from one of her novels.*

Jane was shaking her head as though trying to cast the terrifying images of a deranged man from her mind. She said, "We have to tell Papa."

Lucinda pulled Jane into a tight embrace. "Of course you want to tell your father. But then he will have to tell Euphrastus about Elam. Elam might be tried as a killer and sent away to an asylum, at best, or even prison." She took Jane's face between her palms. "Jane, can you imagine Elam in prison? He saved our lives. Would we repay his bravery with that kind of hell?"

Jane looked at her, stricken, and began to cry.

"Only we four know what happened." Lucinda looked at the body of the German. "How many times have you heard your father say that the bayou resurrects death into life in endless cycles? All we need do is drag the body to the water..." She looked at the sisters, waiting for them to comprehend that once the body was in the water, the alligators and fish would feed on it until there was nothing left of the German but his boots. And in time, even those would disappear.

Jane's eyes widened hysterically and she shook her head back and forth until Lucinda held her again and rocked her, assuring her that all would be well.

Within a half an hour, the three women had filled the dead man's pockets with stones and rolled him into the water. Jane was shaking and pale, crying noisily, but May regarded the sinking remains with a kind of fascination, with no tears or lingering signs of fright. Lucinda knew that if they kept their secret for even a few days, the likelihood was great that they would keep it for a good while longer, their collective silence working like the heavy stones in the German's pockets against the revelation of truth.

Chapter 14

Deerling was buried in the city cemetery north of Houston. For a long time Dr. Tom stared into the pit where the coffin had been laid, ignoring the dust spray kicked up by the damp wind. He was supported by the doctor and the undertaker, one on either side, so he could stand through the brief service. If the ranger's pneumonia had improved at all in the short while that Nate and Deerling had been gone to Harrisburg, Nate couldn't see it.

When the minister stepped away for the earth to be filled in, Dr. Tom turned and was helped into the wagon that had brought him to the cemetery. He lay in the back, eyes trained on the sky, wordless, for the mile's journey into town. Nate rode with him in the wagon, his head buried in his forearms across both knees.

Nate had given his full account of what had happened in Frost Town and Harrisburg to Dr. Tom in his sickroom the evening he had limped back into Houston bringing Deerling's body. To the county sheriff, a man named Taggert, he later gave only a partial story. At Tom's insistence, Nate did not reveal Prudone's telegram to McGill in Lynchburg or his involvement in Deerling's death.

He was not questioned further, and he had no idea what, if anything, the sheriff planned to do about finding Deerling's killer.

When the funeral wagon stopped at the doctor's office, Dr. Tom was carried to bed, and Nate pulled the doctor aside and asked him what his expectations were about the recovery.

The doctor took off his stiff collar to rub at his neck. "Well, he's angry. Sometimes that helps, sometimes it doesn't."

Nate sat by the bedside for two days before the ranger was able to speak to him again. Mostly he lay in a fever, unconscious. Other times, late at night, Nate thought the man's lungs would appear through his mouth, so violent were the coughing spells.

Following Dr. Tom's spitting up blood on the second night, the doctor ordered Nate to hold him down while he forced laudanum down the patient's throat.

After swallowing the laudanum, Dr. Tom rested more quietly, but awake or asleep, he held on to the letter Nate had returned to him, clutching it until it was wilted with sweat.

On the fourth day after his return from Harrisburg, Nate finally received a letter of his own, from his wife. It seemed it was the third letter she had written, the first two, he guessed, delivered to Austin after they had already passed through. He read the letter several times, lingering over the news about his daughter.

Mattie wears the necklace you sent day and night. She will not take it off even at bedtime. Many times she has fallen asleep with her fingers wrapped around the beads. She misses you, Nathaniel, as do I. I wear a necklace made of the time spent without you, and though the beads are invisible, they are weighty on my neck, and it grows longer by the day.

His throat closed at the last, but he imagined the delight in his daughter's face at the moment of the necklace's discovery. He held fast to that image, countering the memory of Deerling's lifeless stare after he'd stopped breathing.

"You've still got George's blood all over you."

Dr. Tom's eyes were open and Nate wondered how long he'd been watching him. Nate looked down at his coat sleeves and at the brown stains that mottled them.

Dr. Tom turned his head to better see. "You wearin' that coat as some kind of penance?"

Nate looked away, his eyes seeking a blank wall but finding Deerling's Whitworth propped in the corner. Dr. Tom coughed once and a grimace passed over his face. Nate started to stand to help him, but the ranger waved him down. The spasm passed, and, after the chest rattling had calmed, Dr. Tom rasped, "You're not to blame."

Nate did stand up then and fled the room. He walked down the street and paced in front of the dry-goods store and the post office, wiping at his eyes with his sleeves when he thought no one was looking. He considered writing his wife. He would pour out his pain to her in the hopes of gaining some relief from the guilt over Deerling's death.

But he started walking north instead and kept going until he had come to the cemetery where they had buried the ranger. He stopped for a brief while at the grave, the clods and raw earth already settling into the spaces that the shovels had made. They hadn't readied the headstone yet, but he knew what it would say: *George A. Deerling, born 1813, died 1870, Comrade in Arms, Father, Friend.*

He found his way back to the road again and continued walking.

Wagons headed for Houston passed him, the travelers inside giving him cautious looks. He was a horseless man walking on narrow, round-heeled boots and wearing a coat stained like an old butcher's apron. His stride was still uneven from the bruising his hip had taken from the fall, but the jagged sensations somehow helped to quiet his mind.

After a few more miles, he came to a farmhouse with a rail fence, and he sat on it, facing away from the road. The fields were flat prairie land, like his farm in Oklahoma.

He thought of his wife and daughter and a feeling like a blow to the chest closed up his throat. Deerling had been right: Nate wasn't much of a farmer. Still, the land was biddable enough, and he was young enough to learn. He could, over time, make a better farm. His true desire, though, was to begin his own herd of horses, to breed the best working animals, combining Texas cow ponies with the Oklahoma-reservation stock. But it would take more money than he could make farming, and his decision to join the Texas police had been a way to earn the seed money to begin the herd.

His mind turned round and round on these topics, like the blind pony he had bought for Mattie who knew only one route: down the path, around the field, and back to the barn. The little horse never stumbled, but he never found new ground either.

The sun had angled steeply to the west before he climbed off the fence and walked the miles back to Houston. When he entered the sickroom, he pulled off his coat and wadded it into a corner. Dr. Tom looked at him through pooled, glassy eyes, but his color was better.

Dr. Tom nodded for him to sit in the chair. When Nate had settled, he said, "You should take George's horse. No, now, listen. That horse is too big for me, and mine is already set to my ways. I wouldn't entrust him to anyone else." Dr. Tom faltered and looked at the ceiling, struggling to quiet a sudden wash of grief.

He cleared his throat, wiped his face with the bedsheet. "I'm going to be in this bed for a while yet, and you need to go on to Lynchburg alone. You can't be walkin' the distance, and that big bay would take you to Canada if you asked him to. I want you to listen good, 'cause I'm too winded to repeat myself. You're going only to see if McGill and his men are encamped there." He pointed a finger at Nate. "You don't engage. Hide your badge, keep your head down, and get back here to me." He paused, his breathing labored. "There's one last thing. A woman's been traveling with McGill, and I want to know if she's there in Lynchburg."

"A woman?"

Dr. Tom palmed the sweat off his face. "She's George's daughter."

Nate sat back in the chair and stared at Dr. Tom. "I thought his daughter was dead."

Dr. Tom shook his head. "She turned bad and ran away. George tried bringing her home, but she always left again. A while back, she took up with McGill. George's mission in life was to redeem her or see her in prison."

"He would have sent her to prison?"

"She's a grown woman involved with a man that's killed eleven people along with two children. You saw that widow in Frost Town. What makes you think that a woman with any decency left would cleave to an evil man like McGill?" Dr. Tom paused, his hand clutching his chest as if to will himself into a calmer state.

Nate recalled that Deerling's exact words were "I had a daughter"; he didn't say that she had died, and Nate saw in ways that he wished he didn't how the world could swallow a child just by spinning from one day to the next. Deerling's single-minded mission to find McGill suddenly made sense.

Nate asked, "What about Taggert? I still don't know why you didn't want me to tell him about McGill in Lynchburg."

"Nate, we've come too far to let a county man have McGill. That's why I asked you to keep quiet about the telegram."

"And Prudone?"

"First things first. We put an end to McGill, and then I'll settle with Prudone in my own way. That son of a bitch will be going to hell already torched."

Nate sat quiet for a moment. "I don't know about this, Tom. It all feels too..."

"Personal?" Dr. Tom asked. He struggled to sit up in the bed. "Isn't that what you told me that first day out of Franklin? You said, 'Hell, it's *all* personal.' Getting to McGill was not personal just to George; it's personal to me too. More than you could possibly know. And with you or without you, I'm settling on McGill and then Prudone." He let Nate think on that a bit and then asked, "Why did you go after those horse thieves in Arkansas, Nate? They only took a few horses. They shot a kid, but you were just a kid yourself. Why didn't you just let it go?" He closed his eyes for a moment, his chest moving erratically. "You didn't let it go, because it would have eaten at you the rest of your natural life. This I know about you. You have a fire in you to make things right. Don't you think going after George's murderer is as right as reclaiming a few horses?"

Nate sat with Dr. Tom until he had drifted off to sleep and then spent the rest of the night sprawled in the chair.

The next morning early, he walked to the livery and took some time letting Deerling's horse settle to his touch and smell; although his own saddle had been retrieved from the Harrisburg-to-Houston road, he steadied the bay with Deerling's familiar tack.

He mounted and touched his heels to the horse's flanks, and the bay crouched and bolted, ears flattened, nose forward, and Nate reined him to a stop, saying, "Let's try that again."

He tapped him once more, and the bay started an easy trot, the muscles in the shoulders and rump bunching and releasing under the rippling hide, like a steam engine under velvet.

Following the roads and cow paths by Buffalo Bayou and skirting the swampier tracts, he reached the old San Jacinto battlefield in a few hours. The ferryman who took him across the confluence of the San Jacinto and Buffalo Rivers was a survivor of Shiloh. He had two wooden legs, and he told Nate cheerfully that he'd quickly drown in the river if he ever fell in, so heavy were his replacement appendages. "But," he said, "it would take another cannonball to sweep me off the deck."

Nate rode into Lynchburg at midday and, after tying his horse to a post, walked slowly up and down the main street, looking into storefronts. His story, if asked, was that he was just another cowboy from West Texas looking for work on one of the big cattle farms south of Houston.

He'd been given a description of two of McGill's men, Purdy and Crenshaw—stunted and weasel-mouthed in the first case; Gallic-nosed and Cajun in the second—as well as of McGill himself. He was a man of average height, slender, dark-haired, with no identifying scars or marks on the face or hands—a description that could have applied to half the men in Texas. Both Deerling and Dr. Tom had seen McGill's image on Wanted posters but had never looked him in the face.

Of the daughter, Dr. Tom told Nate that she was twenty-three years old, fair-skinned and dark-haired, with a small mole under her right eye.

The only other bit of information Nate possessed was that Crenshaw had a rare grulla mare, a horse he had most likely stolen from one of his victims. As Nate walked the main street, he saw no gray horses and very few people. He ordered a beer, which was warm and flat, at the one saloon in town. The barkeep, a top-heavy man with a dirty towel draped over one shoulder, offered the news of the day, all of it unremarkable.

Nate thanked him, and after walking around some more and drifting through the small hotel, he mounted his horse and rode back to the ferry. To his thinking, the whole town seemed too open, too transparent, for McGill and his men to hide in.

Nate was surprised to see another man waiting at the ferry ahead of him. Once afloat, they dismounted from their horses, both looking at the murky water rushing by.

The man finally said, "Makes me a little dizzy watching these currents." He turned to Nate and smiled amiably. "You don't want to get too close to the edge. The currents here at this spot are so powerful that even a strong swimmer would fail to gain either shore."

"That so," Nate responded, taking a step back from the shoddy railing.

The man stuck out his hand. "The name is Estes."

Nate clasped the man's hand. "Nate. Nate Cannon."

"You here looking for work?"

Nate nodded. "You?"

"Always." Estes smiled again, and he and Nate chatted comfortably for a while about their recent journeys.

When the ferry docked on the western side, Estes waved and said, "Good luck. Keep a close eye on those deep waters."

He rode away to the south and Nate felt an immediate downward turn of emotions that he recognized as simple loneliness, the want of cheerful company.

When Nate returned to Houston, he found Dr. Tom sleeping. He sat quietly by the bed until the ranger opened his eyes and then he recounted the events of his trip to Lynchburg. Nate could see the disappointment in Dr. Tom's face as he rubbed his hand over his mouth in frustration.

Nate began telling him about the return trip on the ferry, but he stopped when he saw his partner's face.

Dr. Tom hiked himself up to a sitting position. "What did you say?"

Nate repeated his last bit of information. "The traveler's name was Estes."

"What did he look like?"

"Bearded, spectacles, my height. Said he was a surveyor."

Dr. Tom reached out and grabbed Nate painfully around the wrist. "Do you know what McGill's full name is? It's William Estes McGill. The only reason you're still sitting here and not floating in the Gulf somewhere is that you didn't make him. But I'll bet he made you. Christ Almighty, Nate."

The face of the surveyor on the river had seemed to Nate placid, the eyes behind the spectacles keen but friendly, and he had felt an immediate liking for the man and a desire, once he arrived at the other side of the river, for continued conversation. The sense of isolation and apartness he had experienced during the past few months seemed to sharpen after his fellow passenger had ridden away.

Even Prudone as he rode towards Deerling had given telltale signs indicating impending violence. But Nate had been completely at his ease during the crossing, the memory of Deerling's death dropping away for the briefest while.

He sat quietly, looking at his hands, thinking of the two rivers that joined at the ferry crossing, waters so opaque and muddy that his falling body would have cast little reflection and left only the parting of eddies to signify he had ever been there.

Chapter 15

*L*ucinda's eyes were closed, but she was acutely aware that Bedford Grant was staring at her. She sat on a worn chaise, her head tilted back to expose the full length of her neck, her legs stretched out before her, ankles neatly crossed. The hem of her skirt had been carelessly raised, revealing the curves of her insteps in her heeled, kid-leather boots. She arched her foot more appealingly and felt the laces tighten against her skin.

May reclined next to her, her head in Lucinda's lap. Occasionally, Lucinda would let her fingers find their way to May's hair, and she would stroke it as she would have a cat.

Jane was also in the sitting room, opposite her, quietly sewing. Lucinda suspected that Jane was staring at her as well, but with a different intensity and purpose.

Lucinda had begun spending quite a few evenings with the Grants, eating supper with them and taking long walks with Bedford afterwards. The evenings spent at the Wallers', when Bedford came to call on her, were an exercise in monumental restraint—restraining herself from giving exasperated replies in response to both Euphrastus's puffed-up jealousy and his wife's and daughter's ridiculous swooning over Bedford's courtship.

She was frustrated by the continued reluctance of Bedford to give her any more accounting of the gold coins other than to promise her that he would eventually reveal where they were hidden. She had given faithful reports of her progress in her letters to her supposed brother, Bill, but it had been a while since she had received a response, and the silence was filling her with anxiety, keeping her awake at nights.

May stirred and sat up. "Miss Carter, come for a walk with me."

Lucinda opened her eyes and stretched. "Only if your sister comes with us."

Jane looked up from her work, her expression wary. The shooting of the German had at first left her terrified and clinging, needing reassurance from Lucinda almost hourly that they had made the right decision in hiding his body, but then she'd become silent. Jane had made herself ill with worry, and now it was Lucinda's turn to be Jane's nursemaid. She encouraged the girl to eat and take walks after she had confined herself to her bedroom for days. After a full week of fearfulness, Jane embraced despondency; she was indifferent towards her family, and increasingly cold and guarded with Lucinda, avoiding her whenever possible.

May, however, seemed unaffected by the incident, or at least undisturbed by it; she used every opportunity to revisit the events with Lucinda, talking about it in hushed and eager tones, as though she were discussing a bolt of fabric she'd been forbidden to buy. The constant talk of the shooting was fraying Lucinda's nerves, and she hoped May's troublesome excitement would soon diminish.

Lucinda smiled at Jane, who ducked her head closer to her sewing. "Jane," she prodded, "you look pale. Come with us."

Bedford asked Jane, "Have you not been feeling well?" He sounded surprised; his daughter's anguish had gone completely unnoticed.

"I'm well," Jane murmured. She frowned, but she put her sewing aside and stood.

After gathering up her hat and shawl, Lucinda took Jane's hand and led the sisters out onto the porch. The late-afternoon air was chilled, and Lucinda pulled her shawl higher around her shoulders.

They walked for a while in silence, moving towards Red Bluff Road and away from the bayou. It was an unspoken agreement among them that they would not return to the clearing by the water.

They crossed the road and walked onto the adjoining stretch of prairie grasses, the remaining shafts yellowed and fragile under their shoes. The feeble smell of marsh water threaded the breeze. They slowed their steps only when a snake crossed their path. Its tail thrashed against the dry vegetation, making a vibrating sound, and Lucinda thought it a rattlesnake. But Jane shook her head and declared it a king snake, harmful only to the rodents that burrowed in the fields. She turned and leveled her eyes at Lucinda. "Don't worry, Miss Carter. It's just a pretender."

Three herons lifted their heads in unison to watch the women approaching, their feathers blue-gray under the slanting sun, and May exclaimed, "That will be us in thirty years: skinny-legged and stoop-shouldered." Raising her shawl like a flag, she shrieked and ran, chasing the birds into flight.

Lucinda smiled and turned her face to catch more of the sun. "Such a pleasant day. I almost hate to begin the week at the school tomorrow."

Jane hugged herself tighter with her crossed arms. "I don't suppose you'll have to be teaching much longer."

"Jane, look at me. Look at me." When Jane raised her chin to return the gaze, Lucinda asked, "Haven't I always been kind to you, and to your family?"

Jane hesitated but answered, "Yes."

"Then why have you become so sour towards me?"

Jane exhaled sharply but said nothing and turned to stare across the field.

Lucinda placed her hand on Jane's arm. "That man would have killed me." When there was no response, she dropped her hand, and they watched May chasing grasshoppers from their hiding places.

Jane took a few breaths and turned to Lucinda. "When that man attacked you, he said, 'Where is it?' What did he mean? What was he talking about?"

Lucinda looked at her blankly; her main recollection of him was of his hands closing around her throat.

Jane impatiently drew a strand of hair from her face. "He wanted something back that you had taken from him, didn't he?"

Lucinda felt her face redden and she turned away, trying to veil a sudden burst of anger.

Jane clutched at her hand. "You're only after the gold, aren't you?"

Lucinda looked at the work-worn girl in surprise, realizing she should have known all along that Bedford would have told Jane, his closest ally and confidante, about the treasure, although he never would have revealed his discovery to his unpredictable younger daughter.

She gathered her shawl more tightly around her shoulders. "I don't know what you're speaking of. And the only thing I took from my attacker was myself. That you should question me in this way distresses me no end. It will distress your father as well."

There was an edge of a threat at the last, and Jane flinched, but her eyes narrowed.

May approached them, flushed and breathless, her eyes alert to the tension between the two women. She looked at her sister calculatingly and then linked her arm through Lucinda's. Pulling her back towards the house, May said, "Don't mind Jane, Miss Carter. She's just jealous that you're getting Father now. She'll have to find her own man soon."

In the last hours of daylight, Bedford walked Lucinda back to the Wallers', but she sighed and frowned, and when he asked her what the matter was, she would only shake her head. He invited her to linger on the porch but she pulled away, her hand on the doorknob.

"Lucinda, dear, what's wrong? Is it something I've done?"

Lucinda gave him the back of her head. "It's rather what you haven't done. You don't trust me, Bedford, and by your example, neither does your family. Jane was very cold and thoughtless with me today." She opened the door, but he put his hand over hers.

"Of course I trust you. And as to Jane, I can't imagine why she would be cold with you, but I'll speak with her."

Lucinda turned to face him. "Speak with her all you like, but you must lead by example."

She walked inside, closed the door, and listened to him pacing and then retreating down the steps. She could play the slap-and-tickle game as well as anyone, and tomorrow she'd greet his anxious looks and reticent air with warm smiles and gentle encouragement. She had let him only kiss her cheek so far, his hands restrained by hers over the stays cinching her waist. But beginning tomorrow, she'd start to bring the pot to a full boil.

There were too many threats of discovery now, too many chances to be thwarted by Jane, by Tobias, by the Wallers; she had to move more decisively. If she had to pour whiskey down his throat (something he'd been doing on the sly himself more and more in recent days) and dance naked, she'd get Bedford Grant to reveal to her where the gold was hidden.

The following morning, she left for the school early. She made her way to the greenhouse first to write another letter, but as she approached the structure, she smelled the familiar odor of lit tobacco. She walked to the far side and saw Tobias seated in his usual place, his back against the wall.

She approached him slowly, careful not to alarm him. "I wanted to thank you for carrying me to the Grants'."

He looked at her for a moment, one eye closed against the smoke, and nodded. "I had a cousin who had the shakes."

She moved a few paces closer. "It's been a long time since I've had any tobacco."

He took another deep drag, let the smoke curl out between his lips, and then held it out to her. The smoker's end was wet and glistening from being in his mouth, and in his one open eye was a challenge. She hesitated for only a moment, then stooped down and took the cigarette between her fingers. She drew deeply on it once and handed it back.

She looked around, laid the shawl on the ground, and sat next to him. She stared at his profile for a while. "Are you going to tell anyone about me?"

He looked her full in the face. "Who would I tell?"

"I don't know. Whoever is most likely to reward you for the information."

A slow creeping smile brought his lips apart, showing the tips of his teeth. "No one will thank me for that bit of news."

She took the cigarette from him again. "How did you know?"

He let his head fall back against the wall and closed his eyes. "You ever walk along on a hot day and smell honeysuckle? You can't always see it, it grows underneath sometimes, but you can sure smell it. It hits you sudden-like, and it stops you dead in your tracks." He opened his eyes, turning his head to her. "It's been a long time since I've felt the presence of a come-hither woman."

She looked away but smiled and handed back the small butt end of the cigarette. "Why are you telling me all this? What do you gain from it?"

He squinted at her again. "I feel sorry for you. That surprise you? A black man feelin' sorry for a white woman? But I do. These farmers get wind of what you are, and you'll be out on the road before you can turn around."

He pointed in a sweeping motion across the field. "Besides, all these people here, they can hardly stand the fact that I'm with them day after day, working my fields, raising my crops." He crooked his thumb towards the greenhouse roof; the strengthening sun reflected off the glass negatives embedded there. "Looking at me, they understand they're the upright dead, just like those ghosts there on the ceiling. Everything they knew or had or thought they were gonna have is gone." He took out his tobacco pouch and some papers and began to roll another cigarette. "And you? You're the mold in their bread. The worm in their belly that they live with but don't know is there."

He wet the paper with his tongue, then sealed it. "Yes." He laughed softly. "How the mighty are fallen." He handed Lucinda the cigarette, struck a light for her on the bottom of his match safe. "You and me, an upstairs girl and a slave that was, *we* are the new citizens for the coming of days."

It took only a few days to convince Bedford, through furtive touching and desperate groping, kisses given and received on small, exposed places of naked skin, to take her to the place where he said he had discovered the gold.

On a warm evening after an unexpected rain, Bedford walked her to the clearing where the German had been killed and led her to the very banks where his body had been rolled into the water. At first she was alarmed, thinking the body had been discovered, but Bedford pointed across the water to a small island—what she had thought was simply a promontory jutting out from the opposite bank—and said, "That's where Lafitte's treasure is buried. There amongst the trees."

They stood in the dark, his arm around her waist, and listened to the night sounds coming off the water and to the rustling grasses hiding the multitude of creeping, unseen things. She recalled the persimmons on the banks of Buffalo Bayou, and the alligators that guarded them. The island was so very near, and yet it would have to be approached with caution. She stepped closer to the waterline, ignoring the dense clay mud that leached into her shoes, and made a mental list of what would be needed to dig up the gold: a shallow boat for the crossing, ropes, picks, shovels, and, equally important, a sharp eye and a loaded gun for the swamp guardians. Bill would be pleased.

She shivered in expectation, and Bedford, thinking her cold or afraid, held her closer. He whispered to her, "I told you I would share everything I have with you."

Kissing his cheek, she said, "Yes, Bedford, dear. I am certain now that you will."

The next morning the air turned cool, and Lucinda watched the giant whooping cranes, their white and black feathers in stark contrast to the blue of the sky, gliding onto the bayou waters by the hundreds, heard their raucous calls carried with them from far northern places. Lucinda had been pushing Elam's chair along the path towards Red Bluff Road and the schoolhouse but stopped to watch the birds, describing to him what he couldn't see beyond his stiff, forward-facing view in his invalid's chair.

She mused aloud, "They look too large and awkward to fly. How do you think they manage it?"

She looked down at Elam, smoothed some stray bits of hair off his forehead, and impulsively kissed him on the cheek. She had begun taking him to school with her every morning, placing him next to the stuttering boy, thinking it would do the both of them good. The boy talked to Elam throughout the day, his impediment lessening with practice. And for Elam, it was a rescue from the stultifying and suffocating air of the Waller house.

And because of her closer involvement with Elam, she now knew how the pistol had come to be in his lap. It was Euphrastus who, every morning, before Lucinda wheeled the invalid out the door, lifted the quilt and placed the gun underneath. When she asked him why he would do such a thing when Elam could neither move nor speak, Euphrastus answered that he hoped the constant reminder of his son's unfulfilled duty as a soldier would rally him to, at the very least, claim his responsibilities as a Waller, cause him to shake off his imaginary wounds, raise himself from the invalid's chair, and function as a man.

She took hold of the chair handles and continued rolling Elam into the schoolhouse, then settled him at his usual place. She told her students to work on whatever they pleased, only to be quiet.

She sat in her chair and stared out the window, thinking of the letter she would post that day. She hid a tight, satisfied smile with the palm of her hand; soon she could quit this place and begin a life of protected comfort in New Orleans.

A sudden rush of air caused her to turn. May stood in the doorway, holding on to the door frame with outstretched arms, her hair blown into cascading ribbons around her neck. She wore the dove-gray dress and a fine lavender shawl that Lucinda had given her. May smiled excitedly, her cheeks and forehead wind-reddened and glowing, and Lucinda's breath caught in her throat to see in one body such a perfect balance of color, form, and motion. A true and strong affection for the girl rose up like springwater and Lucinda smiled in return.

May took two steps into the room, seemingly unaware of all the other students staring at her as well. "Miss Carter," she began breathlessly, pointing towards the door.

Lucinda looked through the open space, saw nothing.

"Your brother, Bill, is coming."

Lucinda blinked and stood. On Red Bluff Road, a man walked slowly towards the schoolhouse, leading his horse. He looked closely at everything around him, swiveling his head from side to side, taking in the fields and houses in the distance. When he noticed Lucinda standing outside in the yard, he waved once and continued his same leisurely approach. The sun flared off a pair of spectacles and perhaps a glint of teeth showing through a growth of beard.

May came to stand next to her in the yard, and Lucinda felt the girl slip one hand into hers.

"I met him along the road," she said. "You told him in your letter that you'd befriended someone he'd be interested in. And now he's come to meet that friend."

It took a moment for Lucinda to comprehend that May was speaking of the unfinished letter recovered from the greenhouse. She looked at May's upturned face, rapturous with a girl's expectation of being admired and a woman's fevered hope of being pursued, and she suddenly realized that May believed that the friend referred to in Lucinda's letter to Bill was not Bedford but herself.

Chapter 16

The crisis for Dr. Tom came the day after Nate's return from Lynchburg in the form of a roaring fever and frightening visions that left him moaning and disoriented. Nate and the doctor sat with him through the night, nodding occasionally into sleep, only to be awakened again by the ranger rambling and calling out several times, "Watch it, watch it..."

The doctor warned Nate that the patient could be dead by morning, but by daybreak, the fever had broken, and Dr. Tom gave himself ten days to recover sufficiently to ride with Nate to Lynchburg.

The doctor shook his head but conceded, "I've known stranger things to happen. God moves in mysterious ways, His wonders to perform."

"God, and a lot of opiates," Dr. Tom countered.

He gestured to Nate to help him out of bed, and the two of them shuffled around the room for a few minutes. Winded, Dr. Tom crawled back into bed. An hour later, he leaned on Nate again to walk out of the sickroom and into the doctor's visitation room. By the fifth day, Dr. Tom could walk slowly, with only a little assistance, to the stable to see after his horse.

He ran one hand down the horse's neck and then pointed to his old partner's bay in the next stall. "He looks good, Nate. Few people could handle him. Has he reached around and bitten you yet?"

Nate smiled. "He tried it a time or two."

"George had a scar on his thigh as big as Cleveland that he got from the very first day he was out with that big boy."

Dr. Tom lowered himself onto a crate, supporting his lower ribs with one hand. "This lingering pleurisy is going to be a problem for me." He closed his eyes for a moment, breathing shallowly, then reached into his back pocket and pulled out a vial of dark liquid from which he drank. Holding the vial up to Nate, he said, "As could this."

Nate frowned. "The doctor said you needed it."

"The question is for how long, though."

Dr. Tom sat for a few minutes looking out of the open stable door. "I got wounded at Dove Creek during the war. Caught a ball in the left shoulder. The camp surgeon dug it out but it had broken the collarbone and was painful as hell. We didn't stop until we got to Mexico, and the only way I could ride was if I had enough laudanum to take the edge off the hurt. It wasn't but a week before it got its hooks in me. I spent the next few months taking the edge off everything with those little vials. George caught wise and threatened to shoot any doctor who gave me any more. He took me into his home south of Austin and let me stay there until I got well."

Nate placed another crate next to Dr. Tom and sat down. "Did you ever meet his daughter?"

"Yes." Dr. Tom looked at Nate. "I married her."

Nate blinked a few times and raked his hat off his head. There in front of him was the relatedness he had sensed between Deerling and Dr. Tom.

Dr. Tom backhanded the sweat from his eyes. "Oh, it wasn't a love match, at least not on her part. George thought I could somehow manage to reclaim her, get her to lead a settled life."

"She agreed to the marriage, though."

"If you mean did we tie her down and threaten the minister until he performed the ceremony, then no. Deerling knew I'd take care of Lucinda. And I did my best." He stood up, clung to the boards until his dizziness passed, and again laid a gentling hand on his horse's neck. "I loved her, and I thought that would be enough."

Halfway up the street, Dr. Tom staggered but waved away Nate's offer of a supporting arm. He said, "Nate, you're a good nurse and you've been a good friend. But the next time you try holding me up, I'm going to flatten you."

Five days later, Dr. Tom settled his accounts with the doctor, and he and Nate walked to the stable to retrieve their horses. Their plan was to travel in a wide arc so they could enter the town of Lynchburg not from the ferry side at the south but from the north, and under cover of darkness. It would take them the entire day and part of the night, crossing spongy wet ground and several smaller bayou rivers, but Dr. Tom wanted to give them every advantage should they find McGill's men in town.

They breached the narrow, sandy-bottomed banks of the San Jacinto at its narrows and turned south at sunset, the clouds to their right hanging almost vertically in the sky like a curtain. Dr.

Tom had been quiet most of the day, conserving his strength, but his eyes, sunken from exhaustion and opiates, reflected the yellow light dully, like a shot glass underwater. They stopped to rest for a few hours a mile from town, making a low fire so they could brew enough coffee to keep them awake.

Nate had seen Dr. Tom drink from the laudanum flask several times during the day, and the ranger poured some of the dark liquid into his coffee cup, then drained it in a few swallows. He saw Nate watching him but offered no commentary. They drifted off to a half sleep, huddling under their long coats in the night air, but covered over the fire at the sky's lightening murk in the east.

They tied their horses to a stand of trees, took with them short lengths of rope, and walked past a few small houses at the edge of town. Arriving at the stable, Dr. Tom kicked at the door, rousing the stable boy, who asked, in Spanish, who was there.

Dr. Tom kicked at the door again and said, *"Federales."*

They saw lantern light appear from one of the small windows, and when the door finally eased open, they slipped inside. Dr. Tom asked the boy, *"¿Tienes una yegua grulla aquí?"*

The boy hesitated, but finally pointed to a far stall. Nate walked to the back of the barn and saw the gray mare standing quietly. He turned and nodded to his partner.

Dr. Tom pulled out a coin and gave it to the boy. *"¿Dónde está el hombre ahora?"*

The boy looked at the two of them for a moment, brows knit, but answered, *"En el hotel."*

Dr. Tom put a finger to his lips in warning and they left, crossing the street to the hotel. The door was locked but a low window, its bottom frame flush with the porch, was not. Dr. Tom eased it open, slid a shabby armchair aside, and the two of them stepped into the darkened lobby.

The night clerk was asleep at the desk with his head on his arms, and Dr. Tom took another coin out of his pocket and began tapping it on the desk. The clerk came awake with a start and, seeing the two strangers standing in the ill-lit room, began buttoning his collar, muttering, "I'm sorry, gentlemen. We're closed right now. The door should have been locked."

Dr. Tom scanned the lobby quickly and turned back to the clerk. "We're not here for a room."

"What are you here for?" The clerk looked nervously at Nate and the rope he was carrying.

"Information," Dr. Tom said, his voice low.

"What kind of information?"

"William Estes McGill. Innis Crenshaw. Jacob Purdy. Any of those men staying here?"

The clerk had started shaking his head even before Dr. Tom finished speaking. "Look, you should leave."

"One of the men rides a grulla mare that happens to be in the stable down the street."

"If you don't leave, I'm going to have to call the sheriff."

Tom placed his Colt revolver on the desk. "You don't have a sheriff here. Nor do you have a marshal; he's in Harrisburg. But what we do have is a Texas state policeman."

"A what?"

"A Texas state policeman." Dr. Tom pointed to Nate, who opened his coat to show his badge.

"I've never heard of such a thing."

"Have you heard of the governor of Texas?"

"Yes, of course I have. Governor Davis."

"Well, then, you ignorant son of a bitch, this is one of the governor's hounds, newly appointed judge, jury, and executioner, at his discretion. He's been empowered to act with or without all local officers of the peace. So, if you don't want to be taken out and hanged right now for obstructing state business, you'll give me an answer."

"Who're you?"

"I'm the one that gets to tie the rope."

The clerk swiveled his head from one man to the other. "You won't waken the other guests?"

Dr. Tom tucked the pistol back into his belt. "We'll be as quiet as the grave."

The clerk pointed above his head with one finger. "Innis Crenshaw. Room twelve. Up the stairs and to the left. The other two are gone. Both of them."

"If you've lied to us, or if you make any noise, you're dead." Dr. Tom held out his hand. "Key."

The clerk slipped a master key out from under the desk and handed it to Nate. A window at the top of the stairs showed the sky beginning to turn more gray than black. The men climbed the stairs and walked quietly down the hall to room 12.

Dr. Tom pressed his ear to the door for a few moments, then nodded for Nate to unlock it. The door hinges squeaked, but the form lying in the bed across the room, mouth open, arms flung wide, did not stir. The sleeping man woke only to the unmistakable clicking from the hammer on the navy Colt being cocked and readied at his head.

Dr. Tom said, "Hello, Innis. Nate, take that rope and tie his hands together."

Nate tied Crenshaw's hands tightly in back and pulled him off the bed, then gagged him with a strip torn from a shirt thrown to the floor. After gathering up Crenshaw's pistols and boots, they walked him barefoot down the stairs.

As they passed the desk clerk, Dr. Tom tossed him the key and told him, "You can go back to sleep now."

They collected the grulla mare at the stable, and, once they'd heaved Crenshaw into his saddle, they rode north again along the San Jacinto for several hours before stopping in the shade of some oak trees. Dr. Tom dismounted, yanked Crenshaw from the saddle, and threw him roughly to the ground. He hunkered down and studied the prisoner, saw the gag pulling the corners of his lips grotesquely back from his teeth. Crenshaw's eyes above his beaked nose were alternately frightened and enraged; his black hair, long and pomaded to a greasy sheen, spread out wildly over the ground.

To Nate, he looked like a tethered stud horse about to be gelded.

Dr. Tom stood back up and motioned Nate to walk with him out of earshot. The ranger's face was shaded gray from lack of sleep, and more disturbing to Nate was knowing how much of the laudanum bottle had been emptied since leaving Houston.

Dr. Tom began searching for something in his saddle pack. "You remember Maynard Collie?"

Nate nodded uneasily. A vivid image of Collie's lifeless feet and blue lips came to mind. For the first time in a good while, he thought of the cyanide-filled rifle cartridge in his own pack.

"George spent less than half an hour with him and got him to swallow poison." Dr. Tom pulled from the pack his medical kit and turned to face Nate. "You know how he did that?"

"I imagine with threats."

Dr. Tom nodded. "He threatened his wife."

"His wife?" Nate thought of Maynard's crimes, brutally murdering prostitutes, and had a hard time believing that a man like that would have a weakness for any woman.

"George threatened to shoot her. She was the only one that meant anything to Maynard."

"Would he have done it?"

"He only had to convince Maynard that he would."

"What's his weakness?" Nate nodded to the prisoner.

Dr. Tom looked over at Crenshaw, who had worked himself up to a sitting position, his darting eyes evaluating the options for escape. "His vanity."

Dr. Tom opened the medical kit, revealing a neat array of scalpels, lancets, and probes slotted into green felt. "Nate, you're either in this, or you're out. If you feel your resolve fading, just think of that woman and the children of hers that he helped to murder."

He closed the case and directed Nate to drag and tie Crenshaw to a tree.

Dr. Tom crouched close to Crenshaw, setting the medical kit down where the prisoner could see it. He placed his hat carefully aside and said, "Innis, I'm not going to bother asking you right away to tell me the whereabouts of Purdy or McGill because I know it'd be a waste of my time. Isn't that right?"

Crenshaw moved his tongue against the gag, exhaling air.

"I'll take that as a yes, then. I say this because I know that you know if McGill found out you'd given us his whereabouts, he'd shoot you in the gut and leave you to die a long, slow death. A man can take a whole day to die from a gunshot wound to the belly. It's painful, no doubt. But there are worse things."

Dr. Tom opened the kit. "I want you to think on what I'm going to tell you, and I want you to look at my face to know that what I'm saying is true."

Crenshaw's eyes tracked back and forth between Dr. Tom's face and the kit.

"I went to medical school a while back, and I've had occasion to use those skills from time to time. And it's left an impression on me of just how much suffering a human body can endure before expiring.

"During the war, even though I'm not truly a doctor, I helped saw through shattered arms and legs while the patients were awake, fully aware of their own limbs being hacked off. I once had to remove a woman's cancerous breast with only a pocket scalpel. The operation lasted for over an hour, her screaming the whole time. It saved her life, but I don't think that woman ever regained her power of speech."

Dr. Tom pulled a small scalpel from the box. He spread his fingers close to Crenshaw's face, placing the edge of the scalpel against the big knuckle of his own first finger.

"Do you know how many nerves are in the human hand, Innis? Thousands. That's why it hurts so bad when you scald your palm on your mama's stove. I could sit here and saw on your fingers and hands all day until the only thing left to yank yourself with would be the stumps of your arms. And the beauty of it is, you'd still be alive."

Crenshaw's mouth stretched even wider, chuffing out air, and Nate realized he was laughing, or trying to.

"So here's what I'm going to do for you, Innis. I'm going to remove the gag and you're going to tell me where McGill has gone, and I give you my word I won't hurt you."

Dr. Tom untied the gag from Crenshaw's mouth.

"You go to hell." Crenshaw worked his mouth, spitting and hawking. "I tell you where McGill is and you'll hang me. Besides, you don't scare me with your talk, you runty little bastard—"

The gag was replaced and pulled tighter, exposing more of Crenshaw's teeth. Dr. Tom slipped from the box a pair of pliers with a rounded head. In one practiced move he fastened it onto a tooth, and with his other hand he grabbed Crenshaw's hair.

"I've also been known to practice dentistry." Nate heard a cracking sound as Dr. Tom forcefully twisted the tooth key and pulled the tooth along with the living root from the bone. Crenshaw opened his jaws wider and screamed against the gag. He continued screaming and thrashing for a long time while blood pooled and ran from his mouth.

Dr. Tom took his time removing a piece of linen bandage from the box and soaking it with some of the laudanum from his flask. He carefully packed it into the cavity made by the missing tooth and waited for Crenshaw to quiet down.

After a while, Dr. Tom tapped him on the forehead to get his attention. "I give you my word that I won't hang you. But I also give you my word that if you don't tell me what I need to know, I will carve every protuberance from your face." He pulled out a larger scalpel and held it eye level with the prisoner. "Starting with your nose." He ran the scalpel in a light-handed stroke down one side of Crenshaw's face, and a thin line of scarlet appeared.

The prisoner began to shake his head from side to side, tears seeping from his eyes. Dr. Tom removed the gag.

Crenshaw said, "They went to a settlement to the south called Middle Bayou."

"What for?"

"Some farmer found gold. McGill went to get it."

"Why didn't they take you?"

Crenshaw just looked at him. Dr. Tom smiled tightly. "You were supposed to be watching for us to ride over with the ferryman. Was there a woman traveling with them?"

"No."

Dr. Tom prodded the prisoner with his boot. "You sure about that?"

"No woman, I told you!"

"One last question." Dr. Tom brought the scalpel to Crenshaw's face and lightly etched a matching line down the other side of his face. Crenshaw flinched and the wound trickled blood. "Were you in Frost Town when McGill killed those children?"

Crenshaw nodded once and Dr. Tom looked at Nate and said, "Hang him."

Crenshaw twisted hard at the ropes. The straining dislodged the linen packing in his jaw, opening the wound to bleed again. "You said you wouldn't hang me."

Dr. Tom stood up. "I'm not. He is." He walked to Crenshaw's horse and removed the length of rope from the saddle. He put his hand on Nate's shoulder. "The only sin here is in hesitation."

"Oh, goddamn!" Crenshaw yelled. "My own goddamn rope!"

"Go on, Nate," Dr. Tom said. "This is part of the life you chose. If you falter, just think of those dead children." Dr. Tom handed Nate the rope. "You're not in this alone."

Nate turned his back to the prisoner and, after several tries, managed to pitch the coiled end of the rope over a branch. Fashioning a noose took longer than expected and he soon realized he should have made the noose first. Before he could position the grulla mare under it, he had to listen to ten minutes of bargaining and threatening from the prisoner. He thought of gagging Crenshaw again, his nerves frayed to breaking by the begging, but decided that tolerating the man's last pleading words was the price he paid for killing him. It took both Nate and Dr. Tom to wrestle the noose around Crenshaw's neck and reseat him in his saddle.

Nate thumped the horse and she bolted forward, but Crenshaw dropped awkwardly, desperately squeezing the saddle with both legs. He died badly, kicking and wheezing, scissoring his legs in the air. Nate would have helped him with the drop, but he was afraid of having his jaw broken by flailing feet.

Dr. Tom had his back to Crenshaw, repacking his medical kit, but Nate watched the hanging man dying by measures and wondered how he would tell his wife about it. Describing a hanging, in the general sense, wouldn't be so difficult to convey in a letter. If a man commits himself to service and rides away from his home and family carrying a rope and a gun, he has to expect to use them.

But this hanging couldn't be considered in the general sense, not while he was standing so close to the man's purpling face and bulging eyes, not while he was the one who had fashioned the rope. He understood, watching Crenshaw's purposeful kicks turn to spasmodic jerking, that he had come to a place farther from his family than could be measured in miles. In the few years of his marriage, he had withheld nothing from his wife. But come time for the next letter to her, that would change.

As soon as Crenshaw had quit moving, Nate quietly approached the mare, still wild-eyed and spooked, and settled her only after his own hands had stopped shaking. Then he mounted his horse and turned southward again, leading the mare and following after Dr. Tom, towards Middle Bayou.

Chapter 17

On the evening of Bill's arrival, Lucinda took him to the clearing and pointed to the island.

"There," she said. "The gold is there, somewhere on that island. Bedford says that it's a large cache of coins." She thought for a moment of telling him about the German, his remains snagged somewhere in the water, decomposing slowly, hopefully still submerged. But then she would have to tell him about Mrs. Landry's stolen money in the tapestry bag. He would not be pleased by the risk she had taken.

She watched Bill's face eagerly, looking for signs of approval, waiting for him to slip his arms around her, to palm her hair back from her forehead, to kiss her. But his brow furrowed in concentration, his gaze taking in the thick choke of hanging vines, the floating debris that might or might not be fallen logs. He lit a small cigar and stood looking at the island for a time.

Finally he pursed his lips and said, "I have a man coming in a few days with mules for the gold." He breathed out, exhaling smoke. "My surveying partner." He turned his head and smiled at her: a lifting of the upper lip, revealing straight, unbroken teeth.

His beard, along with the spectacles and the smoke swirling around his chin, worked to mask his features, and she understood the ruse. But it veiled the subtler expressions playing across his face as well, and it seemed for that brief instant that he retreated from her even as she stood next to him.

"Bedford has proposed marriage," she told him. "There is an engagement party in two days."

He smiled again and dropped the cigar, then crushed it out with one boot heel. He cupped one hand behind her neck, pressing her lips to his, and placed the other hand between her legs. "Well, then," he whispered. "I have a gift for the bride."

Bill had been welcomed readily into the Grant home. Soon the settlers began calling on their schoolteacher's handsome brother, the men gathering on the porch to speak with him, attentive to his experience as a surveyor and engineer during the war, the women putting forth their eligible daughters with introductions, to Lucinda's mind, as subtle as cattle being offered at auction. But his hours spent with Bedford at the supper table or out walking aimlessly in the fields—always accompanied by a whiskey bottle—dragged Lucinda into a deep and continual anxiety that Bedford would recognize him. Bill assured her that Bedford had been drunk on his ear in Harrisburg where he'd shown the gold coin, and that he'd keep the old man drunk until he left again. But at times Lucinda could see Bedford regarding Bill with puzzled concentration, a momentary confusion that Jane was quick to observe. Her wariness towards Lucinda—and now towards the newly arrived "brother" occupying her home and constantly feeding liquor to her father—had turned to outright hostility.

Bill had told her, though, that he was tired of waiting, that he had come "to grease the wheels."

The engagement party was held in the Wallers' home, the sitting room filled uncomfortably with invited settlers eager to congratulate Bedford and Lucinda but also there to see with their own eyes the transplanted remnants of old plantation finery. Most of the men, standing or sitting stiffly with their wives, were casting guarded, avaricious glances in May's direction, their overly long hair manfully tamed with what looked to be axle grease. The women, in pieced-together dresses and shawls, struggled to gracefully hold Sephronia's delicate cups and saucers, tiny embossed fruit forks, and slender-stemmed glasses with callused hands that had most recently held buckets, plow handles, or hoes.

Robert McKenzie, the one-armed neighbor that May had wondered about kissing, stood with his back against the green-and-maroon wallpaper of the Wallers' sitting room stealing looks at Jane Grant. He was dressed in a dark suit, his left sleeve pinned neatly to his shoulder, and was indeed handsome, Lucinda thought, in a sickroom, wasting sort of way.

Jane sat at the Wallers' ornate parlor piano, her back to the room, playing something appropriately energetic, although, Lucinda knew, her expression was dour. Lucinda sat next to her, facing the guests, her eyes shifting back and forth like a shuttlecock between the spectacled man newly introduced as Lucinda's brother, Bill Carter, and May. They stood together talking, the top of May's head coming only as high as his collarbone, her upturned face at times rising to meet his as she stood on tiptoe to better hear what he had to say. Bill rested one elbow on the mantelpiece and smiled, his head cocked to one side as May chattered on. *He's watching her,* Lucinda thought, *as a carnival barker would consider a rube, with both amusement and cunning.* He ran the tip of his tongue slowly over his lips and then traced the wetness on his mouth with the pad of his thumb, causing May to blush. Only once did his eyes drift to Lucinda's, where they lingered briefly.

She was about to stand and go to him, but she felt Bedford's hand on her shoulder and she stiffened. He bent down and whispered something unintelligible into her ear, his breath sour from drink. In a few days' time, two whiskey bottles had been emptied.

She reached up, patted Bedford's hand, and then slipped it from her shoulder. She stood and made her way to the opposite side of the room.

"Mr. McKenzie," she said. It shook the one-armed man from his reverie and he blushed, then formally offered his congratulations. She thanked him and asked to refill his glass with punch. She took the glass and promptly handed it to May, instructing her to be polite and return a filled drink to the veteran standing all alone.

Bill leaned forward, looking into his own glass as though he could read the complicated swirls of the liquid inside, and, bringing his mouth closer to Lucinda's ear, said, "What a festive wake."

She smiled uneasily and settled her gaze on the stuffed owl on the mantelpiece, the bird with the staring amber eyes, and thought it an apt totem for the gathering in the room. All of them preserved, stiff and formal, arrayed in their downtrodden best, staring at everyone else with curiosity or with covetousness, but all with eyes seeking to root out the hidden things.

Bill set the glass on the mantelpiece next to the owl and said to her, "Make your excuses and meet me outside."

He nodded brusquely to Sephronia Waller, who was moving through the press of bodies towards him, her weighted, hooped skirt catching and dragging on the legs of the guests around her like a fisherman's net. But he slipped past her without speaking and walked out the door.

In a few minutes Lucinda followed Bill onto the porch and stood watching him smoking a cigar, the smoke curling into the wind away from his slender fingers, and she fought an impulse to cover his other hand resting on the railing with her own.

He stubbed out the live ashes on the railing and pitched the butt into the yard. "The trick will be getting him to point out the exact spot," he said. "I don't want to be digging up the entire island. Especially in the dark."

"It's going to take more time."

"Sister, we don't have more time. Tomorrow night is the night."

"And if he won't tell me?"

"Then he'll have to tell *me*, which will not be as pleasant." He turned, putting his back to the railing, and looked through the parlor windows.

Lucinda saw his expression change and she turned as well to face the house. May stood in the parlor looking outward, her lips parted expectantly, her eyes fixed on Bill.

"I think May should come with us." His smile broadened.

An alarm like the ringing of the fire bell coursed through her and she turned to face the field again. "Why?"

"I think she may be of use."

She drew a breath, and then another. "That was not the plan."

"Plans change."

Carefully, keeping her face turned from the windows, she

walked stiffly down the stairs, her bones as brittle as a bird's, and moved away from the house and into the fields fronting Red Bluff Road. All of the black and perilous spaces that had ever been visited upon her—the abandonment in a madhouse, the years of sinking into uncontrollable fits, the wasteland of half-remembered and loathsome couplings—stretched out before and behind and above her, like a great dark canopy.

Of course there had been other women. There would always be women, bodies used for convenience when she wasn't around. But Bill had chosen her as a partner for her intelligence, for her ability to mold herself capably to any situation, and for her seeming lack of remorse. He had also chosen her because she fed his need to gaze into a person's eyes and see, from a safe remove, Death knocking on the other side. He had promised that he would never leave her, would never desert her.

But now there was a threat she had not anticipated. May was also dissatisfied, restless, and physically without peer. And— Lucinda knew this with a deep, instinctive certainty—May would not hesitate to leave her former teacher behind if it served her own interests.

She felt Bill walking up behind her, and heard the striking of a match to light another cigar. She told him, "She can't come with us."

"Can't? Lucy, don't be tiresome. By tomorrow morning, if the old man hasn't told you exactly where the gold is, you are to leave with the girl for Galveston. Once I tell him you have his daughter, he'll be willing."

"What makes you think she'll come with me?"

"Because you're going to tell her I want her to."

"And Jane?"

"Who?"

"The other sister."

"I'm sure she'll be useful as well."

She turned to look at him. "She'll fight you if her father's threatened."

He ran a finger down the side of her face. "I certainly hope so."

She followed him back to the house and into the parlor, where Jane was at the piano playing "Oh, What a Comfort Is My Home." Lucinda went to stand next to Bedford, a strained smile on her face, accepting congratulations from the neighbors as they began spilling from the house and onto the road for home. When May left, she threw a dazzling smile at Bill, and Lucinda felt panic filling her chest.

After dark, she met Bedford at the greenhouse and led him inside. She turned her face up to his to be kissed, closing her eyes tightly to his avid, straining expression, breathing shallowly against his exhalations of whiskey vapors.

After a time, she took his hand and, after kissing each finger, placed it over one breast, whispering into his ear, "Bedford, please confide in me. Tell me where the coins are hidden. If something were to happen to you, how can I take care of your family?"

He buried his face in her neck. "I can't," he mumbled.

She pulled away. "I've told you everything about myself. My life is an open book to you. But if you would hide this discovery from me...How can I trust you with the day-to-day, if you won't reveal to me the more important things?"

He hung his head, looking wretched and guilt-stricken. "Lucinda, I wish to tell you...I want to tell you that..."

He stammered to silence and she kissed him again until he forgot his misery and resumed running his hands over the folds of her skirt. But to every question about the coins, he remained unresponsive. Another man driven to such frenzy would simply have forced her legs open and taken her. But he stopped his groping as soon as she pushed him away.

She leaned against a wall, closing her eyes, and she realized that Bedford was not going to give her the information she sought.

He sank down to a sitting position, his head in his hands. "You don't understand," he said.

She straightened her hair and clothing and brushed at her skirt. "You must trust me if I am to marry you. I'll not ask you again."

"I can't tell you," he said and looked at her pleadingly, but she walked from the greenhouse without saying good-bye and returned to her room at the Wallers'.

In the morning, she rose early and crept her way quietly to the barn, where she hid her tapestry bag packed with all of her things, as well as some food and water, in the buggy.

When everyone was seated at the table for breakfast, she asked Euphrastus if she could use the buggy for the day, knowing that he wouldn't refuse her in front of his wife.

"I need it to go to Morgan's Point," she explained. She looked to Sephronia and smiled. "I'm meeting the ferry bringing my wedding dress from Houston."

Lavada laughed, delighted. "I can come with you, Miss Carter."

Lucinda ducked her head as though embarrassed. "Lavada, dear, I would be happy to take you. But Bedford will be accompanying me."

Euphrastus looked at her suspiciously. "I didn't know the ferry made passage on a Sunday."

"Commerce never sleeps, Mr. Waller." Lucinda smiled at each of them in turn, relieved she would never see any of them again. "I can harness the horse myself."

She drove the buggy to the Grants' house and waited for Bill to come out into the yard. When he looked at her questioningly, she shook her head.

"The old man's still sleeping off his drink," he said, frowning.

She nodded but kept her eyes averted, afraid of seeing the displeasure on his face. He rested one arm casually across the rear wheel and leaned under the canopy. "I can't wait any longer, Lucy. May's inside. Go talk to her."

After a moment's pause, she stepped from the buggy and walked across the yard and into the house. She called out May's name, and Jane appeared in the hallway, her eyes swollen from crying. But seeing Lucinda, she turned angrily away and walked back into the kitchen. May appeared at the top of the stairs and Lucinda motioned her down. She took May by the hand and led her outside so the girl could see Bill waiting by the buggy.

She took hold of both of May's hands, gave them a reassuring squeeze. "You do know that I care for you like a sister, don't you?" The girl nodded, her eyes slipping past Lucinda's shoulders to where Bill stood. "And Bill's happiness means everything to me." Lucinda's back was to Bill but she could imagine the familiar expression of seduction on his face in that moment as he stared at May: the slow burn of his eyes, the contagion of a creeping smile. "May, look at me. Do you love my brother?"

May returned her gaze and said, "Yes."

"Would you then travel somewhere to marry him, if he asked you to?"

May peered over Lucinda's shoulder once more, her eyes exultant, her breath coming faster. "Yes."

Lucinda ducked her chin, a sorrowful anger narrowing her mouth to an ugly gash, and she reflexively tightened her hold on May's hands.

At that moment Jane came to stand in the doorway, enraged now beyond tears. She stared hatefully at Lucinda, her arms crossed, her mouth moving as though practicing for an argument.

Ignoring her, Lucinda composed herself and said, "You know that Jane and your father would not allow it if they knew. They think you're still a child. But I know better. Bill wants this to happen and can think of little else. But if you want to be with him, you must leave with me today."

"Where will we go?"

"I'll tell you everything once we've left. If Jane asks, we're simply going for a drive."

"Is Bill coming with us?"

"He'll follow after us tomorrow." Lucinda let go of May's hands. She reached out and stroked a loose curl from the girl's forehead. "Hurry now, while your father sleeps. You'll be back to your family soon, and all will be forgiven once you're married."

May looked at her, incredulous. "Why would I ever return to this place?" She turned and ran into the house, brushing wordlessly past Jane, to gather her things, and Lucinda climbed into the buggy to wait.

Bill leaned in and circled his fingers around her ankle with one hand, stroked the calf of her leg with the other. He told her where to meet him in Galveston once they had made the ferry passage from Morgan's Point. They would stay for only a day in

Galveston and then go on to New Orleans. The grip on her ankle tightened painfully and he said, "I'm counting on you, Lucy."

When May climbed into the buggy next to Lucinda, she was carrying a small bag, which she quickly threw to the floor. She turned to Bill, offering her mouth to be kissed, but Lucinda struck at the horse with the whip, and the buggy lurched up the road.

Within half a mile, they saw a man riding towards them leading two mules. He nodded in their direction as he passed and Lucinda recognized the hostile, close-set eyes of Jacob Purdy, Bill's "surveying" partner. Where Innis Crenshaw was, she didn't know, and didn't want to know. After a few miles of traveling southeast, towards Morgan's Point, she made several switchbacks along the paths running through the sprawling Allen cattle ranch, eventually heading the buggy in a northwesterly direction, towards Houston.

Lucinda had expected May to talk on and on about her excitement over her marriage to Bill, and she'd prepared herself for hours of girlish silliness. But surprisingly, May was mostly silent, her mouth curling in secretive smiles.

When Lucinda stopped the buggy briefly to allow May to get out and stretch her legs, she was tempted to whip the horse and drive off, leaving the girl to make her own way back to Middle Bayou. But Lucinda had formulated a different plan for May as she lay sleepless in her bed during the early-morning hours.

She shared some water and biscuits taken from the Wallers' home and carefully began to lay out the journey they were about to make.

"We're going to Houston," Lucinda explained. "There you'll board a train, and then in Hearne you'll take the stagecoach to Fort Worth."

"By myself?" May asked, her eyes widening in fright. "But I've never traveled alone. I've always been with Father. I wouldn't know what to do—"

Lucinda reached out and squeezed one of May's hands to silence her. "Listen and I'll tell you all you need to know. I traveled by myself when I was younger than you and it was the greatest adventure of my life."

May was quiet, but her mouth was downturned, her brows knit together. Her eyes worriedly scanned the prairie, and Lucinda knew that her shortsightedness rendered the surrounding grasslands watery and indistinct, making her all the more vulnerable in unfamiliar territory.

"Have you ever been on a train?" Lucinda asked, tamping down her sympathy for the girl, tearing her eyes away from the frightened face at her shoulder. May shook her head and Lucinda smiled. "It's like flying. The passengers who travel on the rails are the most refined of people. And the view from the windows, May. It's as if you're watching a never-ending tapestry unspooling before you: fields and towns and people working on their farms, tiny from a distance, like dolls. All viewed from your comfortable coach."

She glanced over and saw that the girl's expression had changed from fear to rapt attention. Lucinda then described to her the wonders of rail travel, the excitement of arriving by coach to a city filled with theaters, shops, grand hotels, and beautifully dressed men and women. She was indiscriminate about weaving in descriptions of buildings or events she had seen in various cities and towns. May could not know that the picture Lucinda was painting was more than a little untrue.

"You'll have a first-class ticket with money for food and drink, which you can buy on the train from the most cunning little tea cart. In Hearne, you'll board the stagecoach to Dallas and then go on to Fort Worth."

May's face fell again at the mention of the stagecoach.

Lucinda exhaled sharply, her face disapproving. "Frankly, May, I'm disappointed in you. Bill and I will be only a day behind." She paused for a moment, as though hesitant to reveal more. "He wanted to surprise you by arriving with a trousseau, and he needs my help to do that. He'll be very pained. He thought you were an adventurous girl."

May linked her arm with Lucinda's. "I'll go," she said, uncertainty in her voice. "I'll go."

They arrived in Houston at midday and Lucinda purchased a first-class ticket at the station. She also bought a suitable traveling dress for May and dinner at a hotel, where she wrote down meticulous directions for the exchange to the coach in Hearne. She gave the girl money from the dwindling supply of stolen coins in the tapestry bag.

When the train was ready to depart, Lucinda embraced her former student and helped her as she stepped onto the railcar.

May turned and said, "Soon we'll be sisters."

Lucinda's smile faltered. She looked at the girl in the ill-fitting, hastily bought dress and for an instant fought a powerful desire to pull the girl from the train, tell her that a mistake had been made, that they were leaving instead for Galveston. But she remembered the blushing, triumphant smiles on May's face that morning. She steeled herself by replaying the memories of May and Bill standing together, the girl's eager eyes filled with adoration, Bill's gaze flooded with simple lust. She willed herself away from tender thoughts by imagining herself supplanted by May, deserted and left behind. May was resourceful, young, and beautiful. She would survive.

Lucinda smiled encouragingly. "You must now call me by my Christian name."

May peered nervously from the window, calling out, "Good-bye, Lucinda, good-bye," and they waved at each other until the train had pulled away.

Lucinda stood on the platform for a while, pondering how best to get rid of the horse and buggy, finally deciding to sell them at the stable. The train to Galveston would not leave until the next morning, and she could use the money. None of it would matter, though, once Bill met up with her carrying bags of gold coins. He would be disappointed, and perhaps angry, that May had slipped away from him; however, she knew he'd get over it, and soon.

She took a room in a hotel for the night and dosed herself heavily with laudanum. But it was hours before she could sleep, her eyes open and filled with images of May stepping off the coach in Fort Worth in a few days' time, being stared at and scrutinized by men who would be astonished that such a beauty, barely more than a child, would be making her way through town unescorted; seeking out the boardinghouse that Lucinda had assured her was respectable; presenting herself finally to the boardinghouse mistress, a woman by the name of Mrs. Landry.

Lucinda's last troubled thought before the laudanum did its work was of May handing Mrs. Landry a sealed letter of introduction that read, simply, *Call us even. Lucinda.*

Chapter 18

Whatever was in the open wagon sitting at a distance on a path off the main road had brought a small group of men and women crowding around it. It was still early morning but the sky was a clear, unhindered blue, and the clustered figures were lit by the strengthening daylight.

Nate perched on the lower branches of a tree, the only place that offered him an elevated view across the expanse of dried prairie fields, and watched them through the field glasses. Dr. Tom had not wanted to ride into Middle Bayou so exposed, risking being shot by McGill or his men from some homesteader's attic.

Dr. Tom stood below, peering up at him through the branches. "Well?" he asked.

"There're some settlers gathered around a wagon looking at something."

"A dead something or a live something?"

Nate looked for a few moments longer, taking note of the large turkey buzzards perched on the roof of the nearest house. "Can't tell for sure, but I would guess dead."

Dr. Tom motioned him down and stood for a while with his back braced against the tree, his breathing labored. When Nate had lowered himself to the ground, Dr. Tom told him, "I believe I'm going to let you take the lead on this one. I'm feeling a bit hollow."

Nate took in the pallor of the ranger's face, the pouches beneath his eyes swollen like bruises from a fight, and knew it was more than just the laudanum.

Soon after Crenshaw's torture and hanging, Dr. Tom had slipped off his horse onto his knees, violently heaving the contents of his stomach onto the ground. He had then climbed back on his horse, wiped the back of his sleeve across his mouth, and said, "George used to marvel that I could doctor with a cool head and a steady hand, even with blood up to my ankles, and yet still get weak-kneed after hanging a man who deserved it. But I always sensed that when you willfully kill a man, even for righteousness' sake, and start feeling all right about that, it's time to find different work."

Nate lifted his chin in the direction of the wagon. "Why don't you stay here and let me go talk to them."

In response, Dr. Tom mounted his horse and told Nate, "It's hard to ask questions and keep a vigil at the same time." Leading Crenshaw's mare, he followed after Nate at a gallop across the fields towards the settlers, who scattered briefly at their approach. Some of the men had rifles, which they raised defensively. Nate thought that as a whole they looked astounded, and a few near terrified.

Nate stopped at a distance and shouted, "Texas law here. Don't go poppin' off." He announced their names and purpose and waved at the men to lower their guns.

They rode closer and saw two men, one young, one older, lying faceup in the wagon, both dead, both bloodied and covered by a quilt pulled up to their necks. Two women, a mother and daughter, Nate guessed, were wailing in grief, grappling to hold on to the young man's hand that had slipped over the edge of the wagon.

A settler with the girth of an accountant stood behind the crying women and stared into the wagon, his fine suit covered with clay mud that had dried to a chalky film.

Nate legged himself off the horse and motioned people to clear a path. He climbed into the wagon and hunkered down, pulling the quilt off the dead men. His actions brought a collective outcry from the gathering and a frantic, hysterical pitch to the women's keening. The younger victim had been shot through the chest; pieces of rib showed from the wound made by a shotgun blast. The older one had been shot in the gut with a pistol, and his face was nowhere near peaceful. Nate turned back to the crowd. "What happened here?"

"My son was murdered." The large man crossed his arms protectively in front of his own chest.

Nate motioned for his partner to climb up into the wagon, and, after briefly waggling the stiffened joints of the men's hands, Dr. Tom said under his breath, "They've not been dead but a few hours."

Nate asked the grieving man, "What's your name, sir?"

"Euphrastus Waller." Pointing to the corpse of the young man, he said, "That's my son, Elam." Spittle hung in threads from his lips, and the rawness of it made Nate want to turn his head away. "He was paralyzed, confined to a chair," Euphrastus added, almost as an afterthought.

Nate turned a questioning eye to Dr. Tom and pointed to the mud evenly caking the bottoms of Elam's shoes.

"Who's this?" Nate asked, indicating the other dead man in the wagon.

"His name is Bedford Grant." A pale, straw-haired young woman stepped forward. "I'm Jane Grant, his daughter." She had been crying, her eyes swollen and red-rimmed, but to Nate she seemed very much in control of her emotions and looked more angry than stricken.

Dr. Tom nodded at the wound in Bedford Grant's stomach and said, "Calling card from McGill."

Euphrastus Waller's legs gave out, and his wife and daughter rushed to his side. They struggled to keep him from falling, but the women sank along with him onto the road, their full skirts ballooning out and settling heavily into the dirt. Some of the men moved in to help him to his feet again.

Another settler, his left arm missing from the elbow, moved closer to the wagon and came to stand next to the Grant woman. He hovered by her side, and for a moment, Nate thought he was going to put his one good arm around her.

"Who're you?" Dr. Tom asked.

"I'm Robert McKenzie. I own a farm just up the road. A man came to Middle Bayou a short while back. Said his name was Bill Carter. He claimed to be the schoolteacher's brother."

Jane made an ugly sound through her nose. "I don't believe it for a minute."

Nate stepped down from the wagon. "Why's that?"

Her lips twitched in outrage. "Miss Carter, if that was her

name, was an adventuress posing as a teacher. She and Bill Carter were after something they thought my father had."

McKenzie added, "Yesterday, another man showed up on horseback leading a mule. He told Miss Grant that he was Bill Carter's surveying partner. The Grants took these people into their home. We entrusted our children to that woman..."

"Nate, we need to move this along." Dr. Tom climbed from the wagon, impatiently muttering, "Less hide and more meat."

Nate asked the woman, "What were they after?"

She buried her chin in her neck. "I wouldn't like to say with everyone listening."

Dr. Tom abruptly motioned the settlers to move away from the wagon, directing them to see after the Waller women, who had elevated their agonized crying to a more frenzied level.

Jane waited for Dr. Tom to join them and said in a quiet voice, "My father uncovered a few gold coins on an island he owned in the bayou. Bill Carter believed there was more gold and tried to make my father say where it was buried..." She paused, staring at the bodies in the wagon.

Dr. Tom placed a hand on her arm. "What was the schoolteacher's first name?"

"Lucinda."

Dr. Tom nodded to Nate and asked, "Where are they now?"

"Miss Carter took my sister, May, yesterday morning in the Wallers' buggy to Morgan's Point for the day. They never came back."

"And Bill Carter?" Nate asked.

"Gone. I don't know where." She ran one sleeve across her eyes and nose. "They must have taken my father from the house to the river sometime before this morning. That's where his body was found. I slept at the Wallers' last night. I couldn't abide being in that house alone with those men. Mr. Waller was going to confront them today for my father's sake, but it was too late."

Her anger was turning again to tears, and Nate gave her a moment to collect herself.

Dr. Tom asked, "Did they get your father's gold?"

She raised her chin and smiled tightly. "There was no gold."

Nate thought he had misheard. "What'd you say?"

"There was never any gold." She took a few breaths, ran her tongue over cracked lips. "Last spring, my father found a few old coins while clearing the island for planting. There are legends here about Lafitte's treasure being buried in Middle Bayou. My father believed that he had discovered a part of that treasure. He spent months digging but found nothing more. Once he realized the island was empty, he went to Harrisburg and put about the story that there was gold waiting to be found, hoping to sell the land to someone fool enough to believe it. But he talked to the wrong people. I was the only person who knew the truth."

"Why was *he* shot?" Dr. Tom asked, jerking a thumb at Elam Waller.

"I don't know." Jane brushed her fingers nervously across her face. "There was no reason for him to be shot. He was in the parlor in his chair when I came to Mr. Waller with my fears, but then…he's always in his chair. He can do nothing else."

Nate watched her nervous hands and in that instant a thought came into his head that she was lying about Elam Waller's helpless state. The young man's shoes were muddied as though he had walked along a soggy riverbank. He asked her, "Who found the bodies? Did anyone see the murder?"

"I did."

Nate turned towards the voice and saw a black man in work denim approaching them. He was short and broadly muscled, with a meandering scar, like earthworm castings, across one side of his face.

He stood in front of Nate with what looked to be part of a plow harness across his shoulders. "I'm Tobias Kennedy. I live here." He nodded at the bodies in the wagon and said, "I know how they come to be killed. I saw it. I helped bring the wagon to gather the bodies."

Dr. Tom asked, "You want to tell us what happened?"

Tobias looked at Jane and then motioned for Nate and Dr. Tom to follow him some distance away. "There's another body," he said.

"Another body?" Nate asked, reflexively scanning the surrounding fields. He nervously chewed at the skin on his lips, confounded that one sparse settlement could support so many tragedies in one morning.

"Bill Carter?" Dr. Tom asked.

"No, he's long gone. It's Carter's man. He's still lyin' in the river. What's left of him. The men here just didn't want to say so in front of the women."

"Who killed him?" Nate asked, wondering just how high the body count was going to get.

Tobias pointed to Elam Waller and said, "He did."

Nate shook his head. "Didn't Euphrastus Waller just say that Elam was a useless cripple?"

Tobias dropped the plow harness to the ground. "Listen here. I served with the Thirty-Third Colored Infantry out of South Carolina. You know what I was? A sharpshooter. I got the best eyes in this whole part of the world." He pointed to the settlers still gathered, their collective gaze on the three of them. "They told me I had to be lying. But I told the truth. I know what I saw."

Nate nodded and said, "Show us."

He and Dr. Tom mounted their horses and followed after Tobias, who walked the path towards the bayou. As they rode Tobias talked, turning his chin from side to side, throwing his words over his shoulder.

"I spent last night at the river. I'd put down catfish lines. This time of year, no mosquitoes, the air's cool, I often sleep out. Pull in my lines before dawn after the catfish bite. A few hours before light, I hear men coming up to the clearing. I'd already doused my lantern, but there was a moon and I hid back in the brush. There's no good reason for people to be up makin' so much noise at that hour, especially angry white men in the jug.

"I hear old man Grant's voice and two other voices I don't know. But they're arguin' all up the path. They're carryin' lanterns, and when they get into the clearing, I see Mr. Grant and Carter with his man as surely as I see you."

After that, Tobias continued his walk in silence until they reached the clearing. Nate and Dr. Tom dismounted and stood at the edge of the riverbank, looking at the blood and footprints left in the mud, while Tobias walked up and down the bank, peering into the water.

"There he is." Tobias pointed at something floating in the river, caught in some reeds. "Gator got him. Dragged him off the bank."

He waded into the river to midstream carrying a long branch. The water came up to his chest but he moved easily, and after a few tries, he snagged the floating object and pulled it behind him out of the water.

It was a man, or the top half of a man; the legs were gone. Dr. Tom kicked the truncated bundle over and said, "Jacob Purdy. McGill's man."

Tobias watched Nate stone-faced as he stumbled away, gulping air and swallowing the bile rising in his throat. Nate had seen dead men before, mauled and mangled, but they had been mostly whole. Behind him he heard Dr. Tom ask, "You want to tell us now what happened?"

"Grant was drunk," Tobias said. "So drunk he couldn't hardly stand. Carter kept at him to say where on that island over yonder his gold was buried." He pointed across the water to a promontory of land with steep clay edges and a dense stand of elm. "Kept goin' on about the gold. Finally, Carter quit yellin' and pulled a pistol. Threatened to shoot the old man if he didn't talk."

Tobias raised his chin to a bloody patch on the bank. "Grant fell on the ground pleadin' like a man who knows his time is near, and I hear a voice say, 'Hold there.' I see a man walk into the lantern light and it's Elam Waller, so help me God, carryin' a pistol in one hand. Elam walks right up to them, within a few feet. Carter's taken by surprise, 'cause he's only ever seen the boy in a wheeled chair. Carter's man pulls up his shotgun and, *blam*, both guns go off. Young Elam goes down hard and the other man staggers off into the water holdin' his throat.

"It spooks Carter but he says to Grant, 'We have your daughter. You don't tell me where that treasure is, I'm goin' to kill her myself."

"Grant is crawlin' on his hands and knees cryin'. Says there is no treasure. Never was one. That's when Carter leans over the old man and shoots him in the belly. He stands for a while just watchin' Grant die. Then he rides away. I stayed hidden for a good long while before I had the legs to go get help. I've seen some bad things, but I never saw anyone so keen on watchin' someone die before."

Tobias pulled a derringer out of one pocket and handed it to Dr. Tom. "Mr. Elam's gun. I know that boy was a cripple. I never saw him so much as move a finger, but he reared up out of those weeds and died to help Mr. Grant."

Dr. Tom nodded his thanks to Tobias and pocketed the derringer. He stood at the river's edge, the water reflective but cloudy like mercury glass. Nate joined him and they watched the oily, humpbacked shapes of darkly speckled fish feeding just below the surface and the armored leathery shapes with eyes swimming at the far side of the river.

"Goddamn it," Dr. Tom said. He pulled the familiar flask from his back pocket, an inch or so of liquid staining the bottom, and drained it dry. He pitched the flask into the water, watched it as it was caught up in a circular current. "That's us. Travelin' in circles, like water down a drain. I don't even think I remember how to ride in a straight line. I'm about played out, Nate. And it's not just the pleurisy." He gingerly pressed one hand along his ribs. "There's somethin' else growin' in here..." He looked at Nate. "I sound like an old woman."

"You're gonna need more medicine." Nate hoped that someone

in the settlement would have more "banishment in a bottle," as Dr. Tom called it. Unless his partner stayed behind, now was not the time for him to try to quit the opiates.

Dr. Tom put a hand on Nate's arm. "I need you to stay resolved if you're going to help me end this. Resolved as in no hesitations and no second-guessing, which means that you'd shoot through me to get to McGill if that was the only shot you could take." His fingers loosened their grip on Nate's arm and he ran them across the top of his head. "My thoughts aren't as they should be…"

Nate, keeping his eyes away from Purdy's corpse, said, "The Grant woman talked about Morgan's Point. That's Galveston, I'm thinking. You gonna make it?"

"I'm not going anywhere on a boat. The only thing I'm afraid of is deep water. We can ride like hell and take the bridge train from Houston. Load the horses on a cattle car. We need to find him before he leaves the island and heads for somewhere else."

"Tom, I'll say this one more time. We need someone else on this. Local sheriff, maybe."

"And I'll say this one more time. George and me started this and I plan to be the one who kills that evil son of a bitch before he leaves Texas. It's just McGill now."

"You think he's not gonna hire more men?"

"Not without money, he's not. I think he was counting on that gold. He hasn't pulled a job in a while, which means his getting-around funds are low."

"You know your way around Galveston?"

Dr. Tom ducked his head briefly. "I know my way some. We leave now, we'll make it."

Nate looked over at Tobias and asked, "Anything else you need to tell us?"

Tobias's hand searched the scar on his face in a thoughtful way. "Miss Carter? She's somethin' more than a schoolteacher, if you take my meaning. She talked to me about goin' to New Orleans."

Nate cast a cautious eye at Dr. Tom and he nodded.

"She's a smart woman; had all these people eating from her hand," Tobias said. "But she's not gonna live long with that killer."

Nate thanked Tobias and mounted his horse, then waited patiently for Dr. Tom to clear a coughing fit and mount his own. They headed off for Houston—rushing past the astonished settlers still gathered uncertainly around the wagon—and when they arrived, they sold the saddle off the grulla mare and then the horse itself to a cotton trader with more money than sense. Then they bought the tickets for the train to the island.

Chapter 19

$\mathcal{U}$sing the last of Mrs. Landry's money, Lucinda took a room at the Republic Hotel in Galveston. She had arrived that afternoon off the train from Houston and gone to wait at the hotel, as she had been told to, for Bill to arrive. It was extravagant, but what did it matter? There would be gold enough to see them in comfort for a long time, perhaps years.

She bathed and washed her hair, leaving it down to dry in the warmth from a small corner stove, and through the window, she watched the traffic up and down the Strand. A block away she could see the burned-out shell of the old Tremont Hotel, still standing in partial ruins five years after the fire that destroyed a good part of the town.

She opened the windows, letting in the sharp damp air and the sounds from the wide, evenly spaced streets below. Earlier, she had stepped from the train and walked westward a few blocks to the pier, where she stood looking out at the bay. The island behind her and to the south was flat, devoid of even small hillocks, so that when she confronted the water, the horizon appeared alarmingly elevated and it seemed impossible that the ocean would not rush to overtake the land and everything perched on it.

She watched the ships crowding the harbor: steamers; sailing vessels of every color, size, and dimension; and pilot boats ferrying passengers and crates to and from larger ships anchored far from shore. Stretching her arms along the hand railing, extending them fully to either side, she constructed in her mind a line from her right arm taking her towards New Orleans and from her left towards Mexico. After a while she closed her eyes, feeling the bracing wind at her back and the lowering sun on her face, and imagined herself a kind of polestar drawing Bill to her. "Azimuth," she murmured, refining her thoughts. *I am the bearing of the polestar from which the surveyor takes his plotting.*

Then she had walked back through town, stepping quickly alongside the men and women, native-born and immigrant, who spilled over the sidewalks into the streets. She watched the progress of two Celestials burdened with massive bundles, the men's braids swinging in tandem, until they disappeared into an alley. Entering the hotel lobby, she heard half a dozen languages, and she made mental notes of which new style of hat and waist cincher she would have created once they had settled in New Orleans.

A clock tower down the street gave the time as four o'clock and she had begun to doze when she heard a key in the lock. The door opened, and there was the customary pause that Bill practiced before walking into any room. He passed through the doorway and looked at her before turning his head, searching, and finding no one else there. *He knows,* she thought, *without even asking, that May is gone.*

He took off his coat, draped it onto the bed, and sat in a nearby chair, observing her. Crossing his legs, he then stared out the window, his chin resting on the back of one hand, his fingers curled. She looked closely for whitening or tension around the knuckles, but found none.

Through the window came the sound of a boy calling the newspaper headlines from the afternoon paper. "Edward Rulloff, Bavarian Butcher, hanged in New York! Ulysses S. Grant says Georgia to rejoin Union!"

Bill stood up, retrieved his coat from the bed, and abruptly walked from the room. No words had been exchanged. Lucinda had instinctively waited for him to speak before speaking herself, and when he'd sighed once, exhaling softly over his folded hand, she thought he would tell her his own news. He had brought no bags into the room, and there was no indication that he had anything other than the dirt-streaked clothes on his back. His boots were thickly coated with old mud and he left bits of it on the floor, like a trail.

Within a quarter hour he returned and beckoned for her to come from the room. After pinning up her still-damp hair and collecting her shawl, she followed him down to the lobby and out onto the street, where a small carriage, brought from the livery, stood. He climbed into the driving seat and took up the reins and waited for her to climb in after. She hesitated briefly, allowing herself to think only that he was taking her to the place where the gold had been stored.

He chucked at the reins and they followed the sea road south, the Gulf to their left, the sun blinding them through a wilting sky to their right. Lucinda had brought no hat or bonnet and placed her hand as a shield over her forehead and cheek, keeping her face turned expectantly towards Bill, waiting for him to break his silence.

After traveling a few miles, he finally spoke to her. "Do you know what a boondoggle is, Lucy?" He turned his head to look at her, and Lucy blinked and nodded hesitantly.

"Yes," he said, nodding along with her. "A waste of time and money. Middle Bayou was a complete and utter boondoggle." He drew out the last word, his lips and tongue hard against the consonants. "Bedford Grant fabricated the story of pirate's treasure to puff up the value of land that he wanted to unload."

Shocked, she remained motionless, but the hair on her arms rose as with a chill.

"I have lost a man and substantial resources, leaving me with what I'm wearing on my back, and my horse." He'd taken off his spectacles so that she could see closer into his eyes. "I've also lost a significant asset in the person of May Grant. Or rather, I should say, you have lost May for me. You are lowered in my esteem, Lucy, for not following my instructions." His tone was reasonable: a father reviewing the fractious behavior of a child. But for the first time in her relationship with Bill, she felt afraid, and she fought the temptation to look away, to scan the road for any fellow travelers.

He removed from his pocket a cigar and expertly lit it against the wind. "Have you got any money left?" he asked, and she shook her head. "What about your gun?"

Before she left the hotel room, some formless, self-preserving thought had niggled at her to take the small purse in which she kept the Remington. But she had brushed it aside in her eagerness and expectation, and, when he cut his eyes to her, she met his gaze and again shook her head. Now she did look to the beach for some person to offer assistance, but he clamped one hand over her arm, as though reading her thoughts, and for the first time, it entered her mind that he might kill her.

He dropped the reins to his lap, letting the horse go at his own pace, the hoofbeats sounding a paper-like rattle on the shell-filled road, and lit another match. Handing it to her, he instructed her to keep the flame alive with her cupped hands. Within a moment the wind had blown it out, and he lit and handed her another, instructing her to try it again. The flame stayed visible for only an instant and then went out, leaving a spiral of smoke.

"You see, Lucy," he said, "no matter how hard we try, the outcome is always the same."

After that he was quiet. She dropped her hand from her face and stared dully at the banks of clouds obscuring the sun, turning the white road a liverish pink.

When she was a child, confined inside the walls of the asylum, she dreaded most of all this time of day: the disappearing of the sun and the casting of long shadows. It was a time of claustrophobic despair. Of constrained ice-water baths when she was uncommunicative and cod-liver purges when she lagged in sufficient animal energies; a time of enforced eating, supervised sleeping, and communal, vigilant prayer for her return to normalcy.

In her third year of confinement she discovered the comforting axioms of geometry, the science wherein the properties of magnitude are considered: a line having length, but not breadth; a surface having length and breadth, but not thickness, and so on.

Fixed, constant, and immutable. She would recite them aloud as a way of distancing her mind from her body, which would otherwise be rebellious during her fits and enraged during her treatments.

She recited to herself, as they drove along a parallel path to the sea, the rule of the magnitude of angles, which depended on the *inclination* the lines that formed it had to each other, and not on the *length* of those lines. There had been magnitude between the path of her life and Bill's, even if the length of that path would be short.

When he stopped the carriage, she calculated that they were close to six miles from town. He handed her down and walked with her away from the road and onto the beach. He let go of her and stood pondering the ocean and the sky, both equally dark now.

She stared at his features for as long as she could, until he told her to turn around.

"Watch the stars," he directed, pointing upwards.

She identified the constellation of Perseus and the variable star of Medusa's head. It made her think of the glass negatives of the soldiers in the Wallers' greenhouse and of the white spaces where their eyes would have been.

Then Bill said, "Lucy, look at me."

Chapter 20

The train from Houston to Galveston was to leave at four o'clock. Nate and Dr. Tom arrived shortly after noon, in time to store in the post office's safe room all of their weapons, with the exception of a firearm each, Nate's Winchester and the Whitworth rifle. From the post office, Nate cabled Austin to inform the state police captain there that they would be "off the map" for a week or so but that he would give a full report once they had returned to Houston.

The postman also handed Nate a letter from his wife. The last one he had received from her was during the time of Dr. Tom's convalescence from pneumonia. Nate placed the letter carefully in the pocket of his coat, planning to read it on the train, and followed Dr. Tom to the local apothecary. As he sat on the stoop, though, he decided he couldn't wait any longer and opened the envelope raggedly with one thumb, then pulled out the thin sheet of paper.

Dear Nathaniel,

All is well now, but Mattie was laid low for three days with a griping belly. She is recovered and is back to chasing the chickens. The livestock is

*hearty, the cow giving eight pounds of butter a week. The weather is mild
but with heavy rains.*

*I must tell you I've had troubling dreams these past few nights. Because
of this, I would ask that you take especial care in making any river cross-
ings or in being close to rough water. You have respected my glimmerings in
the past. Please do so now, even if these dark thoughts come from excessive
rains and from too much time spent within four walls.*

*I abide in the belief of your essential goodness, and know with certainty
that you will always make the right and dutiful choice.*

Yours always, Beth

He worried at his lip with a thumb and forefinger over the last
but put the letter quickly away when he felt Dr. Tom's shadow
fall over him. His partner's face was droop-lidded and relaxed; the
man had wasted no time in dosing himself with the newly ac-
quired laudanum.

The most difficulty they had was loading the big bay onto the
cattle car. Deerling's horse, already brutish from the noise and
commotion, balked and almost pulled the stock loader's arm from
its socket. Nate tried patience and bribery in equal measures, but
after ten minutes of the horse's rearing and plunging, they had
moved only the front half of the horse into the narrow entrance
of the darkened car. The lead rope was passed over a pulley, but
the stallion continued heaving backwards, threatening to yank it
from the mounting.

Nate finally moved to the top of the ramp, stood to the bay's
left, and rubbed his hide gently, talking to him in a soothing way.
He motioned for Dr. Tom to do likewise on the right side and
told him to grab hold of the handrail fixed to the side of the

opening. Nate reached across the meaty part of the horse's rump with his right arm and gestured for Dr. Tom to lock forearms with his left and hold fast. Nate counted to three and with their combined momentum forward, they shoved the skittering animal into the stock car.

Dr. Tom clapped the dust from his hands, saying, "You never cease to surprise me, Nate. That's another one I've not seen."

They took their seats in the passenger car with Nate facing in the direction the train was moving.

Dr. Tom smiled and asked, "This your first time on a train?"

Nate nodded and, taking in Dr. Tom's relaxed manner, leaned back onto the bench. Promptly on the hour the train's whistle screamed, and the car bumped violently forward. To Nate's embarrassment, he yelped, slapping the seats with the palms of his hands to right himself, which brought smiles from some of the other passengers.

Dr. Tom nodded and pointed for Nate to look out at the surrounding terrain, which had begun to slip past the window at an alarming rate. Once the train had gained momentum, the lurching stopped, and within minutes Nate began to feel heavy-limbed. He hadn't been subsumed by such a lull since he'd been a child rocked in a chair.

"There's no feeling like it," Dr. Tom said and took a newspaper, abandoned by an earlier passenger, into his lap.

Nate read the letter from his wife again and pulled a stub of pencil from his pocket to write his response on the back. He finally had something he could convey to his wife that hadn't to do with men dying, but the rocking of the train sprawled his writing and caused the pencil lead to break through the paper.

He pocketed the envelope, stretched his legs carefully around Dr. Tom's, and finally stood up in the aisle, knuckling his fist into his bad hip, trying to release the cramp that had threatened to take hold while he was sitting down in the unfamiliar position: knees together and pointing forward. After a short while, though, he felt conspicuous. His standing caused all the other passengers to look at him expectantly, as though he were about to make a pronouncement. He realized that with his coat off, his badge was visible. A man sitting opposite glanced at it briefly and then gave him a hostile gaze.

Nate eased himself back onto the seat and looked at Dr. Tom. He held the newspaper aloft, but he was staring out of the window, his lips moving.

"What'd you say?" Nate asked.

Dr. Tom looked at him, crumpling the newspaper onto his lap. "Charles Dickens is gone. He died this summer past."

It took Nate a minute to recall who Dickens was, and then he remembered their night outside Fort Davis, when Deerling was still alive, and Dr. Tom reading some bit of story, barely legible on the scrap of paper he always kept in his pack. He thought of Deerling sitting by Dr. Tom's bedside, reading from that same paper: *I travel for the great house of Human Interest Brothers...*

"Well, now we won't ever..." Dr. Tom's voice trailed off beneath the train's noises. With some difficulty, he reached and pulled a rag from his back pocket and passed it over his face, pressing his thumbs into the depressions under his brow. He drew a short breath, hiding his mouth behind one hand.

To Nate, Dr. Tom's reflection in the glass made him appear even more gaunt and sickly. In the hours since leaving Middle

Bayou, his partner's body had seemed to diminish, as though the timbre of his thoughts were draining his vigor even more than the laudanum had.

Once, as a child, Nate had spied a frog on a riverbank, poised motionless on a rock. He'd crept up on it, getting close enough to reach out a finger and touch the slick sheen of its head, but still it sat. The frog soon seemed to grow lax in its outer parts and began sinking in on itself. Nate watched horrified as the entire frog, within a quarter hour's time, deflated into a shriveled, glistening mass. When the frog was as hollow as a skin sock, a large beetle crawled out from under it, scurried into the water, and swam away. The image had stayed with him for a long time, haunting him at night, but finally it had slipped away as other, more necessary and compelling, thoughts crowded into his mind. The remembrance of that event unsettled him, and he wished it had not resurfaced.

Dr. Tom had told Nate that Middle Bayou had turned his thoughts dark. The place seemed to be a conjoining of miracles and draining terrors, almost biblical in scope, where crippled men walked, harlots posed as teachers, and giants with claws and teeth pulled grown men into rivers. And if nothing else, it offered a hardened kernel of damnable proof that foolish men like Bedford Grant could wreak as much havoc as malicious ones.

The train began to slow as it approached Harrisburg to take on more passengers, and at the town limits, a man with a long, filthy coat and beard and looking as though he'd been wandering for years faced the tracks and held up a sign. It read *Rouse Yourselves to the Anger of God.*

Lost in his thoughts, Nate was startled by Dr. Tom calling his name. When the train stopped, the ranger bolted up, grabbed the

Whitworth, and, gesturing for Nate to follow, walked purposefully off the train. He moved briskly towards the front of the railcars and stepped up the ladder, disappearing into the engine cab.

Confused, Nate walked as quickly as his seizing hip would allow, and as he came abreast of the engine, he looked up and saw Dr. Tom in animated conversation with the engineer and the fireman. He turned to Nate and motioned him up the ladder. Offering him a hand, Dr. Tom said, "Nate, I am rousing myself to the anger of God."

The cab was cramped with the four men, and the noise was so deafening from the escaping steam, the bell clanging, and the whistle signals that Nate couldn't hear the names of the railroad workers, but he nodded at them and shook hands with the fireman, who was as black with cinder and smoke as the firebox itself.

Dr. Tom shouted into his ear, "I worked for a time on the rails. In Pennsylvania. After I left medical school."

He pointed to the fireman. "That's what I did. Stoked wood and carried coal."

Nate expected they'd soon climb down from the engine and return to the passenger car, but Dr. Tom braced himself against a railing. "Hold on, Nate!" he yelled. "This is somethin' to write your wife about."

The train began its thundering pitch forward and a sensation like falling through the floor of a well passed from the soles of Nate's feet and up his legs. The noise was terrible, making his teeth clash together, and he watched with awe through the forward portal as the train gained speed, pulling the tracks towards and beneath the engine as though they were not being traversed so much as consumed.

The engineer gestured ahead. "Less than forty miles to Virginia Point. Then the bridge to Galveston."

Nate shook his head, amazed, and a kind of harrowing joy overtook him to the point of giddiness. For several hours he watched the passing of fields and houses and even people who had come to stand by the tracks, gawking or waving up at them. Some boys ran alongside for a brief while until their legs gave out and they tumbled all at once into the grass. One fool on a horse chased them and looked to try and cross the tracks ahead of the engine but pulled up at the last minute, the terrified horse lathered and slinging its head.

The engineer shouted to Nate, "We catch one on horseback every few months. Makes a god-awful mess."

Nate watched the engineer expertly twisting valves and wheels and checking gauges for pressure and water levels, and he wished he knew enough to even ask questions as to the function and purpose of the moving pieces. He caught Dr. Tom watching him, and the ranger smiled as though understanding Nate's thoughts.

"I was never happier than when I was riding like this." He leaned closer to Nate, his arms crossed contentedly. "Bituminous coal. That's what we hauled. Soft, powdery stuff. Gets into everything. Especially the lungs." He hooked a thumb at his ribs. "I think that's what's given me the cancer."

Nate jerked his head around and saw his partner was telling him the truth. Dr. Tom placed a hand on Nate's arm.

"Take this as a gift from me. You'll never forget this. Always carry this moment, 'cause you may never in your life again feel this free."

Nate's sensation of falling returned as the engine made the slight rise onto the wooden crossing and the elevated tracks over the Gulf, the pale green colors of the shallows bottomed with sand quickly turning to the dense murk of deeper water. Before them stretched Galveston Bay, and the bridge that ran for miles across it to the island. The whistle was sounded in three long blasts, but the wind that tore in buffeting currents through the cab carried the sound away along with the steam.

The sun was low behind them, lighting the tight, triangular waves obliquely, and a shadow train flowed apace with them over the surface of the water. Giant gulls, their beaks open as though astonished at the train's progress, veered low around the stack vent and followed them across the length of the bridge.

It was another few miles into Galveston along sandy flats and through to the middle of the town, which to Nate's eyes was the finest he'd seen, surpassing even Austin in newness and the scale of its buildings. But a tension had started to grow in his gut that was more than the deep vibratory sensation of riding the engine. All he could think about was how dark the streets and alleyways were becoming as the train passed along them on its way to the rails' end.

The terminus was an immensely long passenger station fronted by a square, red-brick freight building, and by the time Nate had stepped down from the engine, the sun had set and all of Dr. Tom's loose-limbed camaraderie had evaporated. They unloaded the horses without mishap but for the stock loader who had a bandaged shoulder beneath a torn shirt and who came down the ramp swearing. He glared at Nate, saying, "That bastard horse of your'n bit me!"

With apologies, Nate handed the man a few dollars, and he mounted the bay, following after his partner, who rode directly to the nearest livery to feed and water the frayed horses. Dr. Tom paid the stable boy to bring some supper and they sat in the tack room checking their weapons by lantern light.

"First things first," Dr. Tom said. "We ride to the pier and see after those ships leaving for New Orleans tonight."

"And your—" Nate had started to say *your wife*, but he stopped himself. "And Lucinda?"

"If McGill's here, she'll be with him."

Nate repacked dry powder in his revolver and when he was done, he saw that Dr. Tom had been watching him.

"There's something else I need to tell you." Dr. Tom took off his hat and rotated it around in his fingers, crimping the brim unnaturally. "A few years ago, just before she left for the last time, Lucinda came to me and told me she was in the family way. She seemed happy about it. I know I was. But within a few months, she started getting restless. She'd get silent and down in the mouth for long periods. Since she was a child, she'd been plagued with epileptic fits. With her pregnancy, her fits got worse for a while, and then they got better. A month before she was to deliver she ran away. Took George's watch and a horse, some money of mine. I don't know where she went, but more important, I don't know what happened to the child, whether it's even living or dead. I want you to promise me that regardless of what the outcome is for me, you'll not stop trying until you get the answer from her. I have some money put aside at the rangers' bank in Austin, and I have a sister in Buffalo. She should be told if the child is still alive."

Nate nodded, but Dr. Tom said, "I need a promise on that."

Nate in that moment had a presentiment, what his wife would

have called a glimmering, that he was in the presence of a man making a last request. He said, "I promise."

Dr. Tom put his hat back on and worked his mouth around a dry tongue. "I need something sweet to wash out this sour taste. Would you walk up the street to Henderson's Dry Goods and get me some rock candy? Go on, now, Nate. I just need a minute to settle my nerves. When you get back, we'll get this thing started."

Nate walked out of the livery and turned right on the Strand. He hadn't asked the way but decided Henderson's must be farther into town. He walked slowly, giving Dr. Tom the time he asked for, and watched the traffic, the horses, pedestrians, and carts, still crowding the streets.

The sea wind had turned colder and he settled his hat more firmly on his head and turned up his collar. He nodded to a couple on the sidewalk, a boy on a horse, a man in a buggy, and looked on both sides of the street for a sign that said *Henderson's*.

He glanced up at the storied buildings. Even with the few gaslights, the stars were legion, dimensional and sharp, and Nate thought there should be a new word to describe the luster over the Gulf sky.

He walked a few more blocks and then turned back, retracing his steps. He caught sight of his own profile in some glass fronting a shop with a sign that read *Oceanside Lots for Sale. See Surveyor Inside.*

The man in the buggy. The one he'd passed on the street. He'd seen the man only briefly in profile—bearded, spectacled—but the memory of sharing the ferry ride with McGill resurfaced and, immediately following, the recollection of his wife's warning about staying away from rough water.

McGill had been riding in the direction of the livery. Nate turned and began to run, and two blocks away from the livery, he heard three distinct revolver shots, two fast and one following shortly after.

Drawing his own revolver, he cautiously entered the livery through the open stable door, but he already knew what he was going to find.

Chapter 21

There was little doubt in Lucinda's mind that Bill had meant to kill her on the seaside road in Galveston. Instead, he ran the fingers of one hand over her face and told her, "You go to work now, Lucy. And you'll work until you've made up for all that's been lost."

He kissed her, his lips tasting of tobacco and brine, and pinched up her hair in his fingers, yanking it behind every word. "Every. Last. Dollar."

And then he released her; her knees buckled with relief.

"The steamer *Josephine* departs the docks at midnight for New Orleans," he said. "If you keep up a brisk pace, you'll make it in time." He climbed into the buggy. "Walk fast, Lucy. I need to know that you are still with me." He chucked at the reins and headed out, alone, towards town.

She watched the buggy until it had disappeared into the darkness, but even then she could hear the faint sounds of the wheels crackling over the shells, like a plague of locusts departing.

She began walking rapidly, passing no one along the road, watching the tiny lights of boats slipping through the deep currents of the Gulf waters. It was cold, making her teeth clatter together, and she rubbed her hands up and down her arms for warmth. In the third hour of walking, the shells on the road started to cut through the leather of her shoes, and she trailed spatters of dark blood in the shale behind her like tiny starfish caught on dry land. But the wounding of her feet was a distraction from the frigid wind, and she welcomed the pain. She would later reveal her wounds to Bill as visible signs of her penance.

She arrived at the docks before midnight, pulled herself hand over hand along the gangway rope, and limped onto the deck. She knocked timidly on the door to Bill's cabin and felt her head grow dim with fear over his reception. He opened it and she almost fainted, her eyes rolling back in her head. He carried her to the bunk, where he cut the laces of her boots with his knife and took them off her swollen ankles. He put a damp handkerchief over her face and washed her naked feet gently in a bowl of cool water. He cooed to her, stroking her hair, and told her, "I'm the only one left to take care of you. I'll always take care of you, Lucy, but you must never again go against me."

Her wounds, her helplessness, her contriteness, all seemed to excite him, and he pulled up her skirt and took her on the narrow bed, her head rhythmically tapping the wall with every thrust like a metronome.

When he was finished, he got up from the bed and moved to look out the one porthole window. She watched his profile, the tension in the curves of his hip and thigh, and she hid a smile in the hollow of her shoulder. *He's forgiven me*, she thought. *He would never truly hurt me.*

"Tonight I had to kill a man who would have killed me." He

said it quietly, without emphasis on any one word. She sat up, tense with fear again.

"There will be others looking for us," he said. "I've given my last fifty dollars to the captain to keep quiet about us being here, but we need money as soon as we dock." He looked at her and she nodded once that she understood. He would go to the streets and alleyways, anywhere there was gambling, or an easy mark to fall under a confidence game or a robbery. She, in turn, would do the work she did best.

He lay on the bunk again. "I had to do it, Lucy." He circled one arm around her, soothing her, and whispered into her ear, "We need to look to the future. What we need is a wealthy fish, and I know just the fishing hole."

The morning they arrived in New Orleans, Bill took Lucinda to the Fourth Ward, to a grand house that sat on South Basin Street. In front of the building's entrance were two large pagan statues holding gas torches, still lit.

Bill knocked and they were at once admitted to a downstairs receiving room in which every piece of furniture, every ornament, was sharp-edged, glittering, and false. *Cold as death, with more than a whiff of decay,* Lucinda could hear her father saying.

A large black man dressed in evening wear led them upstairs to the madam's office. Hattie C. Hamilton owned the second-finest bordello in New Orleans, after Kate Townsend's palatial crib down the street, and had a long acquaintance with Bill. That Hattie had shot and killed her lover a few months earlier, a senator named Beares who had entirely financed the building, served only to heighten the allure of the place.

Bill made the introductions, and Hattie squinted her eyes at Lucinda and proclaimed her hair and skin exceptionally fine, but she shook her head at Lucinda's torn shoes and wrinkled dress. She asked, "How old are you now? Twenty-seven?"

Lucinda knew it was a negotiating tactic, but it pricked at her vanity. She smiled and answered, "I'm twenty-three today. Tomorrow I might be nineteen."

Hattie had laughed at that, her wide shovel jaw working like the hinge to a tool chest, but her eyes, as well as her handshake, were bloodless. They agreed that Lucinda was to work exclusively for House Hamilton. She'd get twenty dollars per customer for an hourly, and fifty dollars for a night's stay-over, and she'd pay an exorbitant 40 percent of that to Hattie the first month. "For debut expenses," Hattie said.

"But you can keep whatever tips the customers care to give you," the madam added. "You'll need clothes to start and a sitting with my hairdresser. You can't appear downstairs looking like you do now. I'll want you ready to start right away."

By nine o'clock that evening Lucinda was sitting in the parlor, having already received in her room two customers eager to try the new girl. She let her eyes drift about the room to the other men and women in various stages of negotiation and undress, and to the front door, which seemed to be open more often than it was closed. It was attended by the black doorman, Lucius, who carried a double-bladed knife sheathed in his long formal coat.

Bill would not come again before morning—he had his own business to take care of—but she searched the clients walking through the door for his angular form anyway. It was a way to take her mind from the bone-crushing restlessness of waiting, and it gave some warmth to the chill of sitting in the gilt perfection of Hattie's parlor.

Lucinda turned her eyes to a couple nearby: a wealthy customer and his regular, a French whore wearing white-and-red stockings that showed beneath her linen chemise like lurid ribbons under a wedding cake. They were sprawled on a narrow settee, the whore sitting on the man's lap, and she rocked her hips and swung her shoeless feet, making him laugh. One of her hands disappeared into the waistband of the man's trousers, but she frowned when she followed his gaze and saw the object of his attention.

The man shifted in the settee, allowing her hand to slip farther into the pleated folds of his pants. "Who's that?" he asked, pointing to Lucinda.

The whore kissed his neck and answered, "She's no one. She's new." With her free hand she unpinned her hair, which fell in a complicated frizz around her shoulders, and then set about the business of distracting him.

An older man approached Lucinda, disturbing her thoughts, and she turned her head away from him. He'd attempted earlier to engage her, but he smelled of day-old grease and beer, even through his expensive worsted suit, and she rebuffed him. She'd have to be careful about refusing customers. Hattie would not be pleased. But she had in mind another fish, the one she had been watching carefully and who she knew had special, expensive tastes. The fish was now enmeshed firmly in the grip of the whore with legs like a barber's pole, but he snuck a look at Lucinda and she parted her lips, creating a small, rounded O with her mouth. She needed to work fast, and subtle gestures would not achieve the needed results.

She smoothed out her skirt, running her hands lingeringly over her thighs. It was a simple woolen travel suit of evening blue, cut straight and high across her bosom. She looked like a schoolteacher, which was the point.

Hattie had given her a gown in advance of her wages, a dress of champagne silk, the décolletage cut almost to her nipples, and the hem shortened in front to her knees. The same sort of tart casing that every girl in the place would be wearing. But against Hattie's wishes, Lucinda put on the more modest dress, telling the madam it would be more alluring to place herself apart from the other girls.

With studied decorum, she leaned forward and brushed an imaginary bit of dirt from her new kid boots, then let her fingers slowly trace the outline of the seams. They were the only shoes that she could tolerate wearing, as the blisters and swelling on her feet were still painful.

Lucinda's fish had been watching her movements and he smiled broadly at her. She smiled in return, encouraging him, knowing that he had had the French girl for weeks and was in all likelihood growing bored with her. Lucinda caught the huff of tension and anger rising from the whore on his lap.

"Hallo," he said. "Tartine says you're a schoolteacher. Is that so?"

Lucinda dipped her chin, but kept her eyes on the mark.

"How did you get your students to mind you, looking so sweet?"

She leaned forward slightly and said, "Discipline."

Later, when the man followed her up the stairs, Lucinda was aware that Hattie was watching her from the bar, smiling; she had a fist on her hip and one foot on the railing, like a man. The French whore stood at the bottom of the banister observing her with quite a different look.

Chapter 22

*F*or the second time, Nate helped load Dr. Tom's horse onto the Galveston train, but it was oriented on the rails pointing back towards Houston. In the baggage car was a long box labeled *Houston Cemetery*, to be signed for by the same physician who had seen Dr. Tom through his pneumonia; the felt-lined medical kit with all its gleaming, carefully tended scalpels and lancets was going to the Houston doctor in gratitude for services rendered. In the instructions for burial, Nate had included the epitaph for the headstone. He had wanted a passage from Dickens, but the wordiness of the author's sentiments made the job too costly, so he wrote what was on Deerling's headstone: *Comrade in Arms, Father, Friend*. Nate didn't know the year Dr. Tom was born, so below the first line he put only the year of his death: *1870*.

For a good while he lingered on the platform, even after the train had departed, as the state policeman standing next to him shifted impatiently. The officer was a tall, wasp-waisted black man, the first state policeman of color Nate had seen. That officer's partner was also black, blue-black like a grackle's wing, and he carried two cross-draw pistols in his belt. The officers had been summoned to the livery after Dr. Tom had been shot. In checking the ranger's revolver, they found that he had fired off one shot, but there was no evidence that it had found its mark.

The officers carried out, to Nate's mind, a swift and cool-headed search of streets surrounding the stables. But he had no idea how thoroughly they had searched the piers or the ships docked between them.

The lead officer's name was Thoreau, which he pronounced "Thurah." He watched Nate for a while and then cleared his throat. "There's no way to know for sure if your man was on one of those steamers. Captains are bribed all the time to keep quiet about who and what's on board. Besides, even if McGill was on a steamer, as long as he's out of Texas, it's not our problem anymore. Am I right?"

Nate shifted his weight, one foot to the other, but said nothing.

Thoreau gently tapped a finger on Nate's arm. "There's nothing left for you to do here. If you leave Texas, you'll have no authority."

Nate nodded noncommittally and asked, "Are you going to report me?"

Thoreau breathed out through his nose. "Who would I report you to?"

Nate took up the reins of the big bay and set off in the direction of the docks. He heard Thoreau and his partner walking away, back towards town.

"Hey," Nate called, turning and catching up to them. "Letter for my wife." He handed Thoreau an envelope taken from the Republic Hotel.

Thoreau put the letter in his pocket. "She know she's married to a fool?"

"She does now." Nate turned back towards the water, uncertain if he had done the right thing in telling his wife where he was headed. He would have already been gone but for Thoreau's insistence on the formalities of giving a lengthy statement, which Nate suspected was a ploy to keep him in Galveston until his temper had cooled.

Nate left his horse tied to the side of a warehouse and walked out onto the pier to book his passage. He wasn't sure how the horse would take to being on the water after the firestorm in the stock car, but he wouldn't leave the stallion behind. He paid for his passage and then galloped the horse hard down the beach road for miles. When the stallion's breathing became labored, Nate brought him around and trotted him into the wind. The horse's eyes rolled white with the surf and Nate reined him onto the beach, where his nostrils flared wildly at the salty, churning foam, and he set his dark legs into the tidal sand as though confronting an adversary.

Nate, for the briefest of moments, imagined Beth and Mattie there on the beach and himself sitting between them, watching the ships far out in the Gulf. But he pushed those thoughts away, and, when the horse had calmed, he rode back into town. He sat on the docks through the afternoon, waiting for the departure of the evening steamer taking a dozen Texas-bred horses to New Orleans.

He had paid for the fare with the money his partner had pressed on him in the hours before he died. Dr. Tom had lingered for two days, in and out of consciousness, but with the certain knowledge that he would not recover. The ranger had been carried to the Republic Hotel on the Strand, but when he saw they meant to put him in their best room, he protested over the expense and so was taken to a smaller room in the back.

He told Nate through pain-clenched teeth, "I'd stick them with the bill, but they'd just get it from you."

The physician was sent for and he stanched the bleeding from the wounds in the stomach and shoulder and laid on thick the laudanum. He pulled Nate aside, whispering, "It would be no sin, and maybe a blessing, if you were to add twenty more drops to the man's water."

Nate drew up a chair and sat with Dr. Tom through the day-light hours, sleeping on the floor at the foot of the bed through the night.

Once Dr. Tom asked him, "How many hours do you suppose you've sat next to me while I've been sick, and me not even an old man yet, and listened to me talk about myself?"

Nate patted him on the arm but didn't trust himself to speak. He stared at the laudanum bottle for the longest time, but Dr. Tom didn't seem to be in unbearable pain. The ranger lay mostly with his eyes closed, occasionally his lips moving, fingers tapping out some unknown rhythm on the sheets. Once his eyes opened and he asked, "What's the way that song goes?" But Nate didn't know what song the ranger was trying to remember.

Nate stared at the floor for hours, hoping that Dr. Tom would speak again, but mostly he slept. When the ranger finally shifted restlessly, Nate looked towards the bed and saw that Dr. Tom's eyes were on him. He breathed in gasps, saying, "Remember. McGill. You promised."

Nate leaned forward. "I'll find him."

"Lucinda. And the child."

Nate nodded, remembering the pledge he had given to McNally years before: to bring a herd of horses back to Texas, saving an entire bloodline. *As a son to a father*, he had promised McNally, and he repeated the same words to Dr. Tom. "As a son to a father."

If the ranger heard him, he made no reply. He turned his face towards the window, just lightening with the dawn.

"It's the coming of day..." Dr. Tom began, but then he was silent.

The last thing Dr. Tom did before he stopped breathing was brush the back of his palm under his mustache with a slow and steady hand. Nate had seen him do it a hundred times in anticipation of something pleasurable or to order his thoughts in preparation for a necessary but onerous task. Dr. Tom had then laid his arms at his sides, and the blanket slowly sank into the concavity of his chest.

Nate reached out and clasped his hand, and though there was still warmth, there was no returning pressure. He sat at the bedside listening to the rise and fall of the street noises coming from the Strand, hearing the whistle from the approaching train traveling over Galveston Bay, and thought of Dr. Tom in the engine cab, his eyes closed, smiling with the pleasure of the rough vibrations traveling upwards from the bottom of his boot heels. He remembered his partner standing in the streets of St. Gall gazing at the stars overhead, heard Tom's voice telling him that they were all in the black soup together, linking them forever in a kind of kinship through adversity.

Nate's own father had never so much as given a nod to his son's accomplishments and talents, such as they were. And yet this one man, unknown to Nate until several weeks ago, had counseled him, encouraged him, and entrusted to him his last earthly possessions.

Nate pressed the already cooling hand to his own forehead and then laid it back on the bed. Soon after, he walked from the hotel down to the pier to book his passage to New Orleans.

The sun was now low in the west, muted and red through a thin mist of clouds, and he led his horse calmly up the boarding ramp and onto the steamer going to New Orleans. He removed the saddle and stowed it and Dr. Tom's Winchester with the general tack, but he carried the valuable Whitworth with him onto the deck, where he cradled the rifle in his arms like a child and watched Galveston Island slipping away.

Chapter 23

*L*ucinda lay on a day couch, her face toward the ceiling, but she cut her eyes to the side, following the movements of Hattie Hamilton as she paced the floor. The madam had one hand in a fist at her hip, and she pointed and jabbed the forefinger of her other hand like an ice pick.

"I won't have any sick girls in my house, Bill. It was deceitful of you not to tell me."

Bill shifted in the chair set closest to the couch, nodding sympathetically, as though he were merely complicit in the deception and not the perpetrator of it. He exhaled a dense band of cigar smoke and carefully, with his fingertips, plucked a grain of tobacco from his bottom lip.

Hattie added, directing her finger at Lucinda, "You're lucky she didn't have the fit while the judge was still on top of her."

Bill smiled. *"Vero nihil verius."*

"Don't get coy with me. She can't stay here. She'll have to go."

Bill dropped his head back to gaze at the ceiling. "Hasn't she been a good earner?"

"As far as it's gone. Yes." Hattie had stopped pointing and now planted both fists on her hips. "But Bill, it spooks the customers. I get some old piddler on her while she's rattling around with one of her fits, and he's like to die of heart failure. And then I've got a fire stampede out the door."

Bill looked at Lucinda, who met his gaze for a moment and then looked away. "You're not using your imagination."

"What do you mean?" Hattie looked from Bill to Lucinda and back again.

"A specialist."

Bill stood up, and for a moment Hattie looked to move back a step.

He said, "Perhaps someone who would simply want to watch."

Hattie ducked her chin. "To watch?"

"Yes. To simply watch." Bill smiled at her as though he'd solved a complex riddle. He placed an arm behind her ample back and guided her to the door. "Think about it, Hattie. I'm certain that with your contacts, you'll find someone who would, even at a moment's notice, come and see…How should we call it?…Death dancing with the maiden."

He closed the door after Hattie and returned to the couch to stand over Lucinda. He pulled a vial from his coat pocket, placed it on the small table next to her, and said, "Lucy, you don't have the luxury of being sick right now. If we lose your fish because of this, we'll have to start over again, in some other city. We don't have the time, and we don't have the money for it." He reached down and brushed the hair off her forehead but then pinched her ear painfully between his thumb and forefinger.

"Don't make me sorry that I forgave you in Galveston." He kissed her on the mouth. "You seem less excitable when you're on the laudanum. I'd recommend a spoonful every few hours to begin. Perhaps you should start now."

He straightened and turned his back to her, then walked from the room.

She fixed her eyes on the mural of the Muses painted on the ceiling, breathing through her teeth; the sickness in her stomach and bowels rose to her throat, threatening to spill over her tongue and out of her mouth and spoil the satin covering of the couch. Her vision still pulsed; the lines of the painting danced crazily. But to close her eyes brought a more unbearable feeling of being knocked from a water tower. She slowed her breathing, counting the folds in a Muse's cloak, and the nausea retreated.

The attack had come without warning and with none of the usual signs, and she had no memory of what had happened between the time she lifted her skirts to the judge and the moment she'd awakened, an hour later. She had opened her eyes to the madam and some of the other girls standing around the bed, their expressions fearful—the foreign-born girls crossing themselves in frantic succession—but all of them with an unreserved curiosity. The judge had long since fled and one of the girls murmured that Hattie would have to give him free humps for a month of Sundays.

The judge was old and mostly impotent, liking best to look at her body through the film of a nightdress. He tipped her well and was courteous, and she was sorry to have lost him.

She wondered how many other customers she would lose because of the revelation of her illness. She thought it possible that her fish, the skittish and guilt-ridden client she had stolen from Tartine, might use this as an excuse to discontinue their increasingly dangerous games of restraint and orchestrated punishment. She thought of telling him that it was all an elaborate act, that the judge had asked her to feign being unconscious and helpless, but she could imagine Tartine, or any of the other girls, whispering into his ear the shameful details of her sickness: the terrible distortions of her face and limbs, the spittle from her mouth, her loosened bladder.

A cautious knock sounded at the door, after which it opened slowly. A young woman entered the room and stood looking at Lucinda from a distance.

"Hattie asked me to come see after you."

Lucinda remembered that the girl's name was Katrin, but she couldn't recall from which northern, sunless place she had come. Perhaps Germany, or Sweden? Katrin was dressed in a thin linen petticoat, and the curve of her pregnant belly was visible through the fabric. She followed Lucinda's gaze and cupped her mounded flesh with one arm. Lucinda had heard that the girl had followed every bit of whores' wisdom on ending a pregnancy, from tincture of arsenic to repeatedly jumping off a table, to no avail.

She returned Lucinda's gaze and shrugged. "I guess the little bastard still expects to be born."

Lucinda asked for some water and then told the girl to go. Lucinda drank sparingly and soon began to feel better, her vision clearing. The intense nausea was a new, unwelcome visitation. A memory connected to the nausea and brought on by the girl's appearance began to surge into her consciousness, and she reflexively looked to the ceiling, trying to hold the threatening thoughts at bay.

But her thoughts slipped free and she realized she hadn't felt so sick to her stomach since her own pregnancy three years before. And with this breach came a flood of remembrances.

The first few months of it she'd spent with her face over a porcelain thunder mug and she thought she would surely die of starvation. Then one day she woke and had no more sickness. It had disappeared like clouds before a strong wind, leaving only a ravenous appetite and her eyes bloodshot and swollen from the ceaseless retching. She came to feel better than well, to feel as a child does at the outset of a summer's day, a child who has never known illness or injury and is experiencing only the certainty of newly developed muscles, liquid within supple skin.

But the fits returned in her sixth month and worsened in severity and duration until she feared she would be extinguished completely or rendered a simpleton by a brain rupture. She began to loathe and fear in equal measures the body growing inside of her own, was jealous and resentful of it sapping her strength and vitality.

One evening she overheard her father and husband speaking in whispered, conspiratorial tones, saying that, for the infant's own safety, it should be given to a nurse to be raised, and that she, Lucinda, might do better placed again in the care of a "curative" institution.

A month before she was to give birth, she left her father's house accompanied by a Mexican woman who had experience as a mid-wife, and they traveled north to a place far enough, and isolated enough, that Lucinda would not be reclaimed. She had made arrangements to be taken into a home for unmarried mothers and she gave birth on a gentle spring evening, without much pain or any dangerous complications. They had advised her to look away when the baby was pulled from between her legs, as it would make the parting easier. But she did look, and it was a healthy, squalling girl still slick from her womb, and she had felt a clenching ache in her breasts, needing to be relieved of their burden. She watched the nurses clean and swaddle the baby and when they began to carry her from the room, her eyes opened and fixed on Lucinda's with a steady, ancient ownership. Lucinda reached her arm out, fingers extended, and the midwife frowned but let Lucinda briefly touch the downy surface of the baby's head.

For hours she listened for the sound of an infant crying in the nursery, but she heard nothing more than the restless shifting of the still-pregnant women beside her. She left after four days, assured repeatedly by the nurses that the baby would be cared for and placed with suitable parents.

Before traveling, she had bound up her chest to stop her breasts from leaking, but when she stepped onto the coach, the top of her bodice was wet, as though soaked from tears.

Now Lucinda eased her legs over the day couch and sat up. She felt faint for only a moment and, after taking a few more breaths, stood. She reached for the bottle of laudanum on the table, walked to the wash station, and poured the contents into the water pitcher. She straightened her hair, pinched her cheeks for color, and walked from the room to the balcony overlooking the downstairs parlor, where she observed Bill in a gentleman's chair, Tartine draped across his lap. The whore was whispering into his ear, and when she looked over her shoulder at Lucinda, she narrowed her eyes and curled her lips in a triumphant smile.

Chapter 24

On the steamer's deck, soon after boarding, Nate heard a horse screaming and the pounding of terrified hooves down the boat's open corridor. He was certain it was the big bay breaking loose, but it was a speckled roan, mad with terror and on a collision course with him against the railing. He ducked, covering his head with his arms, and felt the wind from the horse as it leaped over the railing, and a second later he heard the splash as it fell into the Gulf.

He grabbed the deck rail, looking for the horse's head to appear, and soon after saw the struggling animal swimming strongly towards the nearest point of land.

Passengers ran onto the deck to watch, and the captain pointed and yelled, "He's making for Pelican Island!"

For forty-five minutes they watched the horse swimming against the tide, and often the body would sink until only the tips of the ears and the nostrils emerged to signal that the animal had not yet drowned.

He looked through the scope of the Whitworth, following its

progress, and one of the passengers mistook it as an aim for a killing.

"Shoot it," the man had urged, laughing. *"Shoot it!"*

A hundred feet out from the island beach the head disappeared under the waves and the man continued his barking laughter, telling Nate that he had missed a fine chance to test his rifle.

Nate pressed the scope closer to his eye, scanning the shoreline for signs of the horse, and when he saw flickers of white light streaking his vision, he realized he had been holding his breath. He thought his eyes were mistaken when he saw two small triangles appear from the waves and then the horse's head rear from the water. With a great intake of air, the horse simply walked up along the sloping sea floor until it came to stand on the beach, coughing and breathing in great sucking gasps.

A jubilant cry rose up from all the other passengers except the barking man, and Nate watched the island through the scope until the horse was lost from view. And then he handed the rifle to a surprised passenger and with both hands pummeled the barking man until he fell to the deck. He hit the man savagely and repeatedly, feeling bones and flesh breaking under his fists; feeling, too, a momentary easing of loss, his grief for Dr. Tom oozing out from some deep place within, like the blood that seeped through the split skin of his knuckles. He kept hitting the man, beating back his uncertainty as to his mission, until the captain and two passengers pulled him away.

Afterwards, he sat against the railing looking at the Gulf sky, the gray clouds mushrooming together in storm formation. He thought about the roan, believing that he'd been meant to witness the horse's struggle. The event recalled to him the thinking of a horse, which is neither reasoned nor reasoning, but steadfast and untiring against all contrary tides. He knew that a horse, if stubborn enough, was capable of running through prickly wire; it would tangle itself until it was shredded hide to bone before abandoning its determined run.

If the roan, like a man, had pondered on and fretted over the difficulty of swimming a half mile to a small island, it most likely would have given up, let the water take it, its churning thoughts working as surely as weights around its legs.

Nate had committed to this path, and he would not think beyond the length of the steps that pointed towards the ultimate capture, or killing, of William Estes McGill. He would not defeat himself with complicated strategies or undo his resolve with worrying over the difficulty of finding his way through a city where he had never been before, where he had no contacts or friends.

He would, like the roan, point his nose to his destination and work muscle and bone to find himself on home ground again.

Chapter 25

*L*ucinda sat in the carriage across from Tartine, staring out the window. She could feel the whore's eyes on her, though, and knew that if she glanced at the girl's face, she'd see her mouth twisted into the same smirking grin she'd carried since spending an entire night with Bill. Tartine crossed her legs as a man would, one ankle over a knee, flashing her red-and-white stockings like a challenge.

Hattie had called them both into her private parlor that morning and told them that Lucinda's fish had requested that they both go to his house—a mansion on First Street—that afternoon. It was an unusual request, Hattie admitted; one, the madam insinuated, that hinted at the unpleasantness of the encounter.

"Unpleasant for you," Hattie had said, looking pointedly at Lucinda.

As they left the parlor, Tartine had whispered into Lucinda's ear, "He will want for you to scream quite a lot."

The fish had not been frightened by Lucinda's fit; in fact, he had specified to Hattie that Lucinda should replay her helpless state in his presence, wearing the same modest schoolteacher's dress she had worn the first evening. She was to remain passive and feign unconsciousness while he worked to revive and reanimate her through "treatments" of his own devising.

The carriage bounced hard over a break in the road and Lucinda looked down at the carpetbag at Tartine's feet, revisiting in her mind its contents: a razor strop and belts of various sizes; rigid paddles, deeply scored; and a pig's bladder with a long, perforated tube attached. She dabbed at the sweat on her upper lip, and her eyes met Tartine's gaze.

She said something in French and Lucinda snapped, "Say what you have to say in English or shut it."

Tartine tilted her head and smiled. "I said only that Bill told me how pretty is St. Louis." She uncrossed her legs and sat with her knees wide apart. "He is very felicitous, wouldn't you say?"

She laughed and Lucinda turned her head towards the window once more. She had tried telling herself that Bill's sudden attentions to Tartine were to be seen as only his escape from boredom or, at worst, a warning to her against attempting further disobedience. But, in truth, she was ill with anxiety that his restlessness and disapproval would edge her towards another series of weakening fits, rendering her useless to his plans and pushing him to seek another partner.

In every brothel she had ever known, she had always felt herself to be above the other girls, certainly the most poised and intelligent of them. And if not the most beautiful, she presented to her clients the appearance of refined accomplishment. She did not look like a whore, nor did she act like one, and the men who paid for her time felt themselves elevated because of it.

But in New Orleans, her cool detachment was looked upon as

an anachronistic and elaborate act that was to be dropped as soon as the customer closed the door. She was not easily shocked, but some of the requests had left her feeling she could crawl out of her own skin.

Soon, soon, she thought. *Bill will get what he wants and we can leave this city and its scheming whores, and all of what I do today will be washed away in perfumed baths and fragrant sheets.*

The carriage had stopped in front of a large house. Tartine hoisted up the carpetbag, stepped onto the street, and held open the door.

"Well…?" she said impatiently.

"…is a deep, dark hole," Lucinda whispered, "into which I would gladly push you."

Lucinda stepped from the carriage and, brushing past Tartine, walked up the stairs and then into the client's house.

Chapter 26

The steamer captain, a *gens de couleur* named Pascal, invited Nate into his quarters to share an evening meal of battered-and-fried catfish steaks and cornbread. With an amused turn of his lips, he watched Nate eating hungrily and set a bottle of brandy on the table.

"That man you pounded on is going to be eating nothing but apple mash for a while," the captain said, pouring them each a glass full. "I know you're Texas law, so what're you doin' going to New Orleans?"

"I'm after a man and his accomplice. A prostitute." Nate tasted the brandy and grimaced. "I made a promise to someone."

"Family?"

Nate nodded. "Near enough."

The captain drained his glass and poured another one for himself. "Who's this man you're hunting?"

"A killer of children."

The captain sat back in his chair, motioning for Nate to drink up. "You know your way around New Orleans?"

Nate shook his head. "Never been there before."

"I was born and raised in New Orleans. I know all the streets and alleyways," he said. "I'll draw you a map."

Nate thanked him and held his breath to take another sip.

"I've spent my whole life on the river," the captain said, warming to his topic. "I've seen every rapid and current, snag, sawyer, and mud bank from the Gulf entry to Natchez, nearly four hundred miles away, so I understand bold action. I'll do what I can to help you."

He took a piece of brown paper and drew a rough map of New Orleans. "You start here," the captain said, resting a finger over a few intersecting lines, "at St. Charles and Canal, and go your way to City Hall. There you'll find the forty thieves. In these few blocks, there are more than forty gambling dens and sporting houses, which stay open all hours. If your man is game, he'll be there sometime, somewhere."

He moved his finger above Canal to Basin Street and he smiled. "This, or thereabouts, is where you'll most likely find your lady." He traced out a rectangle, moving clockwise from the border streets of Basin to Canal to North Robertson to St. Louis. He pursed his lips meaningfully. "Now, if you're lookin' here, I will certainly be happy to help you look."

Nate frowned and the captain's smile widened. "You got some money? 'Cause you're gonna need it."

Nate looked over at the Whitworth propped in a corner of the steering cabin, thinking he'd sell it if he needed to.

The captain moved his finger towards the snaking outline of the river. "Now, you hear me. You stay away from Gallatin Street. Your man, if he owns a watch and can tell time, will not go there.

Even the army stay away from that hellhole." He folded the map up and handed it to Nate.

Nate tucked the map into his jacket and went back out onto the open deck. He sat on the starboard side under a deck lantern, facing the black water of the Gulf, and began writing to his wife.

Dearest Beth,

I am soon to arrive in New Orleans by the steamer Annie Gillette. *You will receive by cable a hundred dollars, a final gift from Dr. Tom, which combined with your widow's take if I don't return will hold you in good stead. Please forgive the few words. You have always known best what was in my heart by what I have not spoken, rather than what I have. I do not mean to be careless or take undue risks with my life, but I am determined to see this through as quickly as I am able so that I may return soon to you and Mattie. I think of you most fondly in the field, the sun on your face, the wind braiding your hair, and the smile you will give to me when I am returned to you.*

My love always, Nathaniel

The steamer docked in the early morning and Nate stood on the pier waiting for his horse to be led off with the others. The big bay, already saddled and bridled, followed the small herd of horses off the steamer with a lowered head, but at the first shrill release of the boat whistle, he reared, breaking the line, and clattered away from the docks. He raced northwards, up Tchoupi-toulas Street, scattering dockworkers and skittering around cargo wagons, his hooves missing traction on the bricked-over streets where they were slick with the mire of refuse and rain.

The steamer captain, standing next to Nate, pointed towards

the thoroughfare. "You better go on for him quick before he get to Canal or he gonna be in somebody's stew."

Nate thanked him and set off on foot as the captain called after him, "Just be glad he don't go the other way. Towards St. Thomas. Then he'd be glue!" He laughed once at his own rhyme and Nate waved his thanks over one shoulder, trying to orient himself to the map of the city the captain had given him. Nate looked back once towards the crowded harbor choked with jockeying vessels, the packet boats and steamers skirting one another like pieces in a chess game played at breakneck speed, and he saw that the captain was still watching him, his mouth downturned, worriedly shaking his head.

Nate continued walking northwards as fast as he dared. He passed warehouses and storage shacks, the workers frantically off-loading bags, barrels, crates, and boxes from wagons and handcarts; the men signaling and calling to one another in a language unknown to Nate.

He shouted to a worker, asked if the man had seen a riderless horse racing by, and the man cupped a palm to one ear and said, "*Quoi?*" Nate repeated the question, and another worker also gestured as though straining to hear and responded the same way. Soon a dozen men were feigning confusion and pointing in different directions, saying, "*Quoi?... Quoi?... Quoi?*" then laughing uproariously, so that the words, sounding like a chorus of wintering ducks, followed Nate up the street.

Nate ground his teeth and continued on his way, red-faced and angry. "Yeah," he said, waving that he got the joke and muttering, "Thank you, you sons-a-bitches."

As he approached Canal Street, he saw a large group of men

gathered in a ring and the big bay's head and neck jerking wildly above the crowd. He ran the last block and heard someone yelling and hurling challenges from somewhere inside the ring.

He pushed himself to the front, his hand on the grip of the Dance, and saw a man with one hand on the horse's reins, the other curled into a fist.

"I am brother to the snapping turtle!" the man roared. "I'm the spawn of the alligator mother and the panther father."

He was large, built like a laborer, and Nate could smell the whiskey vapors rolling from the man's lips even though he was six feet away.

"I'm the bayou bully. I wear the red feather." The roaring man pointed to a denuded turkey feather stuck into the band of his hat as if to a medal. "And this *my* horse now."

"Hey!" Nate shouted. He yanked the pistol from his belt and held it at his side. "That's my horse."

The man turned his walleyes on Nate. "*Say you.*" He swept a large skinning knife from its sheath, staggering with the motion, and jabbed crazily at the air in front of Nate's face. The crowd kept expanding, more people running through the streets to join the circle, and Nate noticed for the first time how wide the avenue was, four times the width of a normal city street.

Nate ducked his head but held out a placating hand. "Did you try to get on him?"

The man blinked, his feet shuffling for balance. His knife hand slowed and then paused.

Nate asked him again, "Did you try and get on him?"

There was a gap of silence wherein Nate could almost hear the groaning path of the man's thoughts. Someone in the crowd coughed once, as though to hasten the confrontation, and the man reared back, blinded by this unconsidered question.

He nodded slowly and Nate asked, "What happened?"

The knife began to waver and the man dropped it to his side. He rubbed his shoulder and said, "The beast bit me!"

Nate made a show of returning his gun to his belt, then he stepped forward calmly and eased the reins from the man's hand before he could gather his thoughts enough to strike. "He won't bite me."

Nate fitted the Whitworth into its leather case and, after draping the reins over the bay's neck, legged himself fluidly onto the saddle and then sat quietly, the horse now complacent.

The man's eyes widened as though to an astonishing thought. He said, "That's your horse."

"It is," Nate said, giving a tell with his eyes that he was ready to be on his way, and the man stepped back and faced the crowd. "Back away, all you bastards!" he yelled. "All you sons of whores and alley dogs. This man's riding his horse. And I will personally gut anyone who tries to take it from him…"

The man's voice continued as Nate headed down Canal Street, and when he turned to look back, the crowd had begun dispersing and the turkey-feather man was grinning and waving to him in a friendly fashion with his knife.

He found his way to St. Charles Avenue and squinted up at the three-story buildings—some new, some with decayed brick- and ironwork—housing the gambling palaces. Men and boys stood in the doorways calling out to him to come in and try his luck.

One barefoot boy trotted alongside him, his head not even reaching the horse's withers. "We got faro on the first floor," the boy said. "Roulette on the second, keno on the third. You don't like that, we got poker. You don't like that, we got ladies." The boy reached for Nate's stirrup and yanked it to make him stop. "Come on, mister, we got split-tail, all ages."

Nate reined the bay to a stop and regarded the boy. "How old are you?"

The boy crossed his arms. "Twelve," he said. "You like boys better?"

Nate thought to plant his boot in the boy's chest and send him ass-first into the street, but instead he asked him where the Buffalo House was. The boy agreed to take him there for a dollar.

The steamer captain had told Nate to go to this place first, as it had housed and succored every gambling man and trickster in New Orleans at one time or another. Nate had been told to talk little, to watch and listen, and, last, to find a seat with his back to a corner.

He tied his horse to a tether ring, walked inside carrying the Whitworth, and ordered a beer at the bar. The palace was spacious, paneled in wood, with mirrors covering the wall in front of him. He scanned the reflected room behind him and saw that even at that early hour, there were twenty or so men seated at drinking or gaming tables, a few girls in shortened frocks sitting with them. The barkeep handed him a beer and a card on which was printed: *The Buffalo House, in the only locality where decent folk do not live.* The back listed the games of chance offered and the names of the women available for "social discourse."

The barkeep looked him over, pointed to a large clock on the wall, and said, "You got one half hour before you order another one. Or..." He finished the sentence by indicating the door.

Nate took his beer, sat at a corner table with the rifle propped next to him, and watched the faro dealer pretending not to observe him. He drank slowly and let his eyes drift over the customers. He set the beer down when he felt his hand shaking, still unnerved by the skinning knife carving the air in front of his face.

Soon one of the girls approached carrying a glass of what looked to be whiskey. She set it down on the table and gestured to a gray-haired man seated at the opposite end of the room.

"From Mr. Gorman." She smiled at Nate but wandered away when he chose to ignore her.

Gorman lifted his own drink and smiled benignly. The man seated next to Gorman was younger and swarthy, with heavy brilliantine in his hair. Nate raised the glass in turn but set it down without tasting it. It had a burned-sugar smell that suggested the liquor was something other than whiskey.

A shout in the street pulled his attention to the open door and when he looked back, the gray-haired man was standing next to the table.

"You don't like our good old Nongela?" Gorman asked.

Nate looked at the glass and back up at the man. "Mr. Gorman, I don't usually drink whiskey this time of day. But I thank you."

"Call me Sam. May I?" He sat in the chair opposite and leaned his elbows on the table in a friendly way. He crooked a thumb over his shoulder. "My partner and I have a bet going. Pierre thinks you're a policeman. A marshal, perhaps. We both agree on your not being from here."

Nate's eyes flicked over Gorman's shoulder, but no one, including Pierre, seemed to have any interest in their conversation.

Gorman waited for a response and, not getting one, continued. "I thought you were a cowboy. But what cowboy carries an English-made Whitworth? They're quite rare, aren't they?"

Nate moved the rifle closer to his chair.

Gorman smiled again cordially as though he hadn't seen Nate drop his right hand off the table and onto his belt. "How far away would you say you could hit a target? Six hundred yards? Eight hundred yards?"

"Mr. Gorman," Nate said. "I thank you for the drink, but I'm waiting for someone."

"Someone?" Gorman looked at the serving girl.

Nate shook his head, pushed the beer away, and began to stand.

Gorman held out a restraining hand. "You have an honest face, Mr. ...?"

Nate picked up the rifle and stood holding it in the crook of his arm. After a moment he said, "Cannon."

"Mr. Cannon, you have an honest face. And so do I, which is why I'm so successful at what I do. I'm a confidence man and a burglar. But I'm seventy-five years old and I have tuberculosis. Now, I'm being straightforward with you because I want you to know that I'm going to offer an exchange that might be to your benefit."

He gestured to the chair and Nate sat down again.

"Someone who fought at Spotsylvania told me that the Union's Major General Sedgwick was killed by a sniper with a Whitworth who was positioned a thousand yards away. Do you believe that?"

Nate had heard the story too, but he cocked his head and waited.

"It captured my imagination, Mr. Cannon, and it's a thing that I would like to see before I die."

Nate propped the rifle against the wall again. "And you, being a betting man, might like to make some money on the show as well."

Gorman grinned and leaned across the table. "I know just about everyone there is to know in New Orleans. So there's a good chance I may know your man."

"And you're so sure I'm looking for a man?"

"As sure as I know you're from Texas, Mr. Cannon."

Nate resisted the impulse to return the smile. He said, "It shoots past eight hundred yards."

Gorman turned and faced his partner, nodding. The brilliantined man got up and walked out the door, disappearing into the street.

Nate reached for the whiskey, and as soon as his hand closed around the glass, Gorman placed his palm over the rim, holding it down.

He smiled apologetically as he slid the glass out of Nate's hand. "Don't drink that."

Nate pushed the beer glass away as well and asked, "What's your offer, Mr. Gorman?"

"To give you the whereabouts of your man, and believe me, if he's still in New Orleans, I can find him."

"In exchange for…?"

"Nine hundred and eighty yards."

Gorman's smile had hardened and he tipped his head back in a watchful way. "Nine hundred and eighty yards to your target."

Nate opened his mouth to ask what the target was, but Gorman stood abruptly and motioned courteously for Nate to follow him out onto the street, saying they had but a short way to travel.

"I'm not leaving until I know where we're going."

"Why, to church, Mr. Cannon." Gorman's guileless smile had returned and Nate stared hard at him for a moment, but he finally stood and followed Gorman into the street.

After Nate was assured that his horse and tack would be left entirely unmolested, the two men walked along St. Charles Avenue, passing the gambling places Nate had done his best to ignore on the way to the Buffalo House. He saw the barefoot boy standing in the same doorway as before, gawking at Nate walking alongside Gorman. The boy gave Nate a tentative wave as though greeting a newly useful acquaintance.

Gorman walked at a leisurely pace towards Canal, and when they reached the wide thoroughfare, he turned left, away from the river. To Nate it seemed that every woman, man, and child greeted Gorman in the same friendly, deferential way, as they would any respected elder, and Gorman often stopped for lengthy conversations that, instinct told Nate, were encoded with some deeper meaning.

They skirted the towering statue of Henry Clay, planted in the middle of the common area behind a simple post-and-chain barrier, and moved beyond hotels, inns, restaurants of every description. Gorman turned right at North Rampart Street and, once the noise of Canal Street had faded, began to talk.

"Mr. Cannon, ahead of us lies our destination." He pointed up the street. "The Old Mortuary Church, the oldest church in New Orleans still standing, built to conduct the funerals of swamp-fever victims." He winked at Nate and stepped expertly over a man dead drunk in a doorway, his legs jutting onto the sidewalk.

Nate stepped over the man as well and asked, "What was in that drink you sent me?"

"Neutral spirits, sugar, dried fruit, and tobacco for the bead and sparkle." Gorman touched Nate's elbow to guide him around a vegetable cart. "And, of course, knockout drops of my own design."

When Nate pulled up short, Gorman shrugged. "You would have slept, Mr. Cannon. It wouldn't have killed you, but I would have taken your rifle. I changed my mind when you ignored the girl. I told my partner, Pierre, that you were a man of singular character."

They had come to stand in front of a mission-style church, compactly built with a single spire. Nate followed Gorman inside. The interior was dark, with only a few candles burning, and Nate stopped in the open doorway to let his eyes adjust to the gloom, his hand instinctively going to the pistol grip. The church seemed to be filled to capacity with men and women sitting quietly in the wooden pews or standing against the walls. Their heads all turned expectantly to the door when he walked in, their clothes rustling in one swelling movement.

Gorman's partner, Pierre, stood in the center aisle holding paper and pencil, a basket at his feet filled with coins and paper money. He nodded once solemnly to Nate and then went back to his tallying.

Gorman waved cheerfully to the priest standing by the altar and said, "You're quite a draw, Mr. Cannon." He motioned for Nate to follow him through a small door leading to a narrow passageway.

Nate turned once to look at the crowd dressed in the flamboyant, extravagant manner of whores, jailbirds, bounders, and worse, and he felt Gorman's hand on his shoulder. "You're safer here, son, than in anyplace else in the city, I assure you."

Nate followed Gorman up to the bell tower and stood at the railing, open at all sides, looking at the expanse of the city, and then he gripped the railing, dizzy and winded. Gorman pointed to the river, to the great building works in all directions, and to the towering spire of the St. Louis Cathedral; Nate, who'd thought that Galveston was an impressive town, with its gaslights and railroads and storefronts, abandoned all expectations of ever seeing another city of such monumental scale.

"That is Conti," Gorman said, pointing to the street bisecting Rampart. "It runs in a straight line to the river. Look through your scope to the top of the last building on the right and tell me what you see on the roof."

Nate knelt on one knee, propped the barrel of the Whitworth on the low railing, and sited down the street. Squinting through the scope, he said, "Looks like some kind of bird." It appeared to Nate to be a large statue of a rooster, facing towards him, with a body of tainted copper and a head of what looked to be luridly colored red glass.

"It's a capon," Gorman said. "A castrated rooster. And the man who put it there is one Gaspar Duverje, a man of great wealth and property, with one of the largest plantations right across the river in Algiers. I've had, over the years, occasion to rob him many times." He smiled at Nate and motioned for him to stand again. "I was never caught and he hated me for that. He made it his life's work to exact his revenge, and he tried in numerous ways to do so." He pointed to a scar on his forehead.

"I was married in this church to the most beautiful Creole woman you could imagine. What she lacked in spotless character, she made up for in good-natured enthusiasm. And Gaspar Duverje stole from me the one thing I would have traded everything else to keep. He took her to Paris and she never returned. Shortly after, he had the capon made and shipped at great expense from France and mounted it on that island building, four stories tall, knowing that every time I came up to the bell tower, which I often did, I would see his insult to me.

"The building is guarded night and day, and every other building around it for blocks is one-storied. The distance between this church and the bird is nine hundred and eighty yards. Mr. Cannon, I've schemed for years on how to knock the head off that bird, and the minute I saw your Whitworth, I knew I had my chance. You give me what I want and I promise you, you'll get what you want."

"So all you want me to do is shoot the rooster?"

Gorman nodded and crossed his arms. "If you overshoot the mark, all you'll hit is water."

"And if I undershoot it?"

Gorman shrugged. "New Orleans is a dangerous place, Mr. Cannon. Anyone who lives here accepts that."

Nate thought about how few tries he'd get. His mind told him it was an impossible shot; he'd fired the gun only once at just over six hundred yards, and, though he'd hit the mark, the shot only nicked the outermost edge of the target. There were four hexagonal bullets left for the rifle, but some quiet caution whispered to him to keep one back, even if it meant losing his chance for information on McGill.

"I have only three bullets," he said. "And the farthest target I've hit was six hundred yards. What happens if I miss?"

Gorman shrugged. "I have every confidence in you. However, I have placed quite a sizable bet on your succeeding. If you were to miss, I wouldn't encourage you to stay in New Orleans."

Pierre appeared at the bell-tower door, nodded to Gorman, and then looked expectantly at Nate. There had been a slight morning wind that seemed to be strengthening with the rising temperatures, but in his favor, it was blowing towards the water. The sun was moving westward and before long the reflection off the rooster's head would be a hindrance.

The people in the church had begun spilling onto Conti Street, walking in the direction of the river, their heads turned expectantly towards the church tower at times, as though waiting for some kind of signal.

Gorman said, as though it were an afterthought, "One more thing, Mr. Cannon. If you do manage to hit the target, it will not sit well with Duverje. He's threatened to kill anyone who brings down the rooster."

Nate rubbed a hand across his forehead. "Anything else you want to tell me now to steady my hand? God Almighty," he muttered. He stared out at the crowd, and one man cupped his palms around his mouth and shouted up at the bell tower, "Go on, you son of a bitch, I've got money riding on this here."

He looked back at Gorman. "You'll find my man?"

Gorman nodded once and Nate cleared his throat, saying, "All right, then. I need a runner to get my cartridge pack off my saddle. I'll want some bunting tied to the railing to cradle the barrel, and a rug to kneel on. And some water. I need some water."

Pierre turned and called down the bell-tower stairs, where a chorus of voices repeated the instructions and Nate realized that there were people lining the stairwell, passing information like a fire brigade handing along buckets of sand.

Folded rugs were placed at Nate's feet, and cotton packing covered with a cloth—an ornate strip of embroidery that Nate suspected had been taken from the altar—was lashed to the railing, a sloping V couched in the middle. Within twenty minutes a boy had brought his cartridge pack, and Nate carefully measured out the powder and poured it down the barrel. He started to ramrod the wadding down the bore, but thought better of it and added more grains of black powder. He tamped down the stiff wadding, loaded the bullet, and fitted a percussion cap onto the nipple.

He took his position and sighted down the scope at his target. He took a few deep breaths, pulled the hammer back, squeezed the air out of his lungs, and fired. When the smoke cleared, the rooster's head was still intact, and Nate had no idea how far he had deviated from the target, whether above it or to the side. He didn't think he had undershot the mark, as he could see no damage to the building below the roofline.

Deerling had once told him that the side scope sometimes influenced the shooter to drag to the left at the moment of firing, so after he repeated the loading process, he edged the centering reticle a thread's distance to the right. He stared at the target until his open eye began to water and then he squeezed off another shot. Again, the clearing air showed the rooster intact.

He looked up at Gorman, who was staring at him, expressionless. Nate stood to stretch and loosen the muscles in his neck and shoulder, and he drank deeply from the glass of water left for him.

The sun had moved farther across the sky and Nate could see the rooster's head beginning to glow like a whorehouse beacon, the faceted glass reflecting light in reddish flares. He thought about his next shot and whether he should use the fourth bullet if he missed.

He reloaded, knelt at the railing, and propped the barrel onto the padding. He exhaled until he felt the bellows of his lungs played out, pulled off another shot, and heard the distant dull ping, barely audible, of the bullet hitting something solid. When the smoke cleared, there was a jagged hole in the rooster's body, but the head remained, and Nate cursed and dropped his head below the stock that was still pressed against his shoulder. He cupped his forehead in one hand, feeling what little grace he had left hopelessly lost against the enormousness of the city below and the task set before him.

From the corner of his eye, he saw Gorman lean down and place something on the rug next to him, and when he looked, there were three more hexagonal bullets.

"The man from Spotsylvania didn't have the rifle," Gorman said. "But he did manage to part with these. For a price."

"You've had the bullets the whole time?"

"You're not a cardplayer, are you, Mr. Cannon."

Gorman leaned against the railing once again, waiting, and Nate struggled to dampen the anger that rode his frustration and tension like barbs on a tight wire.

Gorman said, "I imagine your shots have begun to claim some attention." He pointed to the distant building, and when Nate looked through the scope again, he saw two men with rifles on the roof, one with a spyglass pointed in his direction.

Nate had used so much black powder for the last three shots that he told Gorman he'd have to clean the rifle bore so it wouldn't foul. He quickly cleaned the gun while Gorman stood impassively looking out towards the river, the people in the streets craning their necks up to the tower, trying to make sense of the delay.

Nate deliberated for a moment and then loaded a hundred grains of powder into the barrel, ten more grains than the last shot. To his great relief, the new bullet fit down the bore as well as the old, and when he had seated the cap onto the nipple, he raised the barrel once more to the railing. The view from the scope showed Nate that the spyglass man on the target building had seen him take his shooter's position, and the man frantically waved his partner down, out of sight.

The sometimes buffeting wind had paused. Nate had heard no sounds from the street since a woman's loud laughter was cut off midbreath with a sharp and exuberant curse. Deerling had once told him regarding the Whitworth not to think about the distance being traversed, that his common sense would try to tell him that it couldn't reasonably be done. But he reminded Nate that the gun was made for distance, like a good relay horse was made for long travel, and to imagine the bullet as a thought flying easy and sure to his beloved, though the beloved be far away.

He fired off the Whitworth and a second later heard a faint sound like the scattering of leaves, and, without waiting for confirmation, Gorman pulled a white handkerchief from his breast pocket and waved it to the crowd below. Conti Street erupted with cheering and yells, and Nate saw that the number of specta-tors had grown to fill the avenue like an invading army. He stood up, still holding the Whitworth, his knees and hip popping like corn out of hot coals. He turned away from the street and Gor-man nodded, smiling his gentleman's smile, and extended his arm to the bell-tower door.

Nate followed behind Pierre, who cleared a way through the people standing two abreast on the stairwell, and, with Gorman at his back, they walked out of the church onto the street, where the bounders and footpads clapped him on the back and the whores pressed his hand warmly and whispered into his ear things he couldn't quite make out above the swelling noise and confusion.

He was taken to a nearby saloon, and a whiskey was pressed into his hand, which he quickly drank. And then he drank an-other, and another, all the while accepting with a growing sense of amazement the sly, excitable good wishes of Gorman's ever-expanding street court, all of them assuring Nate he was now one of their own. When Gorman finally asked him the name of the man he sought, Nate shouted into his ear, "William McGill," and told him about Lucinda traveling with him. Gorman turned his head away for a moment but finally nodded and moved off.

A fiddle, and then a squeezebox, began to scratch and wheeze above the din and he later remembered dancing with a woman, his feet moving faster than his lagging mind, until his knees could not support his weight and Gorman guided him to the door, signal-ing to a girl to take him home. Nate thought that home sounded like a good idea and staggered behind her for several blocks before thinking to ask her whose home he was going to. The girl put one of his arms around her shoulders and guided him into a small, one-story house, the front door unlocked, the two rooms modest and tidy.

She sat him on a chair and knelt in front of him to take off his boots, and he took her chin in his hand and raised her high-cheeked face to the light.

He asked her who her people were and she said she was Caddo. He then told her that his wife was Cherokee, and the girl nodded as though the revelation were only right and proper. She unpinned her hair and moved him to sit on the bed. But he took her arms to stay her movements and asked if she would sit on the chair for a while, just so he could look at her. She slipped down her petticoat, baring herself to the waist, and he could vaguely see the small globes of her breasts behind the black hair that fell over them.

When the yearning to touch her became too terrible to bear, he mumbled his thanks and lay on the floor, his back to her. Through the girl he was able to summon the image of his wife under lamplight: the particulars of her features, her softly rounded moon face, and the jet hair that cloaked her shoulders falling straight as rain.

He finally closed his eyes to sleep, and sometime in the middle of the night, the girl rose up and covered him with a blanket.

Chapter 27

The staircase was wide and curving, made of marble and carpeted down the middle with a runner of majestic blue. Lucinda stood at the top of the stairs holding a small tin box in one hand and gripping the banister tightly with the other. She had purposely set her naked feet on the exposed marble, hoping its brittle chill could distract her from the recent memory of what had been done to her body—what she had allowed to be done—and her growing anxiety coiled and uncoiled in her stomach like a worm.

She shivered inside her nightdress, tissue thin and stained with sweat that was not her own, preparing to place one foot down the riser, and the memory of standing atop Mrs. Landry's stairwell slid into her mind. That moment, too, had been a supposed beginning, a stepping from one life into another. She had made an expert copy of the German's key from an impression scored into a thin bar of soap in a tin box, just like the impression she had made of the key belonging to her fish, the key that opened the front door to the house with the curving marble staircase.

Clutching the banister, she followed the first step with a second, but she could go no farther until she slowed her breathing, bringing her mind into sharper focus, ignoring the pain of the abraded flesh on her buttocks and thighs. She had had no fall for days now, but she felt clenched and ragged, as though a new kind of sickness had seeped into her pores along with the damp and the cold.

It seemed to her that everything of import in New Orleans had been built of marble: the monuments, the interiors of the mansions that lined First Street, the mausoleums in the cemeteries. To stand within a marble hall was to be comforted by the exquisite coolness of the veined white stone. But to Lucinda, looking across the grand foyer of the house, with its marble floors and columns, softly luminous in the lamplight, it now gave her the feeling of being entombed alive.

She moved her hand down the banister, her feet following suit another few steps until she stood at the midway point. She heard a door open somewhere on the second landing and she gripped the tin box until its edges broke through the skin of her palm, like a shard of metal piercing a crust of ice, and then the door closed again and she realized it was Tartine using the water closet. Minutes passed and there were no further sounds.

She padded softly to the bottom of the stairs, and though the servants had all been sent away, she peered through the darkened foyer for any moving shadows. A sudden cramping in her abdomen caused her to double over in pain, and she stared at a pinpoint of blood at her feet before realizing that the hand holding the tin box had been cut.

A hollow sensation began building in her head, and pressing her injured palm with the bottom of her shift, she leaned against a column and closed her eyes. This, then, was the moment that had been approaching since the day William McGill lay with her in her bed staring into her face, which was contorted and grinning in a stricture of pain like a death's-head mask, promising to care for her as long as she remained loyal. She had never asked the cost of that loyalty; had never wanted to know. He was the one person who, in the moments of confronting her waking terrors, would not turn away, did not shun or pity her. He would hold her more closely, in those unmarginned spans of time, peering readily into her eyes as they stared unfocused and vacant towards the ceiling.

It was more than anyone else had ever done—more than her own father—and now the bill for the partnership had come due. Her belly cramped again and she clutched the tin more tightly.

Bill would take the impression she had made and fashion a key that would gain him access to the very house in which she stood. He would rob her fish, silently and expertly, taking all the jewelry and gold he could carry in one large carpetbag. Then they would leave for Atlanta, or St. Louis, or some other city of their choosing.

Her spine, pressed against the marble column, began to ache, and she tried to remember the last time she'd felt something other than cold. Her mind summoned an image from Middle Bayou: lying close to May in a hay field on a warm afternoon, the girl's arms around her neck, her body expressive with the heat of youth and perfect health.

She pushed herself off the column and made her way carefully across the foyer. She slipped the bolt, twisted the brass knob, and opened the heavy door, stepping to one side as she did so, but the space remained unfilled by the expected form, and she moved out onto the darkened porch. She heard her name called softly once and saw the glow of a cigar in the crape myrtles fronting the house.

Lucinda eased the door closed and moved shivering into the deeper shadows of the trees, her hands clasped around her arms. She saw Bill reach out with one hand as though to touch her face, but his fingers closed around her throat and he shoved her hard against the wall.

He said, "Keep me waiting like that again and I will hurt you in ways you can't even imagine."

She handed him the tin box and he pocketed it. "Tomorrow is the night," he said. He looked at her stained shift and shivering form and whispered forcefully, "You know, Tartine says she's never been sick a day in her life. Stay the course, Lucy, or I'll be taking her to St. Louis in your stead."

He turned and walked quickly along the avenue, soon disappearing into a poorly lit alley.

Lucinda stood against the wall, which was colder by far than the marble column of the house, with her head tilted back, looking at the sky, sensing the sweat and the deeper wetness of the blood on her shift being lifted away by the wind. She considered for a time remaining propped against the stones until all the parts of her vital self were likewise evaporated into the air, leaving behind only the shell. But after a time she roused herself and walked back into the house.

Chapter 28

Nate woke to a whitewashed room and a prolonged pounding on the door, which was eventually answered by the black-haired girl. He sat up rubbing the shoulder that had been pressed to the floor all night and saw the barefoot boy walking across the threshold as though familiar with the house and its owner.

He nodded to Nate but cut his eyes away in a nervous reflex, jamming both arms stiffly into the pockets of his trousers. He said, "Mr. Gorman is waiting for you. He says come now."

Nate got up and began folding the blanket he had slept in when the girl shook her head and took it from him. He gathered up his hat, fit the Dance into his belt, and followed the boy outside. He had a thought that he should pay the girl something for the evening, but she had already closed and bolted the door and so he followed the boy back towards St. Charles Avenue. He squinted against the light and asked, "What time is it? And where's my horse and rifle?"

The boy spit. "It's past noon. And your gun and horse are with Mr. Gorman."

Nate followed the boy for a few blocks, and after watching

him nervously scanning the streets, Nate took hold of him by the shoulder and asked, "Something you need to tell me?"

The boy licked his lips, his eyes restless and searching. "Mr. Gorman says to come on…"

A cold, smattering mist had started falling and Nate pulled up his collar against the chill. He kept a close eye on the thoroughfares, though he wouldn't have known which of the pinched or restless faces signaled a threat until it had crawled up his back.

The boy led him to the Buffalo House and Nate saw that its porch was filled with half a dozen men who wore their pistols exposed to both the elements and passersby. A few also had Enfield rifles held in the crooks of their arms. The boy chucked his chin for Nate go on inside and then he vanished into the street crowd. Gorman was sitting at the same table as the day before, and Pierre stood up, his face as shuttered as a bank window, and gestured for Nate to take his chair before wandering back to the faro table.

Gorman gestured to Nate's face. "You've got a black eye."

Nate touched the tender flesh and said, "From the recoil on the Whitworth, I guess."

Gorman waved to a serving girl and she brought to the table steak and eggs and coffee.

Nate took off his hat. "Those men out there because of me?"

"Everyone in New Orleans has heard of your shot." Gorman smiled tightly. "Duverje has his men looking for you." He eased a small bundle wrapped in paper across the table in front of Nate. "You embarrassed my enemy and made a lot of money for me, Mr. Cannon."

Nate pushed the bundle away. "I don't need that. I just need to know where McGill is."

Gorman poured a cup of coffee for himself and took his time blowing it cool. "There have been of late some unexplained killings in the district. Men murdered and robbed in alleyways and on dark streets. Their throats slit. I think it may be your man McGill, though it's unusual for a man-killer of his ilk to change his tactics. From what I've been told, he likes to gut-shoot his victims."

Nate started to eat from his plate, nodding tensely in agreement.

"McGill is here, I can tell you that, but no one has seen him since he brought a girl, your girl, to Hattie Hamilton's sporting palace. The girl has not shown up for several days, but Hattie believes she and McGill are working a game to bilk one of her regular clients. The mark, if he's still alive, will not remain that way much longer."

Nate thumbed his plate away. "Where is this client?"

Gorman paused for a moment, seemingly to study the pattern on the coffee cup. He said, "Better than most, I understand the desire for settling disputes in a more time-honored fashion. The war robbed us of a great many things, but one thing we in New Orleans mourn the loss of, perhaps more than anything else, is the ritual for regaining our pride. McGill certainly does not respect those rules, but I believe you do."

Gorman set down his cup.

"Therefore, I will admit to certain grandfatherly feelings towards you, Mr. Cannon. And I will tell you in all earnestness that instead of encountering McGill face to face, you should shoot him in the back. Lie in wait for him in the dark if you must, because if you don't, he will be the one to kill you."

Gorman propped his elbows on the table and leaned closer. "I will tell you that as much influence as I may have over some of my people here, I have very little over the police, even the ones I pay. There is also the complication now of Duverje, who does not put too fine a point on honor."

Gorman gestured to the serving girl and she brought a bottle of brandy and poured some into both cups. "You should stay here until dark. Then the boy will take you to Hattie's. You'll have until first light tomorrow to find McGill and do what you came to do. After that, you must leave; for your own safety, and because those men out there are costing me a small fortune. You'll get back your rifle and horse once you're on the boat for Galveston. You'll not see me again, I'm afraid, Mr. Cannon. But I wish you *bonne chance.*"

He walked out of the Buffalo House and disappeared into the street, and Nate passed the afternoon drinking coffee until he felt his hands shaking when he loaded fresh powder into the Dance. He sat watching the clock and the people that wandered in and out of the Buffalo House, some of them to find a drink or a girl, some of them to take a turn at cards. He suspected more than a few had come to gawk at him while passing pleasantries with Pierre, even placing bets on whether or not he would make it onto the steamer the following day. He tried to find a place of rage or even grief that he could sharpen his intent on, but in the well-ordered and functional arena that was the Buffalo House, the best he could find was a kind of nervous expectation.

The barefoot boy appeared at his table just after dark, and he led Nate past the armed men—who nodded to him with a kind of professional wariness—into the rain-swollen alleyways of

Canal. They weaved their way through the numberless outhouses, stables, and sheds of Basin Street to Hattie Hamilton's palace. He pointed for Nate to go in through the front door and then leaned against the gate in an attitude of alert waiting, hands in pockets, one bare foot cocked over the other.

The entranceway to the sporting house was flanked by two life-size statues of disrobed women, each holding in her outstretched hands live gas torches, and Nate followed after a man in evening dress, surprised that the door was not locked but rather opened readily on its oiled hinges.

The reception hall led to a grand parlor the likes of which Nate had never before witnessed. Seated on velvet couches and satin chairs were women of such confounding, artful beauty, their near nakedness reflected in infinite tides through the gilt mirrors filling every wall, that Nate was stunned to immobility, and a feeling of confined desperation swelled in him when several of the women looked in his direction and smiled through parted lips.

He removed his hat, and a shadowed motion caused Nate to turn. A tall black man had come to stand at one shoulder, but before Nate could take a step back, the man placed a restraining hand on Nate's right arm. The man's other hand was hidden under his long coat, gripping what Nate was certain was a knife concealed in the waistband of his trousers.

He said, "No guns allowed, sir."

The man relinquished his hold on Nate's arm, and Nate handed him the Dance. The man pointed up the stairs. "Miss Hattie will see you directly."

Nate walked across the parlor, his boots striking loudly on the marble floor, conscious of the women and their customers watch-

ing him with hooded eyes. Before he had stepped onto the first
riser, a woman joined him and led him up to the second floor.
Her dress, what there was of it, was nearly transparent and cinched
broadly with a corset of scarlet whalebone, the back laces falling
between the curved, swaying cheeks of her backside. Nate took a
steadying intake of air, breathing in the musk of her body, and he
let her gain a few steps before following after her again. She led
him to a door, opened it, and gestured for him to go in alone.

He walked into a spacious room, heated with an elaborately
painted corner stove, and saw a large rawboned woman smoking
a small cigar seated at a man's desk, both her feet propped up on
a tufted stool. She rested her elbow on the desk, and gestured for
him to sit in a chair facing her.

She looked him over and tipped the ashes of the cigar into a
crystal bowl. She said, "Sam has asked me to help you find someone."

She squinted at him for a minute through the smoke and Nate
heard the door open and close behind him, and he sensed, without seeing, that the tall black man had stepped softly into the
room.

"What will you do when you find him?" she asked.

"I'm going to kill him," he said. "Given the chance."

She ducked her mule's jaw into her neck and smiled at him in
a way that might at one time have been considered coy. "What
makes you think Bill hasn't offered me a lot of money to keep that
from happening?"

For the first time, Nate saw a Colt on the desk within arm's
reach, and he calculated the likelihood of his reaching the gun before the madam could. She was as big as a man, and from the size

of her thighs and shoulders, he guessed her reflexes might be as quick as a man's as well. Nate listened for movement from behind but heard nothing.

"He has, you know," she said, brushing more ashes into the bowl. "Offered me money to be his eyes and ears. Quite a bit of money." She drew on the cigar and waited.

Nate reached into the pocket of his jacket and tossed a coin onto the desk as he stood up, saying, "You might as well go ahead and take all your clothes off. A whore is usually naked when she's diddling with a man."

He heard the rushing footfalls of the black man approaching, but Hattie yelped with laughter and held up one hand to stay him. She waved Nate down again and wiped at her streaming eyes with the back of one hand. She said, "When you get to my age and stage in life, you can't put a price on peace of mind. I want William McGill gone. He's bad for business. He scares the customers. And he ruins my girls."

Nate said, "And he scares you as well, doesn't he? Which I'm guessing is not easy to do."

Hattie's mouth tightened, and Nate jerked a thumb over one shoulder. "Why don't you send your man to do the job?"

"I need Lucius here. He never leaves this place." She said it with her chin raised, as though Nate would challenge her.

"Then it's on me." Nate stood up again. "You know where McGill is?"

"I know where he's going to be. McGill's girl is setting up a client to be robbed tonight. I'll tell you where the client is, but I want something in return for it. Or, rather, I want something returned to me that's mine. Lucinda has a contract to fulfill."

"A contract," Nate said.

Hattie stood up and came around the desk to face him. "I invest quite a bit in my working girls, Mr. Cannon. I want her brought back here afterwards."

"She's going back with me to Texas."

She shook her head. "It never fails: a man with a stiff prick always wants to rescue a whore."

"I've never even met the woman."

She crossed her arms, propping one meaty thigh on the corner of the desk. "Goddamn me," she muttered. She cut her eyes to Lucius and then back to Nate, as though making a decision. "My loss, then. The client's house is on First Street. Number twenty-three."

Nate put on his hat and turned to face Lucius, who stood barring the door.

Hattie waved the black man away. "Mr. Cannon," she said. "One last thing. The client requested another of my girls earlier today. She should have returned by now. I'd go in wary if I was you."

Lucius followed Nate down the stairs and across the grand parlor, the big man making no more noise on the marble floor than a woman in evening slippers. He opened the front door, his face as expressionless and smooth as the statues fronting the entranceway. He handed Nate his pistol and closed the weighted door.

Chapter 29

*L*ucinda was alone with the man in the bed, which was massive and ornate, like the rest of the furniture in the room. A fine sheen of sweat covered his naked pale body. He was blindfolded with a silk handkerchief, his hands tied to the elaborate headboard with soft leather straps. He told her to stand closer and described how he wanted her to touch him. He began his customary rhythmic grunting as she stroked him, muttering for her to slow down or speed up or grasp him more firmly.

She turned her head towards the door, looking for Tartine to return. As much as she hated the woman, her presence made the time spent with the fish less frightening, less repugnant. What she had experienced in the past few hours was something she could never have imagined in even her most depraved moments. She thought of his flesh under her hands and envisioned gouging the skin with her nails the way her own flesh had been peeled away by the leather straps.

It could not be much longer before Bill would slip into the house and take his pick of the rare, jeweled objects that lay scattered about, the money carelessly piled on the man's desk, and then she could put on her clothes and leave.

The man shifted impatiently under her touch and she worked her hands more forcefully and he exhaled with pleasure.

She pulled her thoughts away from the room and thought of Bill and his erratic treatment of her the past few days. She had known for some time that he was a killer but had willed herself to believe that it had always been in self-defense. Just as she had willed her mind to separate his charm from his character, his facile warmth from his cold efficiency, his ready passions from his utter incapability to feel love or even liking for another.

But he had cared for *her*, had promised her that he always would—until her disobedience regarding May, and his discovery that there was no gold in Middle Bayou. His coldness and threats had worsened ever since. Even her recent illness had made him impatient and distant. Her constant need for reassurances was weakening her and pushing him farther away.

She again looked impatiently towards the door and saw a form in the doorway that was not Tartine. It was a man lingering in the half-light of the hallway. At first she thought it was one of the servants loitering, spying on them, but the man stepped into the room and she saw it was Bill.

He quickly put a finger to his lips and she continued stroking the man on the bed, but she was suddenly acutely aware of her own dirty, matted hair, the film of old sweat on her face and body, the scratches on her arms with their ugly crisscrossing patterns. Bill watched her at work, his eyes as steady and emotionless as a serpent's, and then the features of his face changed. A look of distaste, even disgust, shadowed his mouth, and in that moment she knew he was going to leave her.

She had become motionless, staring at Bill, and the fish shifted on the bed and said, "Don't stop. I didn't tell you to stop."

Bill pulled a long slender object from his pocket, and as he approached the bed, the object caught the light and resolved itself into a folding shaver's blade, which he opened gracefully in one fluid movement. He slipped it into Lucinda's hand and closed her palm over the handle with both of his hands, and when she looked at it there was already blood drying on the blade.

Pushing Lucinda onto the bed, Bill leaned over her and whispered, "Do it. Prove to me you'll do anything for me."

The fish, startled by the sudden pressure on the bed, began to protest. Bill quickly removed the blindfold, and, seeing the intruder, the man began to scream.

Lucinda, crouching on the bed, looked at the blade, unable to move. Bill knelt behind her, reached around, and grasped her hand in his own with a crushing grip to guide her movements. He directed the blade at the fish's throat and made a rapid, sweeping pass. The fish stopped screaming in that instant, his eyes wide in terror, and began thrashing violently, a thin wash of blood starting to seep through the shallow wound.

She could feel Bill's breath in her ear and he said to her, "Look at him."

But she closed her eyes, her hand still gripped tightly in Bill's own, the bed bucking with the fish's struggles, and he made another pass with the blade and she felt it catch and progress haltingly, as though it were cutting through something denser than flesh. She felt the warm wash of blood over her hands, but still she kept her eyes closed, heard Bill's voice saying, "Look at him...*look at him.*"

The fish still hadn't begun screaming again, but he thrashed weakly, his legs kicking for a surprisingly short time.

Her head fell back onto Bill's chest, his work now done; their hands rested quietly together on his thighs, the movement of his chest deep and even and satisfied, as after their lovemaking.

When she finally opened her eyes, it was to stare up at the large canopy overhead, the parallel lines of the struts, intersected by cross supports, looking near perfect in their execution, and she soundlessly recited, *If a transversal line cuts across parallel lines at right angles it is called a perpendicular transversal...*

Her breathing calmed and she rested awhile in a vacant, cool place.

Chapter 30

*I*t had begun to rain in earnest, but the boy was where Nate had left him. They came to Canal Street, where the boy hailed a carriage with a whistle and Nate followed him into its dark swaying interior. Nate had never been in such a covered carriage before and he felt it undignified, the conveyance somehow feminine, and it sharpened rather than diminished his sense of exposure. But he was soon glad to be out of the rain, the trip being too far a distance to cover quickly on foot. The carriage moved down St. Charles Avenue, and once the boy pointed to a group of armed men just exiting a saloon.

"Duverje's men, looking for you," he said.

The carriage turned back towards the river on First Street but pulled over after a short distance when the boy leaned out the window and told the driver to stop. He instructed Nate to pay the fare and they stepped onto a street lined with gaslights and large houses tucked behind lush growths of still-green magnolia and live oak.

There were few walkers and even fewer carriages, and the boy moved without hesitation across the street to a two-story columned house. They stood beneath a dense stand of crape myrtles and the boy looked at Nate expectantly.

Nate scanned the second-floor balcony for any open doors but everything seemed closed tight, the windows shuttered and dark. The front of the house was elevated from the ground by a few shallow stairs and, though it was exposed to the street, Nate realized that there were no lights coming from the front windows either, leaving the narrow porch deeply shadowed. A steep brick wall encircled the back of the house, but enough trees grew alongside it to aid anyone wishing to scale the barrier.

He looked up and down the deserted street and whispered to the boy, "What's your name?"

"Alger."

"I need you to try and scale that wall, circle round to the back, and see if any doors are unlocked." He grabbed Alger's collar and brought the boy's face up close to his own. "And Alger, you stay in the shadows. You see any movement, you take off, hear?"

The boy nodded and disappeared into the blackness along the side of the house, his bare feet making no sound on the soaked earth. He easily gained a toehold on a magnolia tree and climbed effortlessly up the lowest branches, then dropped to the far side of the wall.

Nate hunkered down, uncertain how and when McGill would approach the house. He had a good view of the street from both directions within the stand of trees, which were dense enough to keep him from being observed from anyone inside the house as well. The wall surrounding the back garden made it difficult for a man to get in unless the back gate had been left open or unlocked, but still, there was no guarantee that while he kept a vigil at the front of the house, McGill wouldn't gain entry from the back.

The rain pelted first one side of the street and then the other, as though poured from a sweeping, celestial watering can, and the earth and the rotting leaves blanketing it had a keen, wasting odor, like coffee grounds boiled in fish oil, so unlike the astringent, metallic scent of the desert of West Texas or the peppery fragrance of the Big Thicket to the east. It was the smell of long unattended decay, of people living too near one another; the effluvia of extravagant wastefulness.

The minutes passed and the boy still did not reappear. The house remained silent and Nate shifted in restless anxiety with a feeling of worsening dread taking hold in his chest. He stood, determined to follow the boy over the wall, when a hazy figure on the porch caught his eye. The boy had emerged from the opposite side of the house. He paused once, as though listening for sounds, the cameo of his pale face contrasting sharply with the surrounding shadows. He crept to the door and pressed one ear to it before grabbing the knob and twisting it. The door opened easily, and, turning once to signal Nate to come on, he slipped inside.

"Shitfire," Nate said. He yanked the Dance from his belt and ran, sliding in the mud, for the porch stairs. Quickly scanning the streets, he gained the porch in a few steps, and then stood to one side of the door frame. He took a breath and stepped into the entranceway, his shooting arm extended, the gun cocked. It was dark in the hallway but a lamp was lit to the far side, next to a curving staircase. Alger stood motionless within the halo of light, his back to Nate, looking at something on the floor.

Nate remained still for a moment, listening for any sounds that were not their own, and then toe-heeled his way towards the lamp-light. He grabbed Alger around his chest, pushed the boy behind him, and saw what was on the ground. It was a woman seated against the wall, her arms at her sides, her legs sprawled and un-bent, the toes of her red-and-white-stockinged feet turned out like a dancer's. Her head was bowed, as though in prayer, and a solid sheet of drying blood had flowed down her bosom and around her body like a cape carelessly thrown.

Keeping an eye to the stairs, Nate uncocked the hammer on the Dance, knelt down, and pulled at the woman's hair, tipping her head back and exposing the slit in her throat, which opened like a gaping mouth. There was no mole under the eye identifying her as Lucinda, and he guessed it was Hattie's missing girl.

He dropped her head, stood, and grabbed Alger by the back of his neck. He shook the boy and whispered, "You get out of here. Wait for me in those trees. If I'm not out in fifteen minutes, go get help."

"From where—" the boy started, but Nate gave him a push and Alger ran, skating once on the wet marble, and slipped out the door.

Nate moved to the bottom of the stairs, straining his ears for anything to indicate someone else alive in the house. Hugging the wall, he moved up the steps onto the second floor and saw lamp-light from an open door at the end of the hall. There were no sounds, no winking eclipses onto the carpet thrown by someone moving in front of the lamp. He walked carefully to the door, in-haled, and moved gun-first into the room.

It was a bedroom containing a massive canopied bed, its heavy satin covers spilling onto the floor; lying motionless on its sheets was a bulging form, fish-belly white. He approached cautiously, his shooting arm testing the room, and saw that it was a man, spread-eagled and naked, his throat cut raggedly from ear to ear. On the far side of the bed was a standing mirror, and a wan oval shape reflected in the glass composed itself into a face with staring eyes.

He wheeled around and saw in the corner opposite the bed a woman painted in blood, her dark hair wild around her head, her knees drawn up defensively to her chest. He held the gun on her for a moment, but her eyes remained fixed and unblinking and he knelt down, placing his cheek close to her mouth and nose, feeling for breath.

He felt nothing and pulled his face back to check for the identifying mark that would prove she was Deerling's daughter. He looked in her eyes and with a jolt realized that they were now focused with calm lucidity on his own. A rasping sound from behind caused him to turn, and before he felt the blow to the side of his head, he reflexively discharged his revolver, then lay in a throbbing, half-aware state.

He was rolled onto his back, the Dance taken from his grasp, and when his vision cleared, he was looking at the man from the Lynchburg ferry crossing, now beardless and without spectacles. McGill smiled in a genial way, and Nate remembered the liking he had felt for the man, the sense of immediate kinship with a well-spoken and sympathetic traveler.

McGill hunkered down next to him, holding the gun casually, loosely, and said, "Hello, Officer."

Nate started to sit up and McGill shook his head. He said, "That shot may or may not be answered. New Orleans has such a shocking disregard for the sounds of violence. Nonetheless, I shall be brief. I admire your tenacity. It took courage to follow me into a darkened house. But it was very foolish.

"You now have two choices. I can shoot you, and if I do so, you will die slowly and painfully. Or I can cut your throat, which will be quicker, but I can't speak to the pain." He smiled brightly and made a sweeping motion across his throat. "Neither could my most recent encounter. Severs the speech organ, you see."

Nate raised his head and looked at Lucinda, whose eyes had returned to their glassy unresponsiveness. The blow had fractured his thoughts, but it was McGill's effortless affability, driving the flow of events swiftly and cheerfully before him, like trained sheep to a corral, that made his stomach clench and heave. Nate said, "There will be others coming."

"No. I think you are quite alone." McGill waggled the gun like a finger. "I will give you a few more minutes to decide. Otherwise, I'll have to choose for you." He raised the pistol, pointed it at Nate, midbelly. "I'm sure your partner would have decided on the latter, given the opportunity. How long did it take him to die? I'll bet it took more than a few hours." He stood then and dragged a small dressing chair a safe distance from Nate. He sat and crossed his legs comfortably, brushing lint from his pants with his fingertips.

"Have you ever pondered your own death, Nate?" he asked. "Not death in the abstract, but the final, inevitable moment when you are confronted with the rushing formlessness of what's coming next. How is it, do you think, that we have the will to live from day to day through the horrors of life when at the same time we are eaten away by the suspicion, or even the certainty, that after death there is only the eternal black hole?"

He rested his elbows on his knees, holding the gun between his two palms. "I think this deluded belief in an afterlife comes from God. Oh, I believe in God. Or, rather, a kind of god: a malevolent spirit, a trickster that rests in the mind like a disease and whispers to us that we do not stop but continue on in some kind of fever dream in the beyond."

He gestured towards Lucinda. "Ask Lucy what she has seen after returning from some blasted wasteland of nonbeing. Nothing. Absolutely nothing!" He laughed and settled back into the chair. His expression grew contemplative. "In every infected mind, on every dying face, resides the stubborn hope that somehow one's *aliveness* will not end. The constancy of this belief is astonishing, and really quite maddening. But I am the extinguisher of that hope."

He stood up and pulled the chair to one side. "Do you know what I did during the war? I was an engineer, a builder. And yet, all my accomplishments—the roads, the bridges, the aqueducts—were seemingly pointless compared to the lauded feats of our butchers in the field. I killed not one person in a battle, but now I am the hunted man." He cocked the trigger and aimed, shutting one eye in an exaggerated stance.

"It's what I would call the greatest of social ironies." His finger pulled the trigger, but the hammer remained fixed; there was no resulting blast, and Nate realized before McGill did that the thing that Dr. Tom had warned him about repeatedly had happened. The cap from the previous shot had split and fouled in the cylinder.

With that thought came the desperate reflex to move, but a face, haloed in dark hair, appeared behind McGill's shoulder, and an outstretched arm pointed towards McGill's head, the hand curled with graceful fingers around something small and metallic. A dull popping noise was followed by an explosive scattering of the top of McGill's forehead, and he went rigid, falling to the side opposite the concussion. He convulsed for a short time and Lucinda stood and watched, the Remington remaining in her hand, until Nate could stand and yank it from her grasp.

Her lips were moving as though still in conversation with the dead man when Nate pulled back his fist to strike her, fear still coursing through his body. The remembrances of Tom's final hours, of the German woman with the murdered children, made him not want to kill her so much as obliterate her, reduce her vacant features and slackened body to an unrecognizable heap.

Instead, he slowly unclenched his fist and took her hand, seeing for the first time that the blood matting her nightdress did not appear to be her own and most likely came from the man on the bed. He led her down the stairs and out the door, where the boy was waiting for them, still keeping vigil in the stand of sodden crape myrtles.

Chapter 31

The boy took them to a shotgun shack on Pirate's Alley, saying that Duverje's men had taken up spying positions around the Buffalo House and along Canal. It was rumored that the men had orders to shoot Nate on sight, but the boy assured him that they would be safe in the house until the morning.

Nate sat by the door, unable to rest fully, and he jerked awake whenever his head began to nod into sleep. At times he watched Lucinda, lying on a nearby pallet, wearing a clean day dress brought by Alger. But her eyelids remained closed and motionless, like a person gone from the world. He had seen her eyes dim following the shooting, and he suspected she was not truly sleeping but rather retreating from the knowledge of her lover's death, shrouding her awareness in the dark like a coal sled being shoved down into a mine.

Alger sat next to him, keeping the hours by whispering a story he had been told of Jean Lafitte's time in New Orleans and of how he had hidden gold coins within the bricks of the very buildings lining Pirate's Alley.

Nate asked the boy if he thought the stories were true. The boy regarded him with his young-old face and answered that it hardly mattered whether they were true or not. That people would trail after the merest rumor of gold, cleaving to their worst inclinations, like the inevitable and uncontrollable shakes following a strong fever.

After that, the boy was quiet and Nate spent the remainder of the darkened hours listening to the night's thunder and rain, rolling like bands of siege artillery in the far distance, and counting the number of miles he had traveled, beginning in Franklin months ago, and the number of bodies given to the earth in search of a treasure that most likely didn't exist. That he should spend his last night in New Orleans in a place called Pirate's Alley was a thing he was sure Dr. Tom would have appreciated.

Dr. Tom had once told him that no matter how purposeful a course a man chose for himself, time and circumstance would choose their own path and would, like unseen authors, rewrite a man's life to suit their own designs. Like Dickens, he had said, pulling Pip out of a perfectly good bed and into a graveyard at night, onto the path of an escaped killer.

From the moment Nate stepped onto the pier, he had certainly felt stripped of his intentions and placed in a narrative that had already been written. Even lying at McGill's feet with his own pistol being pointed at his belly, he had been confounded by happenstance outside of his control, terror-filled and paralyzed by McGill's rant of the nothingness following death.

Alger disappeared at dawn to alert Gorman's men, who would take Nate and Lucinda to the steamer at the docks, but Nate knew that even a regiment escort would not prevent a well-placed shootist on a roof with an unobstructed view from putting a bullet into his skull.

When it was full light, he took hold of Lucinda's arm and shook her awake. Her eyes opened and she sat up, and Nate wondered how much resistance she would put up to their leaving. But she remained seated at the edge of the bed, waiting to be told how and when to move.

Within the hour Alger had returned with Gorman's men in a wagon, and Nate sat next to Deerling's daughter with Alger at his feet, surrounded by armed men. They rumbled down Tchoupitoulas Street towards the pier and they were almost to the docks before he realized that the warehouse workers had collected in the open bay doors as they passed and were watching their progress silently.

A crowd had started to gather, lining both sides of the narrow lane to the steamer docks, and Nate recognized some of the street denizens from the rooster shoot a few days before. The attending pickpockets and thieves were straight-faced and leaden, their necks craned warily towards a cluster of men holding shotguns, blocking the lane, and Nate knew them to be Duverje's.

Someone from the gathering shouted, "Don't worry, we got your back." And another man called out, "Yeah, *waaaay* back."

There was laughter from the crowd until Duverje's men moved forward, halting the wagon's progress, and the driver pulled up on the reins. Nate looked to the ready steamer in its dock not a hundred paces away and recognized Captain Pascal standing on the open deck, watching the crowd.

A small prim man in an expensive, tight-fitting suit stepped to the front of the cadre of armed men and smiled. He pointed at Nate and said, "You and I have something to settle. You destroyed some very valuable property, property that took a lot of time and expense to acquire, and you will repay me. One way or another."

Nate looked towards the docks and then over the swelling numbers of bystanders; he calculated that the crowd had grown to more than a hundred. He turned to one of the men in the wagon. "Where are my horse and rifle?" he asked.

"Mr. Gorman had them placed on the steamer, as promised."

Nate looked again at Duverje and the growing mob of spectators and, pointing to Lucinda, shouted, "I'm a policeman, appointed by the governor of Texas—"

"You are not in Texas now," Duverje interrupted.

Nate stood up. "This is my prisoner and I'm taking her to that steamer. Anyone who obstructs in this will be shot."

"Not if you are shot first," Duverje said.

Nate then removed the Dance from his holster, cocked it, and waited.

The men in the wagon shifted nervously, and then, one by one, they got out and stood some distance away. Duverje's smile began to fade and he moved behind the protective press of his own men.

Nate scanned the surrounding faces again. Gorman had told him that the demimonde had made him one of their own. But the men and women watching him were wary, and no one had made a move to come to his defense.

To the resounding quiet, he dipped his head for a moment, gathering in his mind the roan's epic swim and agonizing climb out of the surf, and then announced, "I'm going home now."

Nate stepped from the wagon and held his hand out to

Lucinda. She stood and was helped down by suddenly solicitous men, awkward with rifles in hand. Holding her wrist with his left hand, he walked purposefully towards the dock, calling for Duverje and his men to move aside. He swiftly approached the lead man, whose gun was leveled, hoping that the man's protective instincts would take hold and he would back away defensively, but the leader just cocked his rifle and raised it to his shoulder.

A sudden shotgun blast sounded from the dock, and the crowd turned as one towards the *Annie Gillette* and the captain on the elevated steering deck, who was holding a rifle leveled at Duverje's men. Pascal called out, "Duverje, I see you, you little coon-ass. You can't hide from where I'm standing."

A single full-throated, harrowing yell, like a lone battle charge, erupted, and a man began pushing his way violently to the front of the crowd. Shirtless and deeply muscled with a scarred torso shining darkly with animal grease, the man broke ranks and came into the open. He bellowed his ancestry of snake, gator, and river dog, pointing the tip of his knife at Duverje's men. He wore a frayed turkey feather in his cap and paused in his pronouncements to give Nate a nod of recognition.

The docks were still except for the multitude of eyes tracking from challengers to challenged, and an expectant sighing from the crowd began, a collective excitement like heat lightning building along the fringes of the gathering as men and women pressed forward to better see.

"Duverje," the turkey-feather man yelled, pointing his knife like an accusing finger. "Go on back to Algiers. This is *our* city; your cock-rooster is gone. I'm the only bayou bully here and we say this man can leave when and how he chooses."

An ear-shattering blast of the steamer whistle sounded then, and from every throat came a frenzied cry, and the excited crowd surged together across the lane, engulfing Duverje and his men, building a protective wall of swirling bodies.

For a moment, Nate glimpsed Alger straining angrily against the press, shouting something Nate could not make out, but the boy was soon hidden among the taller men and he never reappeared.

Nate was passed from person to person like a log in a swirling eddy, but he and Lucinda were both heaved by the street people onto the boarding ramp, and the steamer soon jerked away from the dock. Nate climbed the stairs to the captain's deck to watch the turkey-feather man circling within the ring formed by the crowd, his knife arm rising and falling, sweeping vertically and diagonally, threatening the largest of Duverje's men, who had drawn his own knife.

The growing distance soon erased the individual features of the dueling men and the crowd surrounding them, turning the scene into a prosaic tableau, one without blood or bones or sweat, reducing death to the smallest speck on the horizon.

Chapter 32

The rain had cleared away, leaving the Gulf waters calm, and the steamer made good time towards Galveston. The captain had food and drink brought to Nate and Lucinda, but he left them mostly alone, asking Nate only if he had gotten his man. Nate nodded but offered no more of the story, and the captain went back to his wheel.

Later, during the night, Nate came out on the deck, and the captain asked Nate if he should see to Lucinda, who was sitting motionless on the lower deck, staring out at the passing water.

Nate glanced at her once and answered, "I don't give a damn one way or another."

The captain opened his mouth as if to say something, but then seemed to think better of it and took it upon himself to cover her shivering form with a blanket.

In the early-morning hours, the steamer passed Pelican Island, and Nate raised the Whitworth and peered through the scope to scan the beach. He saw the roan standing in a small stand of trees cropping at the sea grass, and the horse raised its head at the whistle's blast. Nate watched for a while and for the first time began to shed, like a snake's skin, the dire anxiousness that had plagued him for weeks, and sensed in its place an expectation for a course of life not seated in fear.

He jumped when he felt someone touching the rifle and saw that Lucinda had come on quiet feet to stand with him. She tugged gently at the barrel and he realized that she wanted to look through the scope. He frowned but gave her the rifle and she raised it in one graceful motion to her shoulder and sighted through the scope towards the beach. He watched the dark flow of her hair curling into the wind and saw the mole beneath her right eye, a lone punctuation mark on a clean page. A scent from her like Mayhaw grapes filled his nostrils and he stepped abruptly away, as though she had struck him. She smiled shallowly, her eye still focused on the island, but her brow soon furrowed and she handed him back the rifle and returned wordless to her place on the deck.

In Galveston, Nate took Lucinda directly to the jailhouse, where he found Thoreau eating at his desk. Thoreau paused, a forkful of food halfway to his mouth, his eyes all worry.

Nate motioned for Lucinda to sit in a chair. "This is my prisoner, Lucinda Goddard," he said. "I'm taking her to the mainland as soon as I'm able."

Thoreau set his fork down. "And your man McGill?"

"Dead."

Thoreau looked at Lucinda briefly. "And where exactly are you going to say you apprehended your prisoner?"

"Right here." Nate crossed his arms and waited for Thoreau to weigh the consequences of refuting his story to the officials in Austin.

Thoreau picked up his fork and began eating again. "You say you apprehended her here. Then that must be where it happened. The island is a big place. Do me the kindness, though, of being on the train tomorrow morning."

Nate assured him that they would, but he left Lucinda in a cell at the jailhouse for the night while he walked to the telegraph office next to the Republic Hotel.

The first cable was to police headquarters in Austin: Lucinda Goddard apprehended Galveston. McGill rumored dead New Orleans. Returning to Austin with haste.

He had only a moment's flush of conscience about the lie; that the arrest be considered legal for a trial in Texas was the important thing. He didn't care what Lucinda said. He doubted her word would count for much, if anything.

The second cable went to Harrisburg, to Marshal Prudone, and contained only a few words: McGill dead. Texas law coming.

The third and final cable went to his wife: Leaving Galveston for Austin with prisoner. Will write soon.

After a moment's hesitation he added, my abiding love to you and Mattie.

In the morning, Thoreau accompanied them to the station, and he stood on the platform watching the train depart with relief showing plain on his dark face.

Lucinda sat next to Nate on the swaying train, leaning briefly on his arm in sleep, and he would have rolled his shoulder to wake her but for the woman across the aisle, who smiled at him knowingly, as though witnessing a lovely thing, his sweetheart resting so close to his bosom.

It made him feel low and mean, this revulsion for a woman that his partner had loved and taken for a wife. He tried to call up a feeling of connectedness to Dr. Tom through her presence and to remember the overwhelming, rushing joy that had taken him while riding the engine, but it felt like a year since the first trip to Galveston, the only things left to him a profound sense of loss of fellowship and direction and a building anger that was fueled by the limp body resting against his. It seemed impossible to him that she would not have known McGill was a killer from the very first, and his hostility towards her swelled like a canker.

He let her sleep but pulled her roughly from the train at Harrisburg. He carried the Whitworth in one hand and dragged Lucinda stumbling behind him with the other, moving through the dust towards the jailhouse, steeling himself for the confrontation with Prudone. He had practiced what he would say to the marshal, his warning to him that it wouldn't be that day, or the next, but that someday Nate was going to shoot him dead for the murder of Deerling and there wouldn't be a goddamn thing anyone could do to stop him. He could stand in the next county, aim, fire, and take the top of Prudone's head off, and no one would be the wiser as to who had done it.

But he found only one young deputy in residence—not more than nineteen or so—nervously jangling a ring of cell keys, looking like nothing so much as a kid holding a rattle.

"Marshal Prudone only recently left town," he told Nate. "Rode south yesterday tracking cattle thieves. And I have no idea when the marshal will return. He said it might not be for a good while."

Nate considered this for a moment. He had thought about dealing with Prudone so many times that it had never occurred to him that the man wouldn't be there. In Nate's mind, Prudone was somehow as immutable and fixed as the clock tower over the station. But he was tired, and he looked at Lucinda and realized that his exhaustion was due in part to the hours spent in her company; her passive, hollow presence threatened to sap away his anger like vinegar sucked into a sea sponge.

Nate stepped back into the street, leaving Lucinda behind with the deputy, who awkwardly stood and offered his chair to her instead of placing her in a cell. Nate carried the rifle to the beer hall and found the same barkeep behind the bar that he and Deerling had spoken to weeks before, the barkeep, and former sheriff of Goliad, who had warned that someday someone would settle harshly on Prudone.

Nate laid the Whitworth across the bar. "Do you remember me?"

The barkeep nodded. "You were here with that ranger. Looking for McGill. Did you find him?"

"Yes. I found him. He's dead."

The barkeep exhaled through his teeth. He set two glasses on the bar and poured whiskey for both of them.

Nate emptied the glass and gestured to the rifle. "Would you be willing to trade this for that gold coin? I don't know how much the coin is worth, but this gun is easily worth a thousand dollars."

The barkeep looked at him in surprise. "Why would you want to do that?"

"A lot of people gave their lives for that coin. The ranger I was with is dead. So is his partner. I want it as a reminder of what I've lost." He stuck out his hand to strike the deal, which the barkeep, after some hesitation, took in his own.

"I need a promise from you, though." Nate's grip tightened on the barkeep's hand. "Did you mean it when you said you'd be glad to see Prudone settled with a bullet in his head?"

The barkeep looked briefly over Nate's shoulder, but the hall was empty. He nodded once.

"McGill killed a dozen people, two of them children. The marshal aided him in those murders. Prudone personally killed that ranger I was with. I'll trade you this rifle, but I need your promise that you'll find someone to settle on him. I'd do it myself, but I'm transporting a prisoner to Austin."

The barkeep frowned but asked, "How far will she shoot?"

"Nine hundred and eighty yards."

The barkeep gaped. "That's far enough." He pumped Nate's hand twice and then took possession of the Whitworth, immediately going to hide it in a back room. Nate placed the remaining hex bullets on the bar, and the gold coin was retrieved from its hiding place and placed in his hand.

He thanked the barkeep and walked from the beer hall feeling relieved, not because he didn't have to kill Prudone, but because owning such a rare and expensive weapon had become a burden. It had been a spontaneous decision, trading the gun for the coin, but in truth, the rifle had never felt truly his. It had belonged to Deerling, and in Nate's mind, it always would.

He spent the rest of the day buying supplies and an old mule and spent the night in the livery. In the morning he retrieved Lucinda from the jailhouse, set her on the mule, and rode for Austin. He had briefly contemplated taking her to the cemetery north of Houston where Deerling and Dr. Tom were buried but felt in the end that it would serve no purpose. Upon hearing that

Dr. Tom was dead—shot by McGill—Lucinda had turned her face away, but he heard no crying.

From the first night's encampment she wordlessly took upon herself the task of cooking, expertly singeing the coffee grounds in a pan before boiling them in water with a handful of sugar, frying the cornmeal in fatback with a practiced hand. She even gathered the wood and set the fire, leaving Nate to service the weapons and see after the animals.

But contrary to the seemingly peaceful nature of her face, distant and grave, lit by the coals into a fiery porcelain so that she looked like the Madonna he had seen in a Mexican church, her hands trembled as she held her cup or plate. She wiped her palms repeatedly on her dress or flexed her fingers against the tangles of her hair, snapping at the wisps caught floating into the updrafts of cold evening air.

By the third day, she had begun speaking to herself, toneless and indistinct, her lips in constant motion, her head shaking randomly from side to side, arguing with the unseen.

After dusk, she stood up from the cook fire, holding his dinner and coffee in both hands, and turned to face him. But she remained fixed, only her chin moving in jerking spasms against her neck. She opened her hands, dropping the cup and plate, and he sprang up and moved towards her, arms out to catch her if she fell.

They faced each other, both in rigid confusion, and then she sank down in front of him, clasped her arms around his knees, and buried her face in the creased denim Y of his lap. "Please," she cried, thin ribbons of saliva trailing from her mouth. "Please kill me. If you have any kindness or compassion left in you." She lifted her face for a moment and looked up at him. "You'd shoot an animal beyond redemption."

He stood briefly with his arms out like a man free-falling and then he leaned down to pull her hands apart, to remove her arms from around his thighs, but her grasp was uncannily strong, and as her face pressed again into his thighs, the workings of her jaw agitated him to twin states of arousal and a rage so potent that he thought for an instant that he could remove the Dance, palm her face away with his other hand, and shoot her through the temple.

He raised up a knee, planted it into her chest, and heaved her away from him. She fell, then curled into a ball and wailed the way Nate had heard women giving birth wail, in frantic bursts, ejected half-words and panting breath.

He grabbed up his pack, pulled out the big bite—the buffalo-rifle cartridge packed with cyanide that Deerling had given him—and tossed it to the ground next to her.

"Here!" he yelled. "You want to die, you take care of it yourself. I'm not going to have your murder on my hands because you can't abide the idea of spending your life in a jail cell." He tried to slow his breathing, wiping flecks of spittle from his lips, and fought the impulse to kick the dirt over her head. "Or because you have the morals and conscience of a bitch come into heat, living with a killer of women and children."

She rolled onto her back and became very still, looking up at the sky. Her back began to bow upwards, and her hands clenched; her arms came out straight and beat a tempo-less rhythm on the ground. Her eyes rolled to white, and at first he thought it was just her womanly outburst grown more hysterical, but her lips stretched away from her teeth and she began to foam at the mouth and choke.

He moved forward and then back, his feet shifting in an aimless circle. He knelt down next to her thrashing body, uncertain what to do, thinking she would die after all. He put a tentative hand on her arm, but it was twitched away, and he got his canteen and wet a cloth and pressed it to her forehead. The fit went on for a good half hour in violent waves and then ebbed away slowly, leaving her dress stained dark with sweat.

He straightened her skirt, which had been twisted around her knees like a rope, and when he looked at her face, she had focused her gaze on him, though her body was still in rigors. He had seen that rolled-eyed look once before on the Steel Dust ranch when a yearling got into a green field and foundered himself and he writhed in agony, his guts bloated and crimped up with ballooning air. He had shot the horse out of necessity, and he knew that in her fit, she was gripped in a bodily pain that he couldn't imagine.

He got a blanket when she began to shiver and covered her over and built up the fire again. He felt her eyes, sunken and bruised, on him, following him around the camp, but it was an hour before he could gather the courage to hunker down next to her with some water. He lifted her head so she could drink, and she looked at him gratefully.

He rolled himself into his own blanket and tried to sleep, but he heard her weeping. She quieted after a while, and just as he was about to sink into sleep, he heard her voice, plaintive and indistinct.

"What?" he said, not certain what she was asking.

"The horse on the island. Do you think it will live?"

"I don't know. Maybe." He turned his head and could see her form, bundled like a corpse. "If it has no predators."

"Predators," she repeated. "You mean men."

He paused, remembering the steamer passenger who had wanted him to shoot the horse just because he could. "Maybe," he answered.

"My father once told me that horses can die without companionship."

It took Nate a moment to comprehend that the father she was speaking of was Deerling. He looked up at the night sky, the black soup, as Dr. Tom called it, fighting to keep his anger towards her present, like a shield against her vulnerability. "You can't be worrying about that goddamn horse." He sat up, throwing the blanket from him. "You just lost your father and your husband and you're pining after a horse?"

He could see her eyes glittering in the sullen light of the campfire. "My father was a man of violence." She brushed a length of hair from her face and looked up at the sky. "But he was unfailingly kind to animals."

She made a bitter sound through her nose, and the memory of the horse thief with the pearl buttons shot by Deerling slid into his mind. He lay back down, one arm thrown over his eyes to blot her out of his sight.

"Tom knew all the stars in the night sky," she murmured. "He used to point out the comets to me and say, 'There's another angel falling.'"

"Your husband told me there was a child," he said, and she suddenly quieted. "What happened to the baby?"

"She's safe."

"You mean you abandoned her somewhere."

She turned from her back onto her side, facing him. "I know better than anyone about abandonment, Mr. Cannon. Have you ever been in a lunatic asylum?" She paused as though waiting for him to answer. "My father committed me to several. You can't imagine what they do to young girls…" She stared at him until he looked away. "I made the decision before the baby was born to leave and never come back. I gave birth to a beautiful girl and left her in the care of those who would love her. And there's not been a day that I've regretted my choice."

"Dr. Tom's family…?"

"She's safe, that's all you need to know." She turned away from him, curling her knees up to her chest, and he thought she had drifted off to sleep. But she finally asked him, "Where is your home, Mr. Cannon?"

"Oklahoma," he muttered.

He heard a sharp intake of air, as though his answer had surprised her, but he pressed his arm tighter across his face, willing himself to sleep, to ease his way out of the night and out of her company. The thought of Dr. Tom regarding the night sky with his wife beside him, telling her of comets, made sense, but try as he might, he couldn't fit the image of Lucinda into that picture. She lay not ten feet away, speaking to him of orphaned horses and falling angels, daughter to a famed Texas ranger, wife to another, and yet all he could summon of her former life was an image of her in a bloodstained shift huddled next to a stiffening body.

"Did you know about McGill?" he asked her finally. "Did you know?" But he got no answer, and when he finally lowered his arm to look at her, she was motionless, wrapped cocooned in her blanket.

In the morning, he woke her and saw that she had held the big bite in her hand through the night. He tried to take it back, but she looked so stricken, holding on to the casing tightly with a kind of desperation, as though it were a precious relic of comfort rather than an object of death, and he relented, watched her tear the stitches in her skirt hem open to hide it.

It took another seven days to travel the distance to Austin, but she had no more sickness and they made good time over the well-packed road, the land changing from flat and featureless grasslands to bunched and rolling hills close set with post oak, blackjack, and hickory.

He signed her over to the city jail in Austin to await trial, which, he was told, could take months, as the city was busily processing for trial dozens of man-killers, rapists, and cattle thieves. If she was judged guilty, she would be sent to the women's wing at Huntsville prison, just north of Houston.

Nate arranged for food to be brought to the jail, as well as a clean dress and a Bible, delivered by a lady from the Disciples of Christ church.

In the jail cell, he sat next to Lucinda on the lone bunk for a while, gazing at the floor. He wanted to find a way round to thanking her for saving his life, but the sentiment was hostage to his need to ask her why she had remained so long with a murderer. He had a growing need to hear from her lips that she was, in fact, unaware of McGill's true nature, duped by his affability and cunning. But he'd known the moment he looked into her face that her impulsive shooting of McGill had nothing to do with the protection of his own life, nor was it an outraged response to the discovery of his monstrousness.

And when he finally asked her why she shot her lover, she looked at Nate with her wide-awake eyes and told him simply, "Because he was going to leave me."

He spent another two months finishing his term with a small company of other young state policemen, never firing his Dance pistol again, although he discharged his rifle in the chasing down and arrest of ten horse thieves in the hill country. He apprehended a man who had shot his brother in a drunken brawl, talking him out of a barn where he had threatened self-immolation; he arrested a German immigrant who had killed his wife and four children with a cording ax and then slipped their bodies methodically down his well, like pennies into a clay bank.

He returned to the court for the trial of Lucinda Goddard, expecting to testify, giving lies to the truth about the where and the how of her arrest. But she pled guilty to the charge of accessory to murder, impressing the crowds that had come to see her at the trial when she stated to the court, "I have done wrong and expect to pay heavily for my wrongdoing."

She received from the judge the lenient sentence of ten years at Huntsville.

On the day of her transfer to the prison, she asked to see him and he appeared, hat in hand, amazed to find her clear-eyed and expectant. She had grown full-cheeked, her body no longer gaunt, her hair lustrous and neatly pinned in a bun at the back of her head.

She smiled and took his hand as though they were old friends and said, teasingly, "Prison seems to agree with me."

They stood together awkwardly in silence for a moment and then she said, "I've begun teaching some of the other women in the jail to read. And I'm allowed as many books on mathematics as I want, which is more than I had dared hope for. All compliments of the church lady who brought me my reformation dress." She plucked at the heavy folds of her dark skirt and smiled regretfully, as some women did when caught wearing an unfashionable style.

She and Nate were allowed time together in the small, bricked, and airless exercise courtyard, a matron following close behind them, like an attending duenna, as they circled the walkway.

Once Lucinda pointed to the hem of her dress and whispered, "I have kept the shotgun cartridge. It makes me feel rebellious."

They sat on a bench, the matron wandering some distance away, and Nate realized that she was giving them some privacy, as though he were a suitor.

"How is your wife?" Lucinda asked.

"She's fine," he said. "I'm going back to Oklahoma soon for spring planting."

She asked him a few more questions, listened politely to his answers. But he felt a growing tension in her, and when the matron signaled to them that their time together was at an end, Lucinda asked the matron to hand Nate a small, folded piece of paper.

Lucinda said, "Inside is written the name of the missionary church where I left my baby, as well as the date of her birth." She placed her hand over his. "The mission is in Oklahoma."

He looked at her with surprise; he had assumed the orphanage was in Texas.

"I have no right to ask anything of you," she said. "But I know you are a decent family man. I only want to know that she is well."

He tucked the paper into the pocket of his jacket. "I can't make any promises."

"Of course," she said, but she smiled at him hopefully, as though he had already agreed to her request.

He stood then and walked briskly towards the guard station. At the gate he turned once, but she had already disappeared inside the jail, along with the matron.

He was discharged from the force in good standing and encouraged to rejoin after his crops were in, and he said he'd think on it, although he knew he'd never return to service.

On the day he rode north from Austin, he stopped at Hillyer's Photographic Studio to retrieve the print taken of himself and the two rangers. He had waited all that time to look on the image, knowing that it would pain him.

He was surprised at how young Dr. Tom looked, wearing his new shirt—the old one sacrificed to the snake in the bucket—his dark hair still wet and slicked back from his forehead.

One night on the journey to the Austin jail, Lucinda had mused that she didn't even know why Tom Goddard, an intelligent man who had attended medical school, had moved to Texas and joined the rangers. "His lungs were weak," she had said. "I always supposed he came for the air."

Nate had shaken his head, dismayed that she would not know this elemental thing about her husband, and he told her what his partner had told him. Dr. Tom had said that Texas was the only place he had ever found that, when it killed you, it didn't forget about you.

When he studied Deerling's image on the photograph, he

could clearly see the resemblance to Lucinda, but he noticed what he hadn't been mindful of at the time of the sitting. Along with placing his hand on Nate's shoulder, Deerling had smiled. Not the engaging smile of contentment or even easy, familiar camaraderie, but rather one with a ghosting of pride.

He posted a letter to his wife, telling her of his return.

I live for the day when I can leave Texas. I think now only of our home, and I long for the day when I can stand among our own herd of horses. And if I ever leave you again, it will be to lie in the earth under their hooves, below the fields you have tended so well, for I have seen the wider world and it can offer me nothing compared to what I will find when I am returned to you.

Nate had already crossed the Red River at Colbert's Crossing into Oklahoma before he pulled the paper that Lucinda had given him from his jacket and read by the half-light of a gray and banded sunset what was written there.

Chapter 33

*L*ucinda sat with the letter from General Alvord in her lap, her face half turned to the small cell window behind her. She had put her back to the window in order to capture more light on the page, but she moved her cheek towards the warmth and closed her eyes in pleasure.

With the letter, he had also enclosed his treatise on non-Euclidean geometry, "The Tangencies of Circles and Spheres," along with diary notes from his time collecting botanical samples in the Rocky Mountains. The notes she put aside; she would read them, or not, depending on how personal or speculative they were, Lucinda being interested in only his purer observations of the heretical theorems of the European radicals Beltrami and Lobachevsky.

The tone of the general's letter had been polite and formal but not courtly or presumptive. He was an older man, already fifty by the time he served in the war, and was fascinated by the lady geometrist who had written him, thoughtfully, intelligently, from the Huntsville women's prison.

They began a regular correspondence, one of several she conducted. In the year that Lucinda had been incarcerated, she had become a person of note, a pilgrimage stop for the curious, the alarmists, the outraged. Sometimes the visitors would simply watch her through the cracks in the wall as she made her daily turns about the yard. The bolder ones would throw notes, of declared love or condemnation, over the walls. These she never read but rather walked over them like scattered petals of spring flowers, leaving them for the matrons to gather up and possibly read themselves for their own titillation or amusement.

As well, she had had a few of the women inmates professing their love to her, one woman even hanging herself in her cell in desperation over Lucinda's cold and impersonal rejections.

She had taken to wearing only black—the cloth donated to her by a church group—and it made her look remorseful and pious to the believers who prayed over her. But it was an aesthetic choice more than anything else, a way to further negate the world and its troubling distractions. Her sickness had retreated along with the pressures of the corporeal world. Her life was cloistered, orderly, and, in the pursuit of the life of the mind, even comfortable. The women's prison was new; the food healthful; the matrons, if not kind, were not cruel.

Of course, she was aware that she had been written about in newspapers as far away as Boston and New York, excoriated as the Black Widow of Texas or lauded as the Fallen Dove of Austin, but she heard about these whimsies only in fractured, incomplete pieces from the gossiping lips of the other inmates.

Over the past twelve months, she had toiled to reduce everything and everyone in her circumscribed world—from the regular, right-angled stones and bricks of her cell to the inmates, even herself—to numerical values, just as she had strived to do as a child in the asylum.

She looked up at the buffalo-rifle cartridge, perched upright on its base on the windowsill, one of two possessions from her previous life. Curiously, she had been given permission to keep the cartridge by the warden, who thought it an admonishing object from her father, being ignorant of the fact that it contained a lethal dose of cyanide.

She stared at it thoughtfully. If the equation $a + b = c$ is offered, and if a (the cartridge) is assigned the value of 1, and c (death, the final answer) is assigned the value of 0, then what is her value if she is b? Could a person be a negative number and still walk the earth? She thought that this could certainly be so.

The second object propped on the sill was a portrait photograph, exquisitely hand-tinted, of a girl. Lucinda ran her fingers lightly over the rich pastel colors, textured finely by the brush that had given the portrait depth and brought the girl's face and dress to life.

Lucinda had been in Huntsville for six months when the matron had appeared at her cell door saying that inmate Goddard had a family visitor just arrived. Puzzled, she had run her hands in a smoothing motion over her hair, a hopeful thought taking shape. She had heard not one word from Nate since he had left her in Austin, but she had known it might take time to track down her daughter.

She nodded to the matron; the door was unlocked and opened, and a woman swept into the cell. She was portly and expensively dressed, but gaudily so; her hair, which showed beneath her bonnet, was the color of burned hay. Lucinda had struggled at first to put an identity to the woman, and then the woman raised her upper lip, and she knew the visitor to be Mrs. Landry, the madam from Fort Worth.

She stayed only briefly, long enough to take in the cramped, spartan cell and Lucinda's unadorned black dress and to hand over the photograph. The subject had been posed modestly, dressed in voluminous cornflower blue, mirroring the color of eyes that were incessantly clear and triumphant, a girl beautiful beyond a simple description of lovely attributes in the singular, of teeth or lips or cheek or brow, so that even the matron, craning her neck over the madam's shoulder, gasped.

Mrs. Landry had watched Lucinda's face closely, looking for some strong emotion of grief or guilt, and was disappointed when Lucinda remained unresponsive.

The madam gestured to the photograph. "She asked me to come here. She wanted you to have the portrait to remember her by. And this." She pulled out of her bag the lavender scarf that Lucinda had given May and laid it on the cot. "She died four months back. Yellow fever. We had a lovely funeral. Closed casket, of course. Ruined the face. Pity—May was my best earner."

She paused for a moment and then, as though unable to contain herself, said, "I don't know why she bothered. That was a dirty trick you played on her."

Lucinda had raised her eyes to Mrs. Landry and said, "Yes. But, you see, she loved me."

Mrs. Landry had left immediately after without a backward look or parting comment, and Lucinda sat on her bed and held the portrait, thinking of May's soft-limbed vitality, and of her loveliness, and she wept. She then set the portrait in the window, where she could see it at all times.

Next to the portrait, Lucinda often placed objects, which she changed frequently, like offerings: a small colored stone, a tiny flower, a bit of shiny moss. It had become a shrine where the girl's displayed beauty could serve as a constant reminder of Lucinda's fatal complicity, and she attended the shrine daily in dutiful penance, standing for hours in front of the portrait until her legs throbbed, willing herself to recall May's every gesture, every smile.

Now she pulled the lavender scarf over her shoulders and knocked at the cell door for the matron to release her to her classes. She had been tutoring some of the women of the prison and found that a few had a true talent for mathematics. The teaching gave her a modest satisfaction and the sense that she was serving her term willingly, gracefully, filling her time pro-ductively—making herself worthy—until she could receive word about her child.

The classroom hours shored up the solitary times when clouded recollections of a man's voice calling her name or of tan-gled, blood-filled sheets threatened to send her into a black pit of horror and remorse. She could push away the waking night-mares by seeking out the lines, angles, and elliptical spaces that gave proof to her world, proofs that calmed and comforted her, that helped erase the memories.

But most important, when looking into the faces of the younger inmates, some as young as twelve, she could imagine her own daughter looking to her in gratitude, in understanding, in forgiveness. She had time, and in time, all things were possible.

Afterword

The man perches next to the girl in her bed, the covers tucked around her small frame, telling her, as he often does, stories of his life: of his boyhood spent in want on the heavy, compacted soil of Oklahoma, not fifty miles from where they sit, softly talking in the half-light of her room. He tells her what he learned from his father growing up: how to break a horse to hard service, with rope and a whip. But he reveals how, years later, he learned from his wife, the girl's mother, how to gentle a horse to usefulness by watching and reading the signs that he gave; to move obliquely, and without menace, into the horse's line of sight; to stand calmly, staring into the middle distance, giving the horse a chance to order its quicksilver thoughts inside the passages of its narrow skull.

He tells her how he left home for Texas and at sixteen was called to fight a war in Arkansas. The girl speaks for the first time, recalling that he was too young to fight. *Yes*, the man says, *too young to fight, but not too young to bring three hundred horses back to Texas.*

All but two, the girl says.

Yes, all but two, the man answers.

He recalls how he met her mother at a mission dance and how

she looked in a pale summer dress, her black hair swept back from her face like wings, and the girl smiles and adds, as she always does, *And then I came.*

Yes, and then you came.

He recounts how he left for Texas to serve as a lawman for half a year, and here the girl attends more closely as the man's story becomes more expansive, and he describes his fellow lawmen, Texas rangers who fought for twenty years to bring order to chaotic, lawless places.

The girl offers the names of these rangers dutifully, carefully, *Captain Deerling and Dr. Tom,* as though reciting her own lineage, understanding that, though they were not blood kin, they were of close fellowship to her father; knowing too with a child's innate sense of fairness that blood alone does not make lasting connections between people, any more than does desire or time or proximity. She repeats their names so they won't be forgotten.

He nods at her recitation, describes to her their journey together for months across the entire expanse of Texas: the cactus ringed with purple and blue-tinted agave and saw grasses that when taut were sharp as knives. He recounts seeing striated rock, pink and gray, with overlying dirt the color of blood. He was witness to caves worn into cliff faces, looking like open, staring eyes, and indented spaces worn by cliff-side floods, appearing as doors cut into the rock by giants. Trees would lean over the edges of rocks as though listening to their passage, their twisted, hanging roots looking like nothing so much as legs crossed in timeless waiting, and abutments the shape of horse's heads or pointing fingers piercing the scudding clouds that formed and disappeared and formed again in tumultuous succession.

He tells her of the cities farther east, Austin and Houston and Galveston, and of the legends of pirate's gold in a place called Middle Bayou.

Here the girl holds out her hand and the man places into it the heavy gold coin, old and worn, warmed by his own fingers.

Middle Bayou, he says, stressing the words as though in admonition; the passing-through place, the place of constant sorrows and unexplained miracles, of contrary laws to man and nature, where the lame can suddenly walk, and armored monsters swim in warm and muddy rivers preying on man and beast alike.

And then, the girl prompts, *and then to the city across the Gulf.*

To the city, he agrees, where horses fly from boats and swim to far islands like waterbirds; with streets the width of rivers, and men who do battle in those streets like Old Testament warriors. He tells her of the king of thieves holding sway over his court, residing in a bell tower above an ancient church, and of the king's challenge to him to bring down a terrible rooster, perched on a high aerie over the city, the rooster legion in size with a body of beaten copper and a head of ruby glass so cunningly faceted that at sunset it blinded all the citizens with its light.

He recounts for the girl the preparation needed for the rifle—the heavy powder measure, the six-sided bullet, the copper caps made only in England—given to him by Deerling. The only gun to make the impossible shot…

Nine hundred and eighty yards, the girl whispers.

Nine hundred and eighty yards, the man affirms. He had once marched off the distance carrying her on his shoulders, designating a large tree as the target, and he remembers her disbelief that any bullet, from any gun, could traverse such a distance.

But he makes the impossible shot, he assures her, knocking the head from the rooster, and the king and the citizens rejoice and, as reward, he takes back from captivity a beautiful lady who'd been stolen by pirates from Middle Bayou, a schoolteacher who had, because of the terrible hardship of her journey, become lost in her mind. He had taken her back to Texas, to a high-walled place where she could regain her better self.

And is the lady returned to herself? she asks.

But the girl's eyes have begun to close and he doesn't answer the question, sitting with her instead, watching the soft sheen of her cheek, the spread of her hair across the pillow.

He takes back the coin from her uncurling fingers and slips it into his pocket. She had asked him once about the nature of good and bad and if the coin itself was evil, having moved so many people to violence. He told her what Dr. Tom had once told him: that most things had been placed in the world either to assist in a man's journey to his better self or to tempt him away from it. The danger with gold, and silver, Tom had said, was that they had the ability to do both, with the result that men had always, since the betrayal of the Nazarene, and would always, to the end of time, be the best and the worst of creatures in their presence.

He watches her sleeping and sees the growing angular planes of her face, so different from the moon-shaped roundness of her mother's. He remembers the day-old infant with the pale skin and the dark furze of hair placed in his wife's hands by the missionary workers, his wife who could bring life to the most arid plot of land but who could not grow a child in her belly.

He had read Lucinda's note, the one given to him in the Austin jail, only after crossing the Red River on his return trip to Oklahoma. In the failing light of dusk, he had stared at the letters trailing looped and elegant towards the edge of the paper, like birds rushing for flight, and his hand holding the note had dropped onto his lap. With a growing sense of wonder, he saw what had been hidden before in the face of his daughter: Lucinda's alert, challenging gaze and Dr. Tom's smile of genuine pleasure at a world revealing itself in all its startling complexities.

It was another seventy miles to Tishomingo, but he touched his heels to the bay's ribs and let the horse run himself out. He made camp an hour after sunset south of Marietta to build a fire and slept on top of his blanket in the silky air.

He dreamed that night of an island densely covered with oak and elm, heavily shrouded with winter rains, and a mound of earth between the trees opening up, like a grave in rebellion, pushing the pale bodies of two seamen, long buried, to the surface. The rain stopped and scavengers appeared, beetle, fox, and coyote, to devour the men in unison in a peculiarly slow and stately manner. And in the fashion of dreams, he was not repelled by the sight, but rather awed by the bloodless, almost gentle feeding.

The bones of the once-buried were quickly scattered by wild boars that chased sunning copperheads from the cages of the bleaching ribs. Itinerant ospreys collected for their nests the remaining hair, still intact on the skulls, like lichen on sea boulders.

Left was only the inert detritus of the disappeared—the metal piece of a gun, a buckle, a button, a single gold coin—which in time also mingled with the earth, conjoined with it, related in all its finite parts. Kin.

Acknowledgments

My deepest gratitude to my agent, Julie Barer, for all her support, encouragement, and direction; she is in one person cheerleader, tutor, first reader, and friend. My abiding thanks to Reagan Arthur, my superlative editor, who, through her guidance, patience, and advocacy, has made me a better writer.

My heartfelt thanks also to the wonderful people at Hachette/ Little, Brown: David Young, Michael Pietsch, Heather Fain, Sabrina Callahan, Nicole Dewey, Anna Balasi, Sarah Murphy, Miriam Parker, and Amanda Tobier.

They say third time's the charm, so to Pamela Marshall and Tracy Roe, my copyeditors, I say, How lucky can one writer get!

The idea for this novel and its legends of pirates' gold began with my brother's recounting of the history of Middle Bayou (now Armand Bayou) in southeast Texas. My admiration and thanks go to Kevin (the Captain) Hickman for sharing his knowledge of the Civil War, its armaments and its warriors.

My love and gratitude go to the Cannon family, Danny, Beth, and Mattie, for their hospitality during the many hours in which they revealed so generously their extensive knowledge of horses and horsemanship.

To Tom Godwin, doctor, historian, and archaeologist, and his wife, Patsy, I send my deep appreciation for sharing their knowledge of the early settlers of Middle Bayou. And also to George Dearing, for retelling stories of Texas from an earlier, wilder time.

My research was enhanced immensely by the generous contributions of the following historians: Helen D. Mooty, director of the Galveston County Historical Museum; Don Harper, associated with the Galveston Railroad Museum; and Doug Wicklund, the "Gun Whisperer," senior curator of the National Firearms Museum, expert on the elusive but legendary Whitworth rifle.

My enduring love and gratitude go as well to my sister, Kim Morrison, for her abundant inspiration and creativity, and to all my family and friends who encouraged and supported me during the writing of this third book. And finally to Jim: the adventure is just beginning.

About the Author

Kathleen Kent is the author of *The Heretic's Daughter* and *The Traitor's Wife*. She lives in Dallas.

Reading Group Guide

The
Outcasts

A Novel
by

Kathleen Kent

An online version of this reading group guide is available at littlebrown.com.

A conversation with Kathleen Kent

You have a few titles under your belt now, including your newest, The Outcasts. *Have you always wanted to be a writer? Will you tell us a bit about your background and what led you to write your first novel?*

Writing is something that I've always done for my own pleasure, and I went to the University of Texas thinking I would pursue the Writing Life. But more practical concerns led me to live and work in New York for twenty years, building a career in finance. In the back of my mind, though, a little voice kept whispering, how fine it would be to develop some stories that had always fascinated me, and so I took the leap of faith and moved with my family to Texas to begin writing what was my first novel, *The Heretic's Daughter.* This first novel was about my grandmother, back nine generations, Martha Carrier, who was hanged as a witch in Salem in 1692. I had grown up with stories of Martha and the Carrier family, and I wanted to pay homage to her courage and illuminate the day-to-day lives of her family, her husband and children, who survived the witch trials.

What inspired you to write The Outcasts?

My mother was from New England, and the Carrier family legends inspired me to write my first two novels, *The Heretic's*

Daughter and *The Traitor's Wife*. But I lived most of my childhood in Texas with my dad's family and spent many hours poring over books about the Old West. My dad, a lifelong Texan, was a vivid storyteller himself and used to say—out of earshot of my mom—that all the witches came from her side of the family, but that all the horse thieves came from his side. Some of my favorite authors early on were Louis L'Amour and J. Frank Dobie, and later I was inspired by Cormac McCarthy and Larry McMurtry. With *The Outcasts* I was able to revisit the larger-than-life myths, the heroes and heroines of Texas, with all their faults and weaknesses, as well as their bravery and fortitude. What made the settlement men and women of Texas so fascinating to me was the complexity of their characters—the infinite variety and nuances of good and bad—and their pitched battles against the extremes of terrain and weather as well as against their fellow Texans.

While Nate Cannon is certainly the "white hat" character in The Outcasts, *I couldn't help but fall in love with the strong-yet-vulnerable Lucinda Carter. She's such a survivor, and in spite of her sometimes questionable motives, I found I wanted to see good things happen to her. Did you have a personal favorite character that you enjoyed writing the most?*

I did have a special admiration for Lucinda. She is a survivor and was dealt an unfortunate hand with her physical afflictions and her difficult upbringing. She is not an easy person to like, but she is not without deep compassion (witness her nursing Civil War veterans, and her love for May). But as with so many women of that time, her choices for survival without the protection and resources from a man were few. What surprised me during my research for the book was how many women pursued prostitution briefly and opportunistically to feed themselves and their families. This practice was something Grandma would most likely not have talked about, but most families knew women who had no other choice to keep from starving, especially during those first few years following the Civil War, and who became, if only briefly, "Upstairs Girls."

The character I had the most fun writing, though, was Dr. Tom, a veteran Texas Ranger. A Renaissance man, he trained as a doctor, was a naturalist, and loved to read, most particularly Charles Dickens. I think my inspiration for him was the actor Richard Farnsworth, whom I fell in love with watching *The Grey Fox*. He was the ultimate gentleman cowboy: rock steady, loyal, independent, and not averse to any fight that he saw as morally justified.

The Outcasts is set in the 1800s, and the Gulf Coast settings are almost characters unto themselves. What kind of research did you do for the novel? What are a few things you find fascinating about that time period?

I spent a lot of time doing traditional research about Texas during the mid-1800s, but I also traveled to the Gulf Coast, Middle Bayou in particular (now the Armand Bayou Nature Center), to get a feel of the terrain, the climate, and the critters that inhabit it: wild boar, alligators, poisonous snakes, and banana spiders the size of dinner plates. The thing that most surprised me was how the terrain has changed over the past 150 years. Now the bayou country south of Houston is almost impenetrable with dense underbrush and "trash" trees, but during the years preceding the

Civil War, the land was mostly vast tracts of prairie that wild buffalo inhabited until the cattle men chased them off to raise their herds of longhorn and Angus.

What is your writing process like?

I am normally a plotter, and a slow plotter at that. My normal pace of writing is to write three sentences and erase two, but all the while knowing what ending I am working toward. But I began *The Outcasts* without a strong idea of the ending and began to panic when I was halfway finished with no clear sign of one. I needed something that would tie the characters and the story together in a cohesive way, and I went to bed one night really fretting over what that might be. I dreamt that night of Dr. Tom, and he told me that I had had the answer right in front of me the whole time, and then he gave me the ending. I woke up with a strong sense of wonder regarding the messenger, but it worked in a very satisfying way. It's the first time that that's happened, and it might never happen again. But I'm in debt to Dr. Tom for tying it all together for me.

What, or who, have been some of the biggest influences on your life and/or writing?

As mentioned earlier, I had a special love of writers of the Old West. But there are other authors who left a deep impression on me, Charles Dickens perhaps most of all because of the depth of his character development and his fearlessness in writing for an emotional reading experience over a purely intellectual one. Sometimes I think contemporary authors tend to shy away from emotionally engaging readers in this way as it may appear overly sentimental or maudlin. But nothing is more disappointing than reading an entire novel and not connecting with any of the characters in a deep and substantive way.

What are you reading now?

I just finished reading *The Maid's Version* by Daniel Woodrell, which is a beautifully written novel based on a true-life event—a tragic fire in a dance hall in the 1920s—and the repercussions on the families involved for generations afterward. And I've just begun reading *The Thicket* by Joe Lansdale, a tale of blood and redemption in East Texas, which is where I spent so much time as a child.

When you're not busy at work on your next project, how do you enjoy spending your free time?

I love taking long walks with my boxer, Mattie Belle (it's when I develop a lot of my story ideas), and introducing my sixteen-year-old son to classic movies like *To Kill a Mockingbird*. He would kill me if he knew I said this, but there's nothing more satisfying than having a good cry with your teenage son.

What's next for you, this year and beyond?

I've begun two projects simultaneously, which I've never done before, and at some point I'm going to have to make the decision on which manuscript gets finished first. One is a historical novel set in a Pennsylvania coal community in 1910, with a mining accident and missing children. The other is a real departure for me: a contemporary crime novel based on a short story called "Coincidences Can Kill You" that was published in *Dallas Noir*, an anthology of crime stories by Dallas authors.

This interview was conducted by Kristin Centorcelli and originally appeared on mybookishways.com.

Questions and topics for discussion

1. Most of *The Outcasts* revolves around the separate journeys that Lucinda and Nate take before their paths cross. Discuss the motivations that initially drive the two protagonists toward their goals?

2. Lucinda's moral spectrum has many shades of gray. Dr. Tom sums her up with a question: "What makes you think a woman with any decency left would cleave to an evil man like McGill?" (page 150). Is his assessment of Lucinda fair? Did you find yourself sympathizing with Lucinda or judging her? To what extent should we forgive her capacity for cold self-interest and even brutality?

3. *The Outcasts* takes place in Texas in the 1870s, not long after the Civil War. In what ways does the specter of the war haunt the story? How has it shaped the characters and their world?

4. Nate's first encounter with Dr. Tom and Deerling is marked by distrust and disapproval of their questionable methods, but his relationship with both men evolves as they work together. What does Nate learn from these more seasoned rangers and

from being on the job? How would you describe the portrayal of male friendship in this novel?

5. To what extent does Lucinda fit the mold of the classic nineteenth-century female protagonist, and in what ways does she break it?

6. Of all the people in Middle Bayou, Tobias is the first to see through Lucinda's assumed identity. Why doesn't he expose her?

7. Why do you think the novel is called *The Outcasts*? Which characters does this phrase describe, and why? What would it take for the outcasts to be included, and what would they lose in the process?

8. How does this book compare with other westerns that you have read (or seen)? Which themes does this novel share with them, and which does it reject or reimagine?

9. Are any of the characters in *The Outcasts* "good people" in your estimation? What qualifies as goodness in the universe of this novel? Which character (if any) do you consider the story's moral center, and why?

10. Where do you see Lucinda and Nate ten years from where the book ends? Do you think that Lucinda has found redemption? Has Nate realized his dream raising horses in Oklahoma?

Also by Kathleen Kent

The Heretic's Daughter

A novel

"Gripping and evocative, *The Heretic's Daughter* is a powerful tale of a perilous time."

—Thailan Pham, *People*

"Kent's moving story comes straight from her heart as well as the historical record.... She tells a heart-wrenching story of family love and sacrifice."

—Carol Memmott, *USA Today*

"A coming-of-age tale in which tragedy is trumped by an unsinkable faith in human nature."

—Chelsea Cain, *New York Times Book Review*

Back Bay Books • Available wherever paperbacks are sold

Also by Kathleen Kent

The Traitor's Wife

A novel

"A powerful historical narrative, both love story and thriller, set against the dramatic backdrop of the country's earliest days."
—Steve Bennett, *San Antonio Express-News*

"Kent's novel burns slowly, with polished prose, a gripping plot, and characters—particularly smart, independent-minded Martha—who will linger in your mind."
—Jay Strafford, *Richmond Times-Dispatch*

"*The Heretic's Daughter* was widely—and justly—praised for Kent's lyrical writing and in-depth research, and both of those strengths are on display in *The Traitor's Wife*.... A solid piece of historical fiction, beautifully written."
—Shawna Seed, *Dallas Morning News*

Back Bay Books • Available wherever paperbacks are sold